Widow Creek

Also by Sarah Margolis Pearce

The Promise of Fate

Widow Creek

SARAH MARGOLIS PEARCE

A Lucky Bat Book
Widow Creek
Copyright © 2018 by Sarah Margolis Pearce

ISBN-10: 1-943588-77-5
ISBN-13: 978-1-943588-77-0

Cover Artist: Victorine E. Lieske
Published by Lucky Bat Books
10 9 8 7 6 5 4 3 2 1
Discover more from this author at sarahmargolispearce.com

*To Ellison "Ziggy" Obomsawin-Pearce,
the newest light in my life.*

Author's Note

THE EXCERPTS FROM THE WRITINGS OF Meriwether Lewis and William Clark included in this book were taken verbatim from a version of the journals edited by Bernard DeVoto [1953, Houghton Mifflin, Co., Boston]. The grammar, misspelling of words, and inconsistencies with regard to names of individuals, tribes, and locations is a reflection of the language of the time. Out of respect for this original and historic document, I chose to transcribe entries as they were written by the authors.

St Louis, Missouri
1866

"THE MISSUS TOLD ME ABOUT *THIS*."

The maid held up an oilskin satchel that was large and angular, like a box. It had a bone clasp. It had been stowed within the girl's trunk. When she unpacked the trunk, the maid did not bother folding anything neatly. Instead, she threw everything into a chest of drawers, then dragged the trunk up to the attic.

"She said you ought not to have it and that I was to take it away," lied the maid.

The maid's lanky arms had thick strands of hair hanging like moss from her elbows to her wrists. The girl did not like the grotesque way they looked poking out of the sleeves of her dress. Like an animal pretending to be human.

"You best put all that in the past," the maid said. "That's what *I* think anyways. Filthy lot you come from. Ain't you heard them talking?"

The oilskin satchel with the bone clasp had traveled in a trunk all the way by stagecoach from California. The girl did not know of the satchel's existence until this moment. She wondered why the maid was telling her to forget about it. Her guardian, the woman who'd brought her here, had never mentioned it all those long days in the coach. What was inside the satchel that she mustn't know about?

They were in the attic of the big house stowing away the dirty, battered trunk. Although the girl had not been invited to accompany the maid, she followed her anyway because there was nothing else to do. She was not allowed to go outside. Not that it was an appealing idea: the busy, noisy streets beyond the windows confused and frightened her.

The hairy-armed maid placed the satchel back in the trunk and slammed the lid down. Her eyes narrowed as she saw the girl's attention was drawn to the satchel. "Don't you get no ideas about that," she told the girl.

It seemed ages ago that the girl had packed the trunk with her father while he explained that going to St. Louis was a good opportunity for her. *An education and a chance to see something other than Remington River is best for you*, was how he put it. Her father said that the woman would now be her guardian. *It will be a long journey, but you'll end up in a fine home with a good family*, he told her.

Yet the girl would never forget the dark, glowering looks she received as she and the woman climbed out of the stagecoach. It was different with the woman's family. They were kind. It was the other folks in town who were not.

She heard a loud voice in the crowd when she stepped down from the coach. "Dark, yes. But not quite so dark as to make her unfit. A backwater where nobody cares. That's what will be suitable. As long as she learns her place, she'll do all right."

Much later she would understand what they meant. It would take many years before she no longer cared what they meant.

The maid started to shove the trunk into a corner of the attic. The girl mustered as much courage as she could, for she was about to speak her mind. After all, it was her trunk, and she said to the maid, "But that is my trunk, and I would like to see what is in that satchel. I think it was meant for me to have."

Then the maid stood back. "You think you're better than me? Oh, how they look at you when you can't see them. All of them downstairs do. I know!" she hissed, slamming her hand on the trunk. "I bet if the missus knew what they would say, she'd have thought twice about bringing someone like you here. There's only so much that money can buy." Without warning, the maid gave the girl a backhanded slap across her face.

"Don't you tell me what's yours," the maid sneered, rubbing her knuckle. "See what you made me do? You best listen up. You've got nothing other than what they give you. Now forget about that trunk. And you pray to the Lord that you aren't turned out on the street. Hear me?"

There was the sound of footsteps behind them. A dark, towering form filled the light from the landing below. Slowly climbing the stairs was the woman who'd brought the girl to St. Louis. The girl sat up and took a deep breath.

"Get out," said the woman quietly to the maid, who was now cowering. "How dare you take a hand to this child! Never let me see your face again. And don't ask for your wages. You set one foot back in this house, I'll see you whipped." The maid scurried away.

The woman pulled the trunk out from the corner and opened the lid. She removed the oilskin satchel and handed it to the girl.

"Your father gave this to me and asked that I keep it safe. It is something your mother wrote. She was a good woman and she wanted you to have this when you were old enough. I think that you are. I can't say that you will understand everything written here. But, Lord, she had an interesting life. That she did."

The woman left the girl alone in the attic with the oil satchel. The girl unfastened the bone clasp and removed several items from within. The first was a tattered book with a gray cover bearing faded yellow letters which read *The Journals of Lewis and Clark*. She opened the journals and read the inscription on the first page:

My dearest one.
My mother cherished this copy of The Journals of Lewis and
Clark. There may be nicer and newer copies by now. But this one
saw me through a most troubling of times and experiences. To
that end, I hope it brings you the comfort it gave me.

Then she took out a cup and saucer wrapped in a tattered shawl.
She placed these to the side.

The last item in the satchel was what she was most interested in. It
was a thick notebook bound together by a string laced through three
holes on the left side. The handwriting was neat and bold. The girl
touched the ink as if the color were bleeding from her own fingers.

The story that I have written is, to the best of my ability, true
to fact. My memory might embellish some and I don't mean to
distort the truth. It may be that I just see life a little differently
now and that some of the past is either a little shinier, or a little
more tarnished.
I shall begin in St. Joseph, Missouri, in the year 1849.

The girl moved into a spot of light from one of the attic windows
and began to read.

St. Joseph, Missouri
1849

❧ 1 ❧

I HAVE A REVERENCE FOR THE dead. Well, not all of them. One in particular that I do not revere is Earl Penngrove. Nor do I pay homage to his mortal remains with Sunday visits and bouquets of posies. Truth be told, I don't even recall where on the prairie I stuck that old pine-switch cross with his name scratched in it.

And yet I must thank him for convincing me to head westward. Though his were fibs of the tallest order, without them, I wouldn't have found Remington River, Hasten Peak, or "The Beyond."

Pa owned a dry goods shop in St. Joseph. It was a good business that he built up from a rickety shed selling rope and oil to river folks into a big emporium on Rubidoux Street. Over time, he became a well-regarded shopkeeper in town. My mother and I worked the counter, restocking, keeping books, and tending to the old ladies who spent an hour moaning over the price of a shoe buckle. Pa took care of the inventory, making sure that his shop featured the latest and the best merchandise coming out from the East. "Hardwick Dry Goods Emporium always strives to delight and amaze our customers," the advertisement read on the front window.

The first time I met Earl Penngrove, he walked into the shop just as we opened for the day's trade. I had not seen him before. But people arrived and departed St. Joseph like flies in the summer, and I did not pay particular attention to newcomers.

He was midway through his twenties with a fine beard and high cheeks. He was dressed in what once had been a good top coat. Its cut told me that it came from an experienced tailor. The fit was nearly perfect. The goodness, though, had been beaten out of the garment some time ago. The creases in the lapels were unraveling and bits of lining poked out from the bottom hem. His top hat had seen better days, but it was brushed clean. He gazed around the shop, blinking at our jumbled display of stock. His eyes finally settled on our rack of coats and his expression brightened. When he looked up for assistance, he looked straight at me. The blush that rose up from his throat to his cheeks did not seem to bother him, for he kept his focus on me.

I would have put my head in an empty potato sack if I'd blushed like that in front of a stranger.

Pa made his way around the pickle barrels, bags of seed, and the old stuffed bobcat perched on a table and went toward the man. It was Pa's custom to help the gents with their trousers, jackets, boots, and the like. So I stayed in my place behind the counter. Pa fussed over him and finally persuaded him to try on a gray frock coat. It had just arrived from New York, and I had brushed and pressed it myself before hanging it on the rack.

I did not see him do it, but I know he did it. As the gent pulled the coat on, I heard the plonk of a button hitting the floor planks.

"What have we here?" he commented, bending down in mock surprise. "A loose button on what is otherwise a fine piece of clothing. Perhaps I ought to inspect the seams and lining as well."

"You'll not find a better made item on the rack. But by all means take a good look at the stitching. Top notch through and through," huffed Pa, turning up one of the sleeves to show the hem. He took the button from the gent and inspected it with great scrutiny.

"I'm Hardwick, by the way, sir," said Pa, eyeing the button with suspicion. "Whatever I can do to help, please don't hesitate to ask."

"Pleasure to meet you. I'm Penngrove. Earl Penngrove, Mr. Hardwick. Late of Philadelphia but now here to take up a clerkship with Chalmers and Duncan." Earl examined the hem and then felt the lining.

"Banking, is it?" asked Pa. "Well, now. That's a fine job for a young man as yourself. Fine indeed. Bank there myself, as a matter of fact, Mr. Penngrove. Solid establishment. You'll do well there, I'm sure of it."

Mr. Penngrove, despite Pa's platitudes, replaced the coat on the rack and started for the door. Pa stopped him and a smile crept over Mr. Penngrove's face. I watched them speak in low tones. Then they came toward the counter, and the coat was draped over Pa's arm. Pa scolded me as he handed me the coat and told me to fix the button with good strong thread.

"Now for the bill, Mr. Penngrove," said Pa, writing on a tablet. "I think we can make up fairly for the button issue."

I glanced at the bill and saw that Mr. Penngrove's little trick had reduced the price substantially.

Pa pushed the tablet toward Mr. Penngrove, who nodded with satisfaction. They shook hands in agreement.

Mr. Penngrove leaned over the counter and watched me attach the button.

"You've a nice stitch, miss."

"Funny thing, sir," I said, knotting the thread several times, "it was this very button that I took my needle to just this morning. It arrived loose and I fixed it. Can't see how it could have come off like that."

"Our little secret," he said with a grin and handed me my scissors. I trimmed the thread and began wrapping the coat in paper.

"Is Mr. Hardwick a relation of yours, miss?"

"He is my father, sir," I replied. "My name is Mariah Hardwick."

He cleared his throat. "Oh, I see."

Then he looked around the shop while I tied a string around the parcel.

"A very nice store, I must say, Miss Hardwick. Your father runs a fine business."

I handed him the parcel. His eyes were gray flecked with brown and looked mischievous. I thought about that loose button on the coat. It was a small indiscretion. A bit of foolery from an impetuous young man. A sale was a sale, Pa always said. Even if we get rooked sometimes, he always added.

I doubted I would ever see Earl Penngrove again.

❧ 2 ❧

MY MOTHER HAD A PASSION FOR Captain Meriwether Lewis, Captain William Clark, and their journey to the West in the early years of this century. Pa bought her a book all about the Corps of Discovery. *The Journals of Lewis and Clark* was one of Ma's prized possessions. She was prone to bringing it out at the least provocation and reading an entry aloud. On Meriwether Lewis's birthday, Ma favored this entry:

> *This day I completed my thirty-first year, and conceived that I had, in all human probability, now existed about half the period which I am to remain in this sublunary world. I reflected that I had as yet done little, very little, indeed, to further the hapiness of the human race, or to advance the information of the succeeding generation. I viewed with regret the many hours I have spent in indolence and now soarly feel the want of that information which those hours would have given me had they been judiciously expended. But since they are past and cannot be recalled, I dash from me the gloomy thought, and resolve in future to redouble*

my exertions and at least indeavor to promote those two primary objects of human existence, by giving them the aid of that portion of talents which nature and fortune have bestoed on me; or, in future to live for mankind, as I have heretofore lived for myself.

There was something about the journey of Lewis and Clark that gnawed at Ma's mind like the last piece in a puzzle that doesn't quite fit.

"Off they went and, it's the saints' truth, they weren't thought to come back alive. Imagine that? Maybe a few folks have been to parts out there. Trappers and such. But not so far and not many returned to tell of it at any rate. Every step they took forward got swallowed up from behind. Like as not, they might not ever see the step behind them again. What sort of person gets up one day and says, 'I believe I'll strike out for the next couple of years not having one iota of an idea of what I'll find?'"

"Do you think Captain Lewis ever got afraid, Ma?" I asked, knowing that Meriwether Lewis was her favorite.

Sometimes she would reply, "Oh, my word. Never was that man afraid of anything." Other times Ma would look at me solemnly and declare, "He knew that fear would be with him every day of his journey, Mariah. Every day. Mind you, knowing that, Meriwether Lewis went anyway. Isn't that something?"

The swallowing up is how I pictured it. Like falling into a dark river and seeing the sun disappear above the surface. A little girl might find that terrifying. I guess I might have been more frightened and less curious if Ma hadn't taken me out on the prairie so many times. Ma was raised on the west side of the Missouri on a farm that worked her parents to their early graves. When she'd met Pa, he had just opened his second dry goods store in St. Joseph. Ma was still living on the farm but barely hanging onto it after her folks passed. She'd come to Hardwick's Emporium for some nails. Over a cup of chicory coffee, they sat on pickle barrels and found love. Ma gave up the farm and moved to town with Pa. Her life got a lot easier after that, but she missed the farm and the isolation of the prairie.

She liked to take me across the river to the west bank. She called our excursions "scruffling." After the ferry crossing, we'd go to her old farm. Knock on the dilapidated sod cabin, kick up the dirt looking for something she might have left behind. Ma would pick a few weeds from the front yard. The farm had fallen to pieces with the weather and disuse. The people who bought the farm did not favor the hard work, let it go to ruins and then just abandoned the land. She did not like to think on that. The waste bothered her too much.

As I got older, Ma brought a rifle with her. If Pa knew she was teaching me to shoot, he did not let on. He'd long ago settled, uncomfortably, into the knowledge that he had taken Ma off the land. And he knew she missed it. If it consoled her to return to the prairie and her old farm to shoot, scruffling about and losing herself in old memories, so be it.

We'd do a little hunting and watch the sun bake the grass all around us. Ma would put her hands on her hips and stare to the west.

"There's nothing here for me anymore. It's all moved west. Out there, Mariah," said Ma. "Where the beyond begins. Just over that rise. You can't see it. But it's there. *The beyond.*" She'd look west, eyes on the horizon, and say with a happy sigh, "Out there. Why just look how much *out there* there is! Makes my mind swirl with the glory of it."

Ma and I started to call the westward horizon The Beyond as if it were a strange, new destination.

Some folks are content knowing where their next steps will take them, too afraid of not recognizing the ground or the trees or a river to leave behind what they know. Maybe they can't imagine leaving a new place behind them and wonder if they'll ever see it again. Maybe they think the next place won't be as good, and, well, then they're worried that they won't ever find a better place. I did not think that way. How can you know what is worse or better if you don't get to see enough to know? I wanted to see plenty and plenty more before I decided. I wondered about those thousands of miles Lewis and Clark explored. What was out there in The Beyond? I did not dwell on the enormous space, the lonely miles, and the empty stretches that made your eyes sore from looking. Not then, at any rate. It was the not knowing what was next around the bend that captured my imagination.

By the time I came to share my mother's devout feelings for Captain Lewis, the great man had been dead some forty years. Ma told me that she reckons he died of a broken heart. History may tell a different story about Meriwether Lewis, but she had her own idea.

"You can't come back from something like what he went through, seeing what he saw, the newness of The Beyond. No, I don't think a person could ever see things the same way again. That's what did his soul in, Mariah."

No matter what it did to Captain Lewis's soul, I still wanted to see the things he saw. I wanted to find the person that *I* might become with a journey of two thousand miles behind me.

We would take turns reading from *The Journals*. Ma always took the entries by Captain Lewis. I would try to imitate the gregarious, scientific, and friendly William Clark. My mother would assume the moody drawl of Meriwether Lewis. Pa might, on occasion, listen to our readings. He would scoff at us.

"I cannot for the life of me understand what you two women see in these journals. It sounds like a miserable journey in mean country with Indians abounding, and the men always seem to be sick. I hear no joy or wonderment."

Ma read a favorite passage from Captain Lewis. She called it "The Great Mystery."

During the time of my being on the Plains and above the falls I, as also all my party, repeatedly heard a nois which proceeded from a direction a little to the N. of west, as loud [noise] and resembling precisely the discharge of a piece of ordinance of 6 pounds at the distance of 5 or six miles . . . thinking it was thunder most probably which they had mistaken. at length, walking in the plains yesterday near the most extreme SE bend of the River above the falls, I heard this nois very distinctly. It was perfectly calm, clear, and not a cloud to be seen. I halted and listened attentively about two hours, dureing which time I heard two other discharges, and took the direction of the sound with my pocket compass, which was as nearly West from me as I could estimate from the sound . . . . I have thought it probable that it might be caused by running water in some of the caverns of those emence mountains, on the principal of the blowing caverns; but in such case the sounds would be periodical and regular, which is not the case with this, being sometimes heard once only and at other times several discharges in quick succession. it is heard also at different times of the day and night. I am at a great loss to account for this Phenomenon. I well recollect hearing the Minitarees say that those Rocky mountains make a great noise . . . .

"I tell you every time. That's a thunderstorm he's talking about. Plain and simple," Pa would say.

Mother and I would look knowingly at each other. Captain Lewis always noted the weather in his journal entries: that day was perfectly calm and cloudless.

I liked thinking about the adventure out there for the taking. It only took courage and a will to see the strange, new sights of the West. My thoughts ran to the kind of folks who were out there in The Beyond.

I cannot put a finger on when the restlessness took hold. I think the journal entries seeped into my dreams more than I knew at the time. I took longer and longer walks about town and always ended up at the edge of town. It was here that the wild prairie began and stretched to the riverbanks and westward. As I got older, I began to cross the river without Ma. I wanted to go alone. I imagined the air over the expanse stretching those thousands of miles Captain Lewis talked about. Air that I breathed here that might have touched a wilderness in The Beyond.

I imagined there was an edge, a falling-off place where the grass ended abruptly. I wondered if I would ever travel that far and get swallowed up in The Beyond.

Then the real possibility that I might see some of what I imagined in The Beyond presented itself in the form of Earl Penngrove.

3

It was a Saturday afternoon not long after Earl Penngrove bought that frock coat. Pa let me go early from the shop so I could take a ride on the west bank of the river. I collected our old horse, Daniel, from the stable and made my way down to the ferry pier. The pilot, Hagerty, greeted me as I brought Daniel aboard.

"Well, now. My second fare of the day, Mariah. A gent come a little while ago. On foot, though. You'll probably see him up top of the bank."

I held onto Daniel, for he was not fond of the ferry, and stood next to Hagerty as he pulled us across the muddy river. He liked to gossip as he worked, and he always had a good story to tell about some of the townsfolk. Today, he had a good one: Bru Thomas, the blacksmith, dropped his anvil on his toe but did not quite cut it clean off. What remained of his toe was still attached to his foot and stuck in the dirt. He hollered for his wife, who came in and, not knowing what was wrong, shoved him aside to see what was the matter. "Toe came off just fine," said Hagerty with a nod of satisfaction. "They dug it up so their old sow wouldn't root around for it."

A short time later, I waved to Hagerty and trotted Daniel up the road from the ferry dock and onto the plateau where the prairie grass grew tall and thick. We rode along the path toward Ma's farm. I liked to picture a much younger Ma standing in the front yard, her apron flapping in the breeze coming off the endless vista around her. She liked to say that you can't get clothes properly clean unless you prairie-dry them. Never did she think "town laundry" was as good as "farm laundry."

Then I saw him.

He was leaning against the ruins of Ma's sod house, chewing on an oat stalk and looking westward. When he caught sight of me, he cupped his hands over his eyes in the glare of the sun. He waved. It was Earl Penngrove.

I tied Daniel to an old fence post and loosened his cinch. A pair of fat rabbits darted into a large bush a few yards from where I stood. I took my rifle down from my saddle. "You think you can get them from this distance, Miss Hardwick?" Earl said, eyeing the rifle as he walked up to me.

"I aim to try, Mr. Penngrove," I replied. "I am surprised to see you out here. Hardly anybody comes this way."

"Except you. And sometimes your mother."

I felt a prickle of hair rising on my neck. How did he know I came out here? Had he been following me?

He laughed seeing my concern. "Now, don't fret. A body has a right to come out this way. Wasn't tracking you or anything like that. It was the day before I come to your pa's shop. I just came as far as the top of bank that time. Saw you and your Ma rummaging around. The ferry pilot told me this was her farm. It must have been a nice place at one time."

Knowing now what I came to find out later about Earl, I should have ridden Daniel home at once.

But I did not.

Even as he squinted in the sun, his gray eyes looked at me with curiosity and interest. He certainly couldn't have followed me today.

Maybe he liked this spot, too. Like Ma and I did. A part of me should have been wary, but it pleased me that he wanted to know what I did out here. He did not scoff at the notion. He did not ask why. I wanted to know more about this stranger.

"Well, as long as you're here, I must give you the grand tour," I said, trying to sound confident and unflustered. "The cabin was here. Over there was a pasture for cows. They had chickens and goats, too."

Earl and I walked over a collapsed fence to the old well. He peered inside. "Went dry, did it?"

I sighed. "Yes. But it could have been fixed. The folks who bought the place from Ma did not have what it takes to keep it up. They cleared out within a year. I don't think they even sold it."

"Your pa didn't want to keep it?"

"He likes town. He wasn't much on farming. Ma was alone here for a while once her folks died. I guess she thought it would be better to give it up."

"She miss it much?"

"All the time."

"I reckon she must," he said. "Oh, I don't mind town. It's got its uses, of course. But I do enjoy the space and the quiet out here. I aim to see more of it, too. And soon."

We had stopped to sit on a couple of stumps. The wind kicked up here and there, but it was mostly peaceful and warm. The swooshing sound of the breeze playing in the prairie grass came and went at intervals. At any other time, I would have listened to the song in the grass, but I felt a change coming over me. Anticipation of something about to happen. It was when Earl said he aimed to see more of *it*. Though I did not quite know what he meant, it made me feel excited.

I hesitated for a moment, almost too eager to hear what he would say next. "Do you mean you have plans to move on?"

"Oh yes," he said, sitting forward to pluck another oat stalk. "Very soon, if I can make the arrangements."

"But you've only just arrived. What about the bank and your job?"

"Well, Miss Hardwick, I'll tell you. If you don't mind hearing it," he said slowly.

"Please, go ahead, Mr. Penngrove," I replied.

"About a year ago, I received a communication from a lawyer in San Francisco. He reckons I'm the only relative they can track down of this gent named Lawson. The lawyer asked for some proof of the relation, and I managed to find the same Lawson in an old Bible that belonged to my grandmother. The family tree, you see, was all written there. Sure enough, we are related. It's the best proof I could put together, and I aim to bring it to the lawyer. He already told me it sounded like it was good enough. I got a letter back from him."

"Who is this man Lawson?"

"Turns out he's got a lumber business out west. Or *had* this business. See, he passed away and left no survivors. According to this lawyer, Lawson did very well. Before he died, he mentioned a nephew named Penngrove who lived in New York somewhere. That Penngrove is dead, too. Long story short, I'm related to that nephew and I'm the only one left. Seems like I got an inheritance coming to me from this fellow Lawson. All I have to do is get to San Francisco, bring that old Bible with the family tree, and claim it."

He stood up and paced for a few minutes, scratching his head. "I've been heading west for some time now. I make a little stake and off I go again. Then I stop and make a little more. That's why I'm in St. Joseph. Might be this is the last stop until I can get on one of those wagon trains heading west. I got almost enough."

Earl stopped walking and pointed. "Hey, now! There's one of those rabbits again, Miss Hardwick. Right over yonder."

Sure enough, there was a fat rabbit sunning himself in between two bushes. I raised my rifle carefully and planted my feet far apart for stability.

"Easy now," I whispered as I took aim.

I fired and caught the rabbit below the ear. He tumbled sideways into the bush and did not move again.

"Nice shooting, Miss Hardwick. Somebody like you would make any man heading west proud to have you ride alongside on a wagon. Not only pretty but handy, too." Earl put his hands on his hips and laughed. "Now that was a damn foolish thing to say. My apologies, miss. I shouldn't have said that. I mean no offense."

"Of course, you didn't mean it, Mr. Penngrove," I said quickly. "No harm." I picked up the rabbit and tied it to the back of my saddle.

Earl, on the other side of Daniel now, rested his head on his arms across the saddle. His gray eyes regarded me. "A fine lady such as yourself probably wouldn't want to leave St. Joseph. You've got your kin, and it isn't likely your folks would want you gallivanting into parts unknown. Besides, going west isn't an easy prospect. Why, I can't even imagine the dangers. A lot more than prairie to see, though. It might be the most wonderful thing ever. Or a disaster, I suppose."

I tightened Daniel's cinch and untied his reins. Earl's words hung in the air like a dandelion fairy.

"Still," he drawled, his mouth widened into a crooked grin, "it's pleasant to think about it, don't you agree? So much to see."

Reins in hand, I looked past Earl as far as my eyes could reach. Pa said there was just more damn prairie out there. But I knew that it ended somewhere far away. And what a thrill it would be to roll over that last patch of prairie and onto something entirely new. I smiled. "Mr. Penngrove, I do agree that it is very pleasant to think on."

"A body wonders if he might be as brave as, say, Mr. Lewis and Mr. Clark. They sure saw it all and then some," Earl remarked. He picked another stalk of grass and peeled it back to expose the green shoot.

I dropped the reins.

"It just so happens my ma and I favor Captain Meriwether Lewis and Captain William Clark and their adventures. Are you familiar with their journey?" I asked, trying to calm my breath.

He looked startled. "Oh, yes, Miss Hardwick. Their journals incite my imagination. Indeed, they do," he replied. "Pardon my surprise. But have you read *The Journals*?"

"Yes, sir," I replied. "Ma and I read from them regularly."

I could hardly believe my ears. Outside of Ma and Pa, I hadn't talked about *The Journals* with anyone.

Earl grinned. "Is that a fact? I do declare, we have something in common, don't we?"

I chattered on about some of my favorite passages and quotes. Earl nodded. I liked it that he was interested.

The sky started to darken with rain clouds and I took my leave. As I rode off, I turned back to see Earl sitting back down on the stump, unconcerned that raindrops were falling on him. He certainly wasn't what I expected. That pleased me.

And with that, Earl Penngrove came into my life like a snake in a bird's nest.

4

THE NEXT TIME I SAW EARL, he was talking with Pa in the small room behind the counter at the shop. I could see Pa sitting behind his desk with a thoughtful expression as he listened. I wondered what they were discussing.

Presently, I watched Pa walk Earl around the counter and to the front door where they shook hands. Earl glanced back at me, smiled, and tipped his hat. His eyes grabbed mine and I hung onto that look until he turned and went through the door. My heart thumped. That was Earl. He could charm the legs off a cow without really trying.

"A gentleman always asks first," said Pa to me when he returned to the counter. "Mr. Penngrove would like to call on you. I think that's a fine idea, Mariah. Does that suit you?"

I thought about the other gents who had come to call on me. Each one would sit in our parlor with a plate of Ma's sandwiches and a glass of lemonade. I was expected to make small talk, which I found difficult. How I wished the sandwiches and lemonade would disappear so they would leave. Once there was a farmer who smelled like wet hay and had mismatched boots. Another time Pa brought a long-necked preacher who gurgled while he talked, which made me want to pat his back for fear he was choking.

Earl was something different altogether. It wouldn't hurt to set a spell with him.

"He has invited us to a picnic this Sunday afternoon," said Pa.

Sunday arrived and Earl appeared at our door carrying a basket of picnic provisions. "I hope it'll do, Miss Hardwick," he said, opening the basket for my inspection. Hard-boiled eggs, apples, legs of chicken, and a bottle of cider.

He'd gone to a lot of trouble, I noted. This was a feast. "Thank you, Mr. Penngrove. This looks very nice. Ma is bringing a pecan pie."

"Then you are in favor of a picnic?" he asked.

"Why, yes. It's a grand idea," I replied.

His eyes sparkled and he grinned, showing a straight line of white teeth. "I thought you would."

We heard the snickering of the team harnessed to the wagon in our front yard. Ma appeared with the pie, which she placed in the basket after Earl's profuse compliments over Ma's bonnet and teal-colored dress. He certainly was a pleasing gentleman.

Pa steadied the team as we put the basket in the flat bed. There were benches along the bed. Earl helped Ma into the wagon and then extended his hand to help me. His fingers were long and smooth as he grasped my arm.

"It's your picnic, Mr. Penngrove. Lead the way!" Pa responded with a toss of his head. With a flick of the whip, the wagon lurched away from our drive and out onto Ribidoux Street.

Earl, looking straight at me, said, "What would you say to crossing the river and driving out on the west bank, Mr. Hardwick? I know of a fine spot on the bluffs with the prettiest stand of oak I ever did see."

My face burned. I turned away to hide my smile. Ma elbowed me and laughed.

Pa shouted over the wagon wheels noisily churning up the dried mud, "You'll be pleasing the women folk with your plan, sir. Nothing more than a journey out to the prairie to warm their hearts!"

After we crossed the river, Earl took us to a beautiful spot on the bluffs above the river. St. Joseph spread out below us in the distance. We were very near my mother's old farm. I could see her looking wistfully in its direction. A blue gingham cloth was spread out on the grass beneath a tall oak.

"Mr. Penngrove," said Pa as he ate, "I ran into Seth Chalmers. He tells me you are a fine young man and doing well at the bank. Sounds like you're settling in here in St. Joseph. Are you fixed on staying then?"

"Why, yes, sir," replied Earl. "Settling in as easy as pie. I'm mighty grateful to have made friends with good folks such as yourselves." Pa gave me a wink, which Earl couldn't help but notice.

When we finished, Earl asked Pa if he might me take for a walk. Pa looked at Ma and she nodded approval.

"We'll stay within shouting distance, ma'am," said Earl with a laugh.

I took his arm and we strolled away from my parents.

"I see you are wearing your new coat, Mr. Penngrove. I trust the button hasn't misbehaved again." He touched the button.

"It is stitched to my heart, Miss Hardwick. It won't get away ever again." I couldn't help but laugh.

We found the spot where we sat before, on the stumps near the fallen-down pasture fence by Ma's sod house.

"What do you like best about this place?" he asked.

"I like the quiet of the prairie. Then there's wondering what is beyond the prairie. All the way to where the sun sets. I do a lot of wondering about the places that might be out there. I look as far as I can see, and I think about what it's like to go where I've never been before." I glanced at him. "You must think that awfully foolish, Mr. Penngrove."

"No, I don't, Miss Hardwick. I admire it."

Then he turned to me with a solemn expression. "I aim to make my stake by spring, Miss Hardwick. I truly mean to go west with the first wagon train come April."

"That's very exciting, Mr. Penngrove."

"Would you think it terribly forward if I asked for your assistance in making my preparations? After all, I will be spending considerable time at your father's shop buying what I need. Would you oblige me with your friendship?"

I told him that I would oblige and that any help I could provide him for his journey was his for the asking.

The next day at Pa's shop, my mind wandered as I went about my work. I wondered when Earl Penngrove would appear again and how it would be to help him outfit a wagon for his journey—a journey that was starting to occupy my own thoughts even in the short time since I'd learned about it. I began picturing myself atop a wagon. Sometimes, Earl was sitting next to me. Other times, I was alone. I couldn't decide which image felt best.

I remembered seeing a wagon train set off from St. Joseph last spring. The long line of wagons snaked through town heading north to the shallow crossing upriver. I recalled one wagon. A woman was perched on the seat, reins in hand, with a frightened expression on her face. A man walked alongside the team of oxen guiding them down the road. One of the wheels hit a rock, and the woman bounced hard on the wooden seat and let out a shriek. The man turned sharply and yelled at her to "quit her damn squawking." She bit her lip and I could see tears forming in her eyes. A toll was being taken on their relationship already and they hadn't even left town. I pondered what became of that couple, how they fared and whether they made it to their destination. It was a long stretch to consider myself and Earl, a virtual stranger, in such a situation. But the idea kept coming back to me.

"You're not your usual chatterbox, Mariah," said Pa, eyeing me thoughtfully as he stacked bolts of fabric on the shelf.

When I did not answer, he chuckled. "I reckon I know what's on your mind." It wouldn't surprise me if he knew exactly what I was thinking about. Pa had a way of knowing things about me.

Instead, he said. "Mr. Earl Penngrove. Am I right?"

"Well, I . . ." I stammered.

"You know, Mariah," he said, "you've got more in common with him than you think. And maybe that's enough to, well, make a good start."

"Pa, please," I said. "I hardly know him."

"I ran into Mr. Penngrove at the bank. The day after he bought that coat. We had a good laugh over the button. Oh, sure, I know all about that. Got to get up early in the morning to fool old Hardwick!"

I had to smile. Of course, Pa would have caught on to it.

"In fact, Mr. Penngrove was quite taken with you. We had a fine chat but all he wanted to talk about was you."

I shook my head. "And he told you nothing about this inheritance of his in San Francisco, Pa?"

"No," said Pa, looking up with interest. "He didn't mention it. Just to say that he was thinking on heading west and seeking his fortune. Filled with plans and ideas."

I told Pa about the lawyer's letter, Lawson's company in San Francisco, his death and legacy, the family tree in the Bible, and how Earl was making a stake to leave in spring. "I'm sure he didn't want to put on airs to me," Pa commented. "Humble sort of fellow, I think. But he asked me all sorts of questions about you. Like any eager young man would. I even told him about how you and your mother enjoy the writings of Lewis and Clark. Just to give him a warning in case you two corner him with one of your readings one evening. Prepare him for it."

This gave me pause. I considered the conversation Earl and I had had over Daniel's saddle. The one in which he had brought up Lewis and Clark. As if it were his own idea. A little voice inside me whispered caution. But I paid it no mind.

When Earl started coming around more frequently and brought lists of supplies he needed, I grew excited for him. He said jokingly that it seemed like I was preparing for my own journey and not his at all.

"I'm much obliged that you don't find this onerous, Miss Hardwick," said Earl. He winked. "It makes all the planning more tolerable with you helping me."

I liked his ambition and his interest in all the details. He showed me pictures of the wagon he was having built and how everything would fit neatly inside.

"That's where I'll put the grain barrel for the team. But I should think there'll be good grazing up until the cold sets in. I'm bringing two containers for water. That's where folks don't plan well. Water could be a problem. It's not just the humans but the horses that need it. I'm not much of a cook but I was told that a Dutch oven is the ticket. I guess I'll learn. So I got a place for that . . . over here under the bunk, next to the tool box."

"I must admit, it is exhilarating. I just hope you've got everything you need," I said.

Earl winked again. "Just missing one little thing, Miss Hardwick. Just a one."

It did not take long for me to fall in love. I guess it was a mixture of the planning and my own notion of The Beyond. I couldn't see straight for the adventure of it all. I hadn't thought of marriage as an adventure. I might have saved myself a lot of trouble if I had.

He came to dinner several times, and even Ma said that we were two peas in a pod talking about this trip of his.

"I don't like to think it, Mariah," she said. "But I wonder if you want to go with him. It's such a long way and I might not ever see you again."

"I wouldn't worry, Ma. It's not likely. He's only got enough money for himself. Besides, how could I leave you and Pa?"

"Mariah. You need to start thinking about yourself. Mr. Penngrove seems to be a good man. Pa and I want you to be happy.

Would you go if he asked?"

"I don't know. It would be something to see all the things we've read about, wouldn't it? I haven't made my mind up about Earl. And there's no reason to think he's made up his mind about me."

"Well, I don't know about that." Ma gave me a look and we both laughed.

The snow came early. I was helping Pa bring in wood to heat the stove in the shop. Earl came through the door followed by a swirl of icy wind.

He looked expectantly at me as he brushed flakes from his coat. "Did your father tell you?"

I heard Pa clear his throat and looked at him. He was beaming from ear to ear. Then he went away into his office, shut the door, and left Earl and me alone. "Tell me what?"

"He said that I might . . . and I guess that's what I'm doing. And if it would be all right, that is . . . If you know what I mean, Mariah," he said, fidgeting with his hat.

Despite his stammering, I knew exactly what he meant.

℘ 5 ℘

AFTER OUR WEDDING, WE TOOK UP residence in a small house, just a few doors down from my parents. We told Ma and Pa that we hoped to join the wagon train in April. I must admit Ma was heartbroken, but she understood.

I talked of little else with Earl. We made lists and studied maps. He seemed less fearful of the journey as we plotted it out. It appeared we would be ready as long as Earl was successful in earning the stake we needed to start out.

Ma came over one evening. She brought the journals with her. We let the book fall open, as was our custom, and chose whatever selection was on the page. This one was an account of William Clark upon encountering an animal that was new and strange.

Joseph Fields killed and brought in an animal called by the French Brarow [badger] . . . . This animal burrows in the ground and feeds on flesh (prairie dogs), bugs, and vegetables. His shape and size is like that of a beaver, his head, mouth, etc., is like a dog with short ears, his tail and hair like that of a ground hog but longer and lighter. His internals like the internals of a hog. His skin is thick and loose, his belly is white and the hair short. . . . The hind feet small and toes crooked, his legs are short and when he moves just sufficient to raise his body above the ground. He is of the Bear species. We have his skin stuffed.

It was a rare evening that Earl was home. He often had business at the bank that kept him away until late. He said he was working hard to make the money necessary for our journey west. I was pleased that he lingered in the parlor to hear us reading.

"Imagine that. He'd never seen a badger, Earl," I said. "The French trappers knew about badgers and had a name for it, of course. Still, it was unknown outside of that part of the world. There were so many new plants and animals that they found on their journey. I wonder what else is out there that nobody really knows about? And not just animals. What about new kinds of people who have been so far away from towns and crowds that they just act differently?"

I wasn't entirely sure what I meant. Ma and I were curious about the fate of Lewis and Clark and their men once they returned from their expedition. Or if any of them went back to the wild, unable to adjust to civilization. I had no idea at the time what I would learn about folks who take on The Beyond.

Earl laughed nervously. "No doubt we'll have our share of wild beasts, Mariah. And of a kind of man or woman who lives out there. I'm not sure how much you should look forward to it."

"Don't forget. I'm a good shot, Earl. I'll take care of any beasts that come our way."

He nodded. "I am a fortunate man."

Earl told me he had hoped for a raise so that we could indeed be ready to leave in April. But because the business was poorly managed, as he put it, the partners were keeping him down and would not offer him any rise in salary.

He'd come home late again, smelling of drink. Pacing in the parlor, he was speaking to himself in harsh, angry tones. Something about getting his way no matter what. When he slammed his fist on the table, I jumped from my chair.

"Maybe you ought to find something else, Earl. This is no good, being troubled so. There must be other work for you," I stammered. "If we don't leave by April, it can't be helped. Your inheritance will be there, won't it?"

His eyes bore down on me. "We will leave in April come hell or high water, Mariah. Count on it."

The first hint of trouble came one afternoon. I was hanging laundry when Seth Chalmers, Earl's boss from the bank, appeared at the front gate.

"Mrs. Penngrove?" he asked. "May I have a word with you?"

I put down my basket and hurried to the gate. I wondered why he was here, in the middle of a work day. "Hello, Mr. Chalmers," I said. "Would you like to come in?"

"I'm looking for Earl," he said, his gaze traveling over the house, my basket of laundry, and, finally, on me. "Has he come home?"

"No, sir. He's not here. Is there some kind of trouble?"

He grunted and shook his head. "I know where to look next," he said. Then, tipping his hat at me, Mr. Chalmers set off down the road. Away from town. Away from the bank.

He was going to the river. Why on earth would Earl be down at the river?

I decided to follow him.

He walked purposefully along the road and I struggled to keep up with him. The noon sun beat down and I felt perspiration break out on the back of my neck. I stayed in the shade of the tree-lined road until it gave way to the open track leading down to the river. He did not glance back.

I paused at the rise of the bluff overlooking the river before it descended down to the ferry dock and the tavern on the shore.

Mr. Chalmers entered the tavern by the front entrance. Once I heard the loud and boisterous shouts of men over the clinking of bottles and glasses, I decided I did not want to follow him inside. A poorly tuned piano tried in vain to be heard above the raucous. I went around to the back of the tavern. There was a canvas flap pulled over an opening in the clapboard wall. I pushed it aside and found that I was less than a foot from the back of Earl's head. He was sitting at a table with a group of other men playing cards. I looked with one eye through the small slit. Earl had a large pile of money in front of him. Whatever was happening in the game came to a standstill while all eyes were on Earl. It was his turn, I supposed. He waited a long time, his hand of cards pressed against his coat.

Then he placed the cards face up on the table. There was a great riot of cheers and I saw Earl's shoulders slump. The pile of money was swept away from him.

I was not sure what I had seen, but it was enough to shake me up. I ran back up the bluff away from the tavern and made my way home.

My mind was in a tangle of questions. I managed to finish hanging the laundry and stood trembling beneath the clothesline for a long time wondering what to do. I saw my father arrive at home and thought I should go tell him what I had seen. Something prevented me from doing so. A last attempt at preserving Earl's dignity? Our marriage was our own business and we would deal with problems by ourselves. I sat on the porch and waited to hear what Earl would say. The sun was setting when I spotted Earl coming down the street. Instead of walking to our house, he turned directly into the gated yard of my parents' home. He paused before the porch, straightened his back, and then went up the steps. Again, I fought the impulse to run to their house and foist myself into the conversation. Surely, Earl would be telling my father everything, imploring him to offer some advice. It would be hard for him to confess to Pa. I would give him that time. If anybody would know what to do, it would be my father.

I prepared our dinner and placed it on the stove to warm. It had been nearly two hours since Earl went to my parents. What was being said? Who would tell me about it? A slow rage started to build. I had a right to know, didn't I? We would face it together, Earl and I. *I am not a child*, I told myself. *Go down there right now and demand an explanation!* I tore off my apron and was heading to the door when Earl and my father walked in.

Pa wore a grim expression. Earl stood a little behind him and I could not see his face at first. When I did, he appeared ashen and exhausted.

"What is it?" I asked. "What's been happening, Earl? Mr. Chalmers was here. And then he left. I followed him. He went into Hagerty's Tavern." I hesitated then said, "I saw you there, Earl."

There was a moment of silence. I looked from Pa to Earl and back again.

"Well, Earl. Aren't you going to tell her?" asked Pa sharply

He hung his head and the words came thick and strange, like he was reciting from a book. "I've made a mess of things, Mariah. But it was because I love you and wanted us to get on that wagon train. So much so that I did wrong. Real wrong."

My throat closed up.

"Tell her the whole thing, Earl," said Pa.

"I wasn't going to have enough money." He looked at Pa who crossed his arms and sighed. "And I wanted to have more than enough. For us. So I gambled."

"And where did you get the money to gamble, Earl?" asked Pa, pressing Earl to continue.

"Stole it from the bank. I stole it and I aimed to pay it back before it got noticed. But it didn't work out that way."

Pa said he knew all about Earl's visits to the tavern. We sat out our kitchen table and Pa spelled it out for me. Whatever anger he felt must have been doled out over the previous hours. He was calm now, and my father showed he was what I always knew him to be:

fair and sincere. But I also knew that he was deeply troubled by the grim set of his mouth as he spoke.

He would pay off Earl's gambling debts and cover the funds taken from the bank. He said he would do it to save me from scandal though he knew it would only be the beginning. He hoped that, in time, it would be forgotten. Pa thought that a new horizon brought about by the journey west would harden Earl and make him develop a backbone. Pa gave us a generous stake plus he covered all of the expenses for the supplies, wagon, and fee for the wagon train. Everything that Earl purchased at Pa's store had been on credit. And Earl promised to pay back every penny he owed with the inheritance.

After my father left, Earl placed his hands on the table and looked me straight in the eye. "I'm not going to hang my head down about this, Mariah. It's done and finished. I made a mistake and I'm grateful for your father's help. But I'm going to carry on now and see this journey west to the very end. I will take that inheritance and bring back what I owe your father straight away. I don't ask your forgiveness, Mariah. I don't deserve it. Not now. I aim to be a better man for it, though. God-fearing and truth-telling."

I told him that I believed him. When he asked that we never speak of it again, I agreed. There seemed no point in harping on the situation. If we really intended to set out on this journey, we needed to be a team. I did not want to be like that couple I had seen last year, quibbling at the least little bump in the road. I surmised that, over time and over the long miles ahead, Earl would talk to me about it. And I'd come to understand and forgive.

The next day, I visited Ma. She was sitting in the parlor with her mending. I knew she wouldn't talk about Earl. Ma did not believe in offering an opinion unless asked. Whatever Pa had discussed with her, she'd already made up her mind about it. I think she knew I was determined to make this journey west. Whether she agreed or not, it wasn't her place to stop me. She put down her work and brought out the journals.

"I think we need this," she said.

As was our custom, she let the book fall open and started reading from the page in front of her.

Last evening, Drewyer visited his traps and caught a beaver and an otter; the beaver was large and fat we have therefore fared sumptuously today; this we consider a great prize for another reason, it being a full grown beaver was well supplyed with the materials for making batet with which to catch others. . . . To prepare beaver bate, the castor or bark stone is taken as the base, this is gently pressed out of the bladder-like bag which contains it, into a phiol of 4 ounces with a wide mouth . . . to this you will add half a nutmeg, a doozen or 15 grains of cloves and 30 grains of cinimon finely pulverized, stir them well together and then add as much ardent spirits to the composition as will reduce it to the consistency of mustard prepared for the table. . . . When cloves are not to be had, use double the quantity of allspice, and when no spice can be obtained use the bark of the root of sassafras.

When Ma finished, she closed the book and looked down. For a moment, I thought she was crying. I could see her shoulders were heaving up and down. *Poor Ma. She might be fearful of how Earl will treat me on this journey. I would certainly reassure her that I am well-equipped to take care of myself. It can't get much worse than this. And if it does, I won't hesitate to state my intentions to carry on without him. Fine words for a newly married woman,* I thought. But it was exactly how I felt.

But Ma was not crying. She was laughing.

"Every time I read that part, about them making that beaver bait, I just can't get over how they are directly in the backside of a beaver to get that castor. When I think of the fine ladies at Pa's store buying up castor for their aches and pains, I wonder what they would think if they knew where it came from!"

It was like this when we read from *The Journals*: the words took you away from whatever worried you.

"I thought you were crying. About me and Earl."

She dried her eyes and grew serious. "I know what you're made of, Mariah. You've got the fire in your eyes. Like Captain Lewis. No man's going to get the better of you."

§

By the end of March, we had our wagon, a team of horses, and mostly all the supplies the wagon train outfit suggested we pack.

The snow was melting enough for us to take the wagon out for practice. We spent days out on an isolated track of road training with the horses and the loaded wagon, packing and repacking to make it fit and balanced. We were told that the wagon master would test us with the team and wagon before allowing us to sign on for the long journey. I was starting to like it, hard as it was.

We learned how to turn, back up, rig it up, fix a wheel, mend a harness, and splint an axle. Earl would fight with the horses, cursing if they did not rein in properly. I cajoled them and tried to be patient. We would be dependent on them. We both dreaded pitching our canvas tent. The canvas was still stiff and difficult to manage. Wrestling it up into a precarious shelter with the poles tethered in the baffles was hard enough. Then a light breeze would blow and the whole thing collapsed on us.

As our departure grew near, Ma took me aside.

"Earl is going to work out. I just know it. Give him time. It's a big responsibility taking a wife out on the trail like this. Of course, he's going to be a bit skittish," she said. Then she held my face in her hands and smiled. "I can see that *you're* not afraid, Mariah. Whatever happens, you're going to be just fine. I just know it." Then she said, "Wait here."

When she returned, she had something wrapped in thick oilskin with a bone clasp. She handed it to me. "I'm wanting you to take this and let it be a reminder."

Of course, I knew what it was. *The Journals.* I hesitated. It was her prized possession. "You think of me, Mariah, when you're out there. Sakes alive, I'd be coming with you if I could. Maybe you'll see some of the sights they write about in this book. See some of the things Captain Lewis saw. And you tell me all about it," she said. "And maybe, just maybe, if you don't see that fire in him, in that husband of yours, you've got plenty of your own. You hear? All your own."

The night before we left, we each packed our trunks. I watched Earl put his family Bible, the very thing that he needed to prove that the inheritance was his, beneath his folded trousers and shirts. The book was wrapped up in thick sail-making material and bound with wire. He wasn't taking any chances with it being damaged. In my trunk, I placed a few dresses, a tablecloth that we'd gotten for a wedding present, some other clothing, and the oilskin satchel with the bone clasp that contained *The Journals of Lewis and Clark*. I vowed to keep the tradition of reading whatever passage the book opened upon.

✎ 6 ✎

ONE DAY IN MID-APRIL, EARL AND I sat on a hard bench looking over
the rumps of our horses. We moved in a long line of other wagons
heading westward away from St. Joseph. My parents had come to see
us off and waved to us as we left.

The party of forty individuals making up our wagon train came
from all parts of the country. We had only met a few of them so
far, had talked with them long enough to learn their names but not
much else. Everyone was concentrating on keeping their teams in
line and following the wagon master's instructions. A great cloud
of dust encircled the party of wagons. Earl and I tied kerchiefs over
our mouths and noses and struggled to keep in line. It was not easy.
We watched as the folks in one wagon lost control of their team and
careened away, disappearing over the rise. Presently, they were brought
back by the wagon master himself, hollering and cursing.

The wagon master was a big, brooding man named Flem Keating.
This was his third trip west. He had a dozen or so men in his employ
who kept track of the livestock, divvied up the work groups, maintained discipline, and helped with wagon breakdowns. Our wagons

were organized into three divisions of four wagons each. Eventually, each division would take turns leading the train. Since it was our first day, one of Keating's men rode along with the lead wagon in each division to make sure we kept in somewhat of a straight line. Most folks were skilled at driving their wagons. Others, like Earl and me, were still learning, and Mr. Keating rode up and down the long line of wagons shouting out instructions, forcing teams back in line with his huge horse. He must have ridden twenty miles back and forth that day.

We were not in a lead wagon, so it was our job to stay behind the wagon in front of us. But there was also a wagon behind us and if our speed wasn't constant, the rear wagon could run right into us. They were plenty of white-knuckled drivers that day. Earl and I took turns and even that did not prevent us from developing blisters and raw hands after a few hours.

One thing we learned quickly: you could never tie down the gear on your wagon tightly enough. Twice I had to jump down and run back to fetch something that had bounced out of the ropes. Scrambling along trying to refasten it to a moving wagon was a sight to behold. I wasn't the only one. Mr. Keating rode up and down the line yelling at everyone to attend "tonight's lesson in tying a damn good knot!"

If something wasn't falling off the wagon, there was plenty of stuff falling *inside* the wagon. It did not take long to learn that just because you put something in its rightful place in the wagon did not mean it was going to stay that way. We lost a pound of flour the first day. I turned to see the sack fall out of its little cubby and break open on the floorboards. A fine white trail of dust seeped out from the bottom of our wagon as it bumped along.

At last we stopped for the day. It was early afternoon. We made a corral circle coupling the wagons with tongue and ox chains to form a barrier. Mr. Keating told us that we needed to be able to circle the wagons quickly in case of Indian attack. Indians had not caused much worry in the previous three trips, but we would circle up every night just the same. It was good practice, he said.

Our camp was on a bluff above a bend in the river. Earl and I tumbled off the wagon, stiff and sore.

"Maybe we need to fashion a cushion or something," I told Earl as I rubbed my behind. True to his word, Mr. Keating called for the entire party to gather around his wagon while he demonstrated the correct way to tie gear so it wouldn't fall off. It looked so easy when he did it. Earl and I returned to our own wagon and methodically went through every single item inside and out. We vowed never to lose anything ever again.

It was almost dark when we were finally able to think about eating. We gathered wood and found water. Earl brought out a couple of stools and set the cooking fire. By the time I had a pot of stew nearly ready, we were both exhausted. Our horses were grazing nearby. Most of the activity around us had died down by then as the circle of wagons settled into evening. It was a pleasant sight with the river meandering past below the bluff. Around us rose the quiet sounds of folks tucking into their meals.

The wagon in front of ours held a family with three young children. They were the Johnsons. A lantern glowed beneath the canvas and I could see the mother making up three small beds. The wagon behind us carried an older couple who both were trying to get a fire going. But I could see they'd not gathered enough kindling and the logs were smoldering.

"Earl," I said, "take a few of our small sticks over to them. They won't have a cooking fire unless we help them get it started."

When he came back, he said "My Lord, the kind of people who sign on for this. They've got to be in their seventies. The old man is hobbled up. The wife isn't much better. Didn't they have any children to bring along to help?"

I found out later that Mr. and Mrs. Leon did indeed have a son who was supposed to be accompanying them. But he ran off before they started and so here they were on their own. I feared for them as I knew the journey ahead was just beginning and we hadn't even begun to understand the trials and tribulations before us.

We fell into the rhythm of the days on the wagon and the evenings around our fires. The Leons joined us more often than not for supper. They were heading to Colorado where they had a niece. Mr. Leon kept to himself. His wife said that he kept hoping his son would suddenly show up one day, riding alongside the wagon and begging forgiveness. I saw him looking back sometimes to the track our wagons left behind, in the hope his son would appear.

One evening, Mr. Keating was making his rounds to check on everyone. I asked him about one tribe of Indians that Captain Lewis described in *The Journals*. I had just finished this selection and was curious:

> . . . *[T]he most remarkable trait in their physiognomy is the peculiar flatness and width of forehead which they artificially obtain by compressing the head between two boards while in a state of infancy and from which it never afterwards perfectly recovers. . . . I have observed the heads of many infants, after this singular bandage has been dismissed, or about the age of 10 or eleven months, that were not more than two inches thick about the upper edge of the forehead and reather thinner still higher. From the top of the head to the extremity of the nose is one streight line.*

"Not read these diaries myself, Mrs. Penngrove," he said. "But I reckon they talk about places I been long before I started with wagon trains. That's some good country up there. And as for them Indians with the flat heads, why sure, I seen them. East side of the Rockies. They'll be too far north for us to encounter, ma'am. Trapped up that way for a spell, though. Good, kindly tribe, they were. And they had some mighty fine land for themselves, too."

For me, the land we traveled across was a revelation. It may not have looked much different from the place where I had come from, but it felt different. More alive. As hundreds of miles separated us from any settlements, I felt a release.

I came into my own.

Never had I worked so hard in my life. In the beginning, cooking a simple meal of beans and dried pork required enormous effort. I learned the wise and ingenious marvels of the Dutch oven after several disasters. Each day was the same: Bring the stones from the wagon to build a contained fire pit (wildfire was a great danger), scrounge for firewood, haul water from the nearest source (sometimes this was a good distance), boil the water, serve, and clean up. Start all over again in the morning. In the tradition of these times on the trail, people pulled together and helped. I relished the camaraderie, making friends along the way.

One evening, I was sitting over a pot of soup. Each division was expected to contribute to the Sunday supper, which was cooked over a great fire in the center of the wagon circle. I opened *The Journals of Lewis and Clark* and asked if anyone would care to hear me read. One of the women tending a fussy baby said she would like to hear it. As had become my custom, I would read the first page I opened to.

About five o'clock this evening one of the wives of Charbono [Sacajawea] was delivered of a fine boy. It is worthy of remark that this was the first child which this woman had boarn, and as is common in such cases her labour was tedious and the pain violent; Mr. Jessome informed me that he freequently administered a small portion of the rattle of the rattle-snake, which he assured me had never failed to produce the desired effect, that of hastening the birth of the child; having the rattle of a snake by me I gave it to him and he administered two rings of it to the woman broken in small pieces with the fingers and added to a small quantity of water. Whether this medicine was truly the cause or not I shall not undertake to determine, but I was informed that she had not taken it more than minutes before she brought forth.

After I finished, the woman with the baby said, "Lord, what a tale. But I shall remember it. Should the need arise for one of our friends, I will find a rattler."

One month after departing St. Joseph, we arrived at our first re-supply stop, Fort Kearny. It had been moved from its previous location and rebuilt along a pretty section of the Platte River. Here, there were several forested islands dotting the bend in the river. The fort was still being constructed, with only a few buildings finished.

Earl and I visited the fort and found it to be bustling with activity. There were fur traders, buffalo hunters, Indians with a variety of strange foods to sell, most every imaginable supply, fresh stock and horses, and, to my surprise, a little circus. The troupe of performers were on their way west and put on shows in the parade grounds in the center of the fort. There was a dancing horse, a trio of very small men who dressed as clowns, and a brave, one-eyed woman who walked on a thin rope suspended between the fort buildings.

Mr. Keating told us we would stay near the fort for a week. Everyone was to take an inventory of their supplies and buy what they needed. I was grateful to spend time off the jostling wagon. It seemed like every single thing we owned was covered with a thin layer of dust. I never had the energy to clean after a long day on the trail.

7

FOUR WEEKS OUT OF FORT KEARNY, we began moving along high, rocky bluffs above the river. When I dared to look over the edge, cathedrals of stones reached down to the water. They were the first landmarks signaling the changing landscape ahead.

Our last stop before ascending the Rocky Mountains was Fort Laramie. Here, the draft animals would be let loose to graze and fatten up before the arduous miles ahead. Supplies were restocked, repairs were made, and Keating promised we could catch up on laundry in the river below the fort. We needed to be past the mountain range well before October to avoid snows.

Two days before we reached Fort Laramie, Keating inspected every single wagon and briefed all of us on necessary preparations. The fort would be the final vestige of civilization for a long while.

Keating came to our wagon and crawled underneath, inside, and over the top and checked harnesses and brakes and every inch of axle and wheel.

"I don't aim to leave nobody behind. But, by God, if you haven't made sure that each and every one of you is ready, you just may endanger all of us," he told us.

After he finished combing over our wagon, he said, "You folks are fine, I reckon."

That evening, we put our blankets down under the wagon. It was a fine, warm evening. As I was closing my eyes, Mrs. Leon called out to us. Her husband had taken ill. Earl did not stir, but I got up and followed her back to her wagon. Mr. Leon was sprawled out by the fire drenched in sweat, pale and gasping in shallow, wet spasms. I brought him some water and propped him up to ease his breathing.

Mrs. Leon held his hand and turned to me. "This don't look good, Mrs. Penngrove. I'm fretful that he won't last the night. I should like to read from the scripture, but I just can't seem to find mine. Would you have one that I might borrow?"

I would have called for Earl to bring his Bible from the wagon, but I figured he was probably sleeping by now and I did not want to disturb him. His trunk was easy to get to and after moving aside a few items of clothing, I found the wrapped Bible with the wire around it. It was certainly secured well and it took it a few minutes to unwind the wire. I brought the Bible to Mrs. Leon. By the flickering light of the fire, she read a few passages to her husband.

We brought Mr. Leon into the wagon and settled him for the night. I told Mrs. Leon to stay with her husband in the wagon. I would stay by her fire and keep a pot of hot water going in case she needed it. She handed me Earl's Bible and crawled into her wagon.

Until I handed it to Mrs. Leon, I'd never looked at the Bible. Earl had kept it wrapped up at all times. It was in very good condition. Hardly used at all. He certainly was looking after it well. The Bible was so precious to him that when I asked whether he'd like the pastor to read from it during our wedding, he said an emphatic "No! I won't have anybody else's hands touch it."

I suddenly felt ashamed that I had taken it without asking. Earl would surely understand. I vowed to return it as soon as I could.

I wanted to make sure that Mrs. Leon hadn't mussed any of the pages, so I opened the front cover. In spidery, black cursive, the inscription read: *To our beloved nephew, Charles, on the occasion of his tenth birthday. May God bless you always, Uncle Pete and Aunt Edna.*

It was dated November 10, 1839.

I felt a pulse begin to throb in my head. The name meant nothing to me. Earl had never mentioned any of his family members because he said there *was* no living family. Why did Earl have the Bible of a young boy?

Like all Bibles, the family tree was at the end of the pages, covering both sides of the back cover. The tree itself was an ornate design made with fine pen strokes depicting a large oak. A multitude of limbs branched off from the tree on either side with lines for each entry. Here the names, birth dates, marriages, and deaths of the family would be recorded.

A knot formed in my stomach as I stared at the page. The pain was so great that I could scarcely breathe.

There were no entries. No names such as Lawson or Penngrove. No births, deaths, or marriages.

The tree was completely blank.

I thought of all the possible explanations. Maybe there was another Bible. Perhaps this wasn't the one with the family tree. Earl might have that one hidden somewhere safe as it was the key to his inheritance. Of course, Earl would have an answer. I just needed to ask him. Although I promised to keep Mrs. Leon's fire going, I started toward our wagon. I needed Earl to explain. Holding the Bible, I walked slowly away from the fire and into the darkness. I was startled to nearly run into Earl standing a short distance from the wagon. He was staring at me.

"What's that you have in your hands, Mariah?" he asked in a menacing tone that I'd never heard him use.

The weak light from the Leons' fire caught his eyes. They were piercing and they fixed on me like arrows.

"Mr. Leon is ill. His wife wanted to read from the scriptures. She fears he may pass tonight. She couldn't find hers," I explained, wondering why he was angry.

He took a step toward me. "I heard you in the wagon. Heard you rifling around. I didn't think you'd take what you ought not to. Didn't think you were up to stealing, Mariah."

"Stealing? Is that what you think? I would have woken you but you were sleeping, Earl. I didn't want to wake you," I said.

"You thought I'd say no. Ain't that right? I told you nobody was to touch it. You knew I'd say no. But you went ahead and stole it anyways."

I looked at him defiantly. A moment before, I had been confused about why the family tree was empty. But I forgot about that as my anger rose at being accused of stealing. I thrust the Bible at him. "Take it then. I'll never ask you again for it."

He grabbed it from me, clutching it to his chest. His eyes narrowed. "Did you look at it, Mariah? Spying on me now? You couldn't help yourself, could you?"

I couldn't think what to say.

"And now you know. Don't you, Mariah? You *know!*"

I cried, "I don't know—"

"Don't know what? Or don't want to *say*? Maybe you don't want to *say* you've been as big a fool as that full-blown donkey ass you got for a pa? Why's a man like him pay somebody like me to take his daughter out into this godforsaken hellhole? Never even blinked about it. Not one damn question. Who's the bigger fool? Him for forking over, or you for bending over?"

The shock of his words more than stunned me. They defiled the pure night air, the stars, the peaceful hush of the prairie. Anything that felt good and fine about our journey, the wagons lined up now like we'd been doing it all our lives, the pulling together, the smell of campfire smoke that I loved in my hair, the wonder of what was up ahead over the rise and the promise of The Beyond. It all vanished in an instant. There was nothing left.

I shuddered violently and wondered if I had the strength. *You do it and don't think twice!*

I slapped him hard across the face. Once, twice, and a third time. Earl remained still; it was like I had never even touched him. In a flash, he closed the distance between us, hovering over me with his arm raised. Then he stopped.

"Mrs. Penngrove? Are you out there?" It was Mrs. Leon calling from her wagon. "Would you bring me a cup of warm water? Mr. Leon is chilling."

I turned and ran to the Leons' fire. I poured a cup from the pot and handed it up to her. "Everything all right out there? I heard some loud talk," she asked.

"I don't know what that was. Probably somebody having a nightmare," I said shakily. She looked at me with concern then retreated into her wagon.

Pacing around the campfire, I tried to think. What had just happened? Earl knew the family tree was empty. His vicious words had cut me like a blade. What had he meant?

A lantern sprang to life in our wagon. I strained my eyes to see. There was movement inside. Then I heard someone running away in the dark. A few minutes later, a horse whinnied, and I heard the sound of a rider racing off into the night.

I waited what felt like an eternity, then crept over to our wagon. The lantern was still perched on the hook at the rear of the wagon. Earl's trunk looked like it had been ransacked. I noticed that the horse tack and saddle were gone. It must have been him riding off.

Then something else caught my eye: the cubby where we'd locked up our money was open.

I jumped in the wagon and scrambled to the cubby.

It was empty. All the money was gone.

§

Mr. Leon was much improved by sunup. Though still weak, he insisted on continuing, not wanting to delay the wagon train. I helped the Leons get their wagon ready for departure and left them to return to my own troubles.

I decided to pretend as if nothing had happened. Part of me wanted to believe it. A bad dream. A misunderstanding. Meaningless words. Earl would come back. We'd straighten everything out. He'd explain about the empty family tree, apologize for his mean words, and we'd go on—a bit sore around the edges, but we'd get past it. Ignoring the mess inside the wagon, I secured everything to the sides, loaded up our camping gear, and drew the canvas flap down. As I went to tie it off, I saw the Bible thrown onto a heap of clothes. It was no longer necessary.

I suspected that I'd have one less horse to feed this morning and confirmed that when I discovered only the driving team was still hobbled. I gave them their grain and water then brought them around to the wagon for their harnessing. They gave me no worry for once and I was eternally grateful for their horse sense: they knew I wasn't in my right mind and probably took pity on me.

Climbing onto the bench, I grasped the reins and waited for Keating's call to fall in line. I looked around me in a daze. A light mist crept across the prairie. A flock of grouse took flight at the sound of somebody's frying pan banging on the side of a wagon. The soft whimpering of an infant down the line. In the distance, the crunch of dirt under the hooves of the livestock. I had no clock but I was aware of a ticking inside my skull. Minutes counting down. One by one. All I had to do was get from one minute to the next.

Keating rode down the line yelling for us to get ready to fall in. He galloped past my wagon and then circled back.

"Your husband feeling poorly, Mrs. Penngrove? In the wagon today?" he inquired with concern.

"That's right. He'll be all right soon and back up here directly," I answered, the words coming out in a strangled tone.

Keating paused and looked at me closely. "Nothing serious?"

"Oh, no. Just the usual stomach gripe. He'll be fine. Thank you."

I managed a smile and a nod and that appeared to satisfy Keating, for he took off.

When the call came to fall in, I flicked the reins and guided the wagon in line. As I drove, I went over every detail of my time with Earl, looking for clues. The loose button, the lies about Lewis and Clark, the inheritance, stealing from the bank, the gambling, the empty family tree, and, last of all, the final words he threw in my face. Then I thought about our days on the wagon train. But a veil dropped over them now, for if I had been happy and thought Earl happy, it was all a lie and not worth remembering as happy. It wore away at me, but I wouldn't let it wear me down all the way.

For two days, I kept up the act of pretending Earl was still here. When somebody asked after him, I had excuses.

"Off doing his necessaries."

"Fetching wood."

"Hunting, I suspect."

"Stomach again. In the wagon. He'll be around directly."

"You just missed him."

Mrs. Leon knew. She was a sharp old woman.

"You keeping to yourself, Mrs. Penngrove?" she said one evening.

"I don't mean to, Mrs. Leon," I said. "Just tired, I reckon."

She pursed her lips and leaned over to me. "Are you in the motherly way?"

I snapped my head around with revulsion. "No, ma'am," I replied more sharply than I intended. I knew with certainty that I was not.

Mrs. Leon cocked her head. "I only ask because I know he'll be back. More so if you're in the motherly way."

"Back? What do you mean?" I asked slowly.

"Don't think because I'm old I can't see. He's been gone a while. But they all come back."

I did not say anything.

I'm pretty sure it was Mrs. Leon who told Keating.

The next morning, before the call to fall in, he came riding slowly up to my wagon. I was soaping a harness when he stopped and got off his horse.

He leaned against the wagon watching me work up a lather on the leather. "Why are you doing that now?" he asked.

"It's gone all stiff. Can't get it to fit properly without it being soft," I replied.

"You do a right fine job, Mrs. Penngrove. With everything. Driving, chores, helping the Leons. I might not have known for a good long while."

I stopped soaping.

"How long has he been gone? And don't feed me any of those lines you been using."

"Almost three days."

Keating rapped his hand on the wagon. "You know that you and your husband signed the Articles of Agreement for this wagon train. One of those articles, if I may quote, says that you will do nothing to impede the progress of this train. Do you recall?"

"Yes, sir."

"Your husband running off and then you not telling me directly goes against that article, Mrs. Penngrove. You think you can keep going on like this? On your own? We got tougher miles ahead. What do I do if you can't make it? Leave you? I got an obligation to get everyone through. One wagon falters, everyone does. You see?"

"I see. I didn't mean any trouble. I just didn't know what to do."

"You were supposed to tell me."

I nodded.

"All right now," said Keating. "Let's have it. Where'd he run off to?"

"I don't know."

"Let's try this one. *Why* did he run off?"

"I don't know that one either," I replied but with much less conviction.

"Aren't you worried that he could be hurt or worse? We could have had a search party chase him down if I'd known earlier."

I shrugged. That was my mistake. I should have cried. A worried wife would have collapsed in sobs. But I continued my soaping. Keating caught on that there was more to it. Keating sucked air through his teeth. "Something tells me that this wasn't just a squabble between husband and wife. And I don't have time to go through a gol' darn list of questions. Why don't we just cut to the truth, Mrs. Penngrove? I want to help, but I got a wagon train full of people who want to get on their way."

He took my shoulders and forced me to look up at him. "I been around a lot of different folks and seen too much to not know that something here is bothering you. And you're not sure what it is. Why don't we have it all out right now, Mrs. Penngrove."

"Because I don't know what to think, Mr. Keating. It's all a muddle."

"Try me."

I started from the beginning about Earl's inheritance, the troubles at the bank, my father's assistance with our stake, and then, with a heavy heart, about finding the empty family tree in the Bible. I didn't have to state my suspicions for Mr. Keating. He was a clever man. He put two and two together for me.

"Good Lord, Mrs. Penngrove. You telling me your pa didn't smell a rat?"

"I don't understand."

"Your husband got your pa to hand over money with a promise to repay once he got to San Francisco, saw this lawyer, and got what this Lawson fella left him, is that right?"

"Yes. Earl said he'd been trying to make a stake for a long time. And, well, Pa offered to help him out."

"With nothing but a letter from a lawyer and this family tree in that Bible as proof?"

I nodded.

"And your pa never asked to see the letter or the Bible?"

"Mr. Keating," I said quietly, "my pa wouldn't have thought to ask. He took Earl's word. Maybe he was unwise to do so. But Pa's a trusting man. And I didn't think to ask either." *And I didn't think to ask either.*

"Now, let's not get ahead of ourselves. I only ask it because . . ." He trailed off and hung his head.

"Because why?"

He did not reply, and his silence was all the worse for him knowing something that my mind was still fearful of acknowledging.

"Please tell me, Mr. Keating," I implored. "I'd rather know what's on your mind than guess."

The man kicked at the dirt with his boot. Took off his hat and ran a gloved hand through his hair. Anything to put off what he had to say, it seemed. Finally, he shook his head and said in a quiet tone, "It's just that this ruse's been played all over the place, Mrs. Penngrove."

"What ruse?"

"I hate to tell you. I've seen this kind of business. There was never going to be nothing in San Francisco. Fella comes along with talk of an inheritance. Only he can't get it without someone to stake him to get to it. Finds folks like you and your pa. If the fella plays his cards right, he gets enough to move on and disappear. Sounds like this one, your Earl, well, his eyes got bigger than his belly."

Keating looked down. I understood his meaning. Our marriage had only been a way to get into Pa's deepest pockets.

"Most skip out when the moment presents itself. I reckon there *is* no inheritance and never has been. Your husband figured you saw the Bible and were about to call his hand. And if it was your Pa's money he was after, then he took it and hightailed it out of here. Where he's heading, I couldn't say. But there's a lot of movement around Laramie. He might fix on somebody heading out and join them."

I swallowed. "And had we made it all the way to San Francisco . . ." I trailed off, searching for an answer in Keating's face.

His expression told me what I needed to know. If Earl had planned all this in the way Keating proposed, I might have found myself alone in San Francisco.

"Then I'm thankful that it happened now. I was not favorable toward San Francisco anyway," I quipped.

Keating coughed. "Well, now, I guess that's one way of looking at it." He stared at me and I could sense he was taking new stock of me.

"Well, we'll get a search party out for him. He can't have gotten too far. We'll find him. And then it's up to you what to do next, Mrs. Penngrove. In the meantime, we've got to get rolling here to Fort Laramie."

There was no use in sinking into a mess over it any longer. I hadn't done anything wrong. It was *him*. All my talk about The Beyond, Lewis and Clark, falling off the edge of the prairie and jumping at the chance to go west surely had paved the way for him. He must have thought I was easy pickings for his scheme. *With all your dreams, you certainly got yourself in a dilemma, Mariah.*

I thought about some of the girls I'd known in school, many of them not only with husbands now but with broods of children. Were they sitting across from their husbands, wondering, waiting for some sign from their men? I counted my blessings a thousand times over that I was fighting a team of obstinate horses, driving them over an unforgiving terrain. In no way would I change places with those girls at home. I was seeing, experiencing, drinking in the wild, and finding out what was beyond. It was what I wanted all along. Despite the misfortune of meeting Earl, I was doing what I wanted to do.

Mr. Keating said he'd sort it all out once we got to Fort Laramie. If they found Earl and brought him to his senses, what would I do next? The reins felt good in my chafed and blistered hands. The team had moments where they actually walked with their ears forward and not flat back. As I looked out over them, tall green grass everywhere around me, clouds scurrying above hills, the smell of the earth churning beneath the wheels, I knew I did not want to be anywhere else. I couldn't go back. Earl had left me with nothing other than what I could sell off from the wagon. Even so, I did not want to go back. I wanted to go on. A fool's errand, to be sure. Somehow I would manage, I thought as I picked at the rough patches on my hands.

Then I saw the mountains. They were far in the distance, so far that they might have been a painting or a hallucination. Great splinters of rock, topped with arrows of white, rose up out of a flat landscape. On this day, there were no clouds and we were told that it was unusual to see them so clearly. Mr. Keating came to check on me and noticed that I was transfixed by the mountains.

"It's a sight to see, ma'am. But don't be fooled. They can take you and chew you up, pretty as they are. Now, we'll have to sit down and talk about things as they stand now. That's a rough road ahead and, as you know, I can't be leaving anybody stranded up in the mountains. I want you to think about what you'd like to do."

"You mean about leaving the wagon train and going home?"

"Unless we find Earl and he decides to stay on with you, I can't see you doing this alone."

"I know, Mr. Keating. I know."

I was deeply troubled at the thought of going home. Strangely, I was less concerned about the fate of Earl. Folks came around after hearing about him being missing—though Mr. Keating never let out the details—and offered their sympathy. I was grateful to have such fellowship and I would sorely miss it. My determination to continue on grew. I'd come this far. I was closer than ever to The Beyond.

That evening, our first in the shadow of Fort Laramie, I took out *The Journals*. It fell open to an entry that frightened Ma and me. I did not want to dwell on why this particular page appeared and whether it was a forewarning of what was ahead. Folks around the fire were accustomed to my reading and they encouraged me to go ahead.

In a northerly derection from the mouth of this creek on an emence plain, a high hill is situated, and it appears to be of a conical form, and by the different nations of Indians in the quarter, is suppose to be the residence of Deavels, that they are in human form with remarkable large heads and about 18 inches high, that they are very watchful and are armed with sharp arrows with which they can kill at a great distance They are said to kill all persons who as so hardy as to attempt to approach the hill . . . So much do the Maha, Soues, Ottoes, and other neighbouring nations believe this fable, that no consideration is sufficient to induce them to approach the hill.

"My Ma would say after this entry that they saw this hill on the day after they shot their first buffalo. She always wondered if it was bad luck for them to kill that first buffalo," I told them after I finished. There were murmurs, in disquieting tones, and I hoped I had not alarmed anyone.

A woman stood up. I had seen her before but she rarely said anything. Her name was Hetty Samuels. I recalled that she was alone, too. Her wagon was drawn by mules, which I was told were easier to manage than horses. I'd heard her husband died just before they were to start. There were no children. She'd started off on her own. I thought it strange that Mr. Keating had allowed her to travel alone. I would later learn that she'd paid him twice the usual fare with the agreement that should she become a burden to the group, she would leave. The woman was tall and large-boned with hair of indeterminate length because she never removed the scarf that encircled her head. Her face always seemed to be dark and her mouth in a permanent scowl. She worked hard, though, and never refused to help anyone. Hetty Samuels jammed a stick into the dying embers and a flame burst forth, illuminating her grim expression.

"I don't believe in luck," she said. "Bad luck, good luck, they're all just the same trees in the forest. You can't always pick them out as being different, so why worry? Got to make your own decisions and stick with them."

I nodded. She made a good point. Sometimes what seems like good luck is just the opposite. What looks like a fortunate turn of events can make you take a wrong turn. I thought about Earl and my decision to marry him. Was it good luck to have met him? Or had it been fate's strange hand showing me a path and daring me to take it? And I had, gladly and energetically. Now it was for me to decide whether good luck had turned against me or bad luck had forced to me to choose the right path after all.

ɸ 8 ɷ

AFTER FORT LARAMIE, THE TRIP WAS going to get much more taxing due to unpredictable weather and rougher conditions. No more outposts for resupplying. Turning around on South Pass, our route over the Rockies was out of the question. The snows were snapping at our heels and we had to get through the pass without delay.

At least we'd have a few days at the fort, and this would give me time to think. I had a half hope that Earl would show up, beg forgiveness, explain it all away, and rejoin the wagon train. I had no idea what I would say or do if he came back.

Earl *did* return. Just not the way I expected.

Flem Keating found me a few days after we arrived at the fort. "Mrs. Penngrove, you best come with me. It's Earl. He's been found."

His grim expression and the way he turned quickly and strode off in the direction of the fort told me volumes. Something was dreadfully wrong.

"Where is Earl?" I asked, half running to keep up with Keating.

"He's at the fort," he answered. By the tone of his voice, I could tell that there was more to say.

"Why don't you just tell me, Mr. Keating? Tell me what's happened. It's a long walk up there, and I can't abide with wearing myself out and still not knowing once I get there."

Keating cut his pace in half, allowing me to catch up. "They found him about five miles south of the fort. He was tied onto his saddle and the horse was just wandering around in circles."

I waited for him to continue.

"Who did this?"

"There's a lot of marauders out here. They'd steal your grandmother's knickers," Keating told me.

"What else?" I asked.

"Not a stitch on him."

"His clothes were taken from him? But why?"

"Even his boots was gone."

"What about the money he took from our wagon? Did he manage to hide it?"

"I couldn't tell you that, Mrs. Penngrove. But there was no money."

"Did he say what he'd done with the money, Mr. Keating?"

The big man kept walking although he had slowed somewhat so we could talk. He was trudging more heavily now. He did not answer my question.

"Mr. Keating," I said sharply. I was beginning to get impatient. Why wouldn't this man just come to the point? "Mr. Keating!"

Finally, he spoke. "He'd been strung up, Mrs. Penngrove. Hanged before they looped him on his horse."

A distant memory came to me. I was six years old or so. There was a tree near our house that I enjoyed climbing. One day, my bonnet came off and the sturdy tie snagged on a branch above me. I lost my footing while I tried to pull it loose. My mother made strong bonnet ties, and it was caught under my neck supporting my full weight for a moment or two. Long enough for me to feel the air being squeezed out of me as I thrashed my legs about. When the bonnet tie finally snapped, I fell to the ground, breathless and shaken. The thought of Earl struggling at the end of a noose horrified me.

Earl was dead.

We arrived at the fort and waited at the gates for one of the privates to show us to the quartermaster's office. The army had recently taken over the fort. The rumors of hostile Indians in the area made for a strict and rigid military presence inside the walls. The grim faces of the soldiers were everywhere.

Keating said that I might winter at the fort and wait for an eastbound group heading back to Missouri. I wouldn't have to sell my wagon and the fort would provide shelter and food. The idea of spending months within this fortification did not appeal to me.

We arrived at the quartermaster's office and were shown into a dark, rank, clapboard room that was sparsely furnished. A fire was dying in the hearth, a thin filament of smoke escaping from the ashes. The private shuffled toward a door at the far end of the room. He knocked once, rather softly. When he got no response, he shook his head and banged loudly. The door jerked open by another private, and a flurry of words were exchanged until both of them stopped and turned toward me.

"He's in here, ma'am."

They'd laid Earl out in the back room on a wooden table. I could see the outline of a head, chest, and legs covered with an army blanket. Ten toes poked out from the bottom. Earl was not a tall man, and yet an army blanket could not cover him adequately. Keating held my arm and shook his head as I tried to approach the table.

"I want to see him, Mr. Keating. At least to be sure it is him," I told him. "That would be a wife's duty, I reckon."

The private shrugged and slowly pulled back the blanket. I had never seen a hanging and I had no knowledge of what such action did to a body. Fair to say, I vowed not to seek it out in the future. It was Earl. Through his swollen, half-open eyelids I searched for the gray specks in his brown eyes. His lips were engorged, and if his tongue were pushing through, it looked like he'd bitten it. His neck was scraped raw with an angry open wound, which appeared to have been pecked at or gnawed. I started to draw the blanket further and the private grabbed my wrist.

"Ma'am, I'd advise no further. There were things done to him that no woman ought to see."

I looked at him. "What do you mean?"

Keating cleared his throat, "I think the private means that critters got to him, and there's no sense in troubling yourself over the work of animals. Isn't that right, Private?" The private shot Keating a look of gratitude and nodded.

I inquired no further about what had happened. Evidently it was something too troubling to discuss and that was enough for me. I wished to see no more. I drew the blanket back over his face.

I nodded. "That is my husband."

Keating led me out to a rough-hewn porch. "I'm truly sorry about this, Mrs. Penngrove. The army doesn't cotton to this sort of business, and they will track down who done it."

I felt prickles of sweat chewing at the roots of my hair. When Earl had departed our wagon, I had not thought it would end this way. Not with my viewing what remained of him, with no mercy or dignity shown to him. Robbed, hanged, and left on the plain. An image of his struggle and battle against whoever did this came to me. I had no tears. Just an unsettling opinion of this new world I was seeing.

As if reading my thoughts, Keating said, "Folks come out here for a lot of reasons. Not all of them come with goodness in their hearts. There's a lawlessness out here. So much land, space, and nobody making you account for nothing. This land does strange things to people, Mrs. Penngrove. I guess you've seen some of the worst of it. But, I hate to say, it won't be the last of it, I reckon."

Earl's resting spot was a mound of parched, chunked dirt in a row of other graves. A group of my fellow travelers gathered around as the wind whipped fiercely, blowing debris into the air.

Flem Keating read from the Bible, Book of John, chapter 14:

Let not your hearts be troubled. Believe in God; believe also in me. In my Father's house are many rooms. If it were not so, would I have told you that I go to prepare a place for you? And if I go and prepare a place for you, I will come again and will take you to myself, that where I am you may be also. And you know the way to where I am going.

We sang "Rock of Ages," our voices cracked and raw in the dry gusts. Then Keating rammed the pine-switch cross into the ground.

I waited for sadness. It never came. My heart was closed now. If it remained so for the rest of my life, I'd not regret it.

Say what you will about speaking poorly of the dead, but if it hadn't been for Earl's squirrelly ways, I might not have been on this adventure at all. And, truth be told, my life became a great deal more interesting once we put Earl in the ground. That may be a harsh eulogy to leave my husband, but I had hardened. Keating was right: the land does strange things to people.

Some folks asked me if I wanted to turn back. One family was already intending to go back, done as they were with the difficulties of the journey. I was welcome to join them and return to my parents. The old life. My money was gone, and I might have felt an intense longing for the security of my home, my mother's kitchen, Pa's store, and St. Joseph. But I felt no such longing to return. I had seen the mountains and this was where I wanted to go next. Determined to carry on, I looked west.

❧ 9 ❧

WITH TWO DAYS LEFT IN FORT Laramie, Keating began his long-promised inspection of each wagon prior to this next part of our journey. Everyone who needed repairs made had done so at the fort. Every axle, joint, chassis part, horse, mule, oxen, piece of tack and equipment was scrutinized. This time, however, he was ruthless. In addition to looking for any flaw, weakness, or poorly repaired item, he demanded a detailed inventory of everything in each of our wagons. Anything unnecessary he found resulted in a strong recommendation to leave it behind. This caused much consternation and argument amongst the wagons. Keating was adamant about not leaving anybody stranded on the long journey over South Pass, but that did not mean he was going to stand for wagons overloaded with needless items.

"Either you leave it here or it'll be dumped eventually, if it's weighing down our progress. There are sections where we won't have water or feed for the stock for nearly 100 miles. We need room for both in the wagons," Keating emphasized. "You'll soon see what becomes of anything that delays our crossing."

When he came to my wagon, Keating did not even bother looking it over. "You know what I've come to say, Mrs. Penngrove. I am truly sorry."

He meant that even if my wagon was in acceptable condition, it couldn't be driven alone. He wouldn't take the chance on me faltering as the trail got more difficult and dangerous.

I understood but still couldn't hide my disappointment.

"You could see if somebody else is willing to take you on," Keating said.

It was fine to spend time in the company of others around a campfire or chat with them while hauling water or wood. I had grown close to several folks on the trip. It's quite another idea to hoist your bag onto their wagon and become part of their world. I could see that folks were already anxious about going through the mountains. Tempers were short. Husbands, wives, fathers, and sons could be heard bickering over the least little thing.

A gold and purple sunset spread above the rolling hills around the fort as I built my fire and squatted over a pot of stew. It had been a hot, windless day, but a stiff breeze picked up and swirled the embers. While I waited for my dinner, I took out *The Journals*. This time, I hunted for a particular passage, not sure if it would comfort me or fill me with fear.

In the entry dated June 20, 1805, William Clark wrote:

Not haveing seen the Snake Indians or knowing in fact whither to calculate on their friendship or hostility, we have conceived our party sufficiently small, and therefore have concluded not to dispatch a canoe with a part of our men to St. Louis as we had intended early in the spring.

We fear also that such a measure might possibly discourage those who would in such case remain, and might possibly hazard the fate of the expedition. We have never hinted to any one of the party that we had such a scheme in contemplation, and all

appear perfectly to have made up their minds to Succeed in the
expedition or perish in the attempt. We all believe that we are
now about to enter on the most perilous and difficult part of
our Voyage, yet I see no one repineing. All appear ready to meet
those difficulties which await us with resolution and becoming
fortitude.

Ma and I often discussed whether there was any truth to this or
perhaps whether Clark wrote it to save face in the event of tragedy?
Would Lewis and Clark really consider sending a party homeward?
We did not think so. Clark's entry was, in our opinion, a cautionary
statement to the world, in the event they did not return. From this
entry, I know that all the men, without exception, were committed
to seeing it to the end.

With this thought hovering over my campfire and meal, out of the
diminishing light came someone walking purposefully toward me. It
was Hetty Samuels sloping along with her dress trailing in the dirt,
a shawl tied around her tremendous shoulders. She was carrying a
bundle in her arms along with a stout wooden stool. She dropped the
stool across the fire from me and sat down heavily without invitation.
From the bundle, she produced a well-beaten felt hat and a series
of fur scraps. Hetty began stitching the fur pieces into the brim of
the hat.

She said abruptly, "I've already made one for myself. You'll need
one, as well. This one I'm working on now is yours. I saw one of the
trappers near the fort with one. Told me that it'll help with the cold.
Also, I traded him for a couple of these elk skin gloves, too. I'm not
going to lose a finger. Neither should you."

I watched her stitch. Her fingers were wide and the skin leathery.
Yet her needlework was neat and effortless.

Our eyes met. "I seen your pluck after your man went missing,"
she said. "Then seen you when he turn up dead. It's a bad business.
There's not many that would want to keep on. Flem says you want to."

"I aim to talk him into letting me continue," I said without a great deal of resolve. Keating had already made it clear to me that staying on was not an option.

"I won't be much good company, Mrs. Penngrove. Never have been. But you're welcome to join me. Sometimes two is better than one."

"Not always," I said with a smile.

Hetty Samuels laughed. I don't think I ever saw her laugh again.

"Thank you for the offer, Mrs. Samuels. I believe I will take you up on it. Just call me Mariah," I told her.

She handed me a pair of elk skin gloves and a needle and thread. "There's holes where the trappers burned them. Couple of stitches should do the trick," said Hetty. "You can call me Hetty."

The next day, I moved what supplies and belongings I could fit into Hetty's wagon. I sold off what remained, setting up a rough shop out of the back of my wagon near the gates of Fort Laramie. A brisk trade commenced and much haggling over prices. In the end, I came away with a small amount of money and had disposed of everything down to a broken cooking spoon.

Hetty's destination was a settlement in northern California called Remington River. She had family there. Without Earl, there was no reason for me to continue with our prior plans for San Francisco. I would go with Hetty as far as Remington River and figure out what to do then. She said her brother was a rancher and that he had a fine spread. She told me that she wanted to build her own cabin and settle down to help with ranch chores.

"He's got a couple of young ones by now. Suppose they'll need some tending to, as well ," she added. Her tone struck me as sad, wistful. I sneaked a look at her. Her gaze went over the mules and somewhere far away. I wondered about Hetty and why she had no children.

A week out of Fort Laramie, we set off on South Pass, where there were no trees to provide a buffer from the wind. I could only imagine what winter would be like with snow to add to the harsh conditions. The wide, sweeping plain that we traversed was deceptive. The sharp-edged peaks were closer but still in the distance. One would think we were not in the mountains at all. Until you tried to breathe. The air was thin and always biting. Keating had us fill any nook and cranny in our wagons with buffalo chips for fuel. We had to use them sparingly and mostly for cooking. At night, we huddled in our wagon, barely able to keep warm. Hetty proved to have a steady supply of surprises for me. I nearly fell off the wagon when one day she dropped her usual rough talk and began speaking in a soft but refined voice. I learned that Hetty had been raised in a prosperous family with a large house on one of the best streets in St. Louis. She had been educated and positioned to rise socially when she met a man from the backwoods of North Carolina

"I know," she said. "You'd never guess I was brought up with all the finery you could imagine. A mother who taught me lace work and French. A father who expected me to sit down and entertain beaus in the parlor. I did what I was told. I don't say I wasn't comfortable. But there was something about that comfort that didn't sit well with me. I guess I never really fit in. And it didn't take much for me to drop it all like a hot potato."

She told me that one day she was taking riding lessons out at a horse farm in the country when she met her husband. She was getting nearly past the age for marriage. But her father kept trying new schemes to find her a match. He thought that riding lessons might spark something.

"I was on a devil of an Arabian. He didn't like me and I didn't like him. Next thing I knew, he was flying into the woods and my instructor was gone. The first branch didn't get me but the second one swept me right off, flat on my back. Knocked the wind out of me. Next thing I knew, there was somebody way up in one of the trees, climbing around like a squirrel. A man dressed all in furs and stinking to high heaven. He was gathering eggs. He jumped down to see to me, though. As dirty and grimy as any pig you'd like to meet—that was my first glimpse of Travis." Then she added with a chuckle, "He was a mule skinner."

I nearly choked. "A mule skinner? Hetty!" They were among the lowest of lows by anyone's account.

"Ha! You bet I kept that from my father as long as I could. But Travis was one of a kind. Oh, he wasn't schooled and he could barely sit in a chair. But he could fix things, make a tasty meal out of just about anything, scrounge like no tomorrow, hunt and fish to feed an army. And soft and sweet and funny. We used to laugh about the fine city girl and the rough heathen scampering around the woods. I never did learn properly to ride that old Arabian. But I found something better."

I shook my head. "And you married Travis?"

"Run off," she said quietly. "My folks had a fit. Travis and I homesteaded for a while. We made do but also had some hard times. Never asked for help that we weren't prepared to return in kind. It was a good life."

"But your family. What happened?" I asked, imagining a mule skinner standing in a St. Louis sitting room.

"That's the funny thing. They forgave me," Hetty said. "Sure, they never got used to Travis. But when we told them we were heading west, my folks gave us their blessing and wished us good luck. That meant a lot. They didn't have to do it."

Hetty was quiet for a moment. "Then that man had to up and die on me. Like a big wind come up and ripped the flame away."

One of the mules started to fidget and fight the harness. Hetty went back to her old self and cursed at the animal. "Get up there, mule! Don't make me come down there!"

"And you came along all on your own."

"Yep," she replied. "You can keep all that old St. Louis fluff about me to yourself. I only bring it out when I need to. Travis always said, 'I is the bestest with you and you is the bestest with me.'"

One evening, a trio of Indians appeared on a low ridge less than a mile from our encampment. Astride their horses, they watched us until the light was gone, then they disappeared behind the hill. Keating told us that it had been an unusually rich and plentiful hunting season for the tribes.

"There's been years when you'd see them look awful bad. Skin just hanging off their bones, eyes sunk in like they're near death. A sorry sight, I reckon. Try to help them out with food and such," he said.

Thankfully, crossing South Pass was uneventful. If our wagons were the worse for wear, the weary travelers fared well. We made a few repairs and kept heading west following wide, blue rivers and smaller but still magnificent mountain ranges. Rains became more frequent with fall approaching. Mornings were growing colder, too. Keating was fretful about any delays and pushed us hard. He spoke sparingly about the great desert that we would soon be crossing.

"I hate the heat," said Hetty.

One afternoon, we paused in the cool foothills with the desert spread out before us like a tremendous hand turned up toward the sun. Keating instructed us to fill every spare container with water. He said that he hoped we would not run out of water before reaching the western edge. If we were careful, and if we were lucky enough to find watering holes, we would make it.

The desert proved more fateful than South Pass. The heat sliced into us. The teams needed extra water, which meant rationing. Fights broke out periodically over suspected hoarding of water. Mr. Leon succumbed one stifling afternoon. His death was followed by two children wandering away from the wagon train. Idle chatter in the evening stopped altogether. The stunned silence of our travail was loud and piercing. Even Lewis and Clark provided no consolation. I could no longer read. I had no energy in reserve for anything other than chores. Our group, which had traveled all those long months together, split once we reached the big grassy valley at the western edge of the desert. Here, there was a junction of trails. Along with a few other wagons, Hetty and I took the southern junction that would lead us down to the country around Remington River. We bade farewell to our companions and struck out for what was surely to be a warm welcome from Hetty's family.

◆ 10 ◆

We were greatly mistaken about a warm welcome. Though we had passed several settlements in which we saw that prosperity did not abound, we were not prepared for the dire conditions that we came upon at Remington River. Hetty's brother had struck out several years ago for California. His letters had portrayed the land as rich and plentiful. The tales of his success and happiness had carried Hetty (and me, I might as well admit) through the hard days on the trail. I'd imagined a well-built cabin on a clear, cold stream with a stone hearth and lodgepole corral with horses and stock. A hearty "Hail, weary travelers!" greeting from a smiling man and his wife and brood of children, as they welcomed us from an ample porch. A warm meal in a snug parlor.

There was none of this. Apparently, hard times had befallen them, and when the tattered, battered wagon driven by myself came into the front yard of the homestead, a man on the front porch stood up. He was a skeleton and barely alive. His clothes hung in rags; his feet were bare, his house a dilapidated wreck. The brother's wife had abandoned the homestead and, taking the children with her, retreated to parts unknown. Evidently, the letters home had been intended to paint a rosy picture in order to bring Hetty out west. The brother was far gone in the bottle, it turned out. But family was family, and it was clear that Hetty had her work cut out for her.

We drove the wagon into Remington River in what would be our last time driving the mules. The liveryman haggled over the wagon but settled on a fair price. He bought one of the mules. Hetty took the other one as her brother had only a lame horse and there was plowing to do.

I stood next to the mule and steadied it while Hetty climbed up. We stared at each other. There was so much to say but I couldn't begin. I knew Hetty wasn't much on goodbyes. "You sticking around Remington River? If so, reckon I'll run into you one way or another," said Hetty.

"That'll be fine. Good luck to you, Hetty."

"And to you, Mariah."

She nodded and gave the mule a swift kick.

My bag contained few clothes, some cooking supplies, small odds and ends for trade, and my mother's gift: *The Journals of Lewis and Clark*.

Departing the livery, I came out onto the wide and muddy front street.

Remington River raised my spirits despite its ragged appearance and roughness. The stories of western towns had appeared in the newspapers of St. Joseph. Sketches accompanying the articles had shown ramshackle store fronts, rough-looking men standing next to horses or carts, and what appeared to be absolutely nothing surrounding the towns. Just land. As if the town had sprouted from a seedling and then suddenly shot up to blossom. As I drove into Remington River that morning, the town did indeed appear abruptly. The road went through a heavily wooded area and then came out onto a wide, green meadow with a river running through it. The town began on the other side of a bridge crossing the river. It was early November.

The muddy streets were frozen in spots and patches of snow appeared here and there.

I walked along the wooden walkway by the stagecoach office, the bank, a blacksmith, a general store, a number of saloons, and a hotel. I paused here for a moment. It would be a luxury to sleep in a bed. I could not remember the last time I had slept on anything but a makeshift mattress of straw, usually damp and out in the open. But as much as I yearned for a bath and clean sheets, I vowed to save my money.

I passed by a curious shop. It was dark inside—not inviting as the general store had been, with its heaps of goods spilling out onto the wooden walkway. There was a strange mood to this odd little shop, mysterious and forbidding. But it also was cleanly painted with a red-and-gold pattern of interesting characters across the threshold and around the wooden window frames. A shingle hung above the door that read "The Old Mandarin." I walked beneath the sign twice more before I walked in.

Closing the door behind me, I looked around at the jumble of goods spread over the counters and wooden floor: bolts of cloth, sacks of grain, barrels of biscuits and flour, and a long counter behind which large jars of dried plants, seeds, and powders lined a series of shelves. The man who greeted me was most extraordinary. He wore a full-length dark robe, a pair of cotton slippers, and a bright blue silk cap with a black tassel on top. It was hard to determine his age for his skin was smooth. Beneath his cap, I could see that his head was shaved back from his forehead and a long braid dangled down his back. I had never seen a Chinese man before.

"Good day to you," I said.

"How may I assist you?" he asked.

A pang of homesickness flooded over me. The stocked shelves reminded of my father's shop in St. Joseph. I was at home in such a place.

Something caught my eye on one shelf.

I stopped and peered behind the counter at the objects on the shelf. The man followed my gaze. He saw that I was looking at a cup and saucer, off-white color with a pretty pattern of gold and blue flowers and a delicate handle. The lip of the saucer was edged in gold. I recognized the set immediately and knew they were worth quite a bit. By the way they were displayed rather carelessly, I wondered if their worth was known to the man.

"You like this?" The man took the cup and saucer down. "A man and woman came in to pawn a large chest of possessions. They brought these. The poor woman argued with each item the man pulled out of the chest. 'Surely, we can keep this, my dear? Please?'" He frowned after his singsong imitation of the woman's pleas.

"They had come from the East and, like so many, simply could stretch their money no further. When they finally have to face the harsh truth, the first things to go are their treasures. Oh, how many tears and pleadings come from women standing right here before this counter? It is a business for me, sad to say. I am not a purveyor of sympathy."

I glanced up, hardly looking at the cup and saucer now, feigning indifference. "Not very practical. What on earth would I do with something like this?" I waved dismissively at the objects. "And it is a pity that it's chipped."

"Chipped?" commented the man, pursing his lips. "You must be fatigued from your journey. There is no chip."

"Oh, yes. Small one. Saucer. Right there. On the edge. If it interested me, I might ignore the chip," I said. "And the hairline crack on the cup."

He inspected the cup. He placed it back on the saucer and turned it so the crack did not show.

"A small flaw in what is otherwise a very serviceable cup, missus," he said agreeably. Changing course, he picked up a cloth and began dusting the countertop, careful to leave the cup and saucer on the counter in front of me. He spoke softly as he dusted. "You have just arrived, I take it. Otherwise, I would have seen you. Remington River is not very big, nor does it hide interesting people such as yourself."

I smiled. *Always compliment the customer*, my father would say. Then I nodded and ran my finger along the edge of the counter, a few feet from where the man was dusting.

"I suppose you've heard many a tale about the journey from the East."

I regarded my finger, the one I just pressed into the counter: it was brown with dirt. The man saw this, grunted, and vigorously dusted the area where my fingerprint stood prominently. "Many tales, miss. Many tales," he said wistfully. "And yet you had no sea to cross such as I did, coming from Kowloon. *No sea*. Interesting to me that so many cry about the trip. At least you may stroll around on ground that is not constantly moving."

I laughed. "My journey here was most wondrous, and I would do it again."

He clapped and grinned broadly. "It is the same with me, miss! Great journey! Not so bad. I make it. No problem."

We both laughed now. As his chuckle was dying on his lips, he watched me regard the cup and saucer once more.

"How much?" I asked, not touching the items and not even really looking at them.

The man rubbed his chin and gazed at the ceiling of his shop. "I would have to think."

And then I smiled. "Turn the cup over, sir, and look at the writing on the bottom."

His eyes never left mine as he slowly turned the cup over. He likely half thought I would snatch the saucer off of the counter. He probably thought women coming off the trail were often quite mad and unpredictable.

He read the neat print on the bottom. "Minton and Company. Jeannest," he read. "So?"

"My father is a shopkeeper in Missouri. I learned a good deal from him. I learned that in order to run a decent business, you have to know the merchandise. You, sir, do not know the provenance of this cup and saucer."

I turned to walk away. It was unfair to think this man could possibly know that he possessed part of a tea set belonging to Queen Victoria, I thought. Nor that he would be familiar with a scandal surrounding this particular set. The chinaware had been especially commissioned for the queen in celebration of the birth of a grandchild. A box of it had been stolen years ago in England, and it was rumored to have found its way to the United States. The beautiful design and delicate workmanship, not to mention the notoriety of it being stolen, made it highly coveted. My father came into possession of one of the creamers. He sold it for a fabulous sum. And now, for some fantastic reason, a cup and saucer from that very set was sitting on a shelf in this strange store.

The man grinned and nodded as I told him the story of the cup and saucer.

"So," he said. "A shopkeeper's daughter blesses us with her sharp eye and wit. You will do well here, miss. Cleverer than I."

Then he asked me to tea. We sat at a table beside the front window of his shop and I told him my story. Nothing he had not heard before, however.

"White men can be weak and stupid," he commented when I told him about Earl. "Some of the white women are equally weak in their choice of men," he added. Then he smiled at me. "Yet you have none of this self-pity, no anguished tears about the loss of your husband. You recognized his weakness and moved on. That is something remarkable for one so young."

Could my appearance be one of strength and self-reliance? I felt neither. The fact is I was desperate for a sanctuary, a place to rest and regroup.

I could tell he liked me. He relaxed over the delicious tea that he called jasmine. Fragrant yet light, it was the best tea I had ever sipped. He said his name was Zhao and that he was not a Mandarin at all. He explained that Mandarins were considered royalty in China. But the nickname stuck with him, and he could not argue that such a grand illusion was good for business. Very few people called him by his given name. He was simply the Old Mandarin.

"Adds refinement, I think," he said.

By our second cup of tea, the Old Mandarin had asked me if I would like to work for him. In addition to selling general provisions, he offered customers herbs and other remedies, running a small clinic within the store. He said that a white woman would be good for business. The local women seemed nervous to enter his shop. Perhaps an air of familiarity around the place would encourage them to step through the threshold more often.

The Old Mandarin cleared out a small space in the rear of the shop for my living quarters. It was small but comfortable.

My main occupation was to sit in the window of the shop and make herbal packets. I was highly visible to passersby, hopefully attracting a customer or two. Plus, I was doing tedious work that the Old Mandarin did not care for. The herbal packets were sold to those who worried that their livers might not survive the continual onslaught of liquor inflicted upon them. The Old Mandarin promised that a daily ingestion of these packets would strengthen the liver and allow for a more enduring enjoyment of spirits.

I knew immediately that the herbal packets contained nothing more than ground-up sagebrush, plucked daily from the rear of the store where the high desert stretched eastward for miles. The herbs were soaked, mashed, dried, and rolled into pellets.

There were very few Chinese in the area. I had yet to see another one until a boy named Sing came into the shop. He appeared to be twelve or thirteen. He also wore his hair shaved back from the forehead and down his back in a long pigtail. On his shoulder, I was astounded to see, was a crow. The Old Mandarin greeted the boy in their native tongue.

Sing seemed upset about something and pointed to his pet bird's foot.

"The bird's foot is injured," the Old Mandarin explained to me. "Will you bring me that white jar on the second shelf and a piece of wool batting?"

I brought what he needed and came closer to the boy and his bird. The bird looked at me and opened his beak as if to snap at me. I drew back quickly.

Sing put a finger on the bird's beak and replied in a soft voice in very good English, "He won't bite, miss. That's how he says hello."

"Does your bird have a name?" I asked.

The Old Mandarin laughed as he was preparing a poultice. "Very original name. Yes, Sing?"

Sing smiled. "I call him Bird, miss."

The bird jumped onto the counter. The Old Mandarin started to address the wounded foot but stopped. "My old fingers cannot do this delicate work. Mariah, will you wrap this around the foot and secure it with this ribbon?"

I reached out with my hand and Bird responded by gently tapping my knuckle with his beak. He then cocked his head as if in expectation. He allowed me to apply the poultice and bandage. Raising the foot and inspecting it, Bird was apparently satisfied, for he jumped back onto Sing's shoulder.

The Old Mandarin gave Sing a small packet of fresh materials and instructed him to change the bandage twice a day.

After Sing left, I asked the Old Mandarin about him. "Does he have parents or family here in Remington River?"

"No family. Sing works odd jobs around town. He stays in the livery. I once offered him a job here. He declined. I think he likes to make his own fortunes. Sing is very bright. And engaging, once you get to know him."

The idea of a young boy wandering around town all on his own was distressing. Still, when I would catch sight of him on Front Street running an errand, or down by the river doing laundry, he seemed content.

Working for the Old Mandarin was pleasant. I found him to be well-read and intelligent and quite the conversationalist. He was fond of telling stories of China. He had not journeyed back home since coming to America and he missed China desperately. The opportunity to talk of his home, with somebody interested, was a rare pleasure.

I brought out my tattered copy of *The Journals of Lewis and Clark*. The Old Mandarin was unfamiliar with the expedition, but he was interested in their journey.

"So far! Almost same distance as across the sea from my home. Quite amazing."

I read parts to him in the evenings when we would sit with tea at the table by the window. He asked for me to repeat the story Meriwether Lewis wrote of Sacagawea and the Shoshone chief, Cameahwait, many times. The Old Mandarin seemed particularly taken with the notion of meeting a long-lost family member after so many years and in such a remote place. I wondered if the Old Mandarin hoped such a meeting might take place for him.

[G]lad of an opportunity of being able to converse more intelligibly, Sacjawea was sent for; she came into the tent, sat down, and was beginning to interpret, when in the person of Cameahwait she recognised her brother: She instantly jummped up, and ran and embraced him, throwing over him her blanket and weeping profusely: The chief was himself moved, though not in the same degree. After some conversation between them she resumed her seat, and attempted to interpret for us, but her new situation seemed to overpower her, and she was frequently interrupted by her tears.

Winter came like a dark curtain pulled over the valley. I had endured winters at home, so this kind of cold was tolerable. The snow was dry, which delighted me, and different from the kind that fell in Missouri. The snow in Remington River skidded easily off my coat and hat.

It surprised me how content I had become. I was fed and housed and paid a small amount. It wasn't much, but I was putting aside some when I could. I still had no plan for the future. For the time being, I kept my eyes open for opportunity.

The Old Mandarin once queried if I should like to marry again. I quickly replied that I was in no way looking for a man. I wanted to be independent and move ahead with my own life in my own way.

Remington River was no St. Joseph. But in its claptrap, noisy way, it was interesting and vital. I amused myself at the window, rolling the packets, watching the street parade. I tried to guess the stories of the people walking by.

❧ 11 ❧

I passed the winter in Remington River. I wrote letters to Ma and Pa telling them about Earl, the rest of the trip, and my situation in Remington River. I wondered what they would think about Earl's betrayal.

Spring came at last, and I was bringing a letter to the wagon train that was heading east in a few days. Standing next to the livery, I saw Sing sitting on the walkway with Bird.

A man came riding up on a big black horse. He got down and sat next to Sing. The man was dressed completely in black with black leather chaps decorated with silver medallions. His saddle had the same medallions along the cantle and down the fender. I could see he had a long moustache, and his dark hair was pulled back in a plait secured with strips of leather. I waited for a moment, standing too far away to hear what they were talking about. The man took something from his pocket and offered it to Bird, who plucked it from his fingers and hopped away to peck at it.

After the man rode away, I approached Sing.

"Hello, Sing. And hello, Bird," I said, joining the boy on the walkway. "I've never seen that man before. Is he your friend?"

"He stops to talk with me sometimes. And to give Bird pieces of wild onion."

Sing said he had errands to run. The boy seemed to have friends everywhere and kept busy with any small task that was asked of him.

Bird hopped onto Sing's shoulder and the two hustled away down the street.

Later, I asked the Old Mandarin about the dark man. "That would be Mendonca" was his reply

"Who is he?"

"A complicated one." That was all he would say.

I returned from shopping one evening with a bag of potatoes and onions to find the Old Mandarin sitting at the table by the window with a visitor. It was cold so I hurried to the fire. They were deep in conversation, and the bell clanging above the door as I entered did not deter their talk. I put another log on the fire, and the burst of flame revealed the Old Mandarin's companion. It was the dark man called Mendonca. I tried not to stare at the stranger, but I made one or two prolonged glances at him trying to take in all the details.

If one word could have described him, it was *midnight*. He was dressed, as before, completely in black from his boots to his shirt, vest, and hat. Even the scarf that he wore about his neck was black. His skin was an olive tone. The only objects on him to break up the darkness were the silver medallions I had seen on his saddle and chaps and which now festooned his belt and boots: these were polished brightly, and in the center of each was a piece of black leather.

They paid no attention to me. I retreated to the scullery in the back and began to prepare supper. Soon I heard the rattle of the beaded curtain as it parted and the closing of the door to the back room. This was where the Old Mandarin treated folks with his herbal remedies.

The Old Mandarin did not care for my cooking, and, as I was not versed in the cuisine he preferred, he prepared his own meals. Nonetheless we always ate at the same table. As my supper was nearly ready, I wondered if I should wait, as it was our custom to sit down and review the day's events together.

Presently, I heard the back room door open and the sound of the beads again, and the Old Mandarin appeared in the scullery.

His expression was serious and concerned. "I have no wish to endanger you, my dear. Events may transpire shortly, however, that may result in just that."

"What has happened?"

The dark man came into the room. He was quite tall and moved with the ease of someone with great confidence. He regarded me and raised his eyebrows. His look was not unfriendly. It was more quizzical.

"Is it wise to involve the woman? You know your business, Zhao. But—"

The Old Mandarin turned to me and threw up his hands. "Forgive me. This is Mariah Penngrove. A friend as well as helper. Mariah, this is Pajaro Mendonca." We both nodded to each other in greeting.

The Old Mandarin continued. "Yes, I think I must tell her, Mendonca. If only so she can make her own choice."

Mendonca came into the scullery and sat at the table that I had earlier set for two. Silently, I set a third plate and cutlery.

"You need not, señorita. I will not stay long."

The Old Mandarin took his seat at the table. "Have something to eat. Mariah is a good cook," he said with a wink in my direction.

"There's enough," I said as I ladled out the stew and brought a plate of bread. "And I hope that we will not have to wait to finish for you to tell me what this is all about."

Mendonca grunted approvingly as he tucked into his supper. "Fresh bread. *Dios.* I have not had this in a long time. My appreciation to you, señorita."

"I will explain, Mariah," said the Old Mandarin.

With a nod from Mendonca to proceed, the Old Mandarin began. "This morning, Mendonca and his brothers were riding on the other side of the river going east. They came upon a wagon. With the exception of one, all occupants had been murdered, the wagon driver included. The survivor, a girl, was able to tell her story."

Mendonca reached for the last piece of bread but looked inquiringly at me first. I waved at him to take it.

The Old Mandarin continued. "The girl comes from someone of great means and stature in San Francisco. She had been with four girls traveling by wagon to Remington River from the city. Their wagon was attacked. The driver and the four girls succumbed. This girl pretended to be dead and her attackers fled."

"What do you mean, 'she comes from one of great means and stature in San Francisco'?" I asked.

The Old Mandarin rose and made his pot of jasmine tea then returned to the table. He and Mendonca exchanged glances that made me think they knew a great deal more than they wished to tell me.

"The girl is called Chin. Her mother's name is Po Fong. Po Fong is very unusual in that she is a Chinese woman who is also one of the most powerful people in San Francisco. She did not come to this reputation easily or without making enemies. Po Fong has many. She is also quite ruthless. Why she sends her daughter to Remington River is a mystery to me."

"I can think of only one reason a wagon full of women would be coming to Remington River," I stated bluntly.

Mendonca nodded. "It is what I thought as well."

"Do you know this Po Fong? Is she a friend?" I asked.

"She is no friend of mine," the Old Mandarin replied, acidly. "When I first arrived in the States, of course, one must stop in San Francisco. Naturally, a Chinese like myself goes to where my countrymen congregate. It is called Chinatown.

"There was much talk about the Chinese woman who controlled Chinatown. I learned later that she had a great dislike of her fellow countrymen who had newly arrived. Those who still had the old ways of trust and friendship. She felt that it made us look silly and ignorant to the whites. And she had great need of the respect of the whites. Her business thrived through the pleasure-seeking of the whites. Yes, there was much talk of Po Fong. Her story is probably not all true. Still, considering where she came from, it is astonishing that she found such success.

"She came from a family of wealthy landowners in the remote province of her birth. She was raised very traditionally. But her parents were unable to contain her fierce independence and ambition. Her first act of defiance was to unbind her feet. She had to learn to walk, against the wishes of her family, of course. This was as much an insult as anything: to walk when you are wealthy."

"Unbind her feet? I don't understand."

The Old Mandarin nodded. "Of course, you wouldn't know about this custom, Mariah. I will explain. In China, if you are a highborn woman, you show this status by not walking. You are carried about on a chair. In order to make sure a woman does not walk, her feet are tightly swaddled as an infant. Over time, the bones bend and crack in half. Walking is not only difficult, it is painful. Po Fong removed her bindings. I have heard that she walks rather awkwardly but she manages.

"Her father and mother despaired of her. They need not have worried. An older man paid good money for her. With his sights set on America, she gladly went with him to escape her family. It was an opportunity. As they traveled the long distance to board the ship in Hong Kong, she saw more opportunity. Her husband was kind but stupid. He never suspected her motives as she readily cooperated with all manners of their marriage. Po Fong left China with the husband, but he did not disembark with her. He died mysteriously during the sea voyage. While still at sea, she took up with the ship's captain, who was transporting a large shipment of jade, gold, and gemstones. The captain's death, just one day after putting in at San Francisco, was investigated thoroughly because a substantial portion of the valuable cargo was missing. Po Fong's husband and the captain both died of unknown causes. There were rumors about poison. Well, the fact that Po Fong emerged in Chinatown soon after with a sizeable fortune apparently did not stir up any suspicion. Her brothel business, gambling interests, and extortion of local gentlemen in San Francisco earned her a reputation of possessing few scruples. She learned quickly whom to pay off in exchange for silence. And if the payment was not enough, people had a strange habit of turning up dead when they opposed Po Fong.

"I have thought of her over the years," he continued. "I know of her growing power and also of her conflict with the tongs in San Francisco. She is not well-liked by many of the other Chinese, who have also benefited from the pleasure-seeking whites and see her as competition."

"What is a tong?" I asked.

"An organization with many criminals and all the associated activities. Very bad enemy to make. I think it was a tong that carried out this attack. The tong leaders are always battling one another for superiority."

Mendonca spoke. "Whoever came after these women, they were a brutal sort. There were two whites and a Chinese. Zhao thinks he's from a Chinatown tong. We saw the attack from afar and waited until they were gone. They must have thought they had finished them all off. They took clubs and went around—my apologies, señorita. We went down to the wagon and found the girl barely alive. I saw that she was Chinese. So I brought her to Zhao. She is here. Now. In the back room."

I gulped. I had heard no sounds from the room. "Here?"

"She is resting. Her wounds are severe but I have tended to her," replied the Old Mandarin.

"Why would these tongs come all the way up here to attack a wagon of women?" I asked.

Mendonca wiped his moustache and took out a packet of tobacco. "Yes. There is more to this than meets the eye, señorita." He began to speak again but stopped and eyed the Old Mandarin carefully.

The Old Mandarin sipped his tea. "From what Chin was able to tell us, the women she was with were taken from a rival tong brothel in San Francisco. They were told they were going to be free. Of course, it was just a ploy to get them to go. It was Po Fong's intent to toy with the tongs, for some reason we have yet to understand. They picked the most beautiful and desirable of the women, too. Sad to think that they were just pawns in all this, and now . . . dead."

"The girl says it is only about the tongs and nothing else?" asked Mendonca.

"She has not been able to speak more than a few words," replied the Old Mandarin. "Do you think there is another reason?"

Mendonca said nothing.

Zhao peered into his pot of tea and found it now empty. "We must be careful. For whoever hurt her before may want to do so again. Of course, she must be moved soon. This town cannot hold a secret for very long."

"Yes, I can see that," I agreed. "You did say that others may come after her, didn't you?"

"We will make sure she is secreted away and kept safe, Mariah."

"May I see her?" I asked. "The girl?"

The two men exchanged glances. I followed them to the door of the back room where the Old Mandarin parted the curtains and turned the knob. We entered.

Once inside, my eyes adjusted to the dim light coming from a few candles placed about the room. In a corner was a low pallet and mattress where the girl lay motionless beneath a silk quilt. I approached her and she stirred briefly; her eyes fluttered open and there was terror in them. She started to rise and I placed my hand on her shoulder to calm her. Bandages covered her arms and the head wound she had suffered. I gasped. She was no more than a child, fourteen or fifteen at the most. She was exquisite despite her injuries, with a smooth, oval face, a small mouth, and generous cheeks. The one hand that I could see was fine and fragile. Her breathing became regular, her eyes closed, and she went back to sleep.

"I have given her laudanum. She will sleep for a while. Her wounds looked worse than they are. But they will heal, if tended to properly," said the Old Mandarin.

"Good Lord! She's only a child. What kind of woman sends a girl—her own daughter—out here like this?" I exclaimed. "And for the purpose you're telling me? I don't understand."

"It is not necessary to understand, señorita," said Mendonca. "She likely knows no different life, sad to say."

I thought about some of the saloon girls in town. Some of them might be as young, I supposed. But they had developed a hardened, sour look very soon after arriving. It was not lost on me that someone so beautiful would be a welcome change for the brutes that looked for this kind of thing. I felt a bitter taste rise in my mouth.

As if he read my mind, Mendonca said, "Unfortunately, I know too many who would find her . . . Dios . . . *appealing*."

"Well, she can't stay here, can she? This is not a safe place. You can't just keep her here in this room."

"No, Mariah. It would not be wise for her to leave. There are only a handful of Chinese in Remington River. It would make sense for those searching for her to, at least, stop here and inquire," said Zhao. "They would wonder if she sought refuge here."

"Where do you plan on taking her?"

Mendonca touched my elbow. I turned and he motioned for me to come out of the room. "Let her sleep. I will tell you. Come with me."

The Old Mandarin pulled up a stool next to the girl and gently took her hand. I shut the door and left him by her side.

The hour was growing late. A wind rose up in the late evening sometimes, out of the valley, and I could hear it pressing against the window of the scullery.

Mendonca sat at the table and leaned back in his chair. "Could I trouble you for coffee, Mariah?"

"I will make some. I feel the need for it, myself." I set about grinding the beans and heating the water.

"Your first name, sir? It was said once to me and I cannot recall it. If I may know it?"

"It is Pajaro."

"It is Spanish, I take it. What does it mean?"

He laughed. "Bird. My mother was delivered of me early. I was quite small as an infant. Fragile, I am told. Like a small sparrow, they say. Ha!"

"Where are you from? Originally."

"My father came from Mexico as a stonecutter for one of the missions. I was born in the mission and educated there," he said. His face darkened as he spoke. "Sandro and Lorenzo, my younger brothers, and I left the mission after our parents died. We mined for gold in the foothills. We had a good claim there for a while. All was as we hoped. For a time."

He took out his tobacco bag and prepared a smoke. On closer inspection, he did not appear that old. Perhaps close to thirty. The skin was smooth on his face; his eyes were clear and light brown, in contrast to the pervasive midnight about him. His manner of speaking was quiet and deliberate.

"You don't look like a miner."

"I no longer am one."

He seemed not to want to linger on this particular part of the conversation and proceeded to inquire about my story.

I told him about St. Joseph, the journey, Earl's death, and finding the Old Mandarin. I decided to keep most of the details about Earl to myself. I realized that I had not recounted my story to anybody, apart from the Old Mandarin, in a long time. I feared I had gone on too long. "I'm sorry to bore you. You have most likely heard the same story countless times."

"A few times. Although yours turned out much better than even *you* supposed it would, Mariah." He grinned. "Finding Zhao was fortunate for you."

I glanced toward the doorway and thought about Chin. "It could have turned out much differently. That I know."

"But surely you must want to return to your people. There is nothing keeping you here. Making a stake would take some work, yes. It could be done."

"I have thought about it. But I like it here. I like the mountains, the clear streams, the meadows, even the snow is better here. And I am content for now."

I placed the coffee things on the table and poured out a cup for him and myself. In companionable silence, we sipped. I felt his eyes on me. Like a child, I blushed.

"Now tell me about this plan, Pajaro. I have a feeling I am involved in some way."

Mendonca drained his cup. "If I had any say in the matter, you would not be involved. There is a place a day's ride from here. A stagecoach station called Widow Creek. I know the people managing it, the Monroes. A man and his wife. I have some business with them every now and then. They will cooperate. The girl will be safe there."

Before I could ask him about his business with the Monroes, Mendonca leaned back and pointed at me. "Zhao will ask a favor of you tonight. You must carefully consider your answer. I do not think it is a good plan to involve you."

"What will he ask?"

"He will ask you to drive a wagon with the girl in the back. Drive to Widow Creek Station. She cannot ride a horse in her condition. And it is better if my brothers and I ride ahead to make sure it is safe."

Before I could say anything further, the Old Mandarin returned.

"It grows late. You must be ready at first light." He looked at Mendonca and then at me.

"He has told you?"

I nodded. "I will help, if I can."

Mendonca said, "I will have a wagon ready out back. But it must be *before* it gets light, Zhao. Sandro, Lorenzo, and I will be waiting for you at the crossroads. We will continue on from there to Widow Creek Station."

After Mendonca left, I packed up a few things, as instructed by the Old Mandarin, and prepared to retire, knowing sleep would be difficult. The Old Mandarin called to me from the front of the shop.

I walked out and found him holding a small box. "I want you to have this," he said. I looked inside where I saw some silk fabric wrapped around two objects. I pulled back the corner of one the pieces of silk and saw the cup and saucer that had belonged to Queen Victoria.

He laughed. "The sharp instincts of the shopkeeper's daughter from Missouri!"

"I can't take these. Somebody will buy them and you'll get a fortune."

The Old Mandarin took my hand. "Money is not everything. You've been a good friend, and I hope I have not taken advantage of it with this plan. Your acceptance of this gift will greatly relieve my conscience, Mariah."

"You make it sound like you are not coming."

"I cannot. I need to stay here. You must take all your things with you. If someone comes looking for Chin, they will come here first. There will be trouble if I am not here in my shop. There would be suspicion. I will get word to you, if you can return. And you have Pajaro. He's a good man. He will look after things."

"What is Pajaro's business? I have seen him only one other time in Remington River. You described him to me as complicated. What does that mean?"

By the look on his face, I could tell he was considering how to respond. "He is involved in work that is dangerous but worthy. You may hear things about him. That he is a criminal. That he and his brothers are notorious bandits. But I would never entrust you to a man I did not consider honorable." He patted my shoulder. "Now, please, Mariah. Accept the gift."

"I accept. I will cherish it always," I said, feeling suddenly like my world was changing. Setting off with this strange, dark man with a questionable past seemed foolish. Yet I wanted to help the girl to safety. Zhao had been good to me and I wanted to repay his kindness. "I will be ready in the morning."

When the first gray urgings of morning started to appear, I looked out the window. The wind was high and rain pelted the glass. Then I heard the groan of a wagon and the nickering of horses out back.

❧ 12 ❧

THE OLD MANDARIN WAS BREWING TEA and packing food for the trip. He was pensive and serious.

"I don't like this weather, Mariah."

I didn't either but I did not want to dwell on it.

"How's Chin this morning?"

"Tolerable," he replied. "I will need some assistance getting her into the wagon."

He handed me a sack. "Here's bandages and medicine for her. Change her dressings regularly and apply the poultice. And there's more in there. Now, help me get Chin in the wagon."

The thought of the wagon and the horses sent a wave of uneasiness through me. Driving an unfamiliar team in bad weather did not sit well with me. I took the tea he offered and sipped it, hoping it would brace me for what I knew would be a challenging task.

We settled the injured girl in the wagon, placing her on a mattress stuffed with straw and bundling her with blankets against the morning chill. We had fashioned a peaked canvas cover for the back to protect her from the elements. She woke briefly and moaned, after we arranged for her comfort, and she reached for Zhao. He gave her another dose of laudanum and grasped her hand. He said something to her that I could not hear. Then he climbed out of the wagon and tied the rear flap closed.

I was on the buckboard by this time, with my belongings stowed behind. A thick cloak covered me from head to waist. The reins felt familiar in my hands, but the pulling and jostling of the two horses as they fretted in the harness was unnerving.

The Old Mandarin called up to me. "Be careful, my dear. The brothers will meet you. You have only a short distance to go on your own. I will get word to you soon. Goodbye!"

I gave a halfhearted flick of the reins and was surprised that the horses responded so quickly. With a jolt and slight swerve, we proceeded down the front street as the dark was just easing away.

Once I left town, I was less worried about losing control because there were no buildings to careen into. On the wide and well-worn track out to the crossroads, I gave the team their lead and they went along at a smooth clip. I don't think those two horses ever heard such profuse words of gratitude from a human being.

The road began a gradual ascent and the horses slowed a bit. Then the rain began in earnest. I pulled my cloak more tightly about me, but it afforded little protection from the pelting drops. The weather did not appear to bother the team for they plunged ahead without hesitation. The ascent continued and now the rain was heavy enough that the road was muddy with rivulets running down the wheel tracks. Twice I felt the rear wheels skid in the mud yet we kept our course.

Finally, the road turned toward the tree line and, beneath the great trees, I was protected from the rain, though still soaked and chilled. It was not a foreign feeling to me; many days on the wagon were spent in unbearable conditions that made the anticipation of what was around the next corner both sweet and ominous.

There was a sharp smell of pine along with the scent of sodden earth. Both the forest and the clouds diminished whatever light was gained with the sunrise. Though it was gloomy and damp, the woods gave me a burst of bravery, for they felt strong and full of life, and I felt suddenly more alive than I had been in months. If this was The Beyond my mother and I had talked about so long ago in our little parlor while reading *The Journals*, it was less a destination and more of a way of life.

This helped bolster my courage. I remembered my task and the girl, Chin, who rested in the back. The Old Mandarin had said he trusted Pajaro Mendonca. This certainly was a strange country with values all jumbled up with honor and nobility, as the Old Mandarin had put it. Such goings-on had not touched my life in St. Joseph. I could not have imagined knowing such people as the Old Mandarin and my new acquaintance, Mendonca. And yet here I was helping them escort Chin, whose past was as dark and strange as her future, to an unknown destination.

Presently, I came to the crossroads. It was empty. The opening in the trees afforded a renewed cascade of water from the sky. I hauled up on the team, applied the brake, and wrapped my arms tightly around myself. I looked in the back and could see the even rise and fall of the blanket that covered Chin's chest.

Where was Mendonca?

The sound of hoofbeats came from farther up the road. Four horsemen came into view, and I realized with a knot of fear in my stomach that Mendonca was not among them.

They slowed and approached the wagon. One horseman placed himself directly in front of the team, who began fidgeting with this strange horse in their line of vision. I pulled hard on the reins to keep them in line. The second horseman began to circle back toward the rear of the wagon. The third one waved for me to stay put and indicated with a hand gesture that he was going to come up to me. He paused as the fourth horseman, a Chinese man, pointed at me. The other three horsemen were white. They were all looking for Chin, and I knew that, this time, they meant to finish what they'd started.

I glanced back to see what the second horseman was doing around the back of the wagon.

Where was Mendonca?

I had to think quickly and figure out a way to protect myself and Chin. I did not want to be gunned down on a cold and muddy road.

"Where you headed on such a fine day?" asked the third horseman, who came close enough for me to see that his words held no pleasantries.

Keep your head, Mariah.

"Uhhh," I mumbled and held my head and moaned. "I'm just resting. I don't feel so good. Just stopping for a moment."

I rocked back and forth and gripped my stomach. "I may need to get down here presently and find a tree. I'm just not feeling well at all, mister."

He did not look like the type who would offer assistance.

"What you got in the wagon, woman? Don't lie to me neither."

"That's my father back there!" I exclaimed and drew a hand to my mouth and coughed. "Say you *could* help me, if you would. I'm just tuckered out and probably getting the same sick he has. Do you think you could help me make him more comfortable back there, clean him up some? I'm so weak, I'm afraid I might jostle him too much. Him being so sick and all, I'd like to keep him comfortable. I'm fretful that now that I've caught it, I won't be much good to him."

The second horseman had his hand on the canvas tarp that the Old Mandarin had secured. I cried out in my most dramatic voice turning to the back of the wagon. "I just hope it ain't what killed them folks downriver a week back! Please, Lord, do not deliver us into the hands of that pestilence! Praise Jesus, I've been too good a soul to deserve this!" I added, "Forgive the smell back there, sir. My father has not left the wagon in a few days and he's, well, not terribly clean!"

This prompted the second horseman to withdraw his hand quickly and back away from the wagon.

The man addressing me smirked and eyed me suspiciously. "Where you headed anyway?"

I continued to feign illness and hoped that I was convincing. This time I leaned forward and groaned violently, clutching my stomach. I made a strange guttural sound.

Then I reached down to the bottom of the baseboard and scraped around with my hand until I found what I wanted.

"Mister, I'm heading up yonder to some folks who might help us. Left my ma half-buried back there at the homestead. Powerful sorry about *that*."

I shook violently and grimaced. Then I raised my hand, showed him what it contained and cried piteously. "Oh, mister! My shame is something awful! Guessing I don't need no tree now. Oh, mister. Maybe you got some spare water so's I can clean up my hand!"

"Jesus Christ, woman!" he bellowed, as I held my hand up. He drew his horse back with a swift jerk.

He did not examine my hand too closely before he backed away. He signaled to the other three to follow him. The Chinese man did not move as the others rode past me. He watched me with disgust as I inspected the slop in my hand. Then kicked his horse and took off after the others.

I heaved a huge side of relief but still couldn't stop shaking. I checked on Chin. I watched her move the blanket away from her face and peer up at me, pale and unsmiling. I'm not sure if she understood what had just happened but I was happy to see that she was well for the moment.

The next sounds I heard came from the trees. The light was improving and I looked around anxiously for the source of the noise—the sounds of crunching footfall made by heavy boots, but from what direction I could not detect. It would not surprise me if the horsemen returned. I felt I had not been very convincing. I was positive the Chinese man did not believe my story. I cannot describe my emotions in seeing Pajaro Mendonca striding toward me. I saw who I presumed were his two brothers on horseback in the protection of the trees. Where had he been? Wasn't he supposed to protect me and Chin? And to think the Old Mandarin placed such high confidence in him.

"Eh," he said. "You are not injured?" I did not reply.

"Give me your hand," Pajaro said with a laugh.

I gave him the same hand that I extended to the second horseman. It was smeared with mud kicked up by the team but, from a distance, could have passed as shit, as was my intent. Pajaro took my hand and gently wiped it clean with a kerchief he produced from his back pocket.

"You did well," he said, grinning and seemingly quite pleased with the whole affair. "That's a good trick," as he flicked the mud off his kerchief.

He looked up when I did not respond. Seeing my expression, he said, "We were here the whole time. Up there, in the trees. Our guns were on them. If there was any doubt, we would have taken them out. But we feared for your lives, Mariah. And we did not want to take any chances with bullets if it was not necessary. You thought quickly, señorita."

I wondered whether that was the truth or, in hanging back and watching from the trees, they were merely protecting themselves. I did not try to hide my anger. I could see that I needed to watch after myself. As always, I could only depend on my own resources.

"As you say," I said, bitterly, and took the brake off the wagon, "let's get out of this mess, please. Lead on."

The rain increased. For an hour or so, I drove along the ridge, paralleling the Mendoncas, who rode in and out of the trees, finding intermittent relief from the storm. Shortly, we descended down from the ridge onto a wide meadow. The stream, which on any other day probably meandered peacefully through the center of the meadow, was rushing madly and breaching its banks. The road skirted the stream but was obliterated by the raging waters. The wagon would not do well here and I halted in the downpour. The brothers stopped ahead and held a brief conference.

It was not Pajaro who rode back to the wagon. This one was a bit wider and stouter than Pajaro. He had a pleasant face and kind expression as he approached the wagon. His hair was cut short and he had a ragged beard. Like his brothers, his clothing was entirely black. He rode his horse up to the buckboard. A bit sheepishly, he said, "I am Lorenzo." Water poured off the brim of his hat and down his back as he reached to shake my hand. "I think we must stop and wait for a break in this weather, señorita. Back in the trees? Can you turn this around?"

"I'll try," I said. "I should check on the girl anyway."

The horses were all too willing to turn around, probably aware that we could go no farther. I turned the team and retreated back into the woods.

Pajaro and his brothers dismounted and set about to quickly build a shelter. They cut down several green pine boughs and, using a horse blanket, fashioned a lean-to. I crept into the back of the wagon to check on Chin.

Surprisingly, little water had managed to get in through the canvas. She had been dozing but her eyes fluttered open.

"Do you understand English, Chin?"

She smiled weakly. "Yes. Of course."

She sat up a bit, holding her head. "You were very brave. I heard you with those other men. That was clever."

"Brave? Clever?" I laughed. "Maybe. I must tend to your bandages, now. We have stopped for a bit. The rain is too steady to continue. Will you need more medicine for the pain?"

Chin undid her own bandages and gingerly felt the borders of the wound. "It is not as bad as I thought."

For a child, she had fortitude, and I wondered how in the few short years of her life she had acquired it. Sadly, I considered that often one does not possess fortitude without enduring hardship.

"I have little pain. I am tired, though."

I changed her bandages and gave her some water. "I don't know how much farther we have to go."

Chin nodded. "The old man? Where is he?"

"He remained back in town."

"I wish to thank him for his kindness," she said. "I fear that his kindness has also put him in danger."

I wanted to ask her *Why were you on that wagon in the first place, Chin? With those women? Where were you going?* But I did not think it was the time.

"Rest now. I'll be back."

Emerging from the wagon, I saw the beginnings of a campfire crackling under the lean-to. Pajaro was tending to their horses and Lorenzo was looking after my team. I was silently grateful not to have to try to unharness them and situate them in the trees. My arms were stiff from driving, and I wanted nothing other than to sit on the soft pine duff and warm myself.

Thus, I met the third brother, Sandro.

He did not introduce himself, and his sullen look as I sat by the fire told me that our conversation, if any, would be limited. I only learned his name when Pajaro called to him and instructed him to give me a cup of coffee.

He picked up the pot, inspected its contents, and returned it to the fire.

"Not ready yet, I guess?" I asked.

His eyes responded to my query with a dark stare that left me cold. He was smaller than the other two, wiry, and his quick movements with the pot and now his erratic poking of the fire gave me the impression that he was tightly wound. Then I noticed his hands as he violently stirred the embers under the pot. They were scarred from burns.

Lorenzo and Pajaro came to the fire and sat cross-legged next to it. There was barely enough room for all of us under the shelter. Pajaro and Lorenzo sandwiched me, but I was grateful for their warmth, for our backs were exposed and getting soaked. Pajaro inquired briefly about Chin's condition and I answered shortly that she was fine.

The coffee was ready and we sipped at it wordlessly, each of us in our own thoughts, staring at the fire.

Pajaro stirred next me and adjusted his position. He rolled a smoke. "Eh, we have a change of plans, señorita."

I eyed him warily. "What sort of change of plans?"

"That bunch?" he said, jutting his chin in no particular direction. "In this weather, I am sure they have slowed down. Still, I have no way of knowing which way they went. They may have continued into Remington River. Or they could have circled back, suspicious of you and the wagon and aware of your direction, riding enough of a distance from us that we cannot detect them. There is only one place that way and they will find it—Widow Creek Station. Or they could have split up and gone both ways. I have a worry for Zhao and also for those at the station. I don't want any surprises. Sandro will go to the station, Lorenzo back to town to check on Zhao. We will remain here until they return with what we need to know."

"How do you know they are the ones who attacked that wagon of women? Because of the Chinese? It may be a coincidence, couldn't it?" Although as soon as the words left my mouth, I realized I was speaking with little confidence.

"Sandro and Lorenzo saw them. They are the same bunch," replied Pajaro. "They remained near the wagon after the attack, hidden in the trees, while I brought the girl to Zhao. That bunch came back probably unsure whether they had finished the job. Or maybe looking for something. The Chinese? He tore that wagon apart. Then—"

"He threw all the bodies back in the wagon and burned it to the ground," Lorenzo finished the sentence. I shivered.

Pajaro nodded. "Eh, I tell you one thing. Those other three? We know of them. They are from these parts. Useless drunks most of the time. They are no problem for us, that I can tell you."

Sandro suddenly stood up, snapped a twig, and threw it in the fire. "Dios, we could have finished them off right there at the crossroads! Tell me why we did not? What good is it to let them ride off like that? Your *deal* with the old man? You still have not told us how much we will get for it, Pajaro? How much is this all worth?"

"What deal? What are you talking about?" I asked. Had there been maneuvering behind my back? The Old Mandarin's word describing Pajaro came to mind: complicated.

"Sandro," said Pajaro sharply. "Enough."

With a sick turn in my stomach, I got up from the fire and moved quickly away. Of course, it was all about money to them. To *him*. The one the Old Mandarin also described as "noble." I walked out onto the road and wanted nothing other than to feel clean. I raised my face to the rain, hoping it would wash the sick out of me. I had gotten involved in this scheme and like a fool had never questioned it much, had trusted too much in the Old Mandarin. Why? To help him, yes, as he had been so kind to me. And, I supposed, to help the girl. But was this helping, to drag her out into a storm and nearly get her finished off at the crossroads? I could have argued it, refused to be party to it, but instead I had gone along, and I suddenly realized why. It was *exciting*. The rain couldn't wash away my own selfish reasons for being here. Sandro began saddling up, viciously cinching up the girth. Lorenzo, too, saddled up in silence. They rode off shortly after, and I watched them part ways on the road where I still stood. The fire was still going. Pajaro watched me as I sat back down then unwrapped the oilcloth and removed *The Journals*. As was my custom, I allowed the book to open at any random page and, upon doing so, take heart in whatever message the words bring me. As I hunkered further under the shelter of the lean-to, protecting the pages from the rain, the book fell open to Lewis's entry for Thursday, July 18, 1805.

Pajaro cleared his throat. "May I ask what it is you are reading?"

"Something to take my mind off of this . . ." and I waved my hand.

"Adventure, señorita?"

I looked at him, startled. "Adventure? Is that what this is? I think not."

"Eh, but I think you *do*!"

I shook my head. "I cannot imagine less of one."

"Dios, señorita. Tell me this: why did you come willingly? I heard no argument from you. Frankly, I was surprised. But then I saw the look on your face as you drove into the clearing of the crossroads. If I am not mistaken, you were enjoying yourself."

"Do not presume to know what I think or feel. You know nothing about me."

Pajaro rolled another smoke and leaned onto his saddle. He sighed. "True. I can only guess. I might *guess* about someone who has such a well-cared-for book as that one. I might *guess* that when she takes it out in such a time as *this,* it is not to take her mind off her situation but to find guidance and inspiration." He laughed. "Tell me what you are reading."

I snorted and tried not to consider that his words were actually quite valid. "If you must know, it is *The Journals of Lewis and Clark*. I doubt you are familiar with the book."

"I am not familiar with the book itself. But of Lewis and Clark? Of course. The explorers. Although, that man Clark? Not a friend to the Indians as it turned out."

This caught me off guard and I suddenly felt ignorant, having primarily read only *The Journals* and very little about the later lives of Lewis and Clark. "What do you know of him?"

"In my travels, I have kept company with many Indians. They, like myself and Zhao, are treated like outsiders. It is just the way of this country. But the Indians? Was it not *their* land before the white man? Clark turned against them. You read about it sometime." He pulled on his cigarette and continued, "But it is true that what you might believe about someone may be completely false and, in that belief, you never know the true person. Good or bad."

His remarks unsettled me. I got up from the fire.

"I'll check on the girl."

I walked to the wagon, trying to catch my breath. What was the matter with me? I peered inside the canvas shelter. Chin was fast asleep. Part of me wanted nothing more than to be in deep slumber where my brain would stop churning. What in the world was he saying about Clark?

When I turned back to the fire, Pajaro was craning his head to look at the book. I snatched it up quickly.

He laughed. "I would not dream to touch it. But would you read to me the passage that has caught your attention?"

"Very well. If you insist."

Previous to our departure, we saw a large herd of the Bighorned animals on the immencely high and nearly perpendicular clift opposite to us. On the fase of this cliff they walked about and bounded from rock to rock with apparent unconcern where it appeared to me that no quadruped could have stood, and from which, had they made one false step they must have precipitated at least 500 feet. The anamal appears to frequent such precepices and clifts where in fact they are perfectly secure from the pursuit of the wolf, bear, or even man himself.

I closed the book. Picking up a stick, I knocked about with it in the fire. I could feel Pajaro's eyes on me.

"It must be something truly miraculous to see an animal that one has not seen before," he said. "And to guess the meaning of their behavior, yes?" He stood up and stretched. "Eh, why don't you rest a bit? I will keep watch. When my brothers return, we will make haste then."

He did not wait for my answer but walked toward the horses. My eyes became heavy at his mere mention of rest. But I went back to what Pajaro had said about this being an adventure for me. What had I become? He was right. I was excited to be going forward into something new and strange. As if I were one of Lewis's animals, never seen before and whose behavior can only be guessed at.

The sensation of a hand on my shoulder jolted me awake. The sound of hoofbeats came to my ears.

"It's Lorenzo," said Pajaro.

Lorenzo came flying down the road, and in a splattering of mud and horse sweat he came to a halt. He jumped off his horse and ran to Pajaro. There was much whispering between them. I got up from the fire and checked on Chin. This time she was sitting up.

"It's just one of the brothers," I said. "We may be going soon. Are you ready to travel again?"

"Yes. I am ready," she said. "Miss? I heard some things earlier. When you were talking. About the old man. And a deal."

I felt my heart sink. Was she part of yet another plan in which she was simply a pawn? I did not envy her situation.

"That is just talk. One of these brothers seems to think there is money involved. That was not the Old Mandarin's plan. It was to return you to your mother. Safely."

She shook her head and grimaced. "I know something of the world. If the deal is for me, I can tell you that my mother will not pay. But," she said quietly, "miss, *I* can pay. If you let me go, I will pay you. I'll tell you where it is hidden. The gold."

"What gold?"

"My mother thinks I am a fool. For my years, though, I have learned much from her. To not trust her, for one. She sent me out here. I was expected to look for someone. Someone very important to my mother," she said bitterly. "It did not matter to her whether it was to my liking to come here."

She straightened up a bit. If she were a child, she no longer seemed like it in my eyes. Chin appeared weary. "From my mother, I stole gold. I hid it along the way. Near a stagecoach stop where we paused for the night. I was suspicious of the driver from the beginning. I did not trust him. I feared he was allowing those men to catch up to us. My mother's enemies."

She touched the bandage on her head. "I pretended to be dead. And that one Chinese man in the group? I know him. His name is Ah Wong."

"Ah Wong? You knew him? But why did he attack the wagon and kill those girls? And—"

"And spare me?" She looked at me sharply. "I thought I knew the reason. I thought it was a clever plan to take me away. Ah Wong and I were in love, you see. He told me that he knew my mother was sending me away but he would come after me. And so, I must go and pretend to do what my mother asked. This is what he said. 'Pretend, Chin. Pretend to find this person,' he told me, 'just as your mother asks.' Then, he would come for me and we would go away together. He told me that we could build a better, honest life. Here. Away from my mother and her life. I believed him."

"But it wasn't the truth, was it?" I asked, feeling a chill run through me as she spoke in her low voice, her rage barely disguised.

"The girls I traveled with. One of them told me that Ah Wong was part of a tong that despised my mother. The tong was also looking for this person, the one I was told to find in Remington River. Ah Wong told my mother. He was looking to better himself with her by betraying his own tong. In the end, he betrayed me and everything I believed *about* him. Do you understand? I thought he was coming to take me away. We were going to go together. But it was all lies. In the end, he only wanted to prove to my mother his worth. For money. For power."

Chin laughed bitterly.

"I brought the gold for our future, Ah Wong's and mine. But it is no good now. It is soiled gold with blood on it. And though I have disgraced my mother, I no longer fear her. You may not know what it is to hate your own mother. This hate has driven away my fear. Still, when my mother learns of what has happened, I live on borrowed time. She will come after me." Then she lowered her voice and continued. "I will tell you where it is. The gold. You get it and keep it. Just let me go."

"Here? You're in the middle of nowhere, Chin. And with *them* out there looking for you?"

She smiled. "Not here, miss. I'll know when it is right. And you will let me walk away. Please." She touched her chest and pulled aside the collar of her silk jacket. Around her neck was a string with a pouch attached. "It is a crude map. But you will find it. The gold is there. Safely hidden."

I protested, saying, "You must keep it, Chin. You will need it."

Chin looked at me thoughtfully. "You will need it more, miss."

I wasn't going to argue with her. She seemed so determined.

"What about this person you are supposed to find in Remington River? Do you know who it is?" I asked.

She began to say something when Pajaro appeared. Chin pulled her collar closed. He looked at Chin with a frown. "I am happy to see that you are feeling better. I trust you are ready to travel, for we must leave now."

Chin held her head up. "I am ready, sir."

Pajaro turned to me and motioned me away from the wagon. "I have some bad news."

"The Old Mandarin?" I felt tears form in my eyes. I knew, of course. Lorenzo had looked deeply troubled upon his return.

"Dios. They set fire to his business and, eh, he never got out. Nearly burned down the whole town. I am sorry. He was my friend too."

Pajaro made a movement to let me have my moment of sorrow. I could have broken down in wracking sobs at the mere thought of how he perished. But it would do no good right now. Those men were coming for us now, for sure.

"We must go. Now," I said.

I set about harnessing the damn horses, who fussed and worried over every inch of the process. I sorely disliked the both of them. But with their speed, I could tolerate them for the time we had left together.

Once back on the buckboard, I saw that Pajaro and Lorenzo had broken camp quickly. I thought about what Chin had told me about this gold she had hidden. If it was true, what should I do about it?

I was happy to see that the rain had subsided and the road, though muddy, was clear of standing water. The light was fading as we left the little valley and climbed again over another ridge.

Nearly two hours later, the road dropped down again and the next descent was steep. I was thankful that the road was drier. We emerged into an area where I could see many large and pitted black rocks. It was as if some giant had scooped up a handful of them and thrown them over the landscape.

Presently, we came to a deep ravine. I could hear the roar of water coming from it. The team got too close for my comfort, but enough that I could see a raging creek tumbling over a series of cascades thundering down a hundred feet or more to the bottom of the ravine. We reached another junction in the road. We came upon a plateau of sorts above the ravine. The stream that, farther down, was a torrent crashing over a series of rocky waterfalls was now wide and deep, appearing to nearly breach its banks. The maddening sound of water crashing over the rocks spelled what was beyond the abrupt drop-off: a huge waterfall. Lorenzo rode forward to consult with Pajaro. I slowed up the wagon, fearing the horses would mow the two brothers down.

Then I felt something trickle down my shoulder.

A string. With a silk pouch attached.

I grabbed it before it could slip into the muddy puddle at the base of the buckboard. Then I turned and, through the open canvas flap, I saw Chin.

She was running. It was as if she had never been injured at all. Her hair wildly flying, her arms outstretched. I have heard this about folks. Just before they go, they suddenly get a burst of something.

I jumped off the wagon just in time to see her enter the water. It swept her immediately off her feet and carried her quickly away. I called to her, implored her not to do it. Pajaro, hearing my voice, raced back to the stream. But his horse was slipping on the saturated bank and hesitated.

Chin floated for a few seconds, her head visible above the cresting rivulets of water bouncing off the rocks, and, in my last glimpse of her, she went over the edge of the waterfall.

I would think about this in more detail later. But at the time, it occurred to me how her choices had never been plentiful in her short life, and in the end her last choice had brought her release. I slipped the string over my neck and tucked the pouch down the collar of my dress.

Lorenzo's horse was run hard that day. Pajaro said we must stop for the night. Widow Creek was not much farther, but it would be too difficult in the dark. I heard Lorenzo speak aloud his worry for Sandro. Had that crew of attackers torched the Old Mandarin and then made tracks to Widow Creek? It seemed like a lot of riding to me, but then I was plodding along with the wagon probably slowing down Pajaro and Lorenzo in the process. I had a feeling the wagon would be abandoned in the morning in favor of speed.

We set up camp in silence, each of us consumed by our own thoughts. The image of Chin floating over the precipice to her death haunted me, as did her revelation that her mother would not want her back. I thought of my own mother. I vowed to send a letter at the next opportunity. Lorenzo lit the fire and then promptly found a place to curl up and collapse.

Pajaro made coffee and we shared the food that the Old Mandarin had packed.

When we finished, we sat around the fire. Pajaro lit a smoke.

"Eh, Mariah. The girl? She gave you a hint of her plan? To do what she did? It appears that now we have no reason to continue to Widow

Creek. Except to meet with my brother." None of us had spoken of it until now. It still shocked me. Thinking of the Old Mandarin and now Chin, both their lives ending in such a grisly fashion, made me cold and angry. Mendonca now asked me if I knew of her plan. His mind was working in a different direction than mine. I recalled Sandro's vehemence about *the deal* with the Old Mandarin. "I guess that ruined your deal . . . her running into the water and being dashed to death on the rocks below. How much money did you lose, Pajaro?" I asked.

He hawked a piece of stray tobacco into the fire.

"I have done many things, señorita. Things that in *your* world might seem foreign. Unfair. Unjust. To *you*. I have few regrets because I do what I must for reasons that I feel you would not understand. One of my regrets is Sandro. He sees personal reward or vengeance as the only reasons for anything. This is not the intention of my work. Yet, he cannot change. For him, there are only deals and no actions without them. Think what you will about me, but there was never any deal with Zhao."

He slumped back, leaning against his saddle, and smiled. "You have passed judgment on me already. You wouldn't be the first to get it wrong."

I considered this. In the past, I wouldn't have thought it fitting to ask about someone's motives. People ought to be left to their own business. That's what Pa always said. I had let Earl draw me unwittingly into his business without question. If I had learned anything from Earl, it was to never hesitate to ask.

"Tell me your story, then, if you think it will convince me otherwise."

"I doubt it will."

"Tell me anyway."

"I came north. To the gold. My brothers and me. And my wife and child." He looked up to gauge my reaction. I could not hide my surprise.

"The villain had a family. You are surprised. Cecilia, my wife, was very young. We met in the mission. Her father was a field worker. I was educated. She was not. Still, we were eager to find our fortune. And Lucia was still an infant. A good claim was staked. It was hard work in the foothills. We had a camp and I left my family there while we worked the claim up higher in the mountains. We were successful. We wanted a ranch in the valley. It was so simple. Make a stake and move down to ranch. Eh, we were so hopeful then.

"So we worked the claim. And then they came. White men. They were not so lucky, and I think they expected to find the gold easily. That may have been true early on. But later, one had to go deep into the mountains to find it. My brothers and I worked very hard. And seeing what we had, the white men decided that they deserved it more. Because they were white. To them, being an outsider meant you were less than them. Yet, in truth, *they* were the outsiders. Not us. We were *Californios* and we had a right to our claim. They did not see it that way.

"Lorenzo and I were up at the claim on this day. Cecilia, Lucia, and Sandro stayed behind. The men came. First, they burned our cabin. Sandro was beaten senseless. When he came to, he tried to run into the cabin to save Cecilia and Lucia. He was only able to bring Lucia out . . . she died in his arms, burned alive. You have seen his hands, no doubt.

"I had enough money to take the dispute to court. We did not win. The rule was for the diggings to go to the new claimants. This new law made it difficult if not impossible for Californios to own claims. We lost everything. And I, of course, lost more than the claim."

"What did you do after that?" I asked.

Pajaro looked away. "Revenge. We found the seven men and finished them. A warning to others is what I tell myself. It was not pleasant and I take no pride in what we did. One of my other regrets. After that, we could no longer work our claim. Nor could we live free and at peace."

He continued. "I decided to do what I could for those like me who were in danger of losing all that they had worked for. Now with this new state of California formed, land that was by right owned by Californios through an agreement with the Mexican government was being disputed. There was a need to act in the name of justice.

"With the discovery of gold, many people came to California. For those living in the East, in the United States, it was felt that coming here and claiming land was the same as the homesteaders in other territories. Those homesteaders claimed vacant land in the territories in order to colonize them. Here, in California, this land had been worked for many years. By Californios, owned free and clear by good, hardworking people. Yet those who came from the East took it as their own. And now, Burnett, the new governor in California, does not wish to hear the arguments we have put before him. The titles should never have been in dispute for the Californios. And yet Burnett persists."

He murdered the men who had murdered his family. An eye for an eye, you could say. Still, to believe it, one would have to have little or no trust in justice.

"What about justice? Do you do anything in the name of justice?"

Pajaro's expression was unreadable for a moment, then it went cold. If he thought to win my favor or respect with his tale, he was wrong.

"Steal money and provide funds for those seeking a voice in the courts, Mariah." He laughed at this and gave me a challenging look. Then he added, "Well, we take a small cut for living expenses."

"So you are a robber, too. Who do you rob?"

"The right people."

It struck me that he was calculating and that, even if the Old Mandarin had trusted him, there were parts of him that were ruthless and hard to decipher. Perhaps the Old Mandarin had trusted him too much. Chin would have brought a handsome reward. Had there been a deal in the works for Chin, unbeknownst to the Old Mandarin?

"Chin's mother? Is she one of 'the right people'?"

Pajaro leveled his gaze at me. "In this case, I only considered the girl and her safety." He paused for a moment. Then he said, "You, evidently, did not feel that I had that capacity."

Pajaro arranged his saddle and blanket near the fire and stretched out.

"We will leave at first light. The wagon will stay. You will ride with me. Sleep now, for tomorrow will not be pleasant." He turned over, with his back to me and the fire.

Run, I told myself. *Run now while you have the chance.*

But where would I go? Back to Remington River? How long would that take on foot? Lost in these mountains and perishing beneath the majestic trees? Or should I risk my life with this band of thieves and murderers? Poor choices. I watched as Mendonca's breathing settled into a regular pattern. I could steal his horse and disappear. But they would find me eventually. I remembered that Mendonca had talked about the Monroes at Widow Creek Station. Maybe they could help me. I found that this constant dependence on others to solve my problems was exhausting. And I vowed to put an end to it as soon as I could.

I went to the wagon and took advantage of the shelter. I must have slept soundly, for the first thing that woke me was Pajaro shouting.

He was speaking Spanish, so I was unable to understand except that he sounded frantic. I pulled on my boots and emerged from the wagon in the soupy dawn light with a gentle but persistent rain falling.

As soon as he saw me, Pajaro stopped shouting. Lorenzo was a short distance away in the woods. He stopped and looked first at Pajaro and then at me. Initially, Pajaro appeared angry and then relief washed over him.

"What has happened? Why were you shouting?" I asked, walking up to the fire.

He shook his head and said, mostly to himself, "I had not thought of the wagon."

"What do you mean?" I touched the coffee pot and was grateful that it was warm. Pouring a cup, I looked at him inquiringly.

Pajaro put his hands on his hips and kicked one of the rocks around the fire. "Eh, señorita. You were not here when I awoke. I thought you had gone."

Lorenzo chuckled and began to saddle up his horse. He said something in Spanish to Pajaro, who waved his arm dismissively in response.

I would not let my guard down and presume that he cared for my safety. His story from the previous night had been touching. Tragic. But it had done little to change my vague apprehension that Pajaro Mendonca had a reason for me to get to Widow Creek. I doubted it was for my well-being.

I took a drink of coffee and wiped my mouth with my cloak. "I slept in the wagon. Only a fool would stay out in the rain and cold if there was a better alternative."

Pajaro and his brother drove the wagon into a thicket of trees and let the team loose. Then they mounted and looked expectantly at me. Pajaro offered his hand and I grasped it as he hauled me up. Once behind him, I sensed his horse complaining about the extra load.

He said something in Spanish to the horse and patted its neck.

The morning was cold and still as we moved swiftly along a rough trail that snaked in and out of trees, over ridges, and across fast-running streams. It was a beautiful country of green meadows. Remington River was in a broad valley and part of a high desert terrain. The mountains I saw now were the same ones I had viewed from town but from a greater distance. Once we were clear of the high desert, the mountains took hold of the landscape. While I had crossed mountain ranges on my journey west, they had been rugged and dangerous. Though spectacular to observe, they seemed unfathomable and ungraspable. Here, though, the peaks in the distance conveyed a sense of accessibility; they appeared inviting.

The one peak that dominated them all rose sharply with lower jagged peaks on its shoulders. It was crowned with a dazzling white shroud of snow. I wanted to ask Pajaro the name of the peak but kept silent. Why had he worried about my disappearance into the wagon? Was I going to become part of the *deal* in some way? Or had he actually worried about *me*? As we rode, Lorenzo and Pajaro exchanged snippets of conversation in Spanish. From what I could pick up from their tones, there was some disagreement between them about something. It now occurred to me that once we reached Widow Creek Station, and even right now, I might serve no purpose to them since Chin was no longer a concern. Perhaps I could find a way to go back to Remington River. The thought of it, however, left me empty. Foolishly, I had come to rely on the Old Mandarin and his friendship, and Remington River did not hold the same promise without him there. I chided myself for not having more confidence in myself. There were certainly other things I could do in that town. But what? I felt suddenly alone and, for the first time in a very long while, afraid.

I hugged my bag closer to me and felt the firm outline of *The Journals* through the material. Was it silly to think, or even put faith in, what Meriwether Lewis would do in my position? The trail opened up briefly and I saw again the snow-capped peak framed by a cloudless blue sky. Looking at it, even for that short moment, made me forget everything else.

At every turn, the peak took on a different shape, hue and presence. One minute it was dead rock and the next awash with a new splash of sunlight, illuminating a living facet. I moved my head back and forth trying to catch glimpses of it as we rode.

We stopped for a few minutes in a thicket of aspens, the sound of rushing water taking over the constant percussion of the horses on the trail. The light glittered in the green leaves as the breeze moved through them. I slid off the horse and walked stiffly to a nearby stream to drink and wash. I dried my face on the hem of my dress and was startled to see that Pajaro had come up behind me. He moved like a shadow.

"Once we get to Widow Creek Station, and provided that Sandro is unharmed, my brothers and I have some business to attend to at the station over the next several days." He started to say something else but stopped and rolled a smoke. "It does not concern you and I will not bother you with the details. I only want you to know that you will be safe there, if you wish to stay. Or I can make arrangements for you to go wherever you want, Mariah."

I touched my neck and felt the string, remembering the pouch, the map, and Chin's gold. I almost laughed out loud. Chin had said the gold was near a stagecoach stop. It must be Widow Creek Station. If I could stay on there for a bit, I might get lucky and find it. It was preposterous and wild to even imagine following her map with a shovel and pick and digging around for something that might not even be there. Then I paused and considered that wilder things had already happened to me.

"I think I should like to see what this Widow Creek Station is like before making more plans. And as for your business," I said, giving him a cool look, "it is not my affair, nor will I interfere."

❧ 13 ❧

WIDOW CREEK STATION LAY TWENTY-FIVE MILES west of Remington River. It was the way station for coaches on the Remington River-Red Bluff Road. We cut through the forest, veering off the trail we had been following, and took the stage road for a few miles, still winding through the trees. If we had kept to the road, at this point, it would burst out onto a large, wide meadow, with a stream running down the middle, and the station was easily seen sitting on the eastern edge of the meadow. Pajaro and Lorenzo did not want to be seen until they were able to determine what had happened, if anything, at the station. Instead, we cut into the trees again and came behind the station cloaked by the forest. Had the Chinese and his gang of attackers returned to the station seeking Chin? Or, after murdering the Old Mandarin, had they kept heading east from Remington River?

We left the horses tethered about a quarter mile behind the station and walked through the trees to get a closer look. I trailed behind Pajaro and Lorenzo, clutching my bag, fearful of what we might find. Pajaro stopped, held up his hand, and looked sharply at me.

"Dios, señorita!" he whispered. "Tread lightly. Try to *avoid* the dry branches. Not step on every single one."

I nodded, carefully skirting any stick or pinecone.

We finally got to the edge of the trees and found we were directly behind the cabin, paddock, and barn which comprised the station. A trickle of smoke came from the river-stone chimney. There were no horses in the paddock and, save for a few chickens, the surrounding yard was empty and quiet.

Pajaro gave a series of whistles and waited.

Sandro appeared at the back of the cabin. He looked sharply at his brothers then quickly retreated back inside.

Pajaro and Lorenzo looked at each other, puzzled.

"Eh. He did not give the signal, Pajaro."

"Something is wrong, brother."

They both drew their pistols and started cautiously for the cabin. I was waved back and thankfully remained well inside the trees.

Several minutes passed before Lorenzo walked quickly back toward me. He was frowning.

"You are to come with me. There is no danger. Pajaro says to bring you in."

The rear of the cabin opened into a small scullery and storage room. Through another doorway, we came into the main room of the cabin. A large table was in the center with benches around it. There was a stove, fireplace, and crude sitting area around the fire. Stagecoach passengers were meant to stop and refresh here while the horses were changed out in anticipation of the next part of the journey to Remington River or to Red Bluff. It did not appear a very inviting place to stop at this moment. There was a chill to the room. The fire languished, unattended. My eyes adjusted to the dimness. A man and woman stood in the corner. Pajaro had told me about them. The Monroes, the station agent and his wife. In front of them, on the floor, a body lay face down.

Pajaro and Sandro were in a heated exchange that I could not understand since they spoke in Spanish.

Lorenzo knelt by the body and rolled it over, prompting the man and the woman to turn away. They were startled to see me in the doorway.

The woman asked me, warily, "Who are you?"

"I am Mariah Penngrove. What has happened here?"

She was a small woman with a grayness about her that told me her life had not been easy. I could also tell that while a body in her cabin was unusual, it was more of an inconvenience to her than anything.

"That younger Mendonca. Never trusted him. He's too nervous and fidgety. That one," pointing to the body on the floor, "he come inside. Those others were out there. But only this one come in. There was a fight. Something about that wagon that come around sometime back with all those Chinese women." She shook her head.

"I was trying to get vittles ready for the stage when all the fuss started up. Lord knows what will happen now. Stage is due in a few hours. Them others took the fresh-change horses. I hope the horses already running up from Red Bluff can make it to Remington."

She rubbed her hand over her hair and smoothed her apron. "I'm Philomena Monroe. That there is Wilson, my husband."

Wilson Monroe joined his wife. He looked displeased to see me. "I don't want no more trouble here. I don't know who you are, but you'd best clear out of here. You come with them? You go with them, hear?"

I could hardly think of how to reply. But I managed to say, "Mr. Monroe, I have no intention of causing trouble."

Pajaro now inspected the body, crouching down next to it. "Dios." He slammed his hand on the floor.

"Chinaman got what he deserved, Pajaro," said Sandro with a grin.

"Take him outside, little brother. We'll talk of this later," Pajaro snapped.

Sandro sneered and started to say something but stopped.

They picked up the body and carried it outside, but not before I caught a glimpse of his face. It was the Chinese man whom I had seen at the crossroads. It was Ah Wong, the man Chin had loved and who had betrayed her.

Pajaro came over to the three of us, hands on hips. "Monroe, she is not part of this. I suggest you continue your business and prepare for the stage. Our business will hopefully not be interrupted, yes?"

Monroe stood defiantly and spat, "As you say. But I'm through with it all. You hear? Through."

He stalked out the back door.

Pajaro addressed Mrs. Monroe. "Señora, some coffee for Mrs. Penngrove?"

She looked at him, aghast. "The nerve! After all this?" She looked at me resentfully. "Guess I will. I'm making it for the stage anyways. Make yourself useful, girl, and fetch some wood from out back."

I hurried to respond to her request, thankful for a reason to go outside and breathe some fresh air. I found the woodpile and began loading up my arms. It had suddenly darkened outside and I looked up to see storm clouds gathering. Enormous, dark walls that looked like boulders now filled the sky. Pajaro joined me at the woodpile.

"Eh, this was a bad thing. Wait," he said, placing a hand on my arm. "You should hear this." I put the wood down.

"The attackers came back. Sandro was told not to engage with them. In fact, he was to remain hidden unless it was absolutely necessary. But no. He did not do this. They needed fresh horses. It would have been simple enough to let them take them. But the Chinese came into the cabin. Sandro confronted him. The Chinese was looking for something else. Something one of the women left behind."

"Chin."

"Did she say something to you?" asked Mendonca.

My hand went instinctively to the string around my neck. "No. She told me nothing," I lied, still not sure how much to trust this man.

"Unfortunately, Sandro got in the way. The other three are gone and I think we will not have to worry about them. From what Sandro could understand, they were done with the Chinese and might have finished him themselves had Sandro not done it for them."

I picked up the wood and carried it back to the kitchen. The sorrowful tale of Chin haunted me.

I scarcely had time to think about the pouch that hung about my neck, whether to tell Pajaro about it, or my own future. Mrs. Monroe certainly put me to work helping to prepare for the stage. There were plates to clean, water to fetch for washing up buckets on the porch, sweeping, and the finishing up of the food preparation.

Whatever business the Mendoncas had with Monroe and Widow Creek Station, it all revolved around this particular stagecoach.

Then I saw the brothers saddling up in the front yard. There would be little time to confide in Pajaro about what I knew about Chin's gold. And this was confirmed to me when Pajaro rushed in and took me aside.

"We are off now. You will be safe here. Monroe and his wife have instructions to accommodate you as long as you like."

He continued, "Look. You may see some things today. Trust me, it is for a good intention. I must ask you not to interfere. There is no danger and I have no time to explain. Eh, I think I can trust you. Dios, I *know* it."

He turned to go then stopped. "I don't know when I will be back. I would help you if I could now. But it is not possible. If I return, perhaps I can assist you."

"*If* you return?" I could hardly believe the words came out of my mouth. What was I thinking? This man was a thief, and it seemed like trouble followed him everywhere. Why on earth would I ever want to see him again?

He smiled. "You want me to come back, Mariah?"

I opened my mouth and shut it quickly, afraid more foolishness would come out. "Dios, you are a mystery," he said, and he touched my chin. "I would like to hear more from your book about the explorers. Yes?" And then he was gone.

The rain that had been threatening all morning finally let loose. The Monroes started hollering when they heard the stage coming through the mud. It pulled in front of the cabin, and the passengers had to walk through ankle-deep muck to get inside. There were three men and an older woman. The three men were a party traveling together. One of them, a tall and distinguished, silver-headed gentleman, grimaced as the mud poured into his fine leather shoes. I watched Mr. Monroe climb up on the top of the coach, remove the canvas covering, and hand down the luggage to the driver. Each piece was brought in and placed near the fire to keep it dry.

Once inside, Monroe asked each passenger to identify his or her luggage, as a matter of routine, I supposed, in case something went missing or was left behind. When the silver-haired gentleman identified his black leather bag, Monroe grunted just as he had done for all the other bags.

Since the horses couldn't be switched out, they rested the team longer. Mrs. Monroe and I kept a steady stream of hot coffee, biscuits, bacon, and eggs coming. In the company of the silver-haired gentleman, his other two companions huddled with him and spoke in quiet tones as they ate. They seemed important and refined. I wondered what business they had beyond Widow Creek Station.

At last, the stage prepared to go. The passengers were loaded in. Then Mr. Monroe got up on the top of the stage. The driver retrieved the luggage from the station and handed Monroe each bag. I stood on the porch and watched, mostly to see how this coach was going to get out of the mud.

Then I noticed something curious.

When the driver handed Monroe the silver-haired gent's bag, Monroe tied a white string through the handle. The driver wouldn't have seen it since he was down below. After all the bags were loaded, Monroe placed the piece of canvas over them and fastened it down against the downpour.

I wondered about that string.

It was the following week when we heard the story. Monroe was aghast and nervous.

I was intrigued.

The Monroes told me I could stay on. I guess I wasn't as much trouble as they had expected. Helping out around the station was a good diversion from thinking about Pajaro, Chin, the gold, and what my future might hold. Mrs. Monroe kept me busy with all the household work she was weary of doing. Mr. Monroe had me work around the horses, keeping the harnesses clean and supple, mucking out the stalls, and feeding.

Only once had I looked at the piece of paper in the little silk pouch, and it was one night when I was sitting on the little bunk they had set up for me in the back room. It was a rough map but neatly drawn, and had I been able to study it outside, I might be better able to determine landmarks. Such as it was, I could only guess where the gold might be.

The day we heard the story, the westbound stage from Remington River came in. Mr. Monroe held the horses while the passengers disembarked. The rain had waxed and waned over the past several days, but it was consistent. The muddy front yard greeted the boots of those stepping out. The driver jumped down and stretched his legs. I heard Mr. Monroe call him Clovis King. He had been the driver on the stage the previous week.

King took Monroe aside, away from the passengers.

"I have some news, Monroe. Jesus H. Christ! It's a good one, too," King whispered. "Wait until they all are tucked into their meals and I'll tell you."

It was then that I recognized one of the passengers. He was the same silver-haired gentleman whose bag Mr. Monroe attached with string. The man had a more serious air about him today. I remembered the man and his companions had made a strange picture in the muck, rain, and roughness of the station. The other two, however, were not among the passengers on this particular trip.

With the haggard passengers seated at the table, we started to serve out a thick stew into the chipped crockery along with a loaf of bread and strong coffee. King motioned to Mr. Monroe to follow him outside. I watched curiously and positioned myself near the open door to listen to their conversation.

"Just starting to piece this together myself, Monroe," said King. "You recall I came through here on the outbound. With that one gent who is in there now. The gray-haired one?"

"Sure. I remember." Mr. Monroe sounded nervous.

"We had them two others, too. They was with that gent. Don't know where they got up to," said King. "Well, we get about halfway up the hill out of Spencer Meadows and all of a sudden there they were. Three of them in the road. It was the Mendoncas, I swear, by God. The darkest, meanest bunch I ever did see." King rolled a smoke and lit it.

Mr. Monroe stifled a groan but managed to choke out, "What happened?"

"So they stopped us and I thought we were done. Not carrying anything, mind you. No mail or payroll. Not that day. You know, it was just them gents, an old lady, and their luggage. They made us all get down and stand in the road. They didn't say nothing. One of them jumped up on the roof and was looking through the luggage. I guess he didn't find anything. He got back down, got up on his horse, and said something to the other two. Then, the tall one—the leader, I guess—he says 'Good day, gentleman and madam. We have delayed you far too long.' And then they done rode off. Not a shot fired. Didn't even go through our pockets. I swear it was the strangest thing.

"We was all shaken up, let me tell you. But we made it into Remington River. Couldn't wait to tell the sheriff. But since nothing was taken and nobody hurt, he just shook his head and said, 'You was lucky, King. Plain and simple.'"

King continued. "Funny thing is this: the gray-haired gent had a wad of cash in his coat pocket. He told me later. They didn't go for that, though."

It was at the point that the gent in question came out onto the porch and joined Mr. Monroe and King. The other folks were eating and Mrs. Monroe gave me a cup of coffee, a sign that my work was done for now. I casually walked out on the porch and sat on the step.

"Collier's the name," he said, shaking Mr. Monroe's hand. "King here been telling you about our encounter?"

"Yes, sir," answered Mr. Monroe. "Might say you got real lucky."

Collier shook his head. "It was certainly good fortune that nobody was *hurt*. But I will say that my luck stopped there."

"Was there trouble in town, Mr. Collier? I rode out next day. Never heard if there was," said King.

Collier sat on the bench. "My business that day was with the district court. The governor is trying to settle lands claimed by the former Mexican government. Most will have their titles retained by the owner. But some of these lands, by necessity, will be forfeited to the new California government. After all, a treaty was signed after the war by both sides agreeing to its terms. There was no debate over this. It was arbitrated fairly.

"I was carrying an important document regarding the title to a large holding here in the north with mining interests, water, lumber, and grazing lands. It was my job to have the title entered in Remington River with the district court judge. The newly formed California government was to be named as deed holder. The land is quite valuable and was formerly ceded by the Mexican government but left fallow for reasons unknown."

He furrowed his brow and pressed his hands together. "I appeared before the judge and handed him the documents for his approval." Collier cleared his throat before continuing. "The judge read them and then he looked at me curiously. Almost incredulously. And he laughed. Oh, my word, he was laughing *at* me. You can imagine my confusion. I had been sent by the governor of California, mind you. No small honor. This judge was ridiculing me. At first, I was just astounded. And later came the humiliation." I watched Mr. Monroe go slack-jawed at this point.

King said, "I don't understand. What happened, sir?"

"The documents that I carried, written and signed personally by me to claim the title as agent of the governor, had been changed. They were different."

"Different? In what way?" asked King. He seemed to have some grasp of the gravity of the story.

Collier leaned back and closed his eyes. "The judge read the documents carefully. Slowly. Deliberately. Mind you," and his eyes popped open, "this judge is not a great supporter of the governor. So I was mildly surprised at how seriously he was taking his job in verifying the title. I thought I would have delays and what not. He has publicly chastised the governor, as a matter of fact. I wouldn't put it past to him to declare a holiday in the middle of my business with him.

"Well, then the judge signed the documents with great flourish. The man, in my opinion, is a buffoon. No matter. But before handing them back to me, he started laughing, as I said. It took him a moment to compose himself, the old fool. And then he read the pertinent codicil with the new titleholder. In front of the whole court.

"There are those who decry the ceding of Mexican landholdings to California. I suspect that such individuals were given information about this title and decided to take matters into their own hands. Why, it is inconceivable how such a deed could happen. For it was changed in a most grave manner. Men, I tell you, the document I put into my case in Sacramento *was not the same document I removed and set before that judge.*"

Mr. Monroe finally found his voice. "I don't follow you. Words were changed on the document? What kind of words, Mr. Collier?"

"The title should rightly read *The Honorable State of California.*"

King leaned forward. "But it don't read that? What's it say?"

Collier leaned back and frowned. "The title now reads the name of the person who owns the holding as one Pajaro Mendonca of Marysville."

"Pajaro Mendonca? He's . . . You mean the one who is the leader of the trio?" exclaimed King.

Monroe stood uncomfortably. He noticed that I was sitting on the step, listening, but I couldn't read his expression.

Collier continued. "One and the same. Of course, now I realize the switch was made when they stopped us on the road to Remington River. And we all thought robbery was their intent," said Collier. "That boy, the younger Mendonca. He was up there with the luggage. It was a simple matter if you knew what you were looking for. *And they did.* That is the disturbing part. Somehow, they *knew* what they were looking for."

Collier went on. "You will notice that my traveling companions from the journey to Remington River are no longer with me. Sadly, I have reason to suspect them in this matter, for they disappeared soon after the reading of the title. Vanished. Trusted agents of the governor, too. There were very few people who knew about this transaction. Very few. If it was those two, why . . . I don't know what to think," he said with a deep sigh.

"Probably paid off by the trio. I hope they rot," he added acidly.

Monroe asked, "What will happen now?"

Collier stood up. "Now? Well, nothing. The whole thing is absurd. Of course, Mendonca cannot officially own this property. It is now known as a forgery. But until it can be sorted out by the courts, nothing can happen. Because, officially, until the title can be searched again, nobody owns it. It raises questions again about the sovereignty of the state. Our ability to execute a simple matter of claiming a ceded land-holding. If we can't even do that, our young state is in danger. What Mendonca accomplished was to tie up this property indefinitely. And," Collier said, softly, "made a mockery of the whole state. Unfortunately, the timing of all this couldn't have been worse. There was a journalist from an eastern paper just happened to be in town. The story is likely being carried across the country. The governor will be ridiculed. I can only guess what he will say when I meet with him next."

Mrs. Monroe and I finished cleaning up after the passengers. Mud had been tracked through the entire front room and I was charged with mopping. After the floor was done, we tried to hang some clothes on a line under the eaves out back. Rain blew in gusts, and we resigned ourselves to having clean but damp clothes until the sun returned.

Once all the chores were completed, Mrs. Monroe allowed that I might need a little time to myself. In truth, she wanted to sit in her chair and doze.

I considered taking the little scrap of paper from the pouch and examining it on the porch. There were little signs and notations that I might be able to make sense of if I could look around with map in hand. But Mr. Monroe was cleaning harnesses on the porch. The map would have to wait.

Instead, I brought *The Journals* outside and sat on the bench. I had not opened it since reading the passage about the bighorn sheep to Pajaro. As always, I let the book fall open to a page.

Mr. Monroe looked at me and snorted. "A book? I can't remember the last time I seen a book. Don't read myself. Never learned."

I showed him the book and explained that my mother had given it to me before I left on the wagon train.

"I'll read some of it to you. This is the part of the book where Captain Lewis reaches the Great Divide. That's the place where eastern America meets the West. And he is standing there, looking westward."

[I]mmediately in the level plain between the forks and about a half-mile distance from them stands a high rocky mountain, the base of which is surrounded by a level plain; it has a singular appearance. The mountains do not appear very high in any direction though the tops of some them are partially covered with

snow. This convinces me that we have ascended to a great height since we have entered the Rock Mountains, yet the ascent has been so gradual along the valleys that it was scarcely perceptible by land.

"Who writes like that?" Monroe chuckled.

"A man named Meriwether Lewis. He and Captain William Clark led an expedition west from the Mississippi River. All the way to the ocean."

"They friends of yours?"

I laughed. "Oh, no. They are long gone. This was many years ago. But his words remind me of that peak over there," I said, gesturing to it though it was covered in clouds that day. "If I could get on top of it, what would I see on the other side?"

Mr. Monroe stopped his work. "I'm sure some darn fool has tried to get up there. To that peak. I suppose there would be something to see on the other side. Of course there would. More mountains, I guess. I hear there are some lakes and another big mountain way up north that is covered in snow all year. I'd like to see that. That one there, the one you pointed to, is called Hasten Peak, though."

"Hasten Peak? It has many faces. It changes from moment to moment, too," I commented. "How long have you been here? You and Mrs. Monroe?"

"Going on three years."

"Do you plan to stay?"

He looked sharply at me. "Mendonca say something to you?"

"Why, no! I'm just asking. It's a pretty place even though it's a lot of work. I like it here. I could see why you would want to stay."

He looked through the doorway. The sounds of his wife's snoring apparently satisfied him that he could talk without interference.

"I got no reason to think I can't trust you. I know you saw what I did with that fellow's luggage. And you didn't say nothing to Collier. You know it was part of Mendonca's business. There have been other things, too."

The vigorous strokes that he was applying to the harness made me think he was having difficulty talking about this.

"Mr. Monroe, you don't have to tell me everything. I think you do a fine job here, and I am grateful that you and your wife have let me stay on. I am making plans of my own. I'll not be a burden to you much longer."

Mr. Monroe stopped his work for a moment. "Mendonca has, well, given me enough so's we can move on. I'd had my eye on a little ranch in the valley."

"You mean you want to leave the station?"

"The wife is getting worn out here. I won't say working a ranch will be much easier. But at least it will be ours. I plan to clear out soon. I got a bad feeling about that last business of his." He stood up. "Look. You stay on, if you want. I suppose Mendonca would want that seeing as you're his—"

I held my hand up, feeling a blush creep over my face. "Mr. Monroe. That is not the situation," I said briskly. "I don't know about staying on here. I suppose I could manage . . . I don't know."

Mr. Monroe sat down on the bench. "There's something else you should know. There was a man come around looking for Mendonca and his brothers. Saw him first a couple of months back. Name of Terrence Burke. Works for the stage line. I think the stage line is fed up with Mendonca's business. You don't need to know more. Probably best you don't. This Burke says he'll be back, if he doesn't catch them before. He asked what I knew about them. And miss, I lied. I said I didn't know nothing about him. I can't lie no more. That's why the wife and me best get going. Burke'll be back, especially after this last thing, and I don't want to see him. The station is all stocked up for a while. The schedule is tacked up on the wall. I'll tell you this. Most of the work is the cooking for the passengers. They expect a hot meal for their fare."

He added, "I'd feel easier about leaving if I knew you'd stay on. At least until the stage line comes up with a new agent. They already know I'm moving on. Shouldn't be too long until somebody gets up here."

Although it seemed like Mr. and Mrs. Monroe had been thinking on this for some time, I couldn't help but consider that my coming along had made their departure easier. And sooner. I also wondered if Pajaro knew and that his bringing me here to take on the station to appease the Monroes had been his plan all along.

Three days later, Mr. and Mrs. Monroe, true to their word, packed up quickly, loading what small amount of possessions they owned into their wagon. Apparently, nearly all the furnishings in the cabin belonged to the stage line.

Mrs. Monroe hugged me tightly and said, "I don't feel entirely right about this. But you have to understand, we have to think of ourselves. You'll be fine out here. You're a strong one, I'll wager that."

Mr. Monroe chopped a good supply of wood for me. He even filled the water barrel for me, saving me from hauling up water from the stream for a few days. He promised to stop in at the stage office in Red Bluff and urge them to send someone up as soon as they could. With a wave, they departed in the seemingly permanent rainy weather that had taken hold of this country.

I sat on the porch, alone for the first time in weeks. The green meadow that had captivated me was now so saturated with rain that it was holding onto the water, forming a shimmering, shallow lake.

It seemed as good a time as any to take out Chin's map and see what I could make of it. I took the string from around my neck and opened the pouch. Unfolding the piece of paper, I was careful to avoid the drips of rain coming from the leaking porch eaves. I smoothed it out on my lap. It was drawn carefully enough, but I could not figure out the bearings she marked out on it. A pattern of trees over here? There was a road indicated. I figured they had followed the stage road, so I would go along with that assumption. Wherever she had buried the gold, it was not far off the road. There were some marks, a series of Xs in a row along the road. And then there was a break in the pattern indicated by straight lines. This was a mystery to me. A distance from these marks, she drew an object that looked like a log or a boulder. This object was circled as if to indicate the spot where she might have left the gold.

I finally put the map away. I needed to be patient with it.

Hasten Peak became my anchor. Each day, it seemed to acquire a new character—big brother one day, lonely soul the next. Regal mother on another day and daunting lord of the skies at times.

I opened *The Journals* a few days later and, deviating from my usual habit of letting it fall open, I flipped through the pages searching for the passage I wanted.

The bluffs of the river rise to the height of from two to three hundred feet, and in most places nearly perpendicular. . . . The water, in the course of time, in descending from those hills and plains on either side of the river, has trickled down the soft sand clifts and woarn it into a thousand grotesque figures which, with the help of a little imagination and an oblique view, at a distance are made to represent elegant ranges of lofty freestone buildings, having their parapets well stocked with statuary.

Collumns of various sculpture, both grooved and plain, are also seen supporting long galleries in front of those buildings. . . . As we passed on it seemed as if those seens of visionary inchantment would have an end; for here it is too that nature presents to the view of the traveler vast ranges of walls of tolerable workmanship . . . .

I tried to keep busy in order not to dwell on being alone. It wasn't so much that I was lonely. It was the vague uneasiness about what would happen next that bothered me. Monroe had said someone would come from the stage line eventually. They would have to: there were no fresh-change horses. The next stage wasn't due for a week. In the meantime, I took an inventory of the supplies, cleaned out the stalls and paddocks, and managed to patch a hole in the roof with a piece of plank.

The water covered the meadow now. I wondered how much longer the rain would last and whether the station would get flooded out. Or whether the water would freeze over. It was the end of November. I looked up at the black clouds, and as my gaze wandered down from the clouds, the trees on the far edge of my meadow caught my eye. There were three of them. I could see a pattern, or so I thought. A thrill went through me. There was something in that pattern. I started to study it more carefully and reached for the silk pouch.

Then I heard the sound of an approaching horse.

My gut knotted. I cursed myself for not bringing the shotgun Monroe had shown me propped up in the back room. I would not get caught out here again unarmed.

I made my way along the road and crossed to the house just as a lone rider came trotting along. He pulled up next to the fence and stayed mounted. He was a tall man dressed in an oilcloth coat that was long enough to cover most of his horse's rump. I could not make out his face for it was covered with a hood.

"Good day, miss," he said, pulling off the hood. "Name's Terrence Burke. May I come in out of the rain?"

Burke. Monroe had said he'd be back. "What's your business, sir?"

He smiled. His teeth were crooked and brown. He got off his horse apparently undeterred by my wariness. He held up his hands. "Nothing to fear, miss. Just want to chat and maybe get dry and warm."

Walking up to the porch, I could now see him more clearly. The smile faded as quickly as it had appeared. His face was yellow, pockmarked, and dirty; the skin had a greasy sheen to it.

"You going to invite me in?"

"I just cleaned the floor, sir. I'll ask you to sit here with your muddy boots. I'll bring you some coffee. It's dry enough here for you."

I brought out the coffee and sat at the far end of the bench from him. "What brings you up here, Mr. Burke? If you're looking for Mr. Monroe, he and his wife left a few days ago."

Burke sipped his coffee. "I know."

He seemed in no hurry to explain his visit.

"My name is Mariah Penngrove. I am staying here until the stage line sends a replacement."

"I know that, too. Ran into Monroe a few days ago on the road," he said.

He took out a smoke and attempted to roll it, but his fingers were still wet. He dropped the mess on the porch and tried to kick it off into the dirt with no success except to leave a large smear of mud and tobacco.

Burke sighed and looked at me. "Where is he?"

I met his eyes. They were watery blue but dull and mean. "Mr. Burke. I like plain talk. Where is *who*?"

"As you like," he said, forcing a thin smile. "Mendonca. The Mexican. He's a great friend of yours, I hear."

"I barely know the man, if that constitutes a great friendship. And I have not seen him for nearly two weeks."

"There are a lot of different kinds of friendships. At any rate, whatever he is to you, his days are numbered. He got himself into a bad mess in the valley a few days back. Hard to imagine anything worse than a killing like the one him and his brothers did. For no good reason except sport. Now he's got a federal marshal from Sacramento on his tail. And me." The color drained from my face. Burke could see it and he appeared satisfied. "Tell you what? A man does something like *that*? And if I was a *friend* of his, I'd be watching my pretty little back. Hear me?"

He stood up and stretched. "Yep. Not long for him. The federal marshal is a day's ride behind me with a posse. Mendonca and his brothers can't hide forever."

He walked up to me and bent over to speak. His breath was thick and fetid. "Funny thing, Mariah. I followed Mendonca up from the valley. He's on his way up here. He and his brothers gave me the slip. They know this area better than me, I'll give them that. But he's up here. Close by. You watch yourself."

Burke stepped off the porch into the mud. "Thanks for the coffee."

He paused before getting on his horse. "That meadow sure got full. I don't think I've seen so much rain in my whole life. Ought to get a boat." He laughed.

"Mr. Burke," I called to him. I was not sure I really wanted to know. "What happened in the valley? With Mendonca?"

He got up on his horse. "I was wondering if you'd ask." Burke pulled his hood over his head and leaned on his pommel. "That younger brother? He stabbed a boy and his father in the river. Let 'em float away. Pure evil, I'd say."

"How do you know it was the Mendoncas?"

"They didn't finish the father. He got himself up the bank and hollered for help. Before he died, he told who done it. No mistaking them three."

I steadied myself on the porch post and tried to stop shaking.

Burke tipped his hat. "You'll see me again."

He disappeared around the curve in the road and into the trees. I felt sick to my stomach. Was it true what Burke had said about Sandro? Was it possible that he'd killed the boy and his father?

My mind swirled over the few facts that I knew about the Mendoncas. The business with the governor's document had, at the time, seemed mischievous and no more. To make a mockery of what sounded like a double-cross over land ownership was not a criminal act. Pajaro spoke of robbing, but only to help others. How much did they take for themselves? And I wondered whether people had been hurt in the process of these robberies. Then I remembered the men they had killed in revenge for Pajaro's wife and child. I had to admit it: I knew very little about him, his brothers, or their lives and even less about their motives.

I was so consumed with my thoughts that I never heard the foot-fall behind me before arms encircled my waist from behind, a hand went gently over my mouth, and I was carried inside the cabin. The door was closed behind us and I struggled free, turning with fists raised to face my attacker.

It was Pajaro. He continued to hold me as he put a finger to my lips. We both turned to the window. Burke was down the road turning in to the trees, heading toward Remington River.

I jerked free of his hands. "What are you doing here? Bringing trouble to this place. Burke told me what happened. You should turn yourselves in. But no. You run away. What noble venture is *this* about, Pajaro?"

"Eh, Mariah. You and I, we circle around each other like two cats. Why is that?"

I peered out the window half expecting Burke to be standing on the porch again. "Perhaps it is because I don't know who to trust anymore. People say one thing but have more words and then actions that do not follow what they actually mean."

"You speak the truth. For some. But not for me. I have never lied to you. I *have* kept things from you that were best left unsaid. For your safety."

"Why did you come back? Are you afraid to face the consequences of Sandro's actions? I thought better of you. I was wrong," I whispered, my anger rising.

If I was surprised to see him, I was even more alarmed to see his face sag at my words. His brow furrowed and I could see true sadness and despair in his expression.

"It is true about Sandro. Dios. It is very difficult to talk about. My heart is heavy over this. You must understand. It was not planned this way. None of it."

He leaned against the cabin's wall and pressed his hands over his eyes. "I would give a lot to undo many things, Mariah. Truly."

"Sit down," I said with a sigh. "You look like you're about to fall over. I'll get you some coffee."

Pajaro dragged a chair from the table and sat well away from the window. He stared off into space.

I brought back the coffee and he sipped at it. I had studied him carefully before, at the shop of the Old Mandarin, while we had camped, and here, at Widow Creek. The haughtiness and dry humor. His grins and sly glances at me. Surely they were meant to gain my confidence. Or were they? Now, he was sorely burdened with woe, and though his face was still handsome, it was devoid of that bravado I had come to recognize. It was replaced with concern and worry.

He looked shaken to the core.

"Tell me what happened, Pajaro."

He put his head back and closed his eyes again. Then he began to speak.

"I cannot tell you everything about my business, Mariah. It is not that I don't trust you. But it would put you in danger. Even Lorenzo and Sandro, my own brothers, do not know all that I do. It has been my plan all along to keep them close to me yet distant from some of my other dealings. It is better that way. I only wanted to protect them and then help them start over. Lorenzo, I never worried about. He wants a ranch in the valley. Wife. Children. But Sandro. Sandro is different. I chose to ignore it. With Sandro, *he wanted this life.* Not for helping others but for the excitement. I thought I was guiding him to understand. When all along, he was never listening.

"We knew that Burke was after us. Although, truthfully, his only charge against us was delaying the stage. A small fine or bribe. I think, Mariah, that he would take a bribe. But one cannot be sure with these agents. At any rate, we stocked up in Red Bluff and made plans to start back to Remington River the next day.

"I intended to travel by night to avoid Burke. I knew an old ferry shack down on the river. Just off the Red Bluff-Remington River road. Abandoned now, for a bridge has been built down the river. We holed up there. We played some cards. Sandro does not play with us because he cheats. He was restless. He could not go into town, as he wished. To drink. Gamble. Women. I knew he wanted to. He could not stay still. Pacing the cabin. This was why he heard it first. The sound in the river. Someone swimming toward the pier. We could see the ripples in the water. He was just a boy. The boy called back to someone on the far shore and said, 'Yes, Pa, there are three of them just like you thought.'

"Sandro got up and walked to the edge of the dock and saw a man with a fishing pole standing on the bank staring at us.

"I have known this about Sandro for some time. He was not working it through in his head about the situation, considering alternatives, or consulting us. His mind had been made up in an instant. I wondered at what point Sandro had changed. Become hard and cold. But then, we all changed in our own ways.

"In the beginning, we killed only when it was necessary. To protect ourselves. Yet we put ourselves in harm's way continually. Daring anyone to fight back. Looking for an excuse to kill. I tried to put that from my mind. I consider myself a fair man. If there were an alternative to killing, I would weigh the option. But recently, I had not been doing so. I was wearing down. It was perhaps time to pause and think. But I did not. I only thought about the many who had no voice and lost everything. Like we did.

"I watched as the boy swam back toward his father waiting on the far bank. Sandro dove into the river with a knife in his teeth. We moved to the end of the dock and watched him take the boy down easily. It was over in a moment. Then the boy's body floated face down in the current, carrying it away. The boy's father went into the water shouting. He had dropped his rifle. Sandro swam to the man. Soon the father was floating downstream, too."

My coffee had gone cold. I had gone cold. The rain started up again in earnest. We looked at each other.

"I need to sleep, Mariah. Come with me."

My bed in the back room was hardly big enough for me. Pajaro kicked off his boots and tried to fit into the small frame. He reached for my arm.

"I need to rest, Mariah. Come here with me."

The sad, defeated look from before was still there. And there was a hint of something else. A yearning for a break from his worries. I knew that feeling all too well.

I sat on the bed and felt him pull me toward him. I allowed my head to fall to his shoulder, cradled in his arm, which wrapped around me. I curled up against him. He turned to me and I could not look away. I touched his hair, his mouth, his neck, and, Lord help me, I thought I wanted him. I say that because one cannot know for certain until they see the fire in the eyes. Fire that burned and seared so powerfully, I thought it would cut me in two. I knew. He pulled me on top, settling me on him with strong hands on my hips, guiding me and watching me. His darkness became light, and I realized the light was only for me.

Later, I stared upward at a small chink in the log roof of the cabin. A small wisp of cloud passed over. I imagined it moving toward Hasten Peak, too high to graze its summit but close enough to see it like I never would. I sighed deeply and Pajaro stirred.

He noticed my gaze, still fixed on the roof. "What will you do now, Mariah? Stay here? You'll need to move your bed from beneath that hole, I think."

I laughed. "And to think I might have ended up in San Francisco."

"You still could go there, if you wished."

"No," I said. "That was Earl's plan."

I told him about Earl's deception and how it had turned out for him. Pajaro was quiet for a time and I thought he'd fallen asleep. Then he spoke.

"Your husband," he said. "He made a grave mistake in not trusting you. He never understood your heart." He continued, propping himself up on his elbow to look down at me. "He might have saved himself from the rope. Dios, but he never understood your heart." Once I felt his breath grow regular and deep, I stayed awake watching him. I would not sleep. Burke was out there.

Pajaro woke with a jerk. I drew myself up and sat on the side of the bed. He pulled the curtain aside and scanned the woods. He turned back to me and his shoulders relaxed.

"Sleep is costly to me. But I needed it. Thank you," he said.

I had thought all night about a way to help Pajaro. I had only one solution to offer.

"I want to show you something," I told him.

I pulled the pouch out from inside my blouse. I took the map out and unfolded it. "Chin gave this to me. She said it's a map leading to gold that she hid here. Somewhere in Widow Creek. I don't know why I am telling you this except that it's something that worries me and I'm afraid of being the only one to know about it."

I told him Chin's story about Ah Wong and stealing the gold.

Pajaro's eyes narrowed. "Leave it be, Mariah. Po Fong is a dangerous woman."

"Chin told me to take it, Pajaro. If you could find it, you could take the gold. And you could go far away. Couldn't you?"

Pajaro got off the bed, dressed quickly, and pulled his boots on. He took the map. He walked cautiously from the back room into the main room. The rain was steady. He stayed against the wall, hiding from whoever might be out there, and peered through the front window, consulting the map.

He turned to me. "The meadow was exposed when Chin's wagon came. There was no water. This map points to the meadow. Near the fence. But I fear the gold is underwater. Forget about it."

As if to emphasize his point, he took my face in his hands and looked at me. "Promise me you'll leave it. You do not want to tangle with the likes of Po Fong."

Of course he was right. I looked down at the map again, wishing I had more time to study it properly. There were three very distinct trees depicted as being near the spot where the gold was located. Old ones, thick, and, oddly, all were the exact same proportion. She had buried it in the meadow near the fence by those trees. If

I could only find them. As if it would do any good: the meadow had disappeared.

I put the map away thinking that, for a robber, he did not seem very interested in the gold. I watched as Pajaro braided his long hair and fixed it with a leather strap. He put on his hat and adjusting his bandolier, then said, "I can't say when I can be like *this* with you again, Mariah."

I did not have a chance to say what I wanted. We both heard the horses coming down the road. Either Burke had circled back and joined the posse from the valley or it was just the posse. Pajaro did not look to see who it was. There was no need. He touched my hair and smiled.

"I hope you get to see your Beyond someday, Mariah."

Then he was gone. The downpour suddenly increased and I could no longer make out the road.

When the first shots came, I was in the back room straightening the bed. I finished smoothing out the blanket as more shots rang out. I moved to the front room and tried to find a dry piece of wood to start the fire. Shots from the woods. Shots from the road.

And not one piece of dry wood in the whole pile.

A final volley back and forth and then there was silence.

Except for the rain, washing in squalls over the roof, there was nothing to hear. I pressed my face against the front window and wanted to see Hasten Peak. But it was hidden by the storm. When I needed it most, the peak was nowhere to be seen.

Much later, I heard horses galloping by in the harsh rain. I dreaded looking out to the road for fear of what I might see. Part of me wanted it to be Pajaro and his brothers, hell-bent for speed, racing to get away. Alive and free.

Then there was the other part of me, in a fearful, cold portion of my heart, that wanted it to be over. To be finished with them. Despite the moments in Pajaro's arms in which I had felt the possibilities of a new beginning, there was a hesitation.

I did not know what I wanted.

I stepped to the window.

Burke was in the front leading the posse. They slowed as they passed. He glanced at the cabin window where I stood but did not stop. He was like a ghost behind the relentless curtain of water. A string of riderless horses was being pulled by the posse. I turned quickly away when I saw the three bodies tied to the horses. I did not want to see Burke's prizes.

Darkness came swiftly and a shuddering cold enveloped the cabin. Why were there no dry logs for the fire? I wandered about the rooms looking.

I would have liked some warmth. There was none to be had.

❧ 14 ❧

It was a most tremendious looking animal and extremely hard to kill notwithstanding he had five balls through his lungs and five other in various parts he swam more than half the distance across the river to a sandbar and it was at least twenty minutes before he died; he did not attempt to attack, but fled and made the most tremendous roaring from the moment he was shot. We had no means of weighing this monster. Capt. Clark though he would weigh 500 lbs; for my own part I think the estimate too small by 100 lbs. He measured 8 feet 7 ½ inches from nose to the extremity of the hind feet, 5 feet 10 ½ inches around the breast . . . .

[M]y dog caught a goat which he overtook by superior fleetness; the goat it must be understood was with young and extrremely poor.

I hoped Pajaro and his brothers were spared great agony. They surely must have foreseen their end, and they could not have been surprised at its arrival. The picture in my mind that I will connect to this time is that of Meriwether Lewis's encounter with the grizzly and his oddly placed remark about his dog and the goat.

Pajaro was wrong about the rain. It might back off for a few hours, allowing a smudge of blue sky to appear. Then it would start again. I felt trapped in the cabin. Fortunately, Mr. and Mrs. Monroe had left sufficient provisions.

I would not give in to the anxiety that threatened to overwhelm me. Of course, I needed to consider my future. Surely, the best plan would be to return to Missouri. There was nothing keeping me here. The notion of The Beyond no longer held its appeal to me. Or rather, The Beyond seemed more out of reach than ever, and, as such, I felt it rather pointless to continue wishing for it. I did not want to admit to myself that, perhaps, I had seen enough of it already. And I had seen enough of what it could do to people to last a lifetime.

Roaming around the cabin, then escaping for a few minutes of fresh air when the rain abated, I passed the time slowly and almost in a daze. It seemed that my life was caught in a very fine thread and that soon the thread would give way. I did not know whether to hold on tight or force the break.

Two weeks later, I had company. I watched from the front window as a man and woman on horseback rode up leading a string of pack mules. I opened the door and managed a wave. Suddenly, I was aware of how far I'd let things go. I hadn't bothered to clean around the house, nor had I chopped any more wood than what I needed for a small fire in the morning. Thank goodness there were no horses to feed or tend to, for I might have neglected them. I had spent my days walking from room to room trying to avoid looking out at the woods. In the moments when I couldn't help but picture what had happened to Pajaro and his brothers, I felt like my body was separating from my brain. I did not want to think anymore. I did not want to do anything. Yet I knew that at some point I would regain my senses, and then I would be faced with an uncertain future.

"Hello," the man said coolly as he jumped down from his mule. He walked up the stairs and extended a hand. "The stage line sent us to take over for the other ones." I shook his hand. He was older than Mr. Monroe, thin and weathered.

"Name's White. That's my wife. Burke thought you might have gone off. Wasn't fixing to have nobody here when we arrived. No sir. We were told different. Stagecoach line is mighty sore about what happened up here."

Mrs. White had gotten off her horse and was standing in the front yard looking about, shaking her head, and making sounds of dissatisfaction.

"Were them Mexicans shot right here?" she called out to her husband. She never even looked at me. "That might explain this mess, I suppose. We got our worked cut out for us, Ed. Not to mention all that water out there. How's the stage going to make it around? Lord, this ain't what I settled for. I tell you. We got swindled, Ed. Swindled into this!"

She was a short, stumpy woman with a punched-in face and a mop of unbrushed hair. Her dress was stained. And as she marched up to the house, I could see a mean expression of fury about to unleash.

"You that Penngrove woman?" she said. "We heard what happened up here. We heard plenty. Why, the town is just full of talk about you and that dead Mexican. Ain't fitting. Ain't fitting at all."

She wagged her finger at me. "That stagecoach line is lucky we ain't so picky. Not many would come owing to that shameful business up here. And to think you stayed, eating their food, living in their station, and not paying no mind about the shame."

Mr. White had remained silent, but I could tell he was in agreement with his wife. I was no longer welcome here, and all my days of wandering around in the cabin, at loose ends about making plans, were finished.

While they went about unloading the mules and complaining about any number of things, I packed my small bag of belongings. I think that, had I not announced my departure, they would have not noticed. I took some flour, beans, and a small cooking pot. Those two would probably be more concerned about the missing items more than my absence.

I started off down the road with the intent of making my way to Remington River. As if to urge me onward, the sun broke through the clouds and, for the first time in a long while, Hasten Peak appeared.

I had come a long way to see The Beyond. What had I seen of it that I would remember?

When I came to the curve in the road that I could follow to Remington River, I decided.

There was a rough path cutting into the trees leading away from the road to Remington River. I did not know where it would take me. But it was in the direction of Hasten Peak. I took the path, bound and determined to get as close as I could to that lovely peak. I needed to have something to remember.

The weather improved for the first two days that I walked. The path disappeared a few miles from the road. I would climb a rise through thick bushes and trees and catch sight of the peak and head in its direction. When I found a stream, I camped for the night. It was cold and my cloak was my only blanket. A small fire took the chill off. Sometimes I would come to a meadow or clearing and see deer grazing. The silence, only broken by the call of a hawk or small songbirds, was comforting. I had grown weary of the pounding rain.

Pajaro consumed my thoughts. The knowledge that I would never know more about him, his secrets, the truth about this business of his that he had kept close and hushed about, haunted me. It was like starting a book then losing it and never knowing the ending. Together with having been next to him in the cabin for that one night made the loneliness now maddening. On the third day, I awoke to rain once more. Soaked and now without a fire, I gathered my sodden belongings and started off. The clouds obscured my peak. I had taken to calling it my own, and I wandered from rise to rise hoping to catch a glimpse. That afternoon, I knew I was lost. Using some tree boughs, I made a shelter and hunkered down beside a small fire. Fortunately, *The Journals* remained dry. I took out the book along with the cup and saucer, my gift from the Old Mandarin, and placed them on a log. The book fell open to this passage:

> *It was after the sun had set before these men came up with us, where we had been halted by an occurrence which I have now to recapitulate, and which, although happily passed without ruinous injury, I cannot recollect but with the utmost trepidation and horror. This is the upsetting and narrow escape of the white pirogue. It happened, unfortunately for us that this evening, that Charbono was at the helm of this pirogue instead of Drouillard, who had previously steered her. Charbono cannot swim, and is perhaps the most timid waterman in the world. Perhaps it was equally unlucky that Capt. Clark and myself were both on shore at that moment, a circumstance which rarely happened, and though we were on the shore opposite to the pirogue, were too far distant to be heard, or to do more than remain spectators of her fate. In this pirogue were embarked, our papers, instruments, books, medicine, a great part of our merchandise—and, in short every article indispensably necessity to further the view or ensure the success of the enterprise in which we are now launched to the distance of 2,200 miles.*
>
> *Suffice it to say that the pirogue was under sail when a sudden squall of wind struck her obliquely and turned her considerably. The steersman, alarmed, instead of putting her before the wind, luffed her up into it. The wind was so violent that it drew the brace of the squaresail out of the hand of the man who was attending it, and instantly upset the pirogue and would have turned her completely topsy-turvy had it not been for the resistance made by the awning against the water.*
>
> *[. . .]Capt. Clark and myself both fired our guns to attract the*

attention, if possible, of the crew and ordered the halyards to be cut and the sail hauled in, but they did not hear us. . . .

Charbonneau, still crying to his God for mercy, had not yet recollected the rudder, nor could the repeated orders of the bowsman, Cruzat, bring him to his recollection until he threatened to shoot him instantly if he did take hold of the rudder and do his duty.

To have come twenty-two hundred miles and nearly lose everything in one fell swoop? I chastised Meriwether Lewis and William Clark for storing all their possessions in one boat. And yet, was I not doing something similar? To come this far and for the purpose of seeing my elusive peak without another plan of substance. Sinking everything I had, including my life, into this journey. Foolhardy, to say the least. And now I might be lost.

I looked at the cup and saucer. They were pretty but so out of place sitting on a rotting log. I stared at them, hugging my book. The world started to swim in front of my eyes. I was aware of a deep ache in my chest and slick sweat on my forehead. I had not admitted it to myself the day before, but I could no longer deny that I was ill. Ill and lost.

I must have dozed off, for the sounds coming toward me woke me with the realization that I was no longer alone. There was no mistaking the steady crunch of footfall. My fire had died, and even though it was still early afternoon, the clouds and thick forest made me wish for even a spark of light from the embers.

He called out first. "I sees you there. I mean no harm."

The man who emerged from the woods was carrying an armload of wood so all I could see was his face and legs. He had a long, shaggy, gray beard, eyes the color of a robin's egg, and a worn-out skin cap festooned with feathers. His trousers were made of animal skin as well. His face bore dark marks in a pattern on his cheeks and chin. He approached slowly and stopped suddenly when he drew near. The man looked me up and down; his mouth hung open.

"God almighty! A woman."

He dropped the wood bundle down and set to work with small branches and a great deal of huffing and puffing. Soon a flame took hold and there was light and warmth again beneath my little shelter. Then he sat back and glared at me.

"I guess you know that you're ailing. Just look at you. What in hell are you doing out here? Fixing to do yourself in, is it? Just lay down and hope a critter finishes you off? Only a few set out to do it this way. But a woman. You made a fine mess of it, if you was thinking of offing yourself. And now you just taking the long and hard way to do it. I come in on the middle of it. Damnation. Now I am beholden to do something about it."

It dawned on me that, save for the few words I had exchanged with the Whites, I had not spoken to anybody in weeks. My words came out strange and stiff.

"I'm walking to Hasten Peak," I said.

The man stared at me and shook his head. "Now that there is a fine walk. Just going to the mountain, you tell me. Say, you got a name to go with the walking, miss?"

"Mariah."

"I see. First Mariah I ever met, that's a fact," he said. He poked the fire then reached into his shirt and brought out a piece of hide. He unwrapped it and offered me its contents.

"Jerked it myself. Good deer, too. Go on. Have some."

I took a piece and bit into it. It was soft and chewy and full of a deep, rich flavor. "Thank you. I believe I have run out of food."

"Have you now? I don't reckon that surprises me, either. What were you fixing to do for food? Trap? Got no gun that I can see."

"I don't know how to trap. I'm just walking," I said. Why did my voice sound so strange? Like I was talking in my sleep, slowly and as if I were hearing my words from a great distance.

"I mean no disrespect, Miss Mariah. But you're in a pickle of the worst kind. I don't like any of it and you're a damn nuisance to boot. I guess you don't know how bad you look, do you?"

"Do I?" My hand shook as I raised it to my head. My skin was on fire. "Do I really?"

"Yes, miss. You do. And I reckon I can't leave you out here. You're going to have to come with me. A lot of trouble for me as I've got other things to do besides rescuing fools. But there it is. Got no choice," he said with a grunt. "At least you travel light. What's this? A *book*? A *cup and dish*? My Lord. Just taking a walk to Hasten Peak, were you?" He sucked air through his teeth.

I don't recall walking, but I remember the man's steady arm guiding me through the trees and then warmth, rest, and safety.

Bits and pieces come together in a haze. The man lifting me onto a soft pallet. Water on my face, legs, and arms. Several times, I inhaled a deep, aromatic steam of some kind that made me cough violently but then settled my rattling chest. My head was lifted for sips of something salty and rich or for deliciously cool liquid that tasted like pine. When I'd open my eyes, for the briefest of moments, for I think I slept soundly, I'd look around my environs. Blurry visions of shadows and movement and sounds. Then I'd fall back into darkness.

The first sensation I had was one of heat. Incredible heat. I opened my eyes and I felt awake. My vision was clear. Sweat was trickling down my cheek. I wiped it away and felt my skin. It was cool. I glanced down and saw that I had my dress on but no covering. The heat wasn't from me or from the bedding. There was no light from a fire. I looked around the strange room and saw that the hearth was empty. One wall was made of sod, another of rough stone, a third of logs. A drape made of animal skin covered the last wall, and through this I saw light and felt the first breath of breeze, which was dry and warm.

The other furnishings in the room consisted of a table, two chairs, a bearskin rug, and shelves with crockery. The skin drape moved again, this time with a greater gust of hot wind. I heard the sound of wood being chopped, and I rose carefully, wondering how long I had been down, where I was, and, more importantly, who was outside.

Other than being a little weak, I was thirsty and had a real urge to find a place to relieve myself. Testing my legs, I found them steady enough to carry me past the drape and into bright sunlight. This was where the heat was coming from.

The man had his back to me as he chopped but he must have heard me. Without turning, he said "She lives, does she?"

Then he faced me. Hatless, I saw markings on his face. A series of black lines crisscrossed his face. His age was difficult to determine because of the markings. His blue eyes were sharp and clear. He looked me up and down. "A day ago, I thought you was done for. Fixing to bury you this afternoon. Now I see I can continue chopping wood." He returned to his work.

I stammered, "Sir, I believe I have caused you a good deal of trouble."

"And then some," he grunted. "Water is over there in the barrel."

"Thank you. I need to go into the trees for a moment, though."

He pursed his lips and pointed. "Go thataway. And mind you dig it in the dirt, 'else some bear come a sniffin'."

When I returned, I followed his directions to the water and took a long drink. He stopped his chopping and leaned on his ax. "If you're curious, it's been four days of fever and thrashing and crying and talking. Don't ask me how I slept."

"I'm sorry," I said. I remembered that I had left the road past Widow Creek and started walking. I had been rescued. I recalled the man asking me if I was doing myself in. It had stunned me. Had I been? The shock of Pajaro's death couldn't have been that great. Sad as I was, it was not so much the loss but the now-lingering thought of what might have been. And what was I to do now?

"I don't know your name," I said at last.

"Martin," he replied curtly. "Just Martin. My mother gave me that name, rest her soul. My father gave me the other. Had no use for him and have no use for his name, either. I know your name, so we don't need to go back and forth no more." Martin threw down his ax. "Guess you'll want something to eat."

"It's so hot. The weather changed, didn't it?" I said, watching him swagger toward the cabin.

"Damn high time. I bunked outside last night and then saw fit to chase you down. Hollerin' for your ma, you was."

"For my mother? I see," I murmured, wondering what else I had said.

He ducked inside the cabin, and he emerged with a bowl. "You'll have to make do with cold stew. Don't ask me to make a fire just because I'm chopping."

He placed the bowl on a stump in front of the cabin. The front of the stump was carved out in a likeness of a bird with a great feathered head. Like an owl. I sat down and ran my fingers over the details.

"This is beautiful."

Martin grunted. I tucked into the stew and was surprised at the flavor.

"What meat is this?"

"Venison," he replied.

I ate some more and found a flavoring or herb I had never tasted.

"There's an herb in here that's quite good. What is it?"

This time, he stopped chopping and came over to me. "I haven't talked with another soul since last year. Ain't fixing to waste it on my cooking. I got questions. What are you doing up here, and where you fixing to go now that you're better?"

I knew the answer to the first question. The second one had me stumped.

"I just wanted to see Hasten Peak. You see, I'd come so far, in many ways. And that mountain seemed to call to me."

He squinted at me. "You ain't the first that told me that, miss. But I didn't reckon you for that sort. It's a beauty of a peak, that she is. Something about that peak. You know what? Some folks think there's something or someone living in it. Right down in the center of the peak. A group of fairy people. They fly around at night." Martin stopped for a moment. "I'm not crazy, miss. It's just what some say that don't know that a mountain is a mountain and nothing or nobody can live in it. The kind that believe that, well, probably touched up here." He pointed to his head. "I don't cotton to those tall tales."

He picked at his teeth with a splinter and thrust his chin at me. "And what else? You come up here to see the peak. It called to you or whatever you said. Why's that? Where you from anyway that you ain't never seen a mountain like that?"

"I come from St. Joseph, Missouri."

Martin slapped his thigh. "Well, that explains it all! No wonder. I'm a Virginia man, myself. Never happier in my life to leave that place. Too flat. And don't tell me there's mountains back there. Not a one like any of these around here. Not a one. Somebody tell you different, you spit in their eye."

"We came by wagon. It was my husband and myself, but he died before reaching California." I decided to keep the details to myself.

"He died, did he? Well, I'm sorry for your loss."

After a while, Martin said, "I'll tell you, Miss Mariah. You can't learn wandering. It's just in ya. You don't give a hoot if you get to where you set off. There's nothing better than not knowing where you're going. Because once you get there, well, there you are. The only way you're worse off is if you can't make the best out of where you land. Isn't that right? There's folks that can't stand not knowing what's around the next bend. I got no time for that kind."

"I think you are right, Martin."

"So, with the husband dead, what did you do next?"

"There was a widow in the wagon train. I took up with her. Her name was Hetty."

"What was she running from?"

I looked at him curiously. "Running from?"

"They's always running from something. Always. Can't imagine jumping on one of them wagons and striking out unless you got something you're getting away from. Just don't make sense."

"I wasn't running from anything, Martin."

"Weren't ya? If you don't mind my plain speak, you could have gone back, couldn't ya? What was stopping you from hightailing home after that husband of yours got down in the dirt? I'll tell ya. You were running from something. Maybe not the same as that widow lady. But there was something you didn't want to go back to."

"You speak some truth. I had a notion that what was beyond would make me something different than what I was becoming in Missouri. I guess I didn't want to give that up. So I continued on with Hetty. She had kin in Remington River. She invited me to come with her. Seemed better than going to San Francisco, which was Earl's plan."

"San Franciski? Lord above! There's a place not worth wasting the good breath it takes to say its name. You done right steering clear of it, Miss Mariah. I can't say that Remington River is much better. But it ain't worse by a long shot," said Martin, who had jumped to his feet at the mention of San Francisco. "Why did you leave Remington River? Not much between there and the valley that I would call fitting for someone like you."

"Hetty's brother was in a bad state. I think he didn't write the truth to her. I might have stayed to help, but I didn't want to be a burden to them."

I put down my bowl and wiped my hands. "I don't know where I will go now, Martin. But I won't trouble you much longer. Show me the way back down toward Remington River. I think I've seen enough of the peak."

Martin scratched his chin and said softly, "You feeling up to a little walk? I want to show you something."

I stood up. I was feeling much better. "Yes. I'd like that."

He led me away from his cabin down a short trail that snaked through a large stand of aspen. When we came out of the trees, we were in a beautiful meadow with a stream running through the center. The heat was staggering here in the open. The weather was certainly a far cry from those weeks of freezing rain and clouds.

Then I saw what it was he wanted to show me. Only a thin line of trees separated the meadow from the base of Hasten Peak. Martin lived right beneath it.

"Goodness!" I exclaimed. "Why, it's right here! There is still snow, too. Even in this heat."

"Snow stays most of the year. I thought you'd like to know how close you got. I don't know how you did it. But there you are."

"Have you climbed it, Martin?"

"Some. I clamber around looking for bighorn sheep and such."

"Bighorn sheep? They're here?"

"Oh yes. You look on the mountainside long enough, even from here, you'll see them," he replied.

We sat in the shade of an aspen atop a boulder. For the first time in many days, I allowed Pajaro Mendonca to enter my thoughts. One night of his tenderness and I was left more confused by the man he said he was and the man I thought he was. In time, I supposed, I would understand.

Finally, I shook off the puzzlement. "How did you come to live here?"

Martin reclined on the rock and crossed his legs. He stroked his beard. "Well, for starters, I got pushed out."

"Pushed out? What do you mean?"

"I mean the people. All those people. They just kept coming. Everywhere I looked, I kept seeing them. And I just got fed up. Spent my most of my life out of the way, minding my own business, and then they come and take up space."

"You mean people in towns and cities?"

"Oh, Lord. I have no use for those places. I had a little spread in the valley. I lasted one year. I couldn't see the fellow five miles down the road when I first got there. But soon I was spying him twice in one month. That done it for me. I was a fool thinking I could stand it. No, sir. I come right back up to the mountains. Where I belong."

"What are those marks on your face?"

He scratched his face. "I forget about them sometimes. I ain't got a looking glass to remind me. I guess you'd ask eventually. Shoshone. It was part of the deal. Get marked for every woman. Married two and buried them both. Last one is over there by that bunch of cedar." He indicated a place at the far end of the meadow. "She liked that mountain, too."

"I'm sorry about your wife," I said. "You lived with the Indians?"

"I came out West as a scout. You spend much time out here either you make friends with the Indians or you don't. I like them for the most part. We're sort of the same. They're getting pushed out, too. I wandered around the mountains trapping and scouting and doing more trapping. Now I'm here. Alone, and that suits me just fine. Plus, I don't have the stomach to be that way no more."

"What way is that?"

"Go someplace and just take it because I can. That can't be right no more."

Martin sat up. "I guess you'll go back to Remington River. You never did tell me why you left."

The sound of the stream running through the meadow sounded like glasses clinking together. "I made a friend there and worked for a short time. Then I met some trouble. That trouble is something I can't shake. I think I was trying to get away from that trouble, you see. And I wanted to see the mountain. I had come so far to see something new and different. Before leaving here, I wanted to see this place."

"Your trouble? What sort you talking about?"

"I was caught in the middle of something. I just want to be rid of it. But it seems to follow me. It doesn't seem to be here. Now. But I think it will be wherever I end up." I told Martin about the Old Mandarin, Chin, the gold, the map, Widow Creek, and Pajaro and his brothers.

"Reckon you packed in a lot of living in a short time, Mariah. Ain't no wonder you can't think straight," he said. "I'm going to chew on this. I've got me an idea about your troubles, but we need to get back and feed you again."

Martin made more stew of venison and roots. We took our meal outside, for the cabin was still warm from the day.

The sun went down. The coolness of the evening was a welcome relief.

When we finished, I brought out *The Journals*. "It's about two men who explored the West a long time ago. They were sent by President Thomas Jefferson."

Martin looked at the book. "Military men, as far as I can reckon."

"Why, yes, they were."

"I seen 'em."

"You *saw* Lewis and Clark? Where?"

"I seen 'em come past La Charrette just north of St. Louis. I was working my way upriver and stopped near Femme Osage Creek. Just a boy, I was. Met another famous fellow out there. Name of Daniel Boone, matter of fact. He gone to live with his son in his old age. His son, called Nathan, I believe, give me a job for a month. Saw them two fellows, Clark on the boat and Lewis walking the banks. They passed right by where we was felling some trees. Didn't know nothing about them until later."

I saw Martin's eyes soften as he stared at the fire.

"Read a bit, Mariah."

"I know one that you will find interesting."

[F]rom the cow I killed we saved the necessary materials for making what our wrighthand cook Charbono calls the boudin blanc, and immediately set him about preparing it for supper; this white pudding we all esteem one of the greatest delicacies of the forest, it may not be amiss therefore to give it a place.

About six feet of the lower extremity of the large gut of the Buffaloe is the first morsel that the cook makes love to, this he holds fast at one end with the right hand, while with the forefinger and thumb of the left gentle compresses it, and discharges which he says is not good to eat, but of which in the squel we got a moderate portion; then he takes the muscle lying underneath the shoulder blade next to the back, and fillets are next sought, these are needed up very fine with a good portion of kidney suet; to this composition is then added a just proportion of pepper and salt and a small quantity of flour.

Thus far advanced, our skillful operator Charbono seizes his receptacle . . . and tying it fast at one end turns it inwards and begins now . . . to put in what he says is bon pour manger; thus by stuffing and compressing he soon distends the receptacle to the utmost limits of its power of expansion . . . .

[I]t is then baptized in the Missouri with two dips and a flirt, and bobbed into the kettle; from whence after it be well boiled it is taken and fried with bear's oil until it becomes brown, when it is ready to assuage the pangs of a keen appetite or such as travelers in the wilderness are seldom at a loss for.

"Them Frenchmen got some nerve with their cooking. But that there you're reading about is some good eating, I guarantee." He kicked an ember into the fire. "We come across a fellow once. Near the Moreau River. It was late in the season. We come back from trapping along the Musselschell. Almost too late for us but we was strong and determined to get our beaver back. The fellow? We passed him the first time. He was sitting on the riverbank, snow piling up around him. We called to him, 'Hey, mister!' He didn't wave or say nothing. Just looking up this valley behind him. We paddled on a bit and then one of the older fellows in the group says we got to go back and sees to him.

"So we get back to him and clamber up the bank. And we sees a woman and boy lying next to him. Dead as Tuesday, they were. I looked past them three into the prettiest little valley you ever saw. Ripe for beaver and other game, too. Tall trees, streams, and a big meadow . . . snow did nothing to ugly it, by God. Fellow's wife and boy got caught in the river and drowned. He was a Frenchman but he could talk enough English that we caught his drift of what happened. He pulled the boy and woman out of the river but they was gone. He said he'd lived on the river for years. Funny thing about it. He didn't look sad or nothing. Lord, he didn't even look cold. We begged him to come with us. He would not. He said he would wait.

"'Wait for what?' we asked. He kinda looked strange and smart at the same time. 'If you have to ask, you will not understand what I am waiting for.' I guess he just got plumb to the end of it and didn't want to take no more life."

"He was happy where he was," I said, thinking of the man freezing in the snow next to his dead family. "Even with nobody left to share it, he was content to be in his valley." The sound of wind building above the trees reminded me of the surprise of coming upon a river. One moment there is silence, and then the growing rush of water grows louder and louder as the river gets closer. The breeze flung the tree tops to and fro causing needles to cascade downward. There was no planning for the wind. It just comes and goes at it pleases. The Frenchman on the Musselschell knew this. He was waiting for what fate planned next for him. This was how he lived his life.

§

The next morning, Martin handed me a steaming mug. He'd brewed tea from pine needles. The aroma was so pungent, it brought a cascade of tears to my eyes.

"I've done some considering, Mariah," he said. Noting my watering eyes, he grunted. "Now don't cry about it. Here's what I reckon. I don't think it's this Pajaro character that brought the trouble."

"You don't?" I said, blinking and dabbing my burning eyes. "It seemed to all start with him."

"Nope. That man, as you tell it, he was fixing something. All his talk about the land disputes. That's a bad business in the valley and he's trying to make it right, the way I see it. I know something of the Mexicans. Why, they were here before any of us come west. Had a fellow I knew down in the valley. Miguel. Good sort. Mind you, I didn't like too many people in the valley. Still don't. But he was a good Mexican rancher. Had a nice spread and ran his cattle and treated his people well. Even let a few of the local Indians keep their winter camps on his land. No, the Mexicans didn't want no trouble. But they sure got it. And you know why?"

I thought about this. "Well, from what Pajaro told me, the white settlers came here thinking they could just take land like they were told they could do. That's what *we* were told. We all saw those pamphlets in St. Joseph telling us to just come out and get free land."

Martin nodded. "I know. Brought more than a few of them with them pamphlets out here myself when I was scouting. Of course, that was land that needed settling. And that was a fine deal. But it weren't that way in California. Way different."

"How?"

"Land was settled here already. But now there's gold. And folks who already been out here a long time? Done settled here and built a life, and then folks walk right in from the East and go ahead and take it from them. For gold. There's a greed that comes with it. Never saw nothing like it.

"I believe that gold you got from that girl is cursed. It's no good. Yes, the money ain't bad and not saying that I haven't looked about up here for some of it. But folks go ahead and throw away friends, family, and all sense just to get some of it. Why, it's worse than the bottle or even a woman! Fellow might lose all sense over one or the other. But when it comes to gold, I reckon some folks would throw over a pint and their own mother for it."

Martin slapped his leg. "Tell you what I think. That Chinese girl's gold brought you your bad times. You ain't sure what *is* the truth with it, do you? Way you told me, I ain't got it figured neither. If she's telling the truth about the gold and her mother, then the girl stoled it. Belongs to her mother, don't it? Even if the woman ain't a fit kind of ma, it is her gold fair and square. What if the girl's lying about how she got it, and maybe her mother's a bundle of charm and love and sent her off with her blessings? Then you be doing the ma a favor to bring back her gold."

"Tell Po Fong where the gold is? It would dishonor Chin's memory to go against what she said. She told me I should have it."

"If you wanted it, you'd a gotten it, Mariah. Got the map, ain't ya? You'd a gotten it by now. I don't think you cotton to getting it. And besides, it weren't the girl's to give away. She stole it from her mother. Don't matter if she didn't like the woman. Don't matter why she done it. My way of thinking, that girl settled herself in a nest of snakes doing what she done. Like I say, gold makes folks do terrible things."

Then I remembered what Pajaro said when I told him about the map and the gold. He told me to forget about it. Even he was wary of dealing with it. If what Chin told me about her mother was true, then the gold was never Chin's to begin with, no matter how she felt. And it should go back, with its bad luck, and good riddance to it.

I said as much to Martin and then asked, "How will I go about doing this?"

He scratched his beard. "Simplest way I know is to tell this Chinese woman where her gold's at. Give her the map. And you're done. Wash your hands of it, so to speak. I got it all figured out, Mariah." He got up and went into his cabin and returned with a drawstring bag. "Now this here is *clean gold*. Got it myself. Right up yonder."

He opened the bag and I saw dozens of small nuggets inside. "You will take this, Mariah. Now, no arguing. What am I going to use it for? Been sitting there a year or more."

"I could not take your gold, Martin. You might need it someday."

"Doubt it," he said. "Now, I'll get you as far as the road to Remington River. Don't argue. I ain't going into town this time. I'll go in a month or so. And if I see you there lollygagging around, too scared to go to San Francisco, I'll give you what's for."

We packed up the next day. Martin stuffed some provisions into my bag and we set off. I did not realize how far I had walked. From Martin's cabin, it was a four-day journey to the Remington River road.

When we reached it, Martin put the pouch in my hands. "Go see the assayer first thing. Get your money and tuck it in someplace safe. You got a petticoat or something underneath there, haven't you? Sew it up inside. Keep a few coins in your bag."

I stood for a moment and held Martin's hands. "Thank you. For everything. I will repay you, Martin. I promise."

He laughed. "Good luck on ever finding me again, Miss Mariah! And good luck on your venture." He turned and vanished into the trees.

❧ 15 ❧

I WALKED ALONG THE REMINGTON RIVER road for nearly a day and a half before I encountered a man driving a cart with a hog in the back. He was going to Remington River and kindly offered to take me the rest of the way. My feet were worn out and I gratefully climbed aboard.

We arrived in the early afternoon. The town seemed to be more bustling to me with an increased number of folks on the streets. I shuddered as we passed by the burned-out shell of the Old Mandarin's shop.

The man took me as far as the stable. I asked the stable boy about the assayer's office, for I did not recall seeing it while I resided in Remington River. He pointed down Front Street. "Take a right at McDougal's Store. He'll be open, I reckon."

I found the office and presented Martin's bag of gold to the assayer. He weighed it and slid a piece of paper across the counter.

"That much?" I asked, taken aback at the amount the assayer had written on a piece of paper. He weighed it one more time and tapped his finger on the paper again.

"Two hundred thirty dollars, miss. No mistake, I assure you," the assayer said, smiling. "Where did you say you got this?"

"A friend," I said as he counted out the money. Martin's generosity (for I am sure he knew how much was in the bag) staggered me.

"Pretty good friend," he said as I departed.

The light was fading as I walked away from the assayer's office, but there was enough for me to see Sing standing on the opposite walkway, Bird on his shoulder. Tears filled my eyes as I walked over toward him.

He was staring at me.

"Sing!" I said when I caught up to him.

Bird jumped from Sing's shoulder to a barrel and paced on top of it, claws clicking against the wood. The boy was upset about something. He was shaking.

"Oh, missus," cried Sing. "Oh, missus. You are in the gravest danger. They will be looking for me so I don't have much time. I wish you had not returned to Remington River."

"Why? What has happened?"

"There is much to say, missus. I . . ."

The boy was sweating. I could see the glimmer of beads on his forehead and he wiped it away quickly. "There is someone looking for you. Missus, you have to understand. I did not mean to say anything. But I must bring you to her. Now."

"What do you mean, Sing? Please tell me," I implored.

"I cannot say. For I must bring you now. She knows that you are here."

"Who knows I am here?"

Sing gulped. "It is Po Fong," he whispered. "She has come here to find you. I was told to look for you. And, well, I heard you were here. I wouldn't have said anything. But—missus, you must come with me now. I will be punished if I don't."

"Po Fong?" It appeared that she had saved me a trip to San Francisco. I would give her the map, for I was certain that was what she wanted from me.

"Yes. Please follow me. I cannot be late," said Sing.

He took my arm and guided me down the walkway. We entered a saloon called The White Lily. There was a lively crowd, loud music, and the smell of sweat, perfume, tobacco, and beer. I followed Sing through the throng to a closed door. He knocked once and it opened. Sing stayed back and indicated that I should enter.

The room was softly lit with candles. A table was in the middle of the room with several chairs around it. A tall woman stood off to the side, her back to me. In front of her was a sideboard with two cups and a small teapot. She turned as I entered.

"Mrs. Penngrove?" she asked. "I am Po Fong. Please sit down."

She was over six feet tall and approached the table with an unusual gait, half gliding, almost floating. There was a slight weave to her walk. Like a fish darting against a current. I recalled the Old Mandarin saying that she had removed the bindings from her broken feet and learned to walk despite her culture's tradition. Her black hair was pulled back into a severe knot with a sharp metal stake securing it in place. I could not guess her age, but her regal bearing made her appear much older than me. Yet her skin was smooth and her dark eyes clear. She stood erect and straight-backed, like an animal on alert, her eyes flickering up and down my body. It was most unnerving to be appraised in such a manner.

"Sing tells me that you wish to see me. What is it that you wanted to talk to me about, Miss Fong?" The woman was intimidating, although she'd said few words, and I vowed not to let her get the better of me.

She brought the teapot and cups to the table. Into the pot of hot water she dropped a handful of leaves. Steam rose and she replaced the lid, waiting for it to brew.

Po Fong sat down at the table and said, "I sent an acquaintance of mine to Remington River several weeks ago to make inquiries. I was not satisfied with his results. He was not thorough and did not return with the answers I wanted. Sometimes it is better for me to take matters into my own hands. This is why I am here. In Red Bluff, I learned that a man called Pajaro Mendonca was involved in matters of great importance to me. His reputation is well known even as far away as San Francisco. I have reason to believe that he has something I want. I mean to get it back."

"That doesn't explain why you need to talk to me. I don't understand," I said.

"I have heard about a Chinese man here in Remington River who assisted my daughter after the attack on her wagon. He tended to her wounds and made plans to hide her. For her safety, as I understand it. I also learned that a white woman, previously employed by the Chinese man, took her away from Remington River. Pajaro Mendonca rode with that wagon. Come now, it was not difficult to find out that you were the woman driving the wagon, Mrs. Penngrove. Like it or not, you are now associated with Mendonca."

My mind was working at top speed now. I was conscious of the string around my neck and the pouch containing the map where Chin had hidden the gold. Is this what Po Fong wanted? But why did she think *Pajaro* had something of importance to her? She must think he had something to do with the gold. I recalled the Old Mandarin saying that people who crossed Po Fong had a way of disappearing. Therefore, it would be very dangerous to play games with her. Then I remembered Chin's comments about her mother's cruelty. I tried to remember that it was my intention to return the gold to Po Fong. To rid myself of its curse. It would be a simple matter of giving her the map right now. Yet, I wanted to know how Pajaro was involved. Even though he was dead, my curiosity about him was still alive in me.

"All that is true. I won't deny it. However, I wonder if whatever is of such importance to you is greater than knowing the fate of your daughter, Miss Fong," I said slowly.

Po Fong poured some tea into my cup and into her own. She took a sip and nodded. "Please. Try it. It is a special blend that I think you will like."

I took a sip. Delicious jasmine, hot and clean, poured into me. I realized I had not eaten nor had water in hours. I felt a flood of warmth and, odd for the moment, peace.

Po Fong laughed. "Of course, I know what happened. My daughter was a fool and was so easily led along by Ah Wong. Anybody that stupid is no child of mine. The boy, Ah Wong, he might have been something important in my business. It is a shame he was finished up here. He will be missed."

Ah Wong was missed. But, evidently, not her daughter.

The room was airless and I suddenly longed for a breeze. Sweat started to form on my back. Was I getting ill again? Or just very tired? I had had a long journey. I would welcome rest. I took another sip of tea and tried to stay focused on Po Fong. I needed to tell her about the gold. But I just wanted to hear a bit more of what she had to say.

"I am sorry for your loss. Of Chin, I mean," I said caustically. "You must think I am stupid, for I still have no idea why you wish to talk to me."

Po Fong regarded me with a dark expression. "I won't waste any more time. Mendonca is involved with one of my business dealings and I must find him. I think you can help me. Is that clear enough for you, Mrs. Penngrove?"

Now I was sure that I was more fatigued than I'd thought. My eyes were closing despite my best efforts to keep them open. Did she actually say that she wanted to find Pajaro? I could not have heard that correctly. How could I? My ears were ringing now, even drowning out the raucous music from the saloon.

"There is one small problem, Miss Fong. Pajaro Mendonca is dead. He and his brothers were shot in the woods. So I don't see how I'm going to lead you to him. Unless we go to Red Bluff, track down Terrence Burke, and find out where he buried them."

The words spilled out of my mouth and I wondered how much sense I was making. The room was now spinning. Something was terribly wrong.

Po Fong said, "I met with Mr. Burke in Red Bluff. He was very informative, by the way. Unfortunately, I suspect there was a deal between Burke and that Mexican. That angers me a great deal. I am fairly certain Mendonca paid Burke off in some way in order to escape." The Chinese woman's eyes sparkled in the candlelight, and she leaned forward to meet my gaze. "And, oh, I assure you, Mrs. Penngrove. Pajaro Mendonca is very much alive."

Alive. I could not trust what I was hearing, for the sounds in my ears were like a rushing river, a howling din.

She continued talking as she rose from the table. I could still hear her though she seemed far away now. "I needed to take care of Mr. Burke. He thought he could make a deal with me. Of course, if he was trying to negotiate with me behind Mendonca's back, this is not a man I care to do business with. Particularly if he decided to warn the Mexican. I make my own deals, Mrs. Penngrove. Burke will never make another deal again."

My head was swimming now, but there was no mistaking the cold way in which she spoke of Burke. I knew he was dead.

"Now there is just you, myself, and Mendonca. Burke told me about your, shall we say, *warm* relationship with Mendonca. I am sure he will be quite anxious to see you again. In exchange for what I desire."

From behind me, strong arms took hold of me. I was lifted upright in the chair. I could barely speak now. "He does not know where it is. It is underwater. Under a lake."

"Is that so? Beneath water? It is very noble of you to try to save your friend. No, Mrs. Penngrove. I will waste no more time. I will deal with Mendonca in my own way."

I thought about the pouch. But my hands were too heavy and my head too cloudy to try to show her the map. It was then I noticed that there were three men holding me. I couldn't see their faces but I could hear their breathing.

"Take her now. I have the coach waiting outside," she said.

"You'll be going with me now, Mrs. Penngrove," Po Fong continued. "A long journey. I need to keep an eye on you. Even if I never get my satisfaction from Mendonca, he will know that by crossing me he has caused pain and suffering to those who are dear to him. It will be a lesson to many others as well. It would not be good for my business for my enemies to think I have a weakness."

I tried to say something but my mouth was dry, and the words I tried to form stopped before they left my lips.

"Before you go to sleep, Mrs. Penngrove, let me tell you something. I don't ever give up. You'd better hope Mendonca is the same way. Otherwise, you will never leave San Francisco alive."

San Francisco? But we were in Remington River, weren't we? Why was she worried about Pajaro giving up? The last thing I remember was thinking about San Francisco and how I never wanted to go there. And I sure did not want to die there.

I was vaguely aware of being moved, jostled, carried, propped up, and covered, but it was all in bits and pieces. Like looking in a smudged mirror, I could see forms and blurred faces but not really make out any details. Every so often, a glass dropper was slid between my lips and a squirt of fluid dribbled down my throat. Then there was only darkness.

I have no idea how long I was in this state of twilight. The next time I opened my eyes, I found myself tied to a chair in a room. There was light coming under the door in front of me. I craned my head around to see more of my surroundings. There was a bed in the corner and a window with the curtains pulled closed. Through the window I could hear loud noises of carriage wheels grinding, shouting, dogs barking, and the rhythmic sounds of water being splashed on the ground.

"Hello! Hello! I'm in here. Please help me!" I called out, or rather attempted to call out. My voice was hoarse and cracked and sounded like a bird cackling.

Presently, I heard footsteps outside the door. It opened. A Chinese girl entered. She parted the curtains to allow light into the room. My eyes squinted against the brightness. From somewhere behind me, the girl brought a cup of water and placed it against my lips. I took a deep drink, feeling my peeling, dry lips stinging from the liquid.

I thought I was awake enough to remember what had happened. I realized, though, that I was still fuzzy and could barely concentrate on the girl. She stood for a moment, watching me. Then she left the room. I saw the door close and heard the lock click.

The bright light through the window was so intense that it took several minutes before I could see what was outside. Buildings with rickety porches. Laundry pegged to the porch rails. A window with somebody standing, hand on the glass, looking below to the street. A white bird flew past with something in its beak. There were smells coming from the hallway and perhaps through the window. Strange odors of food cooking, I thought.

Then the door opened again. Po Fong entered the room. She was dressed in a full-length red dress made of a material that shimmered. Her black hair was coiled up, and as she moved near me I saw that two black sticks secured the bun. She had on thick makeup and dark red lipstick.

"We tried to make you as comfortable as we could during the journey. You will be brought food and have an opportunity to bathe, if you wish."

The girl came back and removed the straps that bound me. The skin on my wrists and ankles was red and raw. I stood up and found I needed to steady myself with the back of the chair.

"Where am I? What is this place?" I asked, finding my voice at last.

Po Fong went to the window. "Come see."

I took a few shaky steps toward the window and looked out upon a scene I could not have imagined. The street below was narrow and people were hurrying along it. A woman washed a bucket of greens in the street. Two cats fought over a fish head. A carriage careened by causing walkers to leap out of the way. Everyone I saw below was

Chinese. There were small cooking fires in front of every house, and this was where the strange smells were coming from. The light in the room, which had been so bright, became dull as the sun moved behind the tightly packed structures.

"San Francisco. Chinatown, Mrs. Penngrove. It is unfortunate that you were not able to enjoy the journey here. This part of the West is unique."

"You gave me something. I remember the tea in Remington River. How long have I been asleep?"

"A week or more. You've been tended to. Don't fret. You weren't actually asleep. Just groggy. It was easier to travel with you. We told people you were *ill.*"

I looked about the room and almost wept with joy: my bag was on the bed. I hoped *The Journals* were there and undisturbed along with the cup and saucer from the Old Mandarin. Po Fong glided in her oddly elegant movement to the door. "I will send food and make arrangements for a bath. There will be clean clothes for you as well. For now, Mrs. Penngrove, I'm afraid you will be my guest, and I must ask you to not leave this room. We must wait. Mendonca will either show or not. You will wish him to come here, I'm sure." She started to leave.

"Wait," I said. "I have something to tell you. You didn't give me a chance in Remington River. I think it will change everything."

"I see," she said evenly. "Well, I am listening."

"I must show you this."

I reached for the string around my neck, surprised to find it there. I drew out the silk pouch and took the slip of paper from inside.

"Here," I said, holding the paper. "This is where Chin's gold is buried. It is a map. I tried to tell you. But you wouldn't listen. It is underwater. Like I said. Pajaro does not have it. He couldn't have it. Nobody has touched it, Miss Fong."

Po Fong took the map and frowned. "My daughter never studied her drawing like I wished. She had a good education, you know. But she was stubborn and headstrong. This map was made poorly."

She crumpled it up and threw it down to the carpet. I stared at her. "But I thought you wanted the gold? Isn't that why I am here? To get Mendonca to come out of hiding and tell you where it is?"

Po Fong threw her head back and laughed. "Chin's *gold*? You think that is important to me? I understand now. You have no idea. All the better that you know nothing, Mrs. Penngrove. All you need to know is that in my business, there can never be weakness. Weakness is an opportunity for someone else to come in and take. My daughter stole the gold from me, but that does not matter now. It is what Mendonca has done that matters. My business is in danger because of him. My enemies are laughing at me. He has humiliated me and he shall pay. Dearly, Mrs. Penngrove. Perhaps he will explain it to you. If he gets a chance."

Po Fong cocked her head. "Oh, yes. Your money. I took it from you. It is in safekeeping. I wouldn't want you to try and bribe any of my people."

She turned and left me in the room. The lock on the door clicked firmly in place. I found Chin's map that Po Fong had thrown on the floor and smoothed it and tucked it within the pages of *The Journals*.

A little while later, the Chinese girl returned. She brought a tray of food, which she placed on the table in the corner. Next, a big man appeared at the door carrying a large wooden barrel. He went back into the hallway and carried in several buckets of steaming water. He filled the barrel. The girl arranged a change of clothes on the bed. The man and the girl left.

When the lock clicked, I undressed and soaked in the water.

Afterward, I was refreshed sufficiently to take stock of the situation. I was Po Fong's prisoner. She did not care about Chin's gold. There was something more important that she was after and she believed Pajaro had it.

I was still trying to grasp that Pajaro was alive.

The bodies on the horses? Had it been my imagination? Of course not. Even the Whites confirmed that there had been a shooting at

Widow Creek. If Pajaro hadn't died, then why did he not tell me? In the weeks following Burke's ambush, there had been time. I had been alone. Nobody had come to the station. Foolish of me to think that Pajaro would have risked his life to show me that he lived. And then I'd walked away from Widow Creek, hadn't I? There had been no chance for him to find me then.

I thought of Martin's advice to return the gold and wash my hands of the whole thing. He had been wrong. It was not the gold. It was something else. Something that Po Fong was sure Pajaro had in his possession.

I went to the window and peered out onto the busy alley below. The sun was only allowed to narrowly strike the cobblestones because the buildings were close together and rose high above the narrow street. How would Pajaro ever find his way here? Even if he was informed that Po Fong was looking for him, perhaps he had another plan that did not include me. I had to remind myself that *I* might not be part of his other plan. There was still my old uneasiness about what exactly happened in the woods during the shoot-out. Pajaro survived. What about his brothers? Had there been a deal with Burke? I did not want to rely on sentimentality at this point. I sensed danger in this house.

I decided right then and there that I would not be part of anybody's plan, but I would be master of my own.

Remembering the crude map that Earl and I had studied prior to our departure from St. Joseph, I knew that San Francisco was a very long distance from Remington River. I thought about St. Joseph. I could write my parents for help. We had exchanged only a few letters since my departure. I could sense their worry after hearing Earl had died. Now, however, they were far away and could be of no help to me. It was clear: I was on my own and would remain so indefinitely.

There were few I knew well in this part of the world. Pajaro, for one. Whether or not it was his intent to find me was a mystery. Unless I was completely wrong about the man, I thought at the very least he would try help me. In what fashion that help would be offered, I did not know.

If it wasn't Chin's gold that Po Fong wanted, what was her business with Pajaro? The problem was if he came to San Francisco, he would first have to deal with Po Fong. The woman was as trustworthy as a snake under a log. I had a grim feeling that she would not let either of us live even if she got what she wanted. This alone emboldened me to stay calm and look for opportunity. I was fighting for my life.

My plan took shape: I would try to find Pajaro before he found me. To do that, I would need to escape from the house of Po Fong.

♍ 16 ♌

THE TALL MAN WALKED BRISKLY ALONG the dark streets. A shroud of fog hung low and wooly over the city. He did not like these streets. Discarded animal parts, rotting fruit and vegetables, and human waste, thrown from the shabby buildings, clung to the wet stones. He avoided what looked like a crushed duck head and stepped squarely onto the face of a drunk passed out on the street. The drunk did not register a complaint and the tall man moved on.

If a lantern was lit, it fared poorly against the mist in providing decent illumination. The tall man was wary about looking lost or out of place in this area, and he paid careful attention to each alley sign he passed. He could not ask directions, would not even if he spoke the language of the inhabitants. As luck would have it, a sputtering lantern was affixed to a brick wall and he saw the sign "Compton Alley."

Turning onto it, he moved down the alley, staying close to the buildings. There was no indication about the nature of the business conducted behind the door where the tall man stopped. He turned the handle and entered a smoke-filled room where several men huddled around a table. They were engrossed in their game involving small ivory pieces decorated with colored symbols. He walked past them to another door. His instructions were to knock and wait for a response. The bulky packet in his pocket was starting to stink and he wanted to finish his business quickly. The door opened and a man appeared. He was Chinese, very short and fat and bald. Covering all visible skin, including his face, were intricate ink drawings. The tall man entered the room and sat at a table where a lamp was placed. He noted the instruments of the Chinese man's trade on the table.

The Chinese man sat down. The chair creaked with his weight. He gazed expectantly at the tall man, who reached into his pocket and removed the bulky packet. He untied the string around the cloth and peeled it back to reveal the contents. The Chinese man made no comment about the smell. He turned the object over and saw the design.

"You mix in a bad business, lao-mo," said the Chinese man, pointing at the markings. He knew what they represented.

The tall man brought out another packet. He opened this one and spilled the contents onto the table. The coins rolled and settled near the instruments on the table.

"That is not your worry," said the tall man.

The Chinese man made preparations to do what he was being paid for. The tall man watched him fill containers with red, black, and yellow dye. Next, he selected four sharp needles and tied them together to form the tool for forcing the ink into flesh. Grasping the object in front of him, he pulled the skin taut. He started with the black dye. Dipping the shaft into the dye, he pricked deeply and repeatedly as the desired design began to appear under the flesh: a yellow sun with a black and red snake wrapped around it.

"It is easier when they feel no pain," commented the Chinese man as he worked.

When he was finished, he blotted up the excess ink. There was no need to blot the blood. The object had long since ceased to ooze any. He turned it over and pointed to the symbols etched into the skin on the opposite side.

"These cannot be cut out," said the Chinese man.

"Then burn them off," said the tall man.

A candle was lit.

The Chinese man lifted the object. It was a hand, neatly severed above the wrist. He recognized the hand. He had seen it attached when its owner was alive. There was no mistaking it: the middle finger had suffered an injury in the past. It had healed in a way that made it look like two tines of a fork.

The work of the Chinese man, the new tattoo, was on the inside of the wrist. The old design, on the top, was subjected to the flame, and soon the acrid smell of roasting flesh filled the room. Neither man said anything as they watched the old tattoo disappear. "How long will you keep this thing, lao-mo? How long do you need it?" asked the Chinese man.

"A long time. A very long time," answered the tall man.

Nodding, the Chinese man went to a cupboard in a corner of the room and brought back a jar filled with liquid. "Put it in here when the ink has dried. It will stop the rotting."

∽ 17 ∾

I PAID CLOSE ATTENTION TO PATTERNS of activity that involved me. If I wanted to escape, I would need to find an opportunity.

Besides the girl who untied my hands and the big man with the bathing barrel, I did not see anyone else in the house. Po Fong never returned to my room. The girl brought my meals three times a day, refilled the jug with drinking water, emptied the chamber pot, and saw to my bathing needs. Her arrival was announced by the sound of the key in the lock. She never knocked. When her work was finished in my room, she left without a word. I tried to engage her in conversation but she ignored my efforts.

If my escape could be accomplished by the door, I would have to overpower the girl and run through the house. This seemed like a foolish plan. Not knowing how to exit the house and risking the chance of encountering somebody else made me not favor this plan at all. From what I could see from the window, I knew I was on the second floor of the building. Escaping through the window would be a problem: it was secured with a hasp and a lock. I inspected the lock but it was of good quality and solidly built. Shattering the glass was futile as there were metal bars beyond.

The days were long and I was restless. I had no work, tasks, or chores with which to occupy the hours. There was no hope of conversation. My exercise consisted of pacing the room, passing the window to gaze at the activity outside, and resuming my walk along the walls. One day, I asked the girl if I might have paper and pen with which to write letters. She gave no impression of having heard me. So I was surprised when she brought me a box of paper, a bottle of ink, and a pen. I thanked her and she left without reply. Finding there were no envelopes in the box, I suspected that whatever communication I hoped to reach beyond these walls would be scrutinized by Po Fong. My parents would have no knowledge of where I had been. After my prolonged silence, they most likely feared that I had died. It pained me to think that should I die, a record of what had happened would not exist. I would not be able to tell it. It was then that I decided to write about my experiences after leaving St. Joseph. My memory served me well and I was able to recall interesting details and conversations. Taking a break one afternoon, I opened *The Journals* and the page that fell open was an entry by Clark from July 27, 1805:

> *We begin to feel considerable anxiety with respect to the Snake Indians. If we do not find them or some other nation who have horses, I fear the successful issue of our voyage will be very doubtful or at all events much more difficult in its accomplishment. We are now several hundred miles within the bosom of this wild and mountainous country, where game may rationally be expected shortly to become scarce and subsistence precarious without any information with respect to the country, not knowing how far these mountains continue . . . .*
>
> *However, I still hope for the best, and intend taking a tramp myself in a few days to find these yellow two gentlemen if possible. . . . [I]f any Indians can subsist in the form of a nation*

in these mountains with the means they have of acquiring food,
we can also subsist.

Clark's situation, not unlike mine, meant using what information
was at hand to best advantage. Even with no information about the
land, he resolved to carry on and make do.

Waiting for an opportunity did not mean spending idle time. I
continued to watch the patterns about me.

Finally, a plan started to form in my mind. The bath day routine
offered a possibility.

Every two days, the big man brought up a barrel of water for my
bath. He was not Chinese but a tall, bear-like man with blonde hair
and a golden beard. Trying to talk to him gave me the same results
as with the girl: silence. Unlike the girl, however, he would knock
once when returning after my bath. He would not wait for a reply
to his knock but presumed that in the time it would take for him
to insert his key in the lock and open the door, I would have moved
behind the privacy screen in the corner of the room. He would then
enter the room, unlock the window, and open it. There was another
locking device on the metal bars that allowed him to raise the bars.
Then he emptied the water into the street. He was very careful to
lock the bars and window when he was finished. He carried the keys
on a chain around his neck.

He would leave the empty barrel in the room. Then the girl would
come in carrying a bundle of linens. She would throw them in the
barrel. I noticed that along with the linens, she also put large burlap
sacks in the barrels. One of her many jobs must have been cleaning
the rooms and disposing of the refuse from them. Once she filled
up the barrel with whatever items she wished carried out by the big
man, the girl left the room.

In the few moments I was left alone with the barrel, I inspected
what was inside the burlap pieces. Broken crockery, old newspapers,
soiled materials, candle stubs, pieces of charred wood, and a dead

rodent. There were two more bundles on top of the linens. I lifted them but did not look inside. They each weighed around the same.

The man would return and bring the loaded barrel to the street and place it on the ground. He would not do anything further with the barrel and would disappear back into the house. The girl would come out to the street. Watching her from the window, I saw her look up and down the alley for a moment. A boy came out of the shop at the corner and waved. She glanced behind at the door and, leaving the barrel, scampered down to meet him in the middle of the street. It was too far away to see what they were doing. After a brief time, she ran back, a big smile on her face. In the many days I watched her, she never failed to run to meet the boy.

After saying goodbye to the boy, the girl went back to the barrel and removed the burlap sacks, placing them on the stones. Next, she pulled out the laundry and washed it in a smaller tub. The sacks were collected later but I never saw who fetched them from the street.

From what I could observe, the girl kept to the same routine on my bath days. I had been in Po Fong's house nearly two weeks. Though I had no way of knowing for sure, Mendonca had probably not appeared. I feared that my time was growing short, for if he hadn't come by now, he may never. The words of Po Fong rang in my head. *You won't leave San Francisco alive.*

Bath day was in two days.

My plan was to wait for the big man to empty the water from the barrel. When the girl returned with the laundry and burlap sacks, I would remove the trash from the sacks and hide inside. Then I would be carried out to the street. While the girl ran off to meet her friend, I would jump out of the barrel and escape.

As I waited for bath day, I knew that there were so many holes in the plan, not the least of which was that I had no idea how to get around San Francisco. Where would I go immediately after my escape from the barrel? And where would I go in the days to follow?

I sorely wished I could get a better view of the streets in the immediate vicinity. From what I could tell, the street to the right was a dead-end. Which meant that, should I need to run, I would go left. Once I was beyond this alley, I had to have a destination.

I remembered the time Pajaro and his brothers stopped the stagecoach between Widow Creek and Remington River. The silver-haired gent who represented the governor told us that his documents had been switched, giving the land title to "Pajaro Mendonca of Marysville." I knew that Pajaro went into the valley frequently. Perhaps Marysville was a home base for him. I knew that it would take a journey of several days to get there.

Much to my dismay, I wouldn't have an opportunity to think any further about Marysville. My plans suddenly changed. The door opened and the big man brought in the bathing barrel. A day early! Caught by surprise, I wavered on whether to go through with my plan. The water was poured into the barrel and the big man left. He would return later followed by the girl. I did not waste my time bathing. Instead I packed my things and steadied my nerves. I waited behind the screen.

Soon I heard the heavy footfall! The big man was coming back.

He knocked once and entered. Satisfied that I was finished, he went to the window and unlocked it. I heard him raise the bars and prop them open. Then I waited for the sound of water gushing to the street below. It never came.

Before the man could dump the water, the girl rushed into the room. I had never heard her speak.

"You must come now," she said in a low voice.

The man spoke next. "What is it?"

I couldn't hear what she said. He asked nervously, "Where? Oh damn. It doesn't matter where. That woman again. I'll come right away. I don't want her getting her fur up against me anymore. I'll have to finish this later. Can't keep *madam* waiting."

He did not sound too thrilled to serve *madam*. In fact, he seemed frightened of her. I wondered if I might have made him an ally earlier.

The man left abruptly and the girl followed, closing the door behind her. I heard the door lock.

I came from around the screen with my bag in my hands.

I looked in the barrel and saw the water. If it was full of water, I couldn't use it to escape, could I? The big man hadn't had time to empty it before he was called away.

Then I stopped.

The window was *open and the bars were raised.*

I ran to the window. The delight and sheer joy of fresh air nearly bowled me over. Even the odious smells of cooking below couldn't disguise the clean, brisk air. I allowed myself one breath then climbed out onto the ledge. I saw something that struck me with both hope and utter terror: a plank extended across the alley from the ledge to the building across the way. Most likely a way to save time running up and down stairs. That plank was about ten feet to the right from my window. I would have to crawl along the porch railing to get to the plank.

Tying my bag around my waist with a scarf, I stepped further onto the window ledge and grasped the edge. It was wooden and I could see that it was splintering and very weak. I only hoped the porch itself was of sturdier construction. Inching my way along the porch, I came to the end in a few steps. Another porch was beyond. I inspected it and discovered it was also part of Po Fong's house. There was a window above the porch. I would be taking a big chance to pass in front of it, but I had no time to worry. I climbed over the next railing and crept beneath the window. One more porch to sneak over and the plank would be mine to cross.

As I got to the plank, I looked down once. A dozen feet, more or less, to the ground below. I would survive the fall, but falling was not an option. On hands and knees, I advanced on the plank. It buckled immediately with my weight, but not as much as I thought. Though it bounced, I was able to keep a steady progress. I looked up as I reached the halfway point and my heart skipped a beat. Sitting on the porch where the plank ended was an old Chinese man holding a baby. He was staring at me as he gently stroked the baby's arm. Judging by the narrow confines of the porch where he sat, there would be barely enough room for me. Finally breaching the expanse between the buildings, I breathed a sigh of relief. The man stood up, still holding the baby. His eyes never left mine. With a sweep of his free arm, he parted a curtain to reveal a hallway beyond. I thanked him with a nod of my head and went inside.

It was dark in the hallway and I did not see the people lining it until I started tripping over them. Shoulder to shoulder, along the walls, were men. Some were sleeping, some smoking, and others simply sat, staring at the folks across from them. Nobody was talking. With the dim light of the entrance from where I had just come, I gingerly stepped over the quiet and still figures. Nobody protested or impeded my passage. I came to the end of the hallway and a door. Opening it, I saw a staircase leading to the street below. I ran down and found I was in yet another alley that appeared to come to a dead-end to the right. I turned to the left and saw another row of buildings. A courtyard? I ran to the left and was relieved to see another alley off to the right that opened up to a wider street. I took the alley to the right, noting the sign posted on the side of a building: "St. Louis Alley." Once on the wider street, I saw another street sign: "Dupont Street."

Dupont Street was full of activity. After being in seclusion for so long, the riot of sound and movement nearly overwhelmed me. I stood back for a moment and took stock of my situation. With sick dread, I remembered the money from Martin's gold: it was still at Po Fong's house. I needed money if I was going to go any further with my plan to get to Marysville. It was amazing to me that the little cup and saucer, the gift from the Old Mandarin, had survived all my travails. I needed to find a shop where I could sell them. But where to find such a place? The street rose sharply to my left. I don't think I had ever seen such a steep street. To the right, it descended down into an area with more buildings.

Making my way along that first block of Dupont was as much a challenge as crossing that plank. Every step forward was impeded by hand carts pushed along by Chinese struggling against the weight of all manner of freight. Horse-drawn carriages clopped by. I passed small cafés from which people spilled out onto the street and markets with meat hanging in the window. What animals hung there, I could not fathom. I did not recognize any of the carcasses.

I reached a corner. Had I not felt terror over the prospect of being run down by a cart or wagon, I might not have looked to my right. Indeed, looking down the alley, I realized it was the alley I had crossed overhead on the plank! And there in the street, running in my direction, were the big man and the girl, both looking frantic. Of course, they were looking for me as by now they would have discovered I was missing from the room.

I slipped into a doorway and waited. Surely, I would stand out. I saw no other white people around other than the big man. The doorway was deep and dark enough that the two of them ran right past me, heading up the steep street.

I crossed Dupont and went down another alley. Emerging onto a wide, busy walkway, I found the sign for Clay Street. I could make out a patch of water at the farthest end of this street. From what I recalled from the maps Earl and I had studied, there was a large bay that extended north and east from San Francisco. We had talked about traveling down the rivers from Northern California and into San Francisco Bay to reach the city. The route by land was much longer, and most visitors ferried from the north into the port. Marysville was to the north, that much I knew.

Toward the patch of water, a blue smear in the distance, I headed.

I hurried down Clay Street facing obstacles not unlike the ones I had encountered on Dupont. My eyes darted around as I moved quickly along searching for a particular kind of shop. I passed one or two large stores with imposing displays of fancy clothing and wares. These were not the shops I wanted. As I got closer to the water, I slowed my pace. I came to an area with a row of businesses. The first one was shabby with grimy items in the windows such as old trunks, coils of rope, saddles, and stacks of candles. The second one in the row had a small display of books and newspapers. The third one was what I was looking for. In the window was a small, clean display of well-kept furniture, some pretty oil lamps, and a tall Chinese vase. The sign above the shop read "Curios and Assorted Delights."

The door had a bell above it, which rang as I opened it—a sound that brought back memories of the Old Mandarin and, further in the past, of my father's shop in St. Joseph. How far I had come, how much I had experienced in such a short time, gave me pause. What would the next minutes, hours, days, or months bring?

A man sat at a counter reading a paper. He was an older gent in a suit with a high, starched collar. He looked at me pleasantly at first. Then, noting my disarrayed hair and outfit, he set his face with a tight smile.

"Yes?" he said. "Can I help you?"

Had the man any notion of my need? Those simple words, an offering of help, nearly undid me. *Yes, I need help. Of the direst kind!* But it would be no good to show weakness at this moment. I was here to conduct business. The shopkeeper's daughter in me rose to the occasion.

There was so much to see here, I almost lost heart thinking that it would not be the right shop. There was an area with parlor furniture arranged in such a way that I wanted to sit right down and rub my feet. A fine bedroom set with a marble top washstand looked inviting as well. I walked slowly up to the counter, hoping to find what I wanted. On my right, just before I reached the counter, I found what I was looking for: a glass cabinet containing dishes, porcelain bowls, glassware, and a few delicate statuettes. The ceramics were in poor condition, not well dusted or tended. They looked as if they had not been moved in ages.

I approached the counter. "You have an interesting shop, sir."

He looked me up and down, and, seeing the frightened-looking woman in tatters carrying a bag before him, he read me correctly. "We don't do pawn or trade here. I do sales only," he said, returning to his newspaper.

"Oh, I see," I said. I put my bag on the counter. I removed the oilskin containing *The Journals* and deftly unfastened the bone clasp so the book slid out onto the edge of his newspaper. "Dear me, I am so sorry."

"You have books to sell, you go next door," he said, glancing at the book.

I smiled. "Yes. Your neighbor was quite helpful. While he is gathering the cash for this rare book, he suggested I come here and look around."

The man stopped reading, for I could see his eyes take a closer look at the book. "*That* book?"

"Indeed. It's a first edition. Quite rare. I know it's worth more than the twenty dollars I have accepted. But one must do what one must do to get by," I said, quickly returning the book to the oilskin. "I've had to part with so many nice things since I arrived."

He closed his paper. "*Twenty dollars*, did you say?" Scratching his head, he laughed. "Must be quite a book."

"Oh, yes. Your neighbor drives a hard bargain. But, you see, I must get enough money for passage north and, of course, funds for settling in once I reach my destination. I've been selling jewelry and odds and ends. Flat broke, I would be, if it were not for the quality things I am forced to part with."

"Like I said, I don't usually do pawn, miss. But if you have something worth looking at, I might have a gander at it. Just to be friendly."

I breathed deeply and closed my eyes. "It would mean so much if you would."

Opening my bag, I took out the cup and saucer. The Old Mandarin would understand. He might have preferred that I use them for tea. Unfortunately, Po Fong had ruined my taste for tea. The man picked up the saucer, and, as I hoped, he turned it over, inspecting the marks carefully. He was clever. The dusty cabinet was just for show. He probably had stacks of good crystal and fine crockery hidden in the back, offered by unfortunates like me, saved for loyal customers and sold for double the cost.

He inspected the cup. The small chips and crack did not escape his eye. He knew as well as I the blemishes diminished the worth by very little.

"Where did you get these, miss?" He folded his paper and placed it beneath the counter. A good sign! He was interested.

"As you might gather, I've fallen on dark times," I told him, hoping to maintain an even tone to my voice and not get too excited. "My father, rest his soul, was not the most honest of shopkeepers. So much so that I had to make a quick departure from the East. Creditors, I'm afraid. And then there was the *shipment*, you see." I dropped my voice. "I can hardly mention it."

"Shipment?" he asked. There was no disguising his interest now.

"Yes. A shipment from abroad. It came to us by mistake. Should never have opened it. But my father—such a character you have never met! The crate had a most marvelous tea set. Full service for eight. Of course, he saw the royal seal. That should have made him pause. Not he!"

"Royal seal? Which royal seal?"

"Let me think. Of course, it was a monarchy."

The man's expression darkened. "Well, it wouldn't be a royal seal if it weren't a monarchy."

"Naturally, it was an important monarch. Oh, her name will come to me. I'm awfully tired and anxious, though," I clasped my hands together and shook my head in frustration.

"Could it have been Queen Victoria?"

"Goodness. How did you know?" I exclaimed. His eyes narrowed as he looked once more at the cup.

"And the rest of the service, miss?"

"Split up. Father was ruthless and rather dim. He should have returned it forthright. But no. He sold off the service individually. I saved these."

It was apparent that the man knew the story of the queen's tea set and how it had vanished from England. I hoped he did not know that the set had been broken up long ago and had never actually made an appearance as a full set. "You said you were funding a trip north, miss?"

"Yes, sir. I am making my way to Marysville. I would like to leave as soon as possible, as a matter of fact."

He put the cup into the saucer and turned it a full circle atop the counter. "Marysville? Then you'll want to be on the steamer *Jessup*. This afternoon."

The *Jessup*. And it was leaving today? I could be on my way shortly. If I could only make this deal.

"Yes, of course, the *Jessup* it is," I said brightly.

The man crossed his arms and pursed his lips. "No. I won't take a set that isn't full. Who would want it? It's a lovely piece, though. Good luck to you, miss." He reached under the counter for his paper.

If there was ever a moment I wanted to break into sobs, it was just then. I was tired and frightened. I had not bothered to look out the window for my pursuers. Were they waiting just outside for me? Would I find myself dragged back to that dreadful alley and into the house of Po Fong?

Maybe there was another shop I could try. With a heavy heart, I started to return the cup and saucer to the little box when the man glanced up from his paper at me.

"The *Jessup* has been sold out for days, miss," he said quietly.

I paused and looked at him. "I see."

A tremble went through me as I contemplated where I would go next.

Then his face softened.

"But," he continued, running his finger along the rim of the cup, "it just so happens that my brother is captain of the *Jessup*. Captain Jack is his name. If you are willing to part with these pieces, I can arrange for you to be on that boat today. If you wish it." Perhaps he was tricking me. I had thought myself so clever for playing the shrewd customer. Had he seen through my ruse and discovered my desperation?

"I must think, sir," I said. My hands started shaking and I quickly put them at my sides. Tears came to my eyes, not so much from indecision but from fear that this was a deal that could bring me great heartache. It very well might have been a trick. I could take my cup and saucer and find the dock myself. Inquire about the steamer to Marysville.

And risk being found by Po Fong. This was *her* territory. Not mine. I was a sheep in a wolf's lair.

The man had been looking behind me out the front window ever since I'd arrived. I turned to see whom or what he was looking at. There was nobody there. Was he planning something more dastardly than taking my cup and saucer and sending me on a fool's mission for passage on the *Jessup*?

"You are being followed, miss. Did you not see? A tall man with red hair. Clean shaven. Black bowler. He was behind you when you walked in and has passed in front of the shop several times looking in here."

I brought my hand up to my forehead and leaned onto the counter. *They have found me.* "Sir, I am in the most perilous danger. Did you speak the truth about your brother, the captain?"

The man took out a sheet of paper and pen.

"You'll have trouble with the dock master. He's a tyrant. Doesn't particularly care for women traveling alone. Show him this letter at once. He may waver, but insist that you are to see my brother, Captain Jack. Make sure the dock master takes you to him directly. You will be treated well," he said with a kind smile.

I swallowed back the tears and managed to say, "I am very grateful, sir. I don't know why you have been so kind."

"We shopkeepers need to stick together," he said with a grin.

"But how did you know?"

"Oldest trick in the book, miss. A shopkeeper knows to look for it. Come in to bargain and let it be known you've already gotten a good price at the shop next door? Why, it poses a challenge for a shopkeeper to do better with you!" Then he leaned toward me. "Problem is this: Thomas's Book Shop is closed today. He's getting married."

He placed the letter in an envelope and sealed it. On the front of the envelope, he drew a map to the dock. "Go down Clay Street. Follow it to the bay. Turn left onto Battery and continue to Greenwich. Griffin's Wharf. You can't miss it."

The man went to the door and opened it, pretending to inspect his window display from the outside. He came back in casually and shut the door. He wrapped up the cup and saucer and handed them back to me. "Go on. Take them. Won't be any good without the set." He motioned to a doorway behind him. "No sign of him. Best go out the back. Second alley on the left, take it. It'll bring you back onto Clay Street. God's speed, miss. Better days ahead, I hope."

I pressed my hand to his arm and smiled with gratitude.

As I came to the end of the alley, I peered around the side of the building to Clay Street. The earlier crowds had thinned, much to my disappointment. I could no longer fade into the throng. I looked for the tall man with red hair and a bowler. Probably one of Po Fong's dogs sent to chase me down. If he was around, I did not see him.

Following the shopkeeper's directions, I followed Clay Street to the bay. It was windy and white caps dotted the dark blue water. The air smelled of salt and fish. There was also the unmistakable odor that I recalled from the river boats in St. Joseph: pine tar. The harbor here was full of tall ships, dinghies, small fishing boats, and canoes. Barrels of water full of fish and crabs were being unloaded from the boats.

The sign for Griffin's Wharf hung beneath an archway leading out onto the dock. The ship *Jessup* was tied off at the end. The vessel was large but not as big as the river boats I had seen on the Missouri. The steam stack towered over the boat and great plumes of smoke were rising.

Passengers and crew milled about waiting to depart. A woman skipped past me and called to her children to hurry along to get on board.

There was a line of people waiting in front of the kiosk with a sign that read "Dock Master/Tickets/Inquiries." Judging by the rapidity with which the line progressed (with disgruntled folks walking away after they were served by the dock master at the kiosk), I deduced that the shopkeeper was correct about the boat being sold out. When at last I was able to approach the dock master, he was starting to pull down the board in front of the window.

"Wait, sir. Please," I said, putting my hand up against the wood. "I have a letter for the captain!"

It was then that I saw that the man had been accurately described as "trouble."

He was a wrinkled fellow with a white beard, a watch cap, and one good tooth. "Oh, it's the captain that's got a letter, is it, miss?" The man sneered. "That's what we got mail service for, girlie. Off with you. I'll not have you moping around for our captain today."

"Please, sir. I must see Captain Jack. Read the letter for yourself," and I thrust the envelope at him.

He frowned and spat something dark yellow from his mouth to the ground. "Just so's you know, girlie. Ain't no Captain Jack sails out of here. You keep me here one more minute, I'll call the guard. And he's a sight worse than I am, I tell you!"

This stunned me. *Captain Jack doesn't exist?* I had truly been taken.

Trying once more and, in doing so, actually trying to convince myself that all was not lost, I cried, "But Captain Jack's brother sent me here. To Griffin's Wharf. His brother owns the curio shop on Clay Street, sir. Do you know it?"

He had stopped listening and roughly pulled the board down over the window, nearly crushing my hand.

Coming out of the kiosk, which he locked up, he came around the front and glared at me. "Read the letter yourself!" I shrieked. People were turning around to see what the commotion was about.

He put his hands on his hips and grinned. "What makes you think I even knows how to read, girlie?"

My arms dropped to my side. What could I do? I looked at the boat. People were walking up the gangway, turning left and right at the top, looking for seats. My eyes wandered to the topmost deck. A man came out of the bridge in a dark blue uniform with bright buttons. He wore a black cap. I had no way of knowing if he was the captain or not.

I started waving and calling to him. "You, sir! Up on the deck! I'm looking for Captain Jack! CAPTAIN JACK!"

The dock master scurried over to me and stopped short of clamping his hand over my mouth. I moved away from him quickly and held up the letter. People stopped and stared at me.

"I have a letter for Captain Jack! Please help me find him!"

The man in the uniform squinted in the sun and shaded the light with his hand. He saw me at last and gave me a salute and yelled down to me, "I am Jack, miss!"

Captain Jack directed his attention to the mongrel dock master. "Send her up, Marks. Quickly now!"

Letting loose a flurry of curses, the dock master shoved the line of passengers to the side as I followed him up the gangway. Once at the top, he shot me a look of pure venom. "First staircase on the left, missy. Good riddance to ya!"

Happy to be done with the horrible man, I found the staircase and climbed up to the bridge deck. Captain Jack greeted me and read the note.

"My brother asks that I make you comfortable, miss. You're going as far as Marysville, is it? Make your way down this passage. You'll find a sitting room with refreshments. I anticipate a fine sail today."

I looked to where he pointed. The sign read "First Class Passengers Only."

Hesitating, I said, "But it says first class, sir. Are you sure?"

Captain Jack smiled. "My brother rarely asks a favor. If he does, I know it's for a good reason. Please make yourself comfortable. I've a boat to sail shortly."

I made my way to the first-class lounge. It was filling up with people, so I found a chair near the window and tried to be invisible. There were well-dressed ladies and gents helping themselves to food, which was spread out on a buffet covered with a white tablecloth. Silver pots were neatly labeled for tea, coffee, and hot chocolate. I saw sandwiches, hard-boiled eggs, cheeses, little cakes, and thick slices of toasted bread. I decided to wait until the first round of crowds finished before making myself a plate.

A great whistle blew from atop *Jessup*, and I felt the boat pull away from the pier. From the window, I watched the bustling docksides of San Francisco grow smaller and smaller. I was never so glad to be leaving a place.

With a shiver, I wondered if the tall man with red hair was on board.

My eyes grew heavy and, despite my hunger, I pulled my scarf over my head and let sleep come.

It was dark outside when I awoke. The boat had stopped. We were anchored at another pier. I asked one of the porters where we were.

"Benicia, miss. We'll overnight here. Can't go much farther without daylight. On our way at seven a.m. sharp," he said.

The buffet, I noticed, had been replenished with dinner—roast pork, potatoes, beans, and biscuits. I made myself a plate and consumed it so rapidly, I felt my stomach was about to burst. Full and content for the moment, I shut my eyes again.

The next morning, we set off as scheduled. Tall cliffs surrounded us as we made our way through a strait that curved past farmlands. I wandered outside onto the deck. The air was warm. Little boys were fishing off the banks and waved as we steamed past. For the first time in a while, I felt hopeful. Nothing could be worse than San Francisco.

We reached Sacramento in the late afternoon. Captain Jack found me and told me that a smaller vessel would take me to Marysville. His boat was too big for the Remington River, which was the waterway that ran by Marysville. He gave me instructions to find *The Madeline* which was docked a short distance from *Jessup.*

"Take this note with you. You'll find the docks a might bit friendlier up here. Ask for Connelly. He'll get you situated."

"I don't know how to thank you, Captain. You've been very kind. And to a stranger," I said, already starting to miss the *Jessup,* which I perceived as a sanctuary for me. "Whatever is troubling you, miss, I hope it is temporary," he said and waved goodbye. I disembarked onto the pier. Sacramento seemed every bit as busy and chaotic as San Francisco. I made my way along the wharf dodging people, dogs, and horse-drawn carts, ever mindful of the fact that the tall man with red hair could be watching me that very moment. I found the pier where a boat much smaller than *Jessup* was anchored. Its name, *The Madeline,* was painted on the side. A man was sitting on a barrel whittling a stick.

"Are you Connelly? Captain Jack told me to ask for you."

"That I am. What can I do for you?"

I handed him the note. He read it and pointed to the boat. "Take a seat inside. We'll be leaving shortly."

The boat had a small interior cabin and bench seats along the outside deck. It was a pleasant afternoon, so I decided to sit outside on the starboard side, away from the noise of the docks. The opposite shore of the river was bathed in golden light. Ducks circled in the water, bobbing down for their meals. A road ran along the river, and I saw a boy and girl riding tandem on a pony, bouncing along and

laughing. I felt my shoulders relax and some of the tension leave me.
I recalled the hustle and bustle of St. Joseph and how charming it
could be at times. I would not consider it amusing or interesting any
longer. Cities and big towns now left a sour taste in my mouth.

The boat rocked and swayed as more passengers boarded. There
was a murmur of voices and the sounds of people settling into their
seats. The pilot called for the lines to be cast off. Then we started up
the river.

Though partially concealed by a stack of barrels, I sensed a presence standing at the far end of the deck a few minutes after the boat
left the dock. I leaned forward to see who it was and immediately sat
back, striking my head soundly on the wall.

The tall man with the red hair and bowler!

Incredulous that he should have followed me this far and now
had me cornered, I thought of jumping overboard and swimming
to shore. Instead, it seemed, I was about to have a conversation with
him, for he came walking toward me.

The sun chose this moment to drop to an angle that caused a
sharp glare. Blinded, I couldn't make out his features. He sat a few
feet away from me.

"Hello, Mariah," he said and turned to face me.

It was Pajaro Mendonca.

The word *shock* doesn't fully describe my reaction. There was a
mixture of anger, confusion, and joy. His odd disguise and sudden
appearance confounded me. The many questions and doubts I had
about him surfaced. I might have slapped him.

"There is much to say," he said quietly.

"Much to *say*?" I whispered. "Yes, there is. But right now, I don't
know where to begin, Pajaro. You were dead. Or so I thought. Then
I am told you are alive by a mad Chinese woman. I am kidnapped
by her. I escape and am followed. Did you know how terrified I
was? I thought one of that Chinese woman's people was following
me." I pressed my hands to my eyes. "You have so many secrets,

Pajaro. I should not be surprised that whatever motive you had for not making your presence known me, it probably involves more secrets. Am I right?"

Pajaro looked behind me through the window into the interior cabin, then back and forth up the deck. "They can't see us. And nobody has come outside," he said in a low voice. He was turned now so I could see him clearly. His moustache was gone, his hair cut short and dyed a brownish red. It curled up at the ends. Without the facial hair, I could see faint creases around his mouth and on his brow. He looked troubled.

"As I said, there is much to say and, unfortunately, no time to say it. I had good reason to let you think I was gone. There is a person inside who I believe is following you. I can't be sure. After you left Po Fong's—yes, Mariah, I was there watching you the whole time. After you ran away, I saw somebody in the street. He was dressed in a long gray robe and black braid, as Zhao dressed. Chinese, I assume. He was on your trail, as I was, for I saw him stop, as I did, near the curio shop. At the dock, I saw him get on the boat. Had you not caused that disruption, Mariah, I might not have slipped on board myself," he said with a smile. "I lost him after that," he continued. "But I know he was there. He did not get off in Benicia. Once we got to Sacramento, I left the ship immediately and watched for him. And for you. How did you come to decide on Marysville as your destination?"

I was perturbed to be answering his questions when so many of mine had gone unaddressed. "I was looking for you. To warn you about Po Fong. I remembered that after the land title dispute in Remington River, they gave your name as owner, residing in Marysville. It was all I had to go on," I told him. I started to explain about Po Fong, but he put his finger to his lips.

"We will have a chance to talk soon. For now, I am not sure but I think that man is in another disguise and on this boat."

The sun disappeared behind the distant hills. Pajaro leaned closer. "I am going to the front of the boat. We have not been seen together and it must stay that way. I intend to keep near but I want to see if this man follows you. When we anchor at Marysville, walk straight to Front Street and head north. Stay on the east side, go slowly, and make your way to the edge of town."

"Then what?"

"Wait. I will be there."

Pajaro went back to the front of the boat and stood with his back against the rail, watching.

I sat on the bench, every fiber of my body on edge.

❧ 18 ❧

It was just dusk when I sensed the boat slowing. Up ahead, lanterns on the Marysville dock cast glistening darts of light on the water. The sky was a deep purple and, in the far distance, I could just make out the mountains. And then I saw it: Hasten Peak, snowcapped and proud, highest of them all. I felt my heart constrict with the vision of the peak, and a mix of emotions: love, fear, hope, and nostalgia. The best and worst of moments had occurred in the shadow of Hasten Peak.

As I gathered up my bag, a burst of gunfire from the boat's stern shattered the silence. I heard shouting and the sounds of struggling and fighting. There was a lantern on the bow, the only light on board, and it did little to reveal what was going on. I decided to stay put until we docked.

Pajaro appeared and grabbed my arm. "Come now, Mariah." We moved forward and I noticed a body sprawled on the deck. It was Connelly, the pilot. Shot through the throat.

Two stout and formidable men stood before us, breathing heavily. They shouted something and a third person came from inside the cabin. Walking in an odd, gliding gait, it was Po Fong, I knew at once, although I would not have recognized her from her appearance. She wore an ill-fitting, faded dress with a straw hat perched on her head. Her hair was gray beneath the hat and she had on makeup that made her look much older. She said something to the men. One of them gave her his gun and then they disappeared. The boat gave a lurch forward and sped up, away from the Marysville dock. Po Fong leveled the gun at Pajaro.

Pajaro said, "You won't get far. The river is shallow up ahead. The boat will hit bottom." She cocked her head. "By getting involved so intricately in affairs that are beyond your humble roots, you have complicated this business unnecessarily and put yourself in a dangerous position, Mr. Mendonca."

"If you mean that I involve myself in concerns that do not directly benefit me and at the same time put myself in danger for the benefit of others, you are correct."

"And now you have put yourself *and* Mrs. Penngrove in far worse danger than if you had simply come forth yourself with what you know I will discover eventually."

"Madame, by bringing Mrs. Penngrove into this, you caused much delay in what you seek. Had she not been abducted to San Francisco, I would not have had to come find her. Our dealings might have been concluded long ago."

"Your reputation for trickery precedes you, Mr. Mendonca. You of all people must understand the importance of reputation. In my world, it is a matter of life and death. Should my adversaries learn that someone like you was able to trick me, I would be viewed as weak. A reputation for weakness *and* having been played a fool opens too many doors which, in my business, must remain shut. You, however, must maintain a reputation of *honesty*, am I correct, Mr. Mendonca? It would not serve you well if certain questions were to arise about your honesty in, say, your dealings with the land commission, would it now?"

Po Fong's talk about weakness and reputation made me sick. Her notion of how power was earned and maintained was foreign to me, and I truly had no interest in it. She lived in a world I wished no part of. Yet, I *was* part of it now, and in a precarious position at best. Her mention of this land commission and Pajaro's reputation for honesty puzzled me. I had a distinct feeling that there was more going on here than I knew and I didn't like being kept in the dark.

"Your threats cause me no worry, madam. Whatever becomes of me, I know that I served my people to my best ability. It is well known that you enjoy meddling in political affairs—perhaps for your own gain, but I think it is simply to interfere with and obstruct justice. A dangerous game to play with *your* reputation."

Po Fong held up her hand. "Before you continue with your lecture on the trust your people have in you, I must stop you. I am interested in only that which serves me best. I know you have been secretly working for the land commission, gathering documents at the missions, translating them for the courts, helping the Mexican title holders to fight for their lands . . . all very commendable. However, there is one title that I wish you had not pursued: the Cañon de Purisima. Do what I ask about the Cañon and our business will be concluded. Should you choose otherwise, I am afraid you will find your name will no long carry the same, shall we say, reverence among your people."

"The Cañon, is it? And for that you kidnapped Mrs. Penngrove?"

Po Fong laughed. "Arranging a meeting with you is extremely difficult, Mr. Mendonca. Had I requested one with you, I doubt you would have complied without certain *incentives*, shall we say? Her escape was quite daring but has only served to necessitate our meeting under uncomfortable circumstances."

"Since I never had any intention of meeting with you, madam, our current circumstances mean nothing to me," said Pajaro.

"Mr. Mendonca. I will get to the point. The Cañon is mine whether you believe it or not. And I will have it back."

"You are familiar with the conditions regarding the ceding of the deed, madam?"

"Quite familiar," she said. Then she smiled. "You are referring, of course, to the heir?' Pajaro shifted his stance for a moment and, even in the dark, I detected a hesitation in his reply. "What do you know of the heir?"

"I know he exists and I have people searching for him. Trust me, he will be found."

"Unless he has already been found."

"I think you are bluffing, Mr. Mendonca."

"I have you to thank for helping me find him, madam. I thought it strange that somebody of your reputation would send her own daughter to a brothel in Remington River. I had to ask myself why. I would never have thought to look for the heir right under my own nose. There was no sound reason for you to send your daughter to her fate in Remington River except for rich personal gain, am I right? You did not want to draw attention to your search for the heir, but you knew where he might be. Your daughter could ask questions that would seem innocent enough. She never got the chance."

I remembered Chin telling me that her mother wanted somebody found in Remington River.

Then I smelled smoke. A glow of flames was visible from the stern of the boat. A fire had started.

"Don't be too hasty to try and end it now, Mr. Mendonca. I do not make idle threats. A story will appear in the San Francisco newspaper. It will read, 'A Mr. Pajaro Mendonca, esteemed agent in secret for the land commission, is accused of taking bribes with the specific goal of benefiting the governor of California and his colleagues and depriving land titles to the very people Mendonca says he wishes to protect.' I can now add that you corrupted justice and have exercised undue influence over a young heir to valuable property. How will that sound? You will be finished and likely never be able to show your face again. Argue all you wish, but I have many people eager to see your work destroyed. You have only to tell me what you know about the heir and the story will never appear."

"I see," he said quietly.

While the two of them had a staredown, I was worried about burning alive. What possessed me to do what I did next, I'll never know, but I imagine self-preservation played a large role. I took my bag, swinging it wide and hard, and caught Po Fong on the side of the head. I had a momentary pang of sadness about the cup and saucer wrapped in a thick wool cloth. She fell awkwardly over a coil of rope on the deck and landed face down. I looked at Pajaro, who was as surprised as I was, and we both jumped over the side into the river. The water was shallow where we landed and we hastily made our way to the shore.

Pajaro and I crawled up on the riverbank. The boat was engulfed in flames, and before it exploded, we both saw someone leap from the boat and emerge on the other side of the river. The figure stood there staring at us, ghostly and ominous, in the darkness, the outline illuminated by the glow of the burning boat. Then it turned and vanished into the night. "You think that was her?" I asked Pajaro. Like me, he was panting after our climb up the riverbank.

I was cold sitting there on the bank, half soaked. Yet my curiosity persisted. "What was that all about on the boat? What is the Cañon? Why is it so important to her? And who is this heir?"

Before he could answer, I told him what Chin had told me about searching for someone in Remington River.

"Yes," said Pajaro. "It was what I thought."

"What is the Cañon?" I asked again.

"The Cañon de Purisima is a large land grant that was owned by one of the first Mexican settlers here in the north," Pajaro told me. "He kept it a secret, for the land contained a mine. The man who owned it went back to Mexico for reasons unknown. In exchange for favors from the then-president of Mexico, he deeded the land to the Mexican government. In those days, hardly any Mexicans came this far north. The Mexican government had many other problems to deal with at the time. So the Cañon was abandoned and forgotten. Even its location was not well known.

"The deed, as a piece of government land, was sealed by the president. And only the president could transfer its title. Somehow, a few years ago, a man who was trusted by the president was given the deed. When he got to San Francisco, the man encountered trouble, gambling trouble, at the tables run by Po Fong. He gambled away the land. He went to the mission in San Francisco and begged the priest to hold the document for him. The padre put it with all the other documents held safely for those arguing for their titles in court. The mission is the most secure place for these documents. This is where I do most of my work.

"I have not told you about this next part because, as I said, the less you knew the better. I have been working for the land commission as an agent trying to uncover the rightful deeds for Mexicans. Because I am trusted at the mission and by those wishing to return lands to the Mexicans who lost them, I have been successful in discovering documents proving grantees have fulfilled the requirements of the Mexican colonization laws. This is the only thing the California courts need to confirm the title.

"And then I found the deed to the Cañon de Purisima. The padre said it was a valuable deed and he did not want it to fall into the wrong hands. Po Fong is interested in the deed because it was promised to her as a settlement for the man's gambling debt. She believes that she will be able to influence the court system to turn the deed over to her, even though she knows the terms of the deed prohibit it. The man could not put the deed up for collateral because of the presidential seal. However, the terms of the deed allow for an heir to assume the title. I have found the heir, and now I must worry about him. Po Fong has only to eliminate him in order to open a court challenge for the title. She might not win, but the heir is in jeopardy now. He is in danger and I must get to him quickly."

He helped me to my feet and threw his coat around my shoulders. "We must get away. Fast. I will get us horses. Can you ride at night, Mariah? I cannot promise an easy journey."

We walked along the road, a sliver of moon as our only guide, until we reached a bridge crossing the river. Pajaro told me that his friend would help us with horses and packs. The house was dark when we approached it. Pajaro whistled and a man came to the door presently.

"Wait here," said Pajaro.

He returned a little while later with two saddled horses.

My horse was a rangy paint who bit my foot as I placed it in the stirrup. He limped along in a stumping, staggering motion, which caused the saddle to bump my thighs. Within a few minutes, I was cursing the animal.

Pajaro laughed. "I apologize for Amigo."

"That's his name?" I asked, trying to adjust my seat to the rolling gait of Amigo.

"It is Spanish for *friend*," he told me.

I grunted. "Friend?"

Pajaro kept a slow pace to avoid drawing attention to us and said that once we left town we would start moving faster. I took advantage of the time to launch my questions. "What happened in the woods? With Burke? I have a feeling it is all connected to this place called the Cañon."

"That was a troubling time, Mariah."

"I thought you were dead."

"That troubled me, too. That you thought this. In the woods that day, Burke and I met for a parley. He wanted money to let us go. I asked that he make it appear that we were killed. In this way, I could have more time to authenticate the deed to the Cañon and discover the rightful heir."

"You found him."

"Yes. The man who originally owned the land had a son. The son died but left a child. I have been trying to find him. With the rightful heir, the deed cannot be sold."

Pajaro studied my face as we rode. "In the woods, though. Something happened. It was Sandro. He would not listen to me. He did not trust Burke. Lorenzo was willing to go along with me. Not Sandro. He started firing. Burke and his men fired back. Lorenzo was spared. But Sandro took many bullets."

"I saw them bring horses with bodies down the road past Widow Creek."

"That was Sandro and two of Burke's men. Lorenzo and I got away. Burke returned to Red Bluff but he could not keep silent. Po Fong sent men to inquire, to verify my death. And Burke spoke up hoping for more money. Not knowing where to find us, he was in a poor position to bargain. From what I hear, Burke was killed. As I said, one cannot turn his back on Po Fong. And Po Fong, knowing that I was alive, began her pursuit again. This is when I began to worry about you. I came back to Remington River to look for you."

I grimaced.

"After that shootout, I didn't know what to do," I told him. "The stagecoach line sent up a couple to take over for Mr. and Mrs. Monroe. They made it clear that I had to go. So I started walking. I thought I might like to see Hasten Peak up close. I must have been crazy. I think I was crazy."

Pajaro sighed. "Dios, Mariah. I am to blame."

"Anyway, I walked through the forest. Got lost. Then got sick. A man named Martin found me, and when I got better, he thought I should give back Chin's gold to Po Fong. He said it was bad to know about the gold, and that this was probably what was making my life miserable. I was aiming to tell Po Fong about the gold and give her the map. I went back to Remington River intending to travel to San Francisco and find her. But she caught up with me first."

"Yes. I know. Sing told me that he saw you in Remington River."

"Anyway, she didn't care about the gold. Not one bit," I said. "Even when I showed her the map."

"For ones like her, it is never about the money. It is only about what can be used to influence the will of the others."

"Where is Lorenzo?"

"He is safe. And he is waiting. With the heir."

"Who is the heir? And how did you find him?"

"I think," Pajaro said slowly, "that the less you know about this, the better. It is safer. You will know eventually but only when it is right."

Then he added, "One more thing, Mariah. Due to my work for the land commission, I have been granted immunity in criminal court. This was not widely known, for it served my purposes to still be considered a bandit."

"Why? If you could do this work freely, why continue to be known as a bandit?"

"The people I work for, the ones who have lost so much, would find it hard to trust someone working for the very government that is trying to take their land. The land commission is sympathetic, but it is hard to convince others of this. I prefer to remain who I have always been to my compadres. Even if it is a risk to me. The threats by Po Fong to deliver a story to the newspapers about me will not have the consequences she expects."

"I don't understand. Her hold over you was these stories to tarnish your reputation, and now you say they will cause you no harm. Why not just end it now?"

"Po Fong will not stop until she gets what she wants. Or when she finds herself in such a position that she must relent," said Pajaro. A broad smile swept across his face.

"It looks like you have figured that out, Pajaro," I said.

"Do you remember that Chinese man at Widow Creek? The one Sandro killed? Ah Wong?"

I nodded.

"He was playing both sides and rather dangerously. He betrayed his father, the head of a rival tong, in order to place himself favorably with Po Fong. She lured him away from his father. That is a very dangerous situation with these tongs. It is simply a matter of proving to Ah Wong's father that his son had been involved with Po Fong. I think, understanding the betrayal, it could make Po Fong's life much more complicated. She would return to San Francisco to find herself in a difficult situation."

"What proof do you have?"

Pajaro chuckled. "You won't like it much, I'm afraid."

"If you think it's going to take care of Po Fong, I would like to know."

"Ah Wong's hand. I removed it after Sandro killed him at Widow Creek. I brought it to Chinatown and had Po Fong's tong symbol tattooed on it. His father's symbol was removed. It would cause his father a deep and grave insult to find out about his son's betrayal. The tong tattoo is deeply sacred. It will be sufficient proof."

I drew in a deep breath. "His *hand*?"

"As you recall, he no longer needed it," Pajaro said dryly. "I have it stored in something that should keep it presentable for a long time. If I need it."

I looked over at his saddlebag and wondered about the thickly wrapped bundle that was inside. I did not have any desire to see it.

"Would Ah Wong's father kill Po Fong?" I asked.

"I doubt it. I have a feeling this man will enjoying playing with her and torturing her through business and people. Death means nothing to them, as I think you've seen." Amigo stopped to eat some grass. I stared at Pajaro, picturing him hacking off Ah Wong's hand. Then I no longer wanted to think about it. I pulled on Amigo's reins but to no avail.

"How long has Po Fong been after you?"

"One year."

"So when Chin came along, you knew all about her mother."

"Yes. And Po Fong was bound to hear about the heir and start her own search."

"What will happen now, Pajaro? With her?"

"She will follow us. She knows I will protect the heir. And she will not stop."

❧ 19 ❧

WE QUICKENED OUR PACE OUTSIDE OF Marysville and began the slow climb into the mountains toward Remington River. Po Fong was likely going in the same direction.

Pajaro led us along a rarely traveled route to Remington River. We descended from a ridge and entered a narrow gorge with a lovely river lined with large boulders and dense trees. The scents of wild mint and pine were soothing. Amigo pulled over to nibble at the tender greens along the banks, and I was forever steering him away from his intended meal. We rode along the river for the better part of a day and stopped in a thicket of trees. Hasten Peak made its first up-close appearance, and I was elated to see my old friend. We ate a cold meal of jerky and dry tack. A fire would have given away our location. Darkness quickly took over.

Pajaro sat back and stretched his legs. His expression was relaxed although it was still odd to see his appearance so altered.

"Your disguise worked well. I didn't know it was you."

"Lorenzo was very amused, I can tell you," laughed Pajaro.

He craned his neck and pointed to Hasten Peak. "A familiar sight for you. After all your travels. What would your explorer make of this place, Mariah?"

"I think he would be pleased. I saw two or three bucks as we rode today. Captain Lewis was always writing about the game he saw. But I think I understand something about him that I hadn't thought about before. For all his grand descriptions, he was looking for opportunity for settlers. I wonder if, to him, the beauty was an afterthought."

"Eh, Dios. A complicated man. You think about him with great regard, Mariah. I do not imagine he would have disappointed you. I am sure he saw and appreciated great beauty. Pity the man who cannot see it when it is right in front of him."

After a pause, he added, "I have missed your readings, Mariah."

"Then you shall have one."

I fetched *The Journals* from my saddle pack and opened the book to the tenth chapter.

"This is where the party has come to what they believe is the headwaters of the Missouri. When they come to find out that they haven't found the headwaters, Lewis names the river Maria's River, after Miss Maria Wood," I told Pajaro.

The whole of my party to a man, except myself, were fully persuaided that this river was the Missouri but being fully of opinion that it was neither the main stream, nor that which it would be advisable for us to take, I determined to give it a name, and in honor of Miss Maria Wood, called it Maria's River. it is true that the hue of the waters of this turbulent and troubled stream but illy comport with the pure, celestial virtues and amiable qualifications of that lovely fair one. But, on the other hand, it is a noble river, one destined to become, in my opinion, an object of contention between the two great powers of America and Great Britain with respect to the adjustment of the northwesterly boundary of the former. And that it will become one of the most interesting branches of the Missouri in a commercial point of view I have but little doubt as it abounds with animals of the fur kind, and most probably furnishes a safe and direct communication to that productive country of valuable furs exclusively enjoyed at present by the subjects of His Britannic Majesty. In addition to which, it passes through a rich, fertile, and on the most beautifully picturesque countries that I ever beheld, through the wide expanse of which innumerable herds of living animals are seen, its borders garnished with one continued garden of roses, while its lofty and open forests are the habitation of myriads of the feathered tribes who salute the ear of the passing traveler with their wild and simple yet sweet and cheerful melody.

Pajaro smiled. "You see? He is aware of the beauty."

"Perhaps," I agreed.

"Your explorer did not seem to want to take more than his fair share. Is that not right? At least this is what the padres taught us in school. Though the padres may have wished to make a point about generosity and stewardship, with the story of the exploration of the West, that may not have been exactly the truth. For the padres, it was their way to be generous and not greedy. But they knew it was not the way of most."

"The padres?"

"I was educated at a mission school. We had a lesson or two about Lewis and Clark." Pajaro grinned. "Oh, yes. I was a school boy once. Lorenzo attended for a short time as well. Sandro did not. By the time he was old enough, we had moved out of the mission."

"I am sorry about Sandro, Pajaro. Truly."

"I thank you, but do not be sorry, Mariah. Sandro did not want to give up this life. Lorenzo and I were already making our plans. Sandro could not listen, did not want to listen. For him, it was the excitement that drove him. I wish it were otherwise, but my youngest brother had different ideas about life. I could not deter him."

"What plans do you and Lorenzo have?"

"That has yet to be decided. And you? What about you, Mariah?"

"I am writing about my experiences. Starting with leaving St. Joseph. I worried that I would never leave Po Fong's house. Who would know what happened to me?"

"What have you written about a man like me, I wonder?" he chuckled.

Our eyes met and he studied my face. Our night together and the confusion of feelings when I had assumed he was dead troubled me.

"I will hope for an ending in which you find your Beyond and happiness there as well," he said.

"No doubt it will be a surprise and with no little danger in the process," I said, trying to sound light and without worry.

He said softly, "I always meant to return to you. But I would understand if you did not believe it. I have not been the kind of man I wanted to be for you. It would make sense if you have not thought of me in that way."

"I don't understand everything that you do, Pajaro. I think that your ways may not be entirely wholesome. But you tell me that you are trying to help others. I cannot condone the method, but I should like to know if the results are worth it."

"So the bandit must show validation?" Pajaro sighed. "You seem to be looking for something in me to distrust. Is that it?"

I started to speak but couldn't find the words.

"I'll tell you about a man, Mariah. Then you decide. His name is Gallardo. An old man but proud of his rancho in the valley. He lived there thirty-five years. He grew nuts, raised cattle, and had a dairy. The state told him that his holdings were in question because of a poorly drawn survey map from decades ago. He was required to have the land surveyed again, pay a court fee to execute a new title, and arrange for a court appearance. All these things would require fifty dollars. Because his holdings were in question, he could not broker his stock with the cattlemen's association. He could not sell his milk. For fifty dollars, though, he was told all would be settled. Gallardo came to me and asked my opinion. He did not have the money but considered selling part of his rancho to cover the fees. This has been the case for many like him. Forced to sell off little by little, they lose their holdings simply because they cannot afford to fight for them. I visited the surveyor's office and spoke to the man Gallardo thought to hire. He told me that the court recorder regularly took bribes from state officials to 'misplace' documents and, in doing so, delay the process even longer. I learned that a packet of money from the state, just for this purpose, would be delivered to this court recorder on a stage out of Marysville. So, yes, I stopped the stage. Yes, I took the money from the packet and sent the packet empty, other than a note complimenting the court reporter on his *efficiency*. I gave Gallardo the fifty dollars and arranged a court appearance to take legal claim on his property. As he prepared to travel to Sacramento, he was sent a message from the court saying that his hearing was postponed indefinitely due to a full schedule. I went to Sacramento and discovered that Gallardo's name had not been removed from the schedule, and in not appearing, he had forfeited his claim. With the rest of the money intended for the court recorder's bribe, I went to the same court recorder, bribed him, and got Gallardo back on the court schedule. I escorted Gallardo to court to act as his translator. But I did not introduce myself as such initially, allowing the proceedings to occur in English. The court would not know that I could understand every word they said. I wanted to see what would happen. Gallardo's name had been removed from the schedule again. I walked down to the court recorder's office and, let's just say, *persuaded* him to return Gallardo's scheduled time to the list. The old man got his land back, Mariah. He will die and be buried on the land he worked. That, for me, is enough."

§

Two days later, we neared Widow Creek. As we emerged from the forest, I felt the familiarity of the road that turned onto the meadow. Hasten Peak rose above and was bathed in gold light. The meadow was still flooded. As we rode along, I discovered how the Whites had adapted to the water, which made the road impassable to the stage-coaches. From behind the trees, intending to stay out of sight, we saw Ed White poling a small, flat boat across the water. He was ferrying passengers from one end of the swamp to the other. A stagecoach from Remington River met them on the east side and continued the journey to town. I remembered that it was Burke who had suggested getting a boat. We slipped away past Widow Creek and continued on to Remington River.

Once we reached town, Pajaro stopped at The White Lily Hotel and had a short conversation with a man who sat on a bench in front. When Pajaro returned, his face was dark and troubled.

"She was here. A short time ago, too. She hired two guides who know the area well. I have a feeling she knows exactly where to go. And that worries me greatly. Somebody has betrayed me. I fear they are headed to the Cañon where Lorenzo and the heir wait." He mounted his horse and said, "Can you manage more travel, Mariah? You are not obligated to continue. You may stay here, if you wish. There will be trouble ahead. Of that I am sure."

I want to be with you, I meant to say. *My fear is that I will never see you again.*

Instead, I said, "I should like to see this place called the Cañon."

He nodded and jerked the reins. We headed back out of town on a route northward and into the hills.

At first, the ride was easy following the main road until we turned onto a forest path leading into the hills above Remington River. Then we started climbing steeply through areas with large granite boulders and small, clear lakes. There was a lake for every mile we rode. We stopped at one of the lakes and made camp for the night. The sky turned purple in the last minutes of the day and the moon rose, looking like a potato slice. Had I not had considerable concern about what might transpire the next day at the Cañon, I might have felt the beauty of this place with a deeper reverie.

At dawn, we began an ascent through a series of switchbacks to the top of a ridge. At the very top, we rested. My heart stopped. The view was of Hasten Peak, but from a side I had never seen before. Below was a narrow valley that ended right at the base of the mountain, very similar to Martin's meadow. We descended from the ridge and rode out on the meadow. We came to the end of the meadow and dipped into thick forest. All at once, our progress was halted, for in front of us was a hillside of boulders and fallen trees. "We'll go around to the south. There will be a passage there," said Pajaro.

Sure enough, there was a narrow path leading through the rocks upward. We reached the top of the rocky slope and Pajaro signaled to stop. He got off his horse and disappeared behind the rocks.

The horses were tethered to a makeshift hitching post in a clearing surrounded by aspens. The air was crisp and thin. Sunlight flickered off the leaves and the gushing water cascading between the rocks. On any other day, I would have wished to stop and enjoy the scenery. We emerged from the trees into a narrow valley lined with boulders piled one hundred feet high. At the far end, there was a series of cabins clustered near the opening in the rocks. Rising above the valley, boulders, and cabins was Hasten Peak. It was so close, I thought I could touch it.

"This is the Cañon?" I asked.

"Yes. The mining operation is over there behind the cabins. Down below, in the valley, is the rest of the land. A large, fertile spread good for grazing, full of lumber," he said. "It would make a fine ranch someday if worked hard and properly. It is the mine that Po Fong is most interested in."

We walked toward one of the cabins.

Lorenzo appeared on the porch.

"Much has happened, brother," said Pajaro, clasping his brother's shoulders in greeting. I hesitated at the doorway until Lorenzo extended his hand to me and smiled. "You have had a long journey, Mariah. Come inside and rest."

The cabin was roughly furnished with handmade furniture and a river rock hearth, and it smelled of sweat, smoke, and tobacco. Lorenzo brought some chairs to the hearth where a small fire provided warmth. Pajaro recounted to his brother all the events that had brought us to the Cañon.

Lorenzo whistled. "You think Po Fong will come here?"

"She hired guides, and I think our location has been given away. Have the preparations we spoke of been made, Lorenzo?"

Lorenzo nodded. "Yes. There are lookouts on the high points. She will be seen well before she gets here, but it will not give us much time, Pajaro. Why does she follow you here? What is her purpose?"

"She seems to think there is something to be gained by coming here. She knows about the heir. His life is now in danger. Although to what end his death will serve her, I do not know. The title will never be hers no matter how much time she spends in court. Other than sheer revenge or spite, there is no other reason for her pursuit."

"I don't know why we have not put a bullet in this woman before," said Lorenzo.

"Killing her might solve one problem yet pose another one. It is what her tong will do as revenge to *us* that worries me. I have no interest in watching every shadow and movement for the rest of my life. As for Po Fong, she will be made to understand a few things, and, if I am right, she will no longer bother us. That is my desire. When we need to make other decisions, I will know," said Pajaro.

"Decisions for what?" I asked.

The brothers exchanged looks, and then Pajaro turned to me. "Come to the window. I want to show you something."

I followed him and saw that he pointed to a wall of rocks behind the cabin. "There is a shallow cave behind those rocks. You will see the entrance once you get close. When I tell you to run, go as fast as you can to those rocks. You will have company, too."

I heard a noise like a clacking of sticks behind me. I turned to see Bird, snapping his bill, perched on the shoulder of Sing.

"Sing!" I exclaimed.

Pajaro drew Sing forward and put his hands on the boy's shoulders. "When you run, you will take Sing with you."

I looked questioningly at Pajaro and Lorenzo. They sat back down. Sing went to the fire, and Bird hopped around the stones and finally found a place on the mantle above the hearth. It was then that we heard the first shots. "She is here. Those three shots are the warning that she is coming up the mountain." said Pajaro. "It won't be long now."

"Why are all these men up here, Pajaro?" I asked.

"When it became inevitable that Po Fong would not rest until she had the Purisima mine, I made a plan. I have a few trusted friends. They came to help make preparations. If she is willing to drop this claim on the Cañon and leave peacefully, I will be satisfied. If she decides otherwise, the mine will be destroyed. It will no longer be useful to her unless she wants to invest resources in clearing it again. Along with the problems she will face from the tongs, I think she will forget everything up here," he said. "But just to be sure, there are explosives set up and down the gorge. I will give the signal to blow it up. Two shots. Then you and Sing must run to the cave."

"If the mine is so important to her, why not just destroy it now?" I asked.

"I would like to avoid it. For the heir's sake. It is a rich mine and would bring him great rewards. I will give her a chance to back down, leave, and forget this pursuit," answered Pajaro.

Lorenzo stood up and stretched. "I doubt that woman will give up, brother."

We waited several hours until footsteps on the porch announced Po Fong's arrival. Through the window, we could see a group of Pajaro's men surrounding her and two other men who I recognized from Remington River. *Guides probably bought for a high price to bring her here*, I thought.

"Sing! Go to the back room and wait. I will call for you shortly." Sing followed Pajaro's request and took Bird with him.

Pajaro looked out the window and smiled. "You know? I have to admire that woman. She is hard to escape from."

Po Fong barged in the door and glided in her odd manner across the floor despite her heavy boots. "Mr. Mendonca, I truly hope that I never have to ride through the mountains again. You have caused me a great deal of trouble and so needlessly. Why do you persist in raising obstacles?"

"Because, Madame Fong, I dislike you and your ways. As much discomfort as I can cause you is to my liking."

"The discomfort is only making me impatient."

"And it is the same with me," Pajaro replied. "I would like you to meet someone." Pajaro called to Sing. With Bird on his arm, Sing entered the room. Po Fong glared at him.

"Sing has an interesting story," said Pajaro. "His grandfather, Manuel Gonzalvo, was the original owner of the Cañon. Gonzalvo's son, Manuelito, married a Chinese woman, with whom he had Sing. Unfortunately, Sing was orphaned. He remained in Remington River, cared for by friends. If you know the wording of the deed as well as I, Madame Fong, you know that it specifically mentions the heir. The president of Mexico personally amended the document, for he knew there was a boy somewhere in California. And here he is. You cannot take legal possession of this land, even for a gambling debt, despite what you may want. There is nothing but a long, fruitless court battle ahead."

Po Fong dropped her arms to her side, fists tightly balled. "I have much experience with the courts, Mr. Mendonca. I will lodge a challenge and fight it."

"That is your right. But I assure you, this deed is irrevocable. I have made sure of it. It is unfortunate you had to make this long journey to find it out."

The Chinese woman, who up until now had been tightly wound and consumed with anger, took a breath and composed herself.

"Mr. Mendonca, you seem to have no worry that these assertions may bring into question many of your legal transactions, such as this one. You cannot for a moment think that this will not be challenged. This boy's lineage will be questioned. You will need to produce evidence of his parentage. Without a legal guardian, how will the deed be administered? By you, Mr. Mendonca? That would be an interesting story. You will be accused of unduly influencing a boy for the purposes of maintaining control over this lucrative property. Oh, the court costs will be staggering, but, more to the point, you would be in dire straits. Better to let me simply have the deed, and it will save you much trouble."

Pajaro patted Sing's shoulder. "The boy's lineage can be proven. His birth was recorded at the mission in San Francisco. His father made sure of this. Your question of a legal guardian is a good one, though. I thought very carefully about this. A year ago, a good friend of mine agreed to adopt the boy. It was necessary to keep this arrangement secret while we worked out the details. In the meantime, madam, you had begun your relentless pursuit for the Cañon.

"Oh. I have forgotten," added Pajaro, reaching into his pocket. "The deed. This is what you want, no doubt."

The color drained from Po Fong's face as she took the document and began reading. Pajaro nodded and continued. "As you can see, there are some minor alterations in the deed. I needed to do this so that it would remain in safekeeping within our courts. You see, chaos and tiresome court proceedings are a very good hiding place. Of course, all things can be changed, and I am in the process of making the required adjustments to the document. But in this case, the governor of California himself has authenticated it. It is rather humorous, don't you think? Mired in long arguments and full court schedules, it languished. However, can you read to whom the land is ceded? The judge was amused. The governor was not." Pajaro looked at me, and I suddenly realized that the document in her hands had been the one that he had switched out on the stagecoach those many weeks ago. The document that had been recorded as belonging to Pajaro Mendonca of Marysville.

Po Fong laughed as she read it. "This is absurd, and you know it. It is a simple matter of having another judge discover your ruse and set matters straight. That was pointless."

"Unless I needed time to find the heir and secure his standing. And settle his adoption. The delay was very helpful."

Po Fong stood up slowly. "Where is this good friend of yours who adopted the boy?"

"If it is your intention to make threats to this person, save your breath. My friend, the one who adopted the boy, died. Strange, he perished after helping to save your daughter." My mouth went dry. I could hardly believe my ears. The Old Mandarin had taken in Sing?

Po Fong smirked. "Very clever to have a Chinese adopt the boy. Less suspicious that way. You still have a problem with the title laws, Mr. Mendonca. If the heir is a minor, he cannot take possession of the land until he is of legal age. From the looks of this boy, that is a long time. Anything could happen to him."

Po Fong's eyes ran up and down Sing in a way that made my blood run cold. Pajaro grinned. "That worried me, too. Until I discovered the will."

"What will?" asked Po Fong uneasily.

"Zhao made a will," replied Pajaro. "He was no fool. Your reputation caused him to make plans for the boy. Zhao knew someone who would look after the boy if something happened to him. Someone he trusted and admired. Someone with full rights to administer the deed for him until Sing reaches legal age."

Po Fong narrowed her eyes.

"Zhao also made sure that the guardian is a legal citizen of the United States. There's only one person in this room who can claim that, Madame Fong."

All eyes turned to me.

"I knew nothing about this," I said.

"Zhao did not want you to be in danger, Mariah," said Pajaro. "He asked me not to tell you until it was necessary.

"And one more thing, madam," Pajaro added. "Possibly this should be more of a concern than anything else. A detail that you seemed to have overlooked. A detail that, I think, if it were revealed, would cause much excitement in your life once you return to San Francisco."

Po Fong sat down and folded her hands in her lap. "You have thought of everything, Mr. Mendonca. But a good businessman always leaves room to bargain, just in case. Please tell me about this excitement you have planned for me."

Pajaro's saddlebag was on the floor near the hearth. He walked over to it, opened it, removed the thickly wrapped bundle that he'd carefully stowed, and brought it over to the table. He untied the bundle to reveal a glass jar filled with liquid. The liquid was murky, but there was no mistaking what was floating in it. He opened the jar and placed the hand of Ah Wong on the wrapping. The liquid saturated the cloth with a heavy, slightly sweet smell. The tattoo on the wrist, of the sun and the snake, was visible, though marred by the puckered tissue.

"Ah Wong's father would be greatly distressed to see this. Don't you agree, madam?" asked Pajaro.

There was a long silence.

"He would never need to see the hand, madam. You have my word. But you must go and forget this claim. It is finished," said Pajaro. "Leave us in peace."

Then, in a movement that took everyone by surprise, Po Fong leaped across the room, drawing a pistol from beneath her coat. She aimed it directly at Sing.

I screamed. "Don't hurt him. He has done nothing!"

There was a flurry of black wings as Bird descended onto Po Fong, pecking and clawing at her. She fired one shot into the air, missing Bird. Then a second shot, which went into the hearth. Bird kept up a relentless attack, and she dropped the gun as she fled from the cabin.

Pajaro cursed. "That was the signal. For the explosives. You foolish woman! Dios. Run, Mariah! Take Sing! To the cave."

Po Fong was staggering around in front of the cabin holding her bleeding head as we ran out. Pajaro and Lorenzo were close behind. We ran across the meadow, past the cabin, Sing clinging to my hand, Bird flying above us. We reached the cave and dragged Sing in behind us. Po Fong made it to the entrance of the cave just as we heard the first of the explosions. The cave shook violently, causing rocks to fall on us. I shielded Sing and prayed that Bird had flown high enough to escape. More explosions followed shortly thereafter. Then it was quiet.

REMINGTON RIVER
2015

℘ 20 ℘

THEY WERE LONG-DISTANCE HIKERS COMING OFF the trail and headed toward Remington River to check mail, make phone calls, and resupply. They followed the highway east, staying well off the blacktop. Semis roared by as well as gigantic fifth-wheel trailers that looked like small mansions. Trucks towed ski boats. Cars carried kayaks strapped to the tops. Many were headed to the blue waters of Lake Alma. Or they were passing through on their way up to Hasten Peak National Park. It was a four-mile hike into town. Soon, shuffling along the dusty shoulder, they caught a glimpse of the town of Remington River in the distance. The first business one encountered, coming from the West as the hikers did, was Pleasant Pie Bakers. There was no question: the hikers would stop and share a slice of berry pie as they continued on into town.

The forest service headquarters was across the road from the pie shop. A little farther along, they passed the small airfield where the smoke jumpers were stationed. A Chinese restaurant called Lucky Gardens was closed, but the parking lot in front was full of tables and tents for a flea market. Boylston's Service Station was separated from

Lucky Gardens by a vacant lot, where a pile of tree stumps waited to be chopped for firewood.

It was midsummer and the heat rose up from the pavement despite the early hour. It had been nearly four weeks since the hikers had walked on a paved road. The town was just waking up, and the two wouldn't stay long enough to see it go to sleep that evening. They found the post office and carefully stowed their mail away for later.

They shopped at Mike's Market and filled their packs with supplies for the next leg of their hike. Passing by a sign that read "Museum One Block," they looked at each other, then followed the sign down a side street.

"It's a long shot," said one of the hikers, a young man in his twenties whose hair had been trimmed with the scissors from his pocketknife.

The other hiker, a girl around the same age wearing a bandanna and cutoffs, said, "I know. But I'm super curious. Whatever it is we found, it looks old."

They walked down a dirt road surrounded by old, rundown buildings that looked like a soundstage for an old TV western. At the far end, the museum sign hung above a porch.

Starhawk, the museum curator, watched the two hikers approach her door, laden with packs and the worn-out but wild look of those walking the long trail. In her early years, she had been a flower child of the sixties, adopting the name Starhawk until she married a man who insisted she return to her given name, Nancy. When her husband died, she dropped Nancy.

Starhawk liked to say that Remington River "found" her. She was driving north, heading for Bend, Oregon. After decades of living the urban lifestyle, she downsized, decluttered, and headed north. Her pension was excellent and she had nothing to tie her to the city. When engine trouble forced her to stay in Remington River, she checked into a motel and explored the town.

She liked what she saw. Hasten Peak rose above the town, its snowcapped crown against the blue sky like the palm of a hand holding a dollop of vanilla icing. Tall trees abounded along the streets. It seemed like every building and house had a huge pine towering above it.

People were friendly and said "good morning" as she walked along. She bought a cup of coffee at the Pine Cone Drive-In and sat watching a boy on horseback carefully cross the main street and disappear into a meadow.

Starhawk walked the entire main street that first day, back and forth, and nearly missed the dirt alley on the other side of the bridge. A rickety wooden walkway ran along a series of older buildings. There was an old livery that still had horseshoes nailed around the door. At the end the alley, she saw an old storefront with a sign hanging off the porch that read "Museum." Leaves and dirt piled up in front of the door. It looked like it hadn't been opened in ages. She peered through the window and saw display cases with an assortment of objects, but the glass was filthy and she could not see much. The museum appeared to have been abandoned. The door was locked and there was no sign of anybody about. She walked behind the museum and found that the rear of the museum shared a stand of aspens with the sheriff's department headquarters. Starhawk thought she might inquire here about the museum. She opened the glass door to the sheriff's office and met a cool blast of air conditioning. A very tall woman wearing green slacks, black leather boots, and a thick coat with a sheriff's department patch on the shoulder looked up. Around her waist was a heavy belt with a flashlight, nightstick, and pistol. Atop her head sat a campaign hat that met the top of her eyebrows. Looped over her shoulder was a long, blond braid. Standing in front of her were two teenaged boys slumped against the wall, hands in pockets, glaring at the floor.

"You bet you're going to pick it up," said the woman, who towered over the boys.

One of the boys rolled his eyes and made a sound. The other one shot him a look.

The woman bent over and thrust her face directly in front of the eye roller. "I didn't quite hear what you said, Jimbo. But I think you said you're available all weekend. Isn't that what he said, Kyle?" She looked at the other boy who heaved a deep sigh. The two boys were handed large garbage bags and trash grabbers. The woman opened the front door for them. Starhawk stepped aside to let them pass.

"I have nothing better to do today than drive up and down watching you guys. Make me proud," she said. "Up and down the street, remember? I don't want to see a gum wrapper left behind."

The boys walked outside and Starhawk could see them jostling each other, arguing loudly. Then they stopped. A discarded soda can and a paper bag needed picking up.

The tall woman put her hands on her hips and shook her head. She was in her late twenties with fair skin and light blue eyes. Her expression, as she stared after the boys, was one of guarded affection.

"I'm wondering if you could help me. Could I talk to the sheriff?" asked Starhawk.

"You're talking to her. Are you having some kind of trouble?"

Starhawk grinned. "Oh, there's no trouble at all. My name is Starhawk."

It was the sheriff's turn to try not looking surprised. "Etoile Miller," she replied and offered her hand to Starhawk.

"Those boys look like they've got their work cut out for them."

Etoile laughed. "That's what you get for partying it up down by the river and leaving a pile of chicken bones, chip bags, and beer cans. A bear got into the mess and is now roaming around the outskirts of town looking for more. Now, what can I do for you?" asked the sheriff.

"That museum? What's happening with it? It looks abandoned."

"It is," replied Etoile. "We haven't had anyone there in a year."

The sheriff gave her the phone number of the county historical society and suggested she call them. Starhawk had no idea that this phone call would change her life.

It was less a job and more of an all-consuming passion. Starhawk had become keenly interested in local history once she'd taken over the curator job. The two hikers couldn't have found anyone more enthusiastic to hear about their discovery. She smoothed her gray hair and hiked up her pink-and-purple-paisley parachute pants and waited. There was no other reason for folks to walk down this street other than the museum.

"Welcome to the museum. My name is Starhawk. Have a look around, and I can try to answer any questions you might have."

Starhawk was accustomed to the hikers who passed through during the summer. They seemed like fish out of water when they came off the trail. The young man smiled and stepped forward.

"We found something and wondered if anybody around here might know what it is. Seems historical, I guess. Old, at any rate. We took some pictures of it," he said. "I'm Pete and this is Shelly."

Starhawk stood aside to let them in the entryway of the museum.

Shelly dug into the pocket of her pants and produced a phone. She brought out a cable and looked around. "I'm not sure how much battery I have left."

Starhawk pointed to an outlet behind the counter, and Shelly bent over and plugged in her phone. She swiped across the screen and brought up the first picture, then showed it to Starhawk.

"It looks like a stone," said Starhawk.

Shelly swiped through the series of photos and Starhawk pursed her lips. "You know what? I think we can see these better if we bring them up on a larger screen."

After uploading the photos to her computer, Starhawk, along with Shelly and Pete, huddled around the monitor.

The first image was of a series of stone markers, or carved boulders, nearly obscured by a low, thick growth of manzanita. The second image showed the bushes pushed aside, and the stones were now much more visible. There were three, lined up side by side, half buried in the ground with carvings on them. The next images were of the carving detail on each stone.

Weathered to near smoothness, the carvings were difficult to read.

"Well, I haven't a clue as to what these are. Graves, maybe? I'd sure like to see the writing. Hard to see from these photos. Were you able to make out anything?" Starhawk asked, turning to look at Pete and Shelly.

"From what I could see, there was a line of characters—like Chinese writing?—on each of the stones. Those seemed to be carved very deep," said Pete. "Above the line of characters, I could make out a few numbers, like dates. And there were some words. Those were in English. They looked like parts of names. But those weren't carved as deeply, so I guess they just wore away."

Starhawk returned her focus to the images. "Where is this place?"

"It's a few hundred yards off the trail. You'd never know it was there, though. We got lost for a bit and found ourselves in this little valley surrounded by granite. The brush was really thick and we bushwhacked back to the trail when we stumbled on these rocks," said Shelly. "That compass saved us. Right, Pete?"

"Yeah. Way better than GPS. Super easy to get turned around up there."

"Do you think you could point it out on a map? You say it's just off the trail? How far from here?"

"This was Wednesday. That's the day I took the pictures," said Shelly. "Today is . . ."

"Friday," prompted Starhawk.

"So not more than fifteen miles, I figure. I can show you on my map."

Pete produced a deeply creased and well-used map and placed it on the counter. "Right about here, I think. We were looking for a stream. There's the stream, which we found after getting lost. This is where we left the trail because we had directions to the stream. But those directions weren't right. Here's the GPS coordinates on the directions, useless to us. You won't find the stream, but you will find the stones," laughed Pete. "The compass was more reliable."

Starhawk studied the topographical map for a moment and made a note of the quadrangle. "Look, there's a dirt road near there. Not like I'm going to hike all the way up there. But I can get close. Maybe I'll go up there and have a look."

Pete and Shelly thanked Starhawk for her help. They gave her their email addresses and asked politely if she would write to them if she found out anything.

After they left, she opened a cabinet and took out the forest service map for the area. She found the quadrangle of the area in question and saw that an old logging road did indeed cut across the trail a few miles below where the stones were located. It was possible the stones were the markers of some poor soul's final resting place. It was not unusual to run across old graves in this part of Northern California. The numerous mines that dotted the mountains were notoriously dangerous. Miners were buried on the spot with crude memorials constructed of whatever materials were on hand. The same applied to trappers, hunters, loggers, and the many individuals who came to California on the old wagon train trails: where you fell was you were laid to rest.

Yet, these were no crude memorials. The shapes of the markers showed that somebody had worked the stones to smoothness. A great deal of effort had gone into these objects, and Starhawk was curious as to who had made them, if they were grave markers, to whom they were dedicated.

Sheriff Etoile Miller had two reports to finish. One involved a series of vandalisms at Remington River's community park in which graffiti had been seared into the wooden picnic tables. She couldn't figure out what the graffiti said because whoever had used the blow torch had gotten carried away, leaving scorches instead of statements. The other report involved a domestic abuse case, and she was avoiding this one. Etoile had been born and raised in Remington River so she knew just about everybody in town. This particular case involved a couple she had known her whole life. And, after dealing with the incident, they had become strangers to her. She was glad to see Starhawk standing in the doorway. It was a welcome distraction.

Starhawk pulled a chair to the opposite side of the desk and sat down.

"Can you get away for a few hours tomorrow?" asked Starhawk.

Etoile smiled. "As a matter of fact I can. What's in it for me?"

Starhawk laughed. "The chance to spend the day looking for some unusual rock formations way up in the mountains."

She filled Etoile in on the stones and showed her Shelly's pictures, now printed out on photo paper.

"They don't look like rocks that just happened to be there and got carved. They look placed, don't you think?" Etoile suggested, noting the similar sizes of the rocks and the even spacing between them.

"Seems that way. The writing is probably all worn off, but I'd like to see for myself."

"So I should be prepared to hike?" asked Etoile.

"If I can do it, you can do it," replied Starhawk.

Etoile nodded. "I'm game. See you around eight tomorrow morning?"

§

The last of the snow had melted away, Etoile noted as she drove up the dirt road the next day. It would have been impossible to make progress on the road in anything but her high-clearance, four-wheel-drive truck. The way was narrow, rocky, and deeply rutted but they managed to get within a mile of where Pete and Shelly had gone off the trail. They parked and consulted the map. Using a compass, Starhawk indicated their starting point, an area they could now see was heavy with downed timber.

Etoile stepped out of the truck and stretched. It was mid-July, but the mornings were still brisk at this elevation. The scent of sugar pine was strong and a flawless blue sky spread overhead. Hasten Peak, with a jaunty cap of snow, hovered above them.

The two women grinned at each other and set off.

Climbing up and over logs proved slow going, and Etoile was glad they had both brought hiking poles for stability. They came to a spot where a rocky ledge rose above their heads nearly sixty feet, and they skirted along the base of it. Finally, they found the trail used by Shelly and Pete. Walking along the trail was much easier, and the track was dotted with the boot prints of hikers.

They couldn't count on Pete and Shelly's directions, for they had diverted off the trail and weren't exactly sure where that had happened. It would be trial and error. After an hour of following false leads off the trail and then returning to it, Starhawk spotted some broken branches hanging from a dead pine, still green at the point of the break.

"Those look like they were snapped recently. I'll bet they went through there, Etoile." Making their way past the broken branches, they snaked around the thick brush for ten minutes and were rewarded with signs of cleared-off manzanita, below which the three rocks were visible. Pete and Shelly had described the area as a small, narrow gorge with high walls of granite. It was indeed as described. Etoile walked beyond the stones and announced there must have been a landslide, seeing as the end of the gorge was choked with rocks. Meanwhile, Starhawk crouched by the manzanita and cleared more of the brush away. Each stone was about the size of a large watermelon, rounded on the top and half buried in the ground.

"If they are really graves, we should be careful not to disturb much, Starhawk," said Etoile, sitting down before the stones. She bent over and ran her hand over the stones. "The girl was right. The lettering along the bottom is much clearer than the writing on top" Starhawk stood up and turned slowly around, getting her bearings.

"What was up here? There's no mine on the map. There's really nothing around. I mean, it is gorgeous. But why pick this spot?"

"It looks as if, before that landslide, this gorge went on farther. See how the walls continue on past it?" Etoile said.

"Probably could see what's beyond if we climbed up there. But my mountain goat days are long past."

Etoile laughed. "Yep. Mine, too. Too bad we can't fly over it and see what's beyond."

Starhawk opened her backpack and brought out sheets of parchment paper and a box of charcoal.

"What's that for?" asked Etoile.

"I'm going to make a relief of the stones."

Etoile watched Starhawk carefully cover the writing with the paper and gingerly run the charcoal stick over the writing on each of the stones. In relief, it was possible to make out some of the carving.

The first rock had a name, which was hard to read, and the date 1871. Below the date, the words *Mas Alla* were clearly visible. Below that was a line of what appeared to be Chinese characters. The second rock also had a name and the date 1859. The lines below the date were identical to the first rock. The third and last rock bore a drawing with the date 1851 above the same two lines.

They walked carefully around the stones and found nothing else. Etoile pulled the manzanita back over the stones, covering them up completely. "If they are grave markers, we should leave them in peace. Somebody took a great of deal of effort to place them here. It must have a special meaning," she said.

Starhawk spread out the sheets of paper on her lap. "I think if I can put these on a light box, it might help to decipher the letters. The Chinese characters are pretty clear. I can get these translated. If we only knew why this place was picked, we'd probably have a better clue as to what is written on the rocks."

They retraced their steps back to the trail and returned to the truck.

"Drop me at Sam's," said Starhawk. "He might be able to help translate this."

Sam Kong owned the small general store on the other side of the bridge in Remington River. The store had been in his family for generations. Locals were pretty sure that Sam did not need to run the store on a day-to-day basis. He'd made a tidy sum with choice property purchases over the years. Sam's wasn't as big or sophisticated as Mike's Market, but it was still a favorite among the locals. Holding court every day behind the counter, Sam Kong knew everything going on in Remington River. The store hardly made a profit but remained a fixture in town—if only for Sam's personality and good selection of bait.

Starhawk opened the door to Sam's and bells jingled. The familiar smells of the store greeted her: buttered popcorn from a machine bought from the old movie theater, the rich dirt in which Sam's bait lived until skewered on a hook, yesterday's coffee waiting to be refreshed, and the lingering aroma of incense from a little shrine on a shelf above the counter.

"Not here for bait, Sam," she said.

"I know you have no interest in fishing, Starhawk. And I don't have the Sunday papers yet. So I have a feeling that whatever you want is far more interesting than arguing with some fisherman from Sacramento about the price of night crawlers today," replied Sam.

Starhawk brought out the charcoal reliefs and spread them on the counter. Sam put on his glasses and examined them carefully. She told him about the rocks and how she was trying to figure out what they meant.

She pointed to the characters. "Is this something you understand?"

"It's Cantonese. Good thing it's not Mandarin. You'd be out of luck," said Sam.

He traced his finger along and read *"Niou Tzay.* Eternally grateful."

"What is that first word again?"

Sam repeated it. "Niou tzay. Very unusual words. And yet it is familiar. I've heard it before. I can't place it. Maybe I read it somewhere. Give it time and it'll come to me."

"What does it mean, Sam?"

"It means, or roughly translates to the Cantonese word for cowboy."

"Cowboy?"

"Oh, this is going to drive me crazy. I have heard this word somewhere. Where was it now?" Sam looked at the ceiling, eyes closed, trying to remember.

"None of the other words mean anything to you, Sam?"

Sam looked at the paper again. "No. I'm sorry."

"If you think of anything, you know where to find me," said Starhawk, gathering up her papers.

When she'd returned to the museum, Starhawk brought out her light box and plugged it in. She spread the reliefs over its surface. It helped. She could make out some of the lettering from the first rock. *P-A-J* from the first word. Then *M-E-N-D-O-N-C* from the second word. She wrote these down in a notebook. The second relief was of poorer quality. She could make out the initials *M.H.* followed by *P-E-N-N*. Maybe initials were carved instead of the full name to save space on the rock. She wrote these down as well and picked up the third relief. Placing it on the light table, Starhawk was surprised to see that the drawing from the third rock was that of a bird. The dates and the other words, mas alla, were quite clear now. Starhawk wondered what mas alla meant. Was it a word to indicate *Allah* with the *h* left off or misspelled? She turned to her computer and brought up Google. She typed in "mas alla." The first result was a YouTube video of a Gloria Estefan song called "Mas Alla. Spanish." The lyrics were below and Starhawk copied and pasted the lyrics into a Spanish-to-English translation site.

Mas alla translated to "beyond" in English.

≈ 21 ≈

IT WAS A FEW DAYS LATER that Sam Kong's memory was jarred enough for him to remember. He walked briskly to the museum and found Starhawk dusting a glass cabinet.

She stopped what she was doing and listened.

"About a year ago, a Chinese fellow came through town. He walked into the store. I think he was surprised to find another Chinese who had lived here so long. We started talking, and it turns out he was searching for information about one of his relatives. His great-great-grandfather, I believe. And he told me that his relative had been a landowner in the area. He was looking around up here trying to put together a story about the man. He had all kinds of pictures of his relative and lots of papers and files. I looked at a few of them. One picture was of his great-great-grandfather sitting on an Appaloosa pony in front of a barn. He was dressed in chaps and a big wide hat and was throwing a lasso. I told the fellow that the land around the barn could be anywhere, but the mountains behind look like the ones above the high meadow near Susanville. He was quite excited about this. The fellow wanted to write a book about the man. The book was going to be titled *Niou Tsay*."

"A Chinese cowboy?" asked Starhawk.

"Something like that," said Sam. "I directed him to the historical society in Susanville. Perhaps he discovered more information there."

"Do you remember what year the photograph was from? The one of the man on the horse?"

"I think 1870s. Maybe later."

Starhawk thanked Sam for his help and he went back to work.

The display case she had been dusting before Sam's arrival held a row of framed photographs of very old, handwoven grass baskets. They were crafted by the indigenous people of the Remington River area, the Maidu who were known for their beautiful and intricate basket designs. Over the years, the grass baskets had become highly collectible and few had remained in the Maidu Tribe. Starhawk opened the case and straightened one of the photographs. Memories stirred in her. The baskets in the photographs had disappeared for decades then mysteriously reappeared last year in Remington River. Their rarity and value were indisputable, and when the baskets suddenly vanished again, Starhawk began investigating the history behind them. She was able to unravel a complicated story that stretched back to the early 1900s, but not before a series of tragic events occurred involving the baskets. Since that time, she had become a thoughtful and diligent history sleuth not satisfied with merely describing the items in her displays. She wanted to provide a depth and richness to the stories behind the relics she had pieced together in the museum.

Three stones buried high in the mountains with a collection of half-revealed names, Chinese symbols about cowboys and gratitude, and the Spanish translation for *beyon*d. Starhawk felt the thrill of unanswered questions bubbling up. She was going to figure this out.

Starhawk placed a call to the Susanville Historical Society and arranged an appointment with the documents archivist.

The archivist was waiting and introduced herself as Penny Carter. She was in her early thirties with a short haircut that had a streak of pink running across the top. Penny had worked at the society for a year, and Starhawk knew her reputation as an ardent fan of local history. "So," said Penny, "you've come with a mystery of sorts. Where shall we start?"

"I'd like to see if you can tell me anything about these partial names on the stones. And if there is any connection with a Chinese cowboy from the 1870s or so. I seem to have a jumble of bits and pieces right now."

Starhawk had told her about the reliefs on the phone, and Penny thought they might start with them and see what they could find.

They went downstairs to the room where historical documents were stored. Some had been scanned and were available digitally. But many had been restored and were carefully preserved in long, narrow drawers that covered nearly three walls of one of the rooms.

Penny brought out her own light box and looked at each of the reliefs in turn, taking her time with a magnifying glass. Then she looked at the photographs of where the stones were located. "I appreciate the fact that the hikers only took photos and did not disturb the area. They sure do look like grave markers."

Penny went back to the first relief, placing it on the light box again. Starhawk noticed her fingers tremble as she traced the letters.

"My goodness," said Penny softly, almost to herself. "Could it be you after all this time?"

"Could it be who?" asked Starhawk.

"It would be too much of a coincidence. P-A-J and M-E-N-D-O-N-C," Penny spelled out the letters. "I think the name on this first stone is Pajaro Mendonca. That's just my gut reaction."

"Who is Pajaro Mendonca?" asked Starhawk.

Penny laughed and rubbed her eyes. "Oh, I just can't believe it. There are so many tall tales about the man. He was known as a bandit back in the 1840s to 1850s. He was allegedly mixed up in so many things that, if all of it was true, he couldn't possibly have had the time to do anything. He was a Californio, meaning he was of Spanish descent but born in California. He had two brothers who also participated with him in a variety of crimes. Youngest brother was killed in a shootout. Of Pajaro and the other brother, no more was heard about them after the 1850s or so. There are stories about them in old newspapers and one or two about Pajaro himself. But mostly sensational stories and probably little of it factual. I'm sure I can dig up a clipping or two in our archives. But one would have to take them with a grain of salt."

Penny looked at the relief wistfully. "I wonder what you were doing up there, Pajaro?"

"I've never heard of him. What a colorful figure he must have been, though," said Starhawk.

"Oh, he was colorful, but I suspect much of it was made up. He was probably just like anyone else. Same troubles. But he sure cuts a dashing figure in history."

"Would it be difficult to look at some of the clippings about this man Mendonca?" asked Starhawk. "You seem quite taken with him. Now I'm curious."

"Sure. Let's go over to the computer room and see what we can find. You know," quipped Penny conspiratorially to Starhawk. "Mendonca was reputedly the basis for the character of Zorro."

Starhawk sighed. "Guy Williams."

"Who?"

"The actor who played Zorro on television. I was gone on him when I was a kid. That was well before your time though."

Penny and Starhawk sat side by side poring over a variety of websites and archival material. Penny found an article about Mendonca stating he was wanted for robbing a stagecoach near Marysville. It was only a few words and there was no picture. Another article alleged that Mendonca and his brothers had had a shootout in Red Bluff and several men had been killed.

Then she found a wanted poster for the brothers. The picture on it showed three dark men glaring out from the screen. The tall, dark man in the middle was identified as Pajaro, and it described him as the leader. His large, shaggy moustache hid his mouth. The way his hat sloped over his face concealed his eyes. There was no mistaking the swagger. His thumb was hooked in an ornate leather belt dotted with silver medallions.

"He certainly looks the criminal type, doesn't he?"

Penny gazed at the photo. "Yes. But there is something else intriguing about him. A kind of intelligence. He would have been an interesting person to know. You read enough about these figures from the past and you can make up all kinds of tales about them. That's probably why I'm a historian: I'd rather live in the past, where truth is liberally embellished."

Penny went to another section of the archives using "Mendonca" as the search term and found something else. On the screen was a faded, creased document with writing that was so faint, it was hard to tell what it was. "Oh, this is one of those petitions for change of title. People got married and added somebody onto it. Or died and had a name removed. Not sure what this one is about—"

Penny stopped talking. She enlarged the page. "Well, look at this."

Starhawk strained to see what Penny was interested in. It appeared to be a signature.

"I can't make it out, Penny. Your eyes are better than mine."

Penny laughed. "Look closely. See that signature? I see an M and an H. The rest of it sure looks like Penngrove."

Starhawk said, "That would a long shot, wouldn't it?"

"Yes," said Penny, her voice holding a thrill of excitement. "Except look who also signed the document."

Starhawk gasped. "It couldn't be, could it?"

"Now why in the world is this name on a title deed with Pajaro Mendonca? And who is M. H. Penngrove?" asked Penny.

"I don't recognize the name either. What kind of a document is it?"

"A deed of some kind. Gosh, I wish these were better images," said Penny. "Let me see if I can fool with the resolution for a sec."

Penny maneuvered around the settings and was finally able to enlarge and enhance the image. "M. H. Penngrove signed here, and Mendonca signed here. But it says that Penngrove is guardian in name to the titleholder."

"Was Mendonca the titleholder?" asked Starhawk.

"No. There's another name here. I can barely make it out, though." Penny squinted hard and shook her head.

"That's a K. The name starts with a K. But I can't make out the rest."

Starhawk sat back. "Does it say where the land is located?"

"Not that I can read. Too faded and old," Penny said. "There's some kind of a connection between M. H. Penngrove and Mendonca. Interesting."

"What does 'guardian in name' mean?"

"Not sure," replied Penny.

"Is there a date on the document?"

Penny scrolled down. "Looks like 1852."

"I wonder if this M. H. Penngrove knew who they were dealing with? Mendonca was wanted for murder and robbery," mused Starhawk. "Does 'mas alla' mean anything to you? Anything historical? It appears on all the stones. It means 'beyond' in Spanish."

"Doesn't mean anything to me. Maybe it was a Spanish word that Mendonca used or had some connection with. Yet another mystery!"

They looked at the third image. "It looks like a bird, Starhawk."

"It sure does. With the same lettering and phrase below. I don't know what to make of it."

Starhawk rubbed her neck. "I've taken up way too much of your time, Penny. Plus, I think my eyeballs are going to pop out of my head from looking at this screen for so long. And we haven't even discussed the Chinese writing yet."

"Right," said Penny. "You said you had it translated. What was it again?" Starhawk thumbed through her notebook. "Niou tsay. Eternally grateful."

"Niou tsay," said Penny slowly.

"Yes. It means cowboy in Cantonese. The man who translated it for me said he had heard it from someone searching for his ancestors up here somewhere. I think he might have even come to the historical society."

"I might have to do a little digging for that one, Starhawk. Doesn't ring a bell to me."

"Well, this is a good start. At least we know the names on the stone, even if we don't know why or how they got there."

"You might want to check on one of those genealogy sites for this M. H. Penngrove. Might be something there," said Penny. "I'll let you know if I find anything about the Chinese cowboy."

Starhawk emailed Pete and Shelly and told them what she had found out. Knowing they were still on the trail and wouldn't be able to check email for weeks, she wrote anyway and thanked them for bringing her the photos.

While waiting to see if Penny found out anything more about the Chinese cowboy, Starhawk joined a free genealogy site and started a query about M. H. Penngrove from Remington River, California. Since she knew nothing about the sex or the person's birth and could only presume he or she had died near Remington River, her search ended almost before it started. She found a page where you could ask others using the site if they had any information about ancestors, and Starhawk entered the scant details about M. H. Penngrove.

§

Several weeks went by and the investigation into the rocks stalled. Penny Carter said that one of her colleagues would possibly know something about the Chinese cowboy, but he was on an extended leave. Penny said she'd ask him as soon as he returned. Starhawk had gotten no responses on the genealogy website yet.

She met up with Etoile Miller over lunch at the Pine Cone Drive-In.

"You give up on your history adventure, Starhawk? It was all you could talk about for a while," said Etoile in between bites of her burger.

The Pine Cone had a secret recipe for French fries. Etoile ordered some of them and was waiting until they cooled. Many a time she had made the mistake of eating them too soon and paid for it with a blistered upper palate for days.

"You should have seen the look in Penny's eyes when she talked about Pajaro Mendonca. She's a historian, so, to be fair, I'm sure she gets caught up in the past. But she seemed pretty gone on him."

"*Gone* on him?" Etoile laughed.

"Dating myself, aren't I? It's a good word. Why did it go out of style?" asked Starhawk. "Mendonca was a bandit. Robbed stage-coaches. Quite the character. And Penny was truly *gone* on the guy."

"I can see how that could happen," said Etoile. "You read about these people in a one-dimensional way and get hooked on some aspect of them: courageous, brave, selfless, generous, or just plain bad, right? You never meet those people, never get to really know them, can't possibly know the real story, right? Perfect. You can just make up whatever you want. The ultimate fantasy. And, even better, you never actually have to have a relationship with him. It's all one-sided. Maybe there should be a website for singles: the Dead-Dating Society! Find love with the security of knowing they will never, ever stand you up!"

Starhawk stared at Etoile. "Where do you come up with these ideas?"

"Maybe all the good men lived a hundred years ago?"

Starhawk laughed. "Let's not get maudlin about it, shall we?"

After lunch, Starhawk returned to the museum. There were no emails from Penny and no calls either. Starhawk sighed. She logged onto the genealogy website with no expectations. When she saw the little symbol on the top right of the screen indicating that she had messages, Starhawk's heart skipped.

There were three messages about M. H. Penngrove. The first one took Starhawk's breath away. The second one drove her to her feet. And the third one resulted in her immediately picking up the phone and placing a call to Missouri.

22

ETOILE MILLER STOOD IN FRONT OF the mirror, stretched her arms back behind her head and started to braid her hair. When her arms could reach no further, she flipped the braid over her shoulder and finished the job. The result was an odd twist in the middle of the braid. In all her years of having long hair, she could never figure out how to get rid of the twist.

She lingered a moment in front of the mirror examining her face. Etoile looked it over as she might a crime scene. *There are similarities.*

Before heading off to work, Etoile sat down at her kitchen table with a cup of coffee. The house she grew up in, and now lived in alone, was a small ranch-style house on a cul-de-sac on the west side of town. After her mother died, Etoile'd changed little of the furnishings. She had no interest in decorating. A La-Z-Boy sofa, a Formica dinette, a variety of hand-hooked rugs, and a cabinet containing a collection of her mother's Hummel figurines dominated the living room. The walls featured a deer head and mountain lion skin courtesy of her late father's hunting enthusiasm. He had been the sheriff in Remington River for many years. Etoile had grown up in the town and developed into an accomplished basketball player. When offers from Division I colleges started coming in, including one from Pat Summitt and the Lady Vols, Etoile Miller was poised to leave Remington River and embark on a new life.

A bullet from a shotgun accident changed all that. Her leg could be repaired but her basketball career was finished. Over time, she healed, and when her father died, she returned to Remington River and worked her way up in the sheriff's department. She had been the unanimous choice to head the department. Etoile Miller was fair, calm, and well-liked. If she kept her distance and formed few close friendships, it was because she needed to maintain a professional boundary. She reasoned this was the only way to carry out her job. She reasoned that she really didn't need anything more.

The only decorations Etoile had added to the house were photos of the girls' high school basketball team that she coached. The Lady Pulas, as the team was called, had gone to the state finals several times under Etoile's guidance. Outside of Remington River, few people understood the humor behind the name; *pula* meant "basket" in Maidu, a reference to the tribe's culture of basket weaving.

The Pulas were Etoile's family now.

She opened her laptop. She was thinking about the conversation with Starhawk and the lives of people from the past, remote and intangible. Who really understood about people and their stories from the past? What was the truth? In her line of work, Etoile knew that people might tell one version of a story in the beginning. Often, they were so convinced of the truth that even when the storyteller was presented with irrefutable evidence to the contrary, they often could not accept it. They *believed*. So how could history interpret what was *believed* to be true at the time?

She did a search for "criminals of old California."

When she found an entry for Pajaro Mendonca, she clicked on it. A photo popped up. It was a daguerreotype. He stood alone. He was clothed in black from head to toe, and his dark hair was obscured by a large hat, though but a trace of his plait was visible draped over his shoulder. He had an enormous moustache, below which a fine line of white teeth was visible. *Defiant in his stance,* she thought. His eyes said something different. He looked bemused as his gaze was directed behind the photographer. *Who or what was he looking at?*

The text read:

A more treacherous and untrustworthy individual has seldom been seen in these parts. He is reputed to have roamed Northern California eluding capture with his two brothers, Lorenzo and Sandro. Few stagecoach lines were spared from their attacks. The stolen money from these raids has never been traced. Legend has it that Mendonca buried caches of money in the mountains. He was last seen in the Remington River area in the early 1850s but appears to have disappeared from further notoriety after that.

Etoile closed her laptop and rose quickly from the table. *No wonder that name was familiar.* She gathered her work gear and hurried out to her truck. She was anxious to get to the office. There was an old case she wanted to look up.

❧ 23 ❧

WHILE HER CALL TO MISSOURI RANG, Starhawk scanned the three messages again. They were all from a Sharon Hollister of St. Joseph, Missouri. In the first email, the woman asked whether M. H. Penngrove of Remington River could be Mariah Hardwick Penngrove, formerly of St. Joseph, Missouri. In the second message, Sharon said that she definitely had information about Mariah Hardwick Penngrove, if this was indeed the person Starhawk was looking for. Her third message revealed that she had a manuscript she believed to have been written by Mariah Hardwick Penngrove about her early life.

Sharon answered the phone, and after brief introductions, she told Starhawk she had a well-documented family history dating back to the early to mid-1800s.

"The Bibles in that era each had a page for filling in the branches of a family tree. My ancestors kept up the tree meticulously," Sharon told her. "There is no M. H. Penngrove in the tree. She's not my relative. But I have a trunk that has been in my family's possession for generations. The trunk itself belonged to Hetty Samuels Merrimack.

She *is* a relative and is in the Bible tree. Inside the trunk, though, are things belonging to Mariah Hardwick Penngrove. It was shipped from Remington River, California, in 1864. Seems likely we're talking about the same person. Tell me what you know about M. H. Penngrove."

"Three carved rocks were found in the hills above Remington River," Starhawk told her. "Much of the carving has worn off, but we managed to piece together two of the names and some other words. All of them have the same writing in Chinese and Spanish below the names. There's mas alla, which is Spanish for 'the beyond.' And niou tsay, 'eternally grateful,' is written in Chinese characters. One rock says 'MH Penngrove 1859.' One says 'Pajaro Mendonca 1871.'"

Sharon made a sound. "Stop right there. Pajaro Mendonca. He's in the manuscript written by Mariah Hardwick Penngrove. Has to be the same person. The word 'beyond' is also mentioned frequently in the story, and there is quite a large reference to Chinatown in San Francisco."

Then Sharon asked, "The third rock? Did it by any chance have the name Lucia Cravotti on it?"

Starhawk replied, "No. There is a carving of what we think is a bird or other object with the date 1852. Who is Lucia Cravotti?"

Sharon sighed. "I was hoping you'd tell me. I thought perhaps she had come from Remington River."

"Why would you connect Lucia Cravotti to Remington River?"

"In the family tree, Hetty Samuels Merrimack is listed. Below her name, but not linked with a branch of the tree, is Lucia Cravotti. I've searched for her on the genealogy website, like I did for Mariah Hardwick Penngrove. So far there's been nothing."

"What is this manuscript, Sharon?"

"Well, it's a yarn, I'll tell you. If it is true, Mariah had a wild early life. Unfortunately, it ends just as things get interesting."

"Ends?" asked Starhawk.

"Yes. Just abruptly ends. Either she never got a chance to finish it or she just didn't want to."

"What else is in the trunk?"

"An oilskin pouch with an old copy of *The Journals of Lewis and Clark* and a cup and saucer. No letters or any other personal objects. No clue as to why Mariah's things were sent to Missouri. *The Journals* and cup and saucer are described in the manuscript, by the way. Apparently, they were very important to her."

"What's the story about?"

"Goodness, it's a jumble of adventures and musings interspersed with quotations from Lewis and Clark. Pajaro Mendonca seems to be a love interest. There's a Chinese boy named Sing. A Chinese woman is chasing them. But it starts with a covered wagon journey across the country. This is where Mariah meets my relative, Hetty Samuels. She went to Remington River by wagon, too. They met on the trail. Hetty was widowed before the trip and remarried later on."

Starhawk told her, "We are not sure about whether these rocks are graves or just memorials. We're not even sure the years on them are dates of their deaths. We have found some old documents, land deeds, with M. H. Penngrove's and Pajaro's names on them. There's another name but the image is poor. We think it starts with a *K*. The people here at the local historical society are working on enhancing the image. I wish I could help with Lucia Cravotti, Sharon."

There was a pause and then Sharon asked, "Would you like a copy of the manuscript? Since you're piecing together the lives of these folks, you might enjoy reading the story."

Starhawk had been hoping she'd offer the manuscript. "That would be wonderful. It would be an honor to read about them."

Sharon said she'd make a copy and send it as soon as possible. "If you find out anything about Lucia Cravotti, please let me know."

§

"She wrote a book about her life," Penny said.

Starhawk had dropped in to see Penny and ask what she knew about Hetty Merrimack.

"Hetty appears in Remington River sometime in the late 1840s," Penny went on. "She married well and became one of the leading citizens of the town. It was considered classy back in the day to pen a tome about yourself, I guess. She probably sold a few copies to friends and business colleagues of her husband's. It's here in the library if you want to borrow it."

Starhawk took the book and returned home. Over a dinner of scrambled eggs and toast, she started reading about Hetty Merrimack.

The first chapter, which was brief, told of her early life. She'd come from the East in a covered wagon. Widowed shortly before starting the journey, she decided to continue on to Remington River, where she had relatives. She was known as Hetty Samuels upon arrival. Very little of the journey was described, and what transpired once she settled in the area was not well detailed. It was as if, Starhawk thought, Hetty wanted to leave that part of herself behind.

The subsequent chapters talked about meeting Henry Merrimack, a lawyer from Texas who had come to California for the Gold Rush. He was younger than Hetty and, judging from the way she had written about their courtship, he was head over heels in love with her. Starhawk turned to the front of the book, where there was a photo of Henry and his new bride. He was a head shorter than her with gigantic, bristly sideburns and eyes set close together. Narrow shoulders and a skinny neck completed the picture. Next to him was the enormous personage of Hetty. She was thick around the waist, which was probably necessary to support her gigantic bosom and head. Her hair was coiffed in the style of the day, and a large hat with a white feather sat perched atop her head. The feather looked as if it were clinging for dear life, Starhawk thought.

Hetty scowled in the photo while her husband appeared to be perplexed. *Head over heels in love?*

Henry had made a modest strike in the gold fields, enough to open a law office in Remington River. They'd built a house on the outskirts of town and Hetty had worked in her husband's practice. They had been childless.

The book quickly leaped into Hetty's work, overseeing parentless children in the area. Illness, accidents, and poverty after the Gold Rush had caused families to disintegrate, and, for a time, the streets of Remington River had had numerous orphans wandering around them. The Merrimack Benevolent Society had sought to reunite these children with relatives. It appeared that Hetty had put ads in papers around the country seeking aunts, uncles, grandparents, and anyone else with familial connections to these children. Meanwhile, Henry's political life had flourished, and together they had prospered in the glow of respectability and integrity.

Starhawk turned to the last chapter, which contained a list of "success stories" about Hetty's reunification efforts. Sadly, it was a short list with no more than ten names. Starhawk went down the list and found the name "Hollister, St. Joseph, Missouri" next to the name of Lucia Cravotti, age twelve.

She called Sharon Hollister and told her what she'd found out about Lucia Cravotti. "Well, that explains how she ended up in my family's Bible," Sharon said. "But still nothing to indicate why she came to St. Joseph or who she was. I've sent the manuscript, Starhawk. You should get it soon. There were some other things, too. A bookmark, a photograph of the inscription in the front cover of *The Journals of Lewis and Clark*, and a picture of the cup and saucer. Not sure if those will be helpful, but I thought you'd might like them."

"We're sure anxious to read this book, Sharon. I'm not giving up on Lucia. Something will shake loose soon. I feel it," said Starhawk. "I'm going to send you a copy of Hetty's book, too."

❧ 24 ❧

MARCUS CHOY HAD RECENTLY RETIRED AS a civil engineer for the City and County of San Francisco. He was looking forward to unfettered time to pursue his hobby: writing a book about one of his ancestors. He'd started the project years ago but had had to abandon it because it proved time consuming. He'd conducted his research over a series of vacations in which he had traveled around California and even to China, trying to put together a timeline of events chronicling the life of his great-great-grandfather, Sing Kwok.

Marcus had a collection of photographs and letters that spanned generations of his family. According to the records kept over generations, Sing Kwok had become of one the West's first Chinese cowboys, settling on a ranch in the high desert west of Reno. He'd married a woman from Canton Province (the family thought she might have been a mail-order bride but could not prove this). They had raised several children, all of whom lived into old age. Marcus imagined that it had been a difficult life at the time, living as a Chinese man in Northern California. The ranch had prospered, though, from what Marcus could derive from family letters. Sing had been a good and fair employer to many locals in the area. The ranch was sold off in the early 1900s after Sing and his wife passed away. Their children scattered around the state. Marcus's great grandfather settled in San Francisco.

Before he died, Sing Kwok wrote a story about his cowboy days for his family. It stayed in the family and was beloved by the children who were read the tales of horses, stampedes, wildfires, and cattle rustling, all of which had been embellished with photos and drawings by Sing. Particularly captivating to Marcus was the photo of Sing astride an Appaloosa in front of a barn. The man's face was dark, the color of leather, likely from exposure. Marcus thought Sing's story might be of interest to others. He intended to call the book *Niou Tzay*, the name Sing used to describe himself in his story. Marcus had saved and carefully preserved the original manuscript of *Niou Tzay*.

What had proven most difficult was documenting the early years of Sing Kwok. Marcus had not been able to trace Sing's birth in China nor his journey to America. He assumed Sing had been born in China, but there was no record of that or his parents. What had happened to him in the intervening years, up to the point when he established himself as a rancher in Northern California, was a mystery. Sing didn't write about the years when he was a young man before moving to the ranch. Marcus had pursued many dead-end searches.

Marcus's travels to Northern California had included a visit to the Susanville Historical Society as he thought Sing's property had been near there. A fruitless search through countless documents to find the property had left Marcus frustrated. It was as if Sing had suddenly appeared, out of nowhere, as a ranch owner at the age of twenty-one.

Marcus, therefore, decided to concentrate on what he knew about his great-great-grandfather—or, rather, what Sing Kwok had intended his family to know about him. When Marcus got a phone call from Tom Nelson, the Susanville Historical Society's curator, he was surprised and pleased. It had been over a year since Marcus had visited Susanville.

§

Tom Nelson had returned to his job as curator after rushing to Pasadena to care for his elderly father. His father had never recovered from the stroke, and Tom had ended up staying on to tie up his affairs. During his absence, his staff had kept up with the odds and ends of the job very efficiently.

Penny Nelson briefed Tom on the latest news from around town. When she was done and satisfied that Tom was all caught up, she told him about the stone markers found in the mountains above Remington River.

She finished the story with a description of the Chinese characters found carved in the stone and asked Tom if he knew anything about them.

"Niou tsay? Yeah, I do, as a matter of fact," he said. He opened a drawer in his desk and pulled out a file. "I remember this guy. Here it is: Marcus Choy. From San Francisco. His great-great-grandfather lived around here and called himself 'The Chinese Cowboy.'"

"How in the world did that term end up on a rock in the middle of nowhere?" asked Penny.

Tom shook his head. "I'll give the guy a call and see if he's still working on his book. He might know something. Meanwhile, is the site being preserved at all? Or are day-trippers tramping all over it?"

Penny told him that Starhawk and Sheriff Miller were being particularly guarded about talking about it to anyone. "That's good," said Tom.

He called Marcus Choy and told him about the rocks and the carved characters on them, on the outside chance he was still interested in researching his ancestor. Marcus was delighted to hear about the discovery and decided to come up immediately.

❧ 25 ❧

Deputy Purdue was sorting the day's mail for Sheriff Miller. He liked to pile the envelopes in categories: bills, communications, departmental, and junk, all alphabetical and stacked neatly in order. Purdue took great pride in his organizational skills. The office door burst open and a gust of wind threatened to disrupt his piles. Purdue threw his body over his work, a maneuver of considerable athleticism that was completely ignored as his boss bustled past him and shut the door to her office.

"And good morning to you," he said under his breath. Purdue looked over his shoulder and saw that Sheriff Miller had not even removed her coat before starting in on her computer. Something sure was important.

Etoile Miller opened the file on her desktop. She scrolled down until she found what she was looking for, a case from several years back. It was unusual because it involved a bungled bank robbery in Remington River. A crime such as this was rare in the town. The three characters involved were right out of a cheap cops-and-robbers novel. The story had dominated newspapers all over California for a few weeks, though less for the crime than for the comical aspects of it. At the center of it was Jordan Blake. Reportedly a gifted student of California history working on his graduate degree, Blake also had a nasty gambling habit. He was sixty grand in the hole and had a pair of bad dudes, Sal Juarez and Glen Finnegan, after him to repay his debt. In a panic because his family was being threatened over the debt, Blake concocted a wild scheme to settle things with Sal and Glen.

Etoile remembered sitting down to interview Blake after his arrest. As he recounted the story to her, she saw that even Blake found the whole thing crazy, as he repeatedly shook his head in disbelief. He told her that during his research for his degree, he had read about the legend of bandits who had buried money in the hills around Remington River, and about Pajaro Mendonca. Blake knew Mendonca had been fond of robbing stagecoaches in the area. In his haste to find a solution to his money problems, Blake admitted later, he had not thought the details through completely. He had reasoned that Mendonca would not have wanted to carry the stolen goods very far from the stagecoach he robbed.

"Right? Didn't want to lug the stuff all over the place and chance getting caught. This was my reasoning. It was simply a matter of choosing a place that would convince Glen and Sal," Blake said at the time. "I had some evidence that pointed to Widow Creek Ranch but really didn't know where to look on the property."

He was interviewed in a hospital bed because he been grazed by a bullet in the aftermath of his folly. Etoile recalled that he was grateful to have the madness put to an end and didn't mind the wound. He was convinced that the shot he took had stopped everything at the bank. Blake had persuaded Sal and Glen into believing he knew exactly where to dig for Mendonca's cache. And once he found the hidden money, Blake had reasoned, not only would be able to repay his debt, but they all could reap the benefit of whatever was left. Blake found some old maps of the stagecoach routes and used these to bolster his plan. Having no idea on earth where to actually dig, Blake's hope was that he would simply happen upon a likely place that would convince Sal and Glen. The three chose a spot at Widow Creek Ranch and, in broad daylight, began tearing up the place with shovels. They were interrupted by the irate farmer and fled the scene.

Apparently, robbing the bank had been an afterthought as a result of their misadventure at Widow Creek. It was doomed from the beginning. The teller pressed the silent alarm as soon as Blake stepped up to the window, and there was a quick response from the sheriff's department.

One of the deputies asked Blake, as he waited for an ambulance, if he really believed Mendonca's loot was buried somewhere.

Blake responded, "No. Not really. In fact, I doubt he had any money to speak of. Pajaro Mendonca was a good guy. He just never got the right stories written about him."

Now, Etoile wondered what Jordan Blake had meant by "the right stories."

§

Later in the afternoon, Starhawk bumped into Sheriff Miller in the produce section at Mike's Market, scrutinizing a pile of melons. Starhawk had a bag of tomatoes in her cart.

"What are you making for dinner?" asked Etoile. "Something with tomatoes. Maybe sauce. You'll need garlic."

"And breaded chicken breasts."

"Sounds Italian."

"You should come by for dinner," Starhawk said. "I have a lot to tell you. Unless you want to gab here."

Etoile grimaced. "Not really. Jeff Coldwell is in the beer section buying two cases of Pacifico. He's already spotted me and I know he wants me to waive his citation. Part of me would like to avoid him.

Part of me would like to go out to the parking lot and see if he even bothered to get his truck registered and give him another citation. A guy who can buy up like that can afford his registration."

Starhawk smiled. She knew Etoile Miller's dry humor was sometimes mistaken for aloofness and insincerity. She also knew that the sheriff was tough but with a big heart for anybody in trouble or being maligned. But she had little time or patience for complainers.

"Then come by for dinner. You are not going to believe what I have to tell you."

"Don't think you're the only one with cool stuff, Starhawk. I got some tidbits on Pajaro Mendonca."

Starhawk grinned at Etoile. "Is that right? Building a dossier on Zorro?"

"Oh, come on," said Etoile wryly. "What time tonight?"

"Around seven. Bring wine."

§

That evening, after an excellent meal, Etoile and Starhawk sat with glasses of wine on the front porch of the museum. The women had exchanged their news over dinner. Starhawk told Etoile about the book on Hetty Merrimack and the reference to Lucia Cravotti. Etoile mentioned Jordan Blake's comments at the time of his arrest about Mendonca and how she wasn't sure how seriously to take them. In the distance, Hasten Peak was bathed in a pink glow. Bats careened up and down the alley feasting on gnats. The faint sounds of the main highway could be heard from beyond the alley.

"I wonder if this manuscript is going to clear up anything about those rocks," mused Starhawk.

"I guess we'll know soon enough," commented Etoile.

"Jordan Blake," Etoile continued. "The way he talked about Mendonca, he sounded like he almost admired the man. Like there was another side to him that nobody knows about."

Starhawk turned to Etoile. "One does get drawn to these characters from the past. It's like what we were talking about the other day. The stories of these people in history and how we never really know because we weren't part of their worlds. The real story about Mendonca *is* probably less exciting than what we know about him. It's the wondering about what the man was *really* like that is fascinating."

Etoile laughed. "I'm sure he put his boots on the same way as everybody else, Starhawk."

"Oh. But I'll bet you he had some mighty fine boots, Etoile," remarked Starhawk. "I remember that bank robbery. I don't recall many of the details about why they chose to dig at Widow Creek Ranch, though."

"Blake only talked about it when we interviewed him. I guess the press never got wind of it. Thank God! We'd have dozens of would-be treasure hunters roaming the countryside."

"Jordan Blake seemed like such an intelligent young man. I wonder if he was able to get back to his research?"

"He pled guilty, which got him a reduced sentence. He's still at Folsom."

"You checked?" asked Starhawk, glancing over her glasses.

Etoile cleared her throat. "Yes, I did. He's apparently doing well down there. Behaving himself. Didn't fall in with the wrong sort."

"Do you remember I told you that Penny Carter said that man who's interested in the Chinese cowboy is coming here? His name is Marcus Choy. He wants to see the rocks," said Starhawk.

"Really?" said Etoile. "I guess he's got as much of a connection as us, if not more, with the rocks. It's too much of a coincidence that those words are the same ones used by his great-great-grandfather."

"And then there's that third rock, Etoile."

"The bird or whatever it is. There's something about that place. Those rocks were not positioned there randomly. There is a reason for them to be right there."

❧ 26 ❧

MARCUS CHOY CHECKED IN WITH TOM Nelson as soon as he got to Susanville. His plans about how long to stay were open-ended.

"I haven't been up there myself, Marcus," Tom told him. "I've just seen the photos. It's quite a find, though. And I knew the minute I saw the words on the rocks that you would be interested. I think you'll enjoy meeting Starhawk. She's managed to find out about two of the names on the rock. Plus, she's tracked down this manuscript that I told you about."

"After all this time. I won't say that I'd given up on learning anything more about Sing. But you get to a point that you're just looking over the same articles and materials, and I wondered if that was all I would ever know. Now this," chuckled Marcus.

"Etoile Miller is the sheriff in Remington River. She said she would take you up to the rocks. Here's her number."

Marcus thanked Tom and called Etoile. She told him she was available right away, and since it was still early in the afternoon, she'd be happy to drive him if he could come over to Remington River. He agreed and left immediately.

They met up on Remington River Highway where the road turned to dirt. He left his car and got into Etoile's truck for the rest of the journey. Sitting next to her, Marcus stole a few glances at the tall woman with the campaign hat sitting straight and firm on her head. Her long blond hair hung in a single braid down her back. A few wisps from under the hat kept getting caught in the wind and bothering her by getting stuck in her mouth.

"Have you been sheriff for a long time?" asked Marcus.

"A few years," she said and turned to him. "I grew up here. My father was sheriff before me."

Marcus told her about Sing Kwok and the book he wanted to write about him.

"He was legendary in my family. I think a lot of us kids wanted to be cowboys like him," said Marcus.

"Do you have any idea what sort of man your great-great-grandfather was, Marcus? Other than probably having a pretty tough go of it, being a Chinese rancher back then. It's not easy for outsiders coming up here *now*. Even if they're white," said Etoile.

"I cannot imagine what he went through. As to your question," said Marcus, as they bumped along the rough road, "he gave the impression of being a jolly guy. That's the best description I can come up with. I'll let you read his story sometime. He paints a rosy picture of hard work combined with great peace and prosperity. There is no sign of bitterness or resentment at all. What has been handed down through generations in my family is nothing about the real man at all. They would simply say "Oh, Sing. He had a good life. Always smiling and happy."

Marcus sat quietly then continued. "I don't buy all of it, Sheriff. And the fact that there is absolutely nothing of his childhood makes me wonder about the man. Unfortunately, all I have to go on is this perpetual story of sunshine and riding horses across the meadows. I'd have to make up any of the gritty stuff."

They continued on in silence until reaching the spot where the trail crossed the road.

Etoile got out of the truck and staggered on her stiff leg.
Marcus saw her rubbing her leg. "Are you okay?"

"Yes. Just stiff."

She limped around to the front of the truck, seeing him eye her
leg with concern. "Old injury," she said.

Now knowing exactly where to go, Etoile led Marcus on a shorter
route to the rocks. In less than twenty minutes, they were standing
by the manzanita bushes, the rocks barely visible beneath.

"I hid them again," explained Etoile as she pulled back the bushes.

Marcus knelt down and ran his hands over the smooth tops of the
rocks. His fingers grazed the carvings, feeling the rough indentations
on each of them.

"Why were they hidden?" he asked.

"You mean just now? With the bushes? I didn't want them
to be—"

"No," he interrupted, "I mean why were they hidden to begin
with, all the way up here? In the middle of nowhere. Somebody did
not want these found. Ever."

"What makes you say that?"

"I get a feeling that whoever put these here didn't want anybody
to know their location. A private place," said Marcus. His fingers
touched the Chinese lettering. "Niou tsay, just as you said."

Marcus stood up abruptly. "I think Sing put these here. I don't
know why. But I just have a hunch. 'Eternally grateful,'" he read from
the stone. "To Pajaro Mendonca and Mariah Penngrove? Was it for
them? What did they do for Sing that he felt he had to honor them?"
Marcus took a few pictures. He helped Etoile arrange the bushes to
conceal the stones and they hiked back to the car.

Marcus and Etoile stopped at the Pine Cone for a late lunch. As
they sat at the table waiting for their coffee and sandwiches, Marcus
brought out a folder with some photographs. "Here's the one of Sing
on his horse," said Marcus, sliding the photo toward Etoile. The
Appaloosa stood in tall green grass in front of an old barn. It must

have been a windy day because the grass was bent down in places. She also saw that there was a hat on the ground near the horse. A large black hat with silver medallions around the rim. It must have blown off in the wind. Sing grinned to the camera.

"This photo is the only one I have with his children. It's dated 1863."

The photo was taken in front of the same barn. Sing stood in the center, once again smiling broadly. A small woman stood next to him squinting in the sun with a dour expression on her face.

"This is your great-great-grandmother?"

Marcus nodded. "What a harsh life she must have had. I'll bet she was hard-pressed to take a moment from her daily work for a photograph."

There were five children of various ages, lined next to Sing and his wife. "Do you know their names?"

Marcus turned the photograph over to reveal a written list of names. "I can't be sure if they're all in order, though."

They were all names with Chinese origins. Except for one: Lucia. This was the first name on the list. Etoile turned the photograph back over and looked at the girl.

"Who is this girl, Marcus?"

"That's Lucia. Sing and Lily had four children. Lucia was not their child, but she is talked about as being one of their own nonetheless. She was the oldest."

The girl was dressed in a white pinafore, in contrast to her brown complexion. Her black hair was pulled back in a tight ponytail. She wore no shoes. Her piercing dark eyes stared directly into the camera; there was a serious look on her face. She looked to be about thirteen. "I have a letter about Lucia," said Marcus. "I do not know who her parents were. But her mother wrote this letter to her. It is not clear how Lucia ended up with Sing. But he took her in as his own."

"What does the letter say?"

"Here's a copy. I brought everything," said Marcus.

Etoile looked at him while he searched through his satchel. He was short and compact, in his sixties, and he had a wistful air about him. He told her that he had never married and lived in the same house in San Francisco where he was raised. Just being up in the mountains appeared to touch him. She'd heard him breathing in deeply as they'd climbed the rocky road to the stones. He would shut his eyes frequently and then open them as they passed a meadow or crossed a stream. It was as if everything that she took for granted as part of her home, he looked upon with great reverence.

When he handed her the copy of the letter, he smiled. It was written in a clear, cursive style.

My dearest one:

How I have come to admire your quest for adventure. Just the other day, your papa told me you crossed that old log on the river. How bad he felt that he hadn't stopped you in time. How worried he was that you would fall. I laughed and said she is as sure-footed as a bighorn sheep. And how proud you were when you called to him from the other side. I wish I had been well enough to see it. You have grown up to be a fine girl, and I hope you will find as much joy and adventure as I have. Beyond that, I can only wish for you to know love and wisdom and curiosity. The world is so different when you open your eyes and look around you for everything new. Papa will always look after you as well as our beloved Sing. And I may not be here, but I will always be beyond watching over my darling Lucia.

Your loving mother

Etoile finished reading the letter and handed it back to Marcus. Marcus watched her carefully and said, "Whoever Lucia was, she was greatly loved."

§

Etoile Miller entered the required information on the TRULINCS website and waited for confirmation and approval to send the email. The TRULINCS process for communicating with an inmate was a secure server that enabled inmates to correspond. She learned that Jordan Blake, because of his good behavior, was able to receive and send emails. All correspondence was closely monitored by prison officials. Etoile contacted Folsom and was assured that once her TRULINCS account was established, Blake would get her email.

As to whether he would respond, that was another matter.

"He emails his mother and his attorney. Nobody else," she was told. Jordan didn't communicate with anyone from his graduate program at Chico. Jordan Blake, evidently, had abandoned that part of his life.

She kept her initial email brief and to the point, asking whether, during his research, he had ever uncovered further information about Pajaro Mendonca, as well as whether he knew the name Mariah Penngrove. She concluded the message by explaining that her interest centered around a possible burial site where their names appeared on rocks. For now, she did not tell him about the Chinese writing, the odd picture of the bird on the third rock, or anything about the Chinese cowboy. Nor did she mention the manuscript. She first wanted to know how interested Jordan Blake was in talking to her. And how much he still remembered about his graduate work.

∾ 27 ∾

A PACKAGE WAS WAITING FOR STARHAWK at the post office. It was from Missouri and she knew immediately that it was the manuscript. She opened the package. In addition to the copy of the manuscript, there was a note from Sharon plus the photos of the inscription inside the front of *The Journals*, the cup and saucer, and another picture of a small scrap of paper, the bookmark found in the book.

The book's inscription read:

For Mother on her birthday. With love and 'beyond,' Mariah.

Starhawk looked at the picture of the bookmark. It featured a series of markings and pictures of trees and a fence. She would make copies of the bookmark, inscription, and picture of the cup and saucer.

Resisting the urge to read it herself, Starhawk brought the manuscript to Remington River Copy Cat and asked to have four copies made of everything. She decided to invite Tom, Penny, Marcus, and

Etoile to a potluck dinner followed by a group reading of the manuscript. She confirmed that everyone was willing to attend and set the date for the following Tuesday at the museum.

❧ 28 ❧

JORDAN BLAKE STARED AT THE COMPUTER screen in the prison's library and ran his hand over his chin. He pinched the soft flesh. His face was bloated. Obese, flaccid, and irrelevant, like him. The email from Sheriff Etoile Miller made him feel sick and hopeful at the same time: sick because it dredged up a memory that he was trying to forget. The whole damn incident was too surreal to even contemplate, and, when he did, he realized what an utter fool he had been. It involved a Jordan Blake—the one that had it all together until the day it completely fell apart—that hardly resembled the one sitting at the computer in a prison library. Two years ago, Jordan had been the golden boy in the Early California History graduate program at Chico State. He had been on track to apply to the doctoral program at University of California, Riverside. His thesis was fresh and interesting and, according to his advisor, was a natural launch for a larger body of research.

What had started out as a couple of card games in the back room of a college bar turned into weekly forays to a nearby casino, where he proceeded to dig himself into an enormous hole of debt, despair, and revulsion with himself.

At the time, he thought about just swallowing his pride and crawling home to his parents, placing himself at their judgmental and harsh mercy. However, the idea of asking his father for the money, particularly for the reason he had, was not appealing. Sherm Blake was as unforgiving a man as you'd ever want to encounter.

Jordan pictured himself with Sherm sitting by the pool at the family home in Orinda. Maybe he'd wait until morning to have a serious talk with his father, with the sun coming up over the pool house while watching his mother do her laps. Maybe they'd have their breakfast by the pool. He'd wait until his father had scraped the crumbs from his toast with his knife and forked the last bit of cantaloupe into his mouth before saying, "Dad, I've got a little problem."

Sherm would raise his eyebrows and, jumping to the bitter but correct conclusion, say, "Don't tell me you've fucked up. I really can't understand your proclivity for being an absolute cretin at every point where you could have success." Jordan's mother would groan at the F word but would silently agree by stopping her laps, rolling her eyes, crossing her arms over the chest of her wet bathing suit, and pursing her lips. There was nobody on his side in Orinda.

His father didn't understand his interest in history ("Where's the money in *that*, Jordy?"), and he certainly wouldn't understand his passion for gambling. The enormity of the debt, sixty thousand dollars, would be a permanent mark against his character. No, Jordan had to find another way. The way he settled on was the worst possible kind, and it delivered him into the lap of degradation called Folsom.

Sheriff Miller had been one of the arresting officers at the time. Jordan recalled her tall and imposing presence during the initial questioning, her odd limp as she circled his hospital bed. He also remembered her sympathy when he fell apart completely.

Therefore, the email from Etoile gave him some hope. It had been years since anyone had asked him anything about his research. Not that he hadn't thought about it. It had taken him two years to surface, so to speak, from a profound depression where simply placing one foot in front of the other was the most intellectual stimulation he could muster.

Jordan decided then and there to stop wasting time being morose and dejected. The email stirred him into action. He wrote an email to his mother. Once she had gotten over the shock of having a felon for a son, she surprised him by being a kind and sincere correspondent, writing long emails with news from home. No finger wagging or chastising him for his evil ways. Sherm, on the hand, wrote seldom and usually to inquire whether he needed money or cigarettes, which was a nice gesture on his part. Unfortunately, Sherm's idea of prison was based on 1950s films featuring Robert Mitchum chain-smoking in his cell. Folsom was strictly nonsmoking. Money, on the other hand, was useful for toiletries and the charges associated with using TRULINCS. In Jordan's email to his mother, he asked her to arrange for his attorney to send him a box stored in his Orinda bedroom: his research materials.

Then he composed a short reply to Etoile: "Where exactly were these rocks found?"

❧ 29 ❧

Jordan Blake waited patiently for the box to arrive. When it finally did, he was summoned to an administrative office where it was unpacked in front of the prying eyes of an assistant warden, who looked at each piece of paper like it was soiled with feces. Jordan had expected to be excited to see his work but had not counted on being overcome with emotion, and he fought back tears as he saw it scrutinized. The assistant warden carelessly dumped the stack of papers back in the box, and Jordan realized that it would be a considerable task to re-order everything. He didn't care.

Back in his cell, he painstakingly arranged his notes. He had been a serious student. The card games had been his relaxation until they took over his life. He remembered the debt hanging over him. The day he thought he'd found the solution to his problems began in scholarly fashion. Then it ended with lunacy.

Jordan had been in the Chico State library that day looking for anecdotal stories for his thesis. He wanted some choice quotes about the infamous first governor of California, Peter Burnett. He scrolled through old newspapers and assorted documents, concentrating on the time immediately before Burnett resigned as governor. Burnett's unpopular stance on a number of issues, principally his racial and ethnic views, had prompted his early departure from politics. He found a letter that Burnett had written to his old business partner, John Sutter. The usual verses about how intolerable the legislature had been to him and the rueful comments about wasted time and money over petty issues like slavery. Jordan passed over this as it was not very juicy. Then Jordan saw something interesting. Burnett told Sutter he'd like to get his hands on the person who had invited that "egomaniac easterner Troy Willams Turner, late of the Albany, New York press, to write the story which delivered the final blow to me. I shan't ever recover from that, and, as you know, the blows become more savage when one is thrown to the ground."

Cross-referencing Turner, Jordan found that Turner was a reporter for the *Albany Evening Journal*. He discovered a collection of stories by Turner in a book the journalist had authored about his travels west. The book was long out of print. Apparently, the stories had been serialized in the newspaper before he put them into book form. As luck would have it, Jordan found a few of the stories from the paper in the microfiche files under the heading "Politics in Remington River, California."

Turner, apparently trying to channel Frances Trollope, started off with a scathing description of sanitation in the town and continued with a rambling discourse about the poor quality of "vittles." Finally, Jordan found what he wanted. Here was a "sensational series of articles about the bumbling new governor of California." Turner wrote about how a Californio bandit by the name of Pajaro Mendonca of Marysville had "hoodwinked" the governor's agent in a daring exchange of documents on the stagecoach between Red Bluff and Remington River.

Pajaro Mendonca's escapades would make a fine anecdote for Jordan's treatise on the new governor's lack of foresight in finding common ground with the Californios. "The stage had just left

Widow Creek Station, near Remington River, when the nefarious plot unfolded," the article read.

Jordan had come across the name Pajaro Mendonca once or twice in his research. He checked the old Red Bluff newspaper films and found a few more stories about Mendonca, but they were unrelated to the exchanged documents belonging to the governor.

Pajaro Mendonca and his two brothers ultimately met their fate in a shootout near Widow Creek Station, thanks to the heroic efforts of stage agent Terence Burke. Only the body of Sandro Mendonca was recovered. What has become of the leader of the bandits, Pajaro, and his brother, Lorenzo, is as yet unknown. Burke is of the opinion that the surviving Mendoncas were mortally wounded as a result of skilled gunmanship. They managed to hide but ultimately perished. A woman named Mariah Penngrove (of St. Joseph, Missouri) was found managing the station and was reportedly involved with Pajaro Mendonca. The relationship between the bandit and Mrs. Penngrove is not clear, and authorities have not been able to get any information from Mrs. Penngrove as she seems to have disappeared.

The next part made him sit up with interest.

Many parties in the area, including several stagecoach companies, are interested in where Mendonca secreted his loot. The reputedly enormous quantity of gold, from several years of criminal activity, has not been found.

Jordan Blake laughed out loud and then looked around furtively to see if anybody had seen him. It was only a matter of time before the loan shark's crew caught up with him, even in the sacrosanct library.

Mendonca's gold. It was ridiculous to even consider. Unfortunately, Jordan was running out of alternatives. Even a ridiculous one was better than none. The idea of "Jordan Blake, Treasure Hunter" was laughable. Sure, there were legends of bandits hiding their purloined caches all over California. From the sheer number of stories, it sounded like one could trip over millions of dollars in cash and gold simply by taking a walk in the woods. Why couldn't he, Jordan Blake, dangerously in debt, be one of those lucky sods?

If anyone could find a clue to the location of Mendonca's gold, wouldn't it make sense that it would be a graduate student specializing in Northern California history?

Glen Finnegan and Sal Juarez stopped and smiled when they saw Jordan hunkered down in a pile of books and papers. *It was only a matter of time, wasn't it?*

"Professor!" said Finnegan brightly.

Juarez glared.

Jordan felt his gut clench and roil.

"We've been looking you. You need a beer," said Finnegan. "Right now."

They marched him to a nearby bar and ordered drinks. It wasn't quite noon and the place was empty. They sat at a table near the back door. Finnegan got right to the point. "No more talk. You're going to give me something in three days, or I'm going to take it out of your skull. You dig me, chum? Your *skull*," hissed Finnegan as he sipped his beer.

"Now, you're done with your beer, see? Pay the bartender like a nice kid," said Juarez.

Jordan hadn't had a sip. Still, he put a ten on the bar. "Good. You're coming outside with us. Not the front. The back door, bro."

Jordan gulped and felt Juarez place a hand on his shoulder, pushing him along. Jordan opened the door into an alley behind the bar. Finnegan took the first swing and caught Jordan under the chin. He folded to the pavement like a house of cards. Juarez kicked him twice in the side.

Finnegan grunted, "Remember what I said. *Your skull next time.*"

The two walked down the alley and disappeared around the corner.

Jordan stayed still for a minute. One of his teeth was loose. His tongue felt the play in the incisor that now wiggled like a swing. He rolled over and a river of blood came out of his mouth. His hand found a stack of magazines sitting next to the door to the bar. He grabbed one and tried to blot some of the blood. He sat up and leaned against the wall. *Jesus.* What was he going to do now? He picked up another magazine, inspecting its cleanliness, which was minimal, and staunched the blood flow. The magazine was one of those tourist guides for the area around Hasten Peak National Park, about two and a half hours east of Chico. The cover showed verdant meadows, gushing rivers, trout the size of small poodles, and the snowcapped Hasten Peak. Jordan wasn't much on the mountains, but it looked awfully inviting right now.

He tore a page from the magazine and dabbed at his mouth. He looked down at the paper, which was now smeared with blood. There was an advertisement for farm-fresh produce. The name of the business caught his eye: Widow Creek Ranch. Certified Organic.

The advertisement included a map with directions to Widow Creek. It was near Remington River, but was it the same place where the shootout between Burke and Mendonca had transpired? Jordan Blake wiped the last of the blood and began formulating a plan that bordered on insanity. Widow Creek. Of course. It was a deranged idea. Not the least of which was the fact that the plan was born from sheer panic and fear. *These are not solid ingredients for a good solution. Here's the idea, folks: Find the gold that Pajaro Mendonca buried at Widow Creek! Pay off Glen and Sal!* It sounded like some terrible made-for-TV movie. All that was missing was an ad for sea monkeys and a decoder ring.

He went back to the library and reread the articles about Mendonca and Widow Creek and found an old map of the area. Then he found another article.

What he read worried him. It was an article from the Remington River newspaper about Widow Creek Station, dated 1851. The main topic in the press during this time was the weather. Floods, roads washed out, and a general pronouncement by some religious fanatics that God was seeking revenge for the sin and evil in town. The story said the company that ran the stage from Red Bluff to Remington River was going to start charging a toll at Widow Creek Station in addition to the regular fare. Passengers were furious about the increased prices. Jordan found himself looking at a very rough picture of Widow Creek Station. It looked like there was a lake in front of it. The article said that, due to massive flooding at the station, the stage company needed to charge more on the Red Bluff-Remington River run because the road was impassable to Widow Creek Station except by skiff. Stages were halted, passengers loaded onto the boat and punted to the other side, where a new stage picked them. It was costly to the company, since they had to pay the station agent more to paddle across the swamp. But they were hopeful that the swamp that had formed from the previous year's rains would be absorbed soon.

If the gold was buried there before the flooding, Lord knows what condition the strong box is in now. Not that it mattered. It was an absurd plan. *No point in continuing,* he told himself.

Two days later, however, the plan resurfaced as the best idea in the world due to a visit from Glen and Sal.

Jordan was getting into his Subaru in front of his apartment when a black Torino pulled up next to him. Glen and Sal got out and knocked on his window.

"Open up, Jordy," said Glen. Jordan reluctantly opened the door as he felt his tongue push the swinging incisor.

The two got into the back seat. "You aren't leaving town, Professor?" asked Glen.

"No. Just going to the store. Need anything? Pretzels? Duct tape? Brass knuckles?" asked Jordan.

Sal slapped the side of Jordan's head. "You're funny. Now. Not for long. Boss has been patient. But it's all over. You got a plan yet?"

Glen slipped his hand around Jordan's neck and laughed. "Do tell, Jordy."

"If I may explain, Glen?" Jordan said prying Glen's fingers from his throat. He put his hands on the wheel and took a deep breath. He had little more to give other than this harebrained scheme concocted on the fly. The details were loose and vague. Still, there was a chance that the gold was there. Jordan Blake had nothing to lose. He was also banking that the two men sitting behind him were not the sharpest tools in the shed.

When he had finished telling Glen and Sal the entire plan, he lied and said he had detailed maps of the area. Jordan wiped the sweat from his brow and sighed. "So. That's it, Glen. It might be a fortune. Don't you see? We all could benefit here. I pay you back, and then whatever is left, we can split. Or, hell, you and Sal take it all."

Glen Finnegan sat back and shook his head. "That has to be the stupidest thing I've ever heard. What are we, ten years old? Digging for treasure in the back yard? While we're at it, let's build a tree fort and start a club. You think my boss is going to *buy* this idea? Doubt it, Jordy. Strongly doubt it."

Sal elbowed Glen. "Hey. What if he's right? What if there is something up there? I mean, damn, the guy *is* a history nut. Got those maps, too. I've heard about people finding stuff like that . . . gold and shit up in the hills."

"Jordy. There is something else you ought to know," said Finnegan.

Jordan Blake met Glen's gray, cold eyes again in the rearview mirror. "What else?"

"My boss is already taking further steps to get paid up, see. Stuff I don't have much control over. Your, uh, parents have a nice house down there in the Bay Area. That pool is sweet. Your mom's not bad looking either."

"What are you saying, Glen?" Jordan was truly panicked now. He'd never imagined it would go this far. "You've been to my parents' place? Are you shaking them down for this? My father will not pay."

"Nothing's happened yet. All I have to do is make a call, though. And something will happen. Fact is, I was going to make that call today."

Finnegan smiled. "But now you're coming around with this dumb-ass story about gold. And, well, Sal here is sort of excited about it. Aren't you, Sal? Maybe I'm interested, too. Tell you what, Jordy. Start driving. There's daylight left for a few hours."

They picked up a bag of tacos, some sodas, and a shovel. A few hours later, they were a few miles west of Remington River. They found the turnoff from the main highway and left the pavement for a rough dirt road just as it got dark. They decided to pull over and wait for morning.

The three of them slept in the car a few miles down the road from Widow Creek Ranch. As soon as the sun came up, they drove until they emerged onto the Widow Creek property. The large meadow was green and lush with borders of wildflowers hugging the fence. Jordan had produced a "treasure map," a term which delighted Sal. In reality, it was a forest service map dated 2002. But he had doctored it by circling a spot and, like in a comic book, putting an *X* on it. This satisfied Sal, who giggled and rubbed his hands together. Glen, on the other hand, made no comment.

None of them had considered that Widow Creek Ranch was a working farm, and as soon as they drove past the main compound, they saw a group of workers pushing wheelbarrows between a row of greenhouses. Walking into the meadow and commencing to dig would certainly raise an alarm.

Jordan, thinking only of his parents now, glanced at the workers and saw a spot near the end of the meadow where he thought they could dig unnoticed. *God, I'm in deep shit!* He boldly exited the car and, doing his best imitation of Howard Carter entering the Valley of the Kings, tromped out onto the meadow, map and shovel in hand. Pretending to scrutinize both the map and the landscape, he dramatically raised his hand to indicate that he'd found the spot. Glen and Sal started walking onto the meadow. They all heard an ATV revving its motor and turned to see a man racing down the road toward them.

Jordan proceeded to dig furiously, throwing clots of grass and dirt high in the air, hoping that the man on the ATV might save him. Maybe he'd call the police? That would be great. Jordan could explain the whole thing. Sal and Glen would be taken away. Although for what crime, he didn't know.

Maybe he'd just wake up and discover it was all a horrible nightmare?

Glen and Sal didn't want to wait to find out what the ATV driver wanted.

"Get back in the car, Jordy," said Glen. "It's time for Plan B."

Jordan didn't stop digging until Glen stuck a gun into his side. "Now. Go." Jordan dropped the shovel and ran back to the car with Glen and Sal hot on his heels. Jordan careened down the road, dirt and rocks flying as he sped along.

Glen waited until they were clear of the Widow Creek property before he told Jordan about Plan B.

"You were right about your father, Jordy. He won't pay up. That's too bad. Boss has had Plan B in the works all along. You just changed the schedule with this little adventure. Drive into Remington River, kid. You're going to move up in the world. And real quick."

"What does that mean?" asked Jordan, his chest tightening so that his breathing became jagged and painful.

"You're going to rob a bank for us," said Sal, letting out a war whoop.

What transpired would have been comedic had Jordan not been threatened with a gun. Or if he had not felt his parents were in danger. Glen and Sal waited in the Subaru, Glen behind the wheel.

Jordan was handed a pistol and told to show it to the teller along with a note that Glen wrote out. Jordan put the note in his right pocket and the gun in his left pocket. Bile rose in his throat as he watched a woman with a couple of kids walk out of the bank. Jordan was instructed to walk in, show the note and the gun, then come out with the bag of money.

"Easy peasy," said Glen. "They don't want any trouble. They'll hand it over."

Jordan moved in a daze toward the glass doors and was shaking as he pushed them open. He froze when he saw the guard and considered throwing himself at his mercy. The guard barely acknowledged his presence. He had to think of his parents. What would happen to them if he didn't go through with this? He hesitated for a moment longer, then looked back to see Glen getting out of the car. Why was Glen getting out of the car? That wasn't the plan. Jordan moved to the teller's window. He reached into his pocket, his fingers so slimy with sweat that he could barely slide them in. The paper came out in a crumpled mess and he slid it across to the teller. She looked at him briefly then smoothed out the paper. She read it.

"What's this, sir?" she asked.

Jordan, still shaking, hadn't expected to have any conversation with anyone. He looked down at the paper and felt the blood leave his brain.

It was a gas receipt.

He had taken out the wrong piece of paper.

Then he made the worst mistake of his life: he brought out the gun and the teller shrieked as if he'd shot her.

Then he heard the bank doors open and watched with a sickening dread as Glen and Sal walked in. Jordan held up the gun. The guard awoke from his daydream and shouted. Jordan ran toward the guard. And, without intending to, Jordan pulled the trigger of the gun. It discharged and hit a window. The sound of shattering glass scared Jordan so much that he didn't feel the bullet from Glen's gun enter his shoulder.

Sirens. More sirens. Uniforms charging into the bank from both sides. Jordan was down on the ground. Sal tried to run out and barreled straight into a sheriff's deputy. Glen stood still and dropped his gun. The smirk on his face was still there as two deputies descended on him.

Jordan's shoulder was wet. Blood, an explanation for the increasing pain he felt. Shot, like a rat in a barrel. He was so relieved it was all over that, through his sobs, he profusely thanked the deputy who handcuffed him.

Later, much later, Jordan would find out that Glen and Sal had double-crossed their boss and were running for their own lives the day they pulled up next to Jordan's Subaru. Glen and Sal needed cash quickly. The whole thing about shaking down his parents had been a lie. Just as Jordan's premise for going on the treasure hunt had been a lie. Glen and Sal had intended to rob the bank all along. Jordan had been in the wrong place at the wrong time.

As he sat in his cell, looking through the box of research papers, Jordan smiled for the first time in a long while. Sheriff Miller was asking for his help. Maybe she had seen something in him. Maybe she was looking beyond his pathetic, former self. Maybe he had something to offer the world besides the mess he'd left behind.

It's all in the past, isn't it?

❧ 30 ❧

ETOILE MILLER PUT THE MAP SHOWING the location of the rocks into the scanner. Then she uploaded it to her computer. She attached the image in an email to Jordan Blake. She knew a response would probably take a few days.

She stopped by Mike's Market and bought a bag of tortilla chips and a container of guacamole, her contributions to Starhawk's call for potluck, before heading to the museum.

The reading of the manuscript was tonight.

"It's like Christmas, isn't it?" Starhawk said as Etoile walked through the door. Starhawk had made space in her back room for a round table covered with a purple cloth surrounded by five chairs. The sounds of footfall on the front porch signaled the arrival of the others.

Marcus Choy brought a spinach salad and a loaf of crusty sour-dough bread. Penny Carter put a platter of cold cuts, cheese slices, and crackers on the table. Tom Nelson brought a cake and coffee makings for later. Starhawk's enchilada casserole completed the dinner. A stack of spiral-bound books was placed in the center of the table.

"The Merrimack Benevolent Society was not as benevolent as you might think," Tom Nelson said in between mouthfuls. "I'm sure their intentions were noble in trying to connect orphans with relatives. But you have to consider that some of these children were sent great distances only to find themselves with families that really didn't want them or didn't have the resources to properly care for them."

"And I'm sure that, to some degree, Hetty Merrimack started the society to increase her standing in the community. It is interesting that Hetty chose this particular child to send to a family in Missouri, given that the girl was not related. When you called me about Lucia Cravotti, I checked our local birth records and baptismal records and could find nothing on her. Unless Cravotti was not her birth name."

"Well, she was only twelve at the time she was sent to Missouri in 1871. She couldn't have been married, could she?" said Starhawk. "Perhaps she was adopted."

"Possibly. That would explain why we can't find a birth record for her. Then again, there were countless births that went unrecorded during that time. It's not unusual at all," said Tom.

"Maybe we'll find something out about Lucia Cravotti in the manuscript," said Marcus.

Everyone served themselves and sat at the table with glasses of wine. Conversation was light as they ate. The manuscript beckoned to them all.

When they had finished and dishes were cleared, Starhawk distributed the books to each of them, along with photos of the inscription, cup and saucer, and bookmark.

"This does look like a map, you're right," said Tom, holding up the photograph of the bookmark.

"And there's the reference to 'beyond' again in the inscription," commented Marcus.

"I have not read it out of respect for all of you eager beavers," said Starhawk with a chuckle. "It's not often that I get to sit in a roomful of such attentive historians with an as-yet undiscovered bit of history."

Starhawk raised her glass for a toast. "To Pajaro, Mariah, and niou tsay!"

She suggested that they take turns with the chapters. They opened the books.

"My God," said Starhawk. "This is wonderful. It's so clear. The writing just jumps off the page. I'm glad she had good penmanship, our Mariah."

It was decided unanimously that Starhawk would read the first chapter. She could not help but embellish her reading with some theatrics and managed to change voices for each of the characters. She chose a flat Midwestern drawl for the narrator, Mariah. For Ma, she read in a slow, wistful tone. Pa was gregarious. Meriwether Lewis had a Virginian accent, loud and brash.

The table was momentarily quiet after Starhawk finished.

"Can it be determined yet if this is factual or just a novel?" asked Marcus.

"I guess we'll find out, Marcus. For now, it's a pleasant reminiscence," answered Tom. "Who's next?"

They decided to go in order around the table. It was Tom's turn.

Tom read in a serious tone with little inflection. It was a short chapter, and when he finished, he looked up and smiled. "My God. What was it like to not know? Not know what was out there. No real maps or images. Only what you could imagine. I'd like to think that I would have the imagination and urge to discover. But I'll bet it was terrifying for most folks back then. Lewis and Clark opened up a whole new set of hopes and ambitions for some and at the same time a whole new set of nightmares."

"Did he really kill himself? Meriwether Lewis? I remember in school hearing about the controversy," asked Etoile

Penny nodded. "On the Natchez Trace. In a little wilderness inn. He died of gunshot wounds. It is suspected he shot himself. Although nobody can be sure. One of history's dark mysteries."

Penny took the next section and proceeded to read a long chapter in a light, rapid, no-nonsense tone that fit perfectly with the content. It was about Mariah's wagon train trip to Remington River, starting with her ill-fated marriage to a man Starhawk later described as "an imbecile."

Etoile said, "You've got to give her credit for hanging in there. Although I think losing Earl was harder on her than she says."

"Why do you say that?" asked Starhawk.

"Because it seems like she needed to be stronger than him. Like her will to do everything she did was based on showing him that she could do it."

"Defiance breeds strength," commented Marcus. "'Strength doesn't come from physical capacity. It comes from indomitable will.' A quote from Gandhi."

"The quotes from *The Journals*, though. It was like her bible. Her inspiration," said Penny.

"Yes," said Starhawk. "Those words were her anchor, I think. She picked some interesting ones, too. 'The Great Mystery'? What did Lewis hear up there, I wonder?"

Marcus read the next chapter. He started haltingly then continued in a pleasant, quiet manner; when he came upon something unexpected, he stammered. He had come to the part about a boy named Sing and his pet named Bird.

Marcus removed his glasses. "I remember something."

There was silence. He looked over their heads to a distant place on the wall of the room. "He wrote about a bird. I had no idea. He wrote that he was always looking for a wild bird to befriend. But they would fly away when he would approach them." He looked at the group. "I feel that this is factual. And that this boy is Sing. I am sure. My Sing."

Etoile said, "The third rock?"

"Yes," replied Marcus. "It was for Bird, I think."

He read on in the same pleasant, quiet way but with an emotion that resounded with everyone. When he finished, he looked up and smiled.

To Starhawk, he said, "I thank you for this. You may not understand how moving this is for me."

Starhawk squeezed his arm and smiled. "I'm sure this means more to you than any one of us."

Etoile's chapter was about Mariah meeting Mendonca, a story about a dangerous woman in Chinatown, a girl named Chin, and the plans for a daring escapade. Etoile surprised herself by becoming so engrossed in the reading that she altogether forgot she was in a room with other people.

She finished but found herself still seated in the Old Mandarin's shop breaking bread with Pajaro Mendonca, the man who was dark as midnight. An injured girl in the back room. A radically different Remington River on the other side of the walls. Cold, isolated, and wild. And she would be driving a team of horses come dawn.

Starhawk immediately started reading the next chapter, sensing the group's collective anticipation of what was going to happen next.

There was quite a bit of dialogue in this next chapter, and everyone was glad that Starhawk was reading. The drama of the story was once again captured by her vocal characterizations.

"This woman, Po Fong," said Marcus, after Starhawk had finished. "I've read about her. She lived into her nineties. Settled in a small suburb south of San Francisco in humble surroundings. And it was said she ended her days as a faithful grower of prized roses."

"You have heard of her?" asked Etoile.

"Oh, yes. She was a madam. Famous for her brothels and gambling houses during the Barbary Coast days of San Francisco. It is astonishing that she would turn up here in this story. She was notorious, and I have no doubt she had a myriad of strange and complicated dealings. But her own daughter? It is hard to understand the conditions in which one would use her own daughter for such business," said Marcus.

Etoile asked, "That little piece of paper? The one that looks like a map? It was a bookmark in *The Journals.*"

They all looked at their copies of what they now knew was Chin's map.

"It's amazing. Like a time capsule or something," said Starhawk. "Mariah saved the map after all those years."

Tom said, "Widow Creek has gone through a lot of transformations over the years. I wonder if anyone suspected there was a cache out there. That map doesn't give a great deal of detail."

Marcus asked, "What kind of transformations?"

"Well, it was a stagecoach stop, as we know. Then it was a ranch for a time when the stage line went out of business. It was in private hands for a long time. Back in the Sixties it was a commune. I heard Janis Joplin spent a week up there with friends, as a matter of fact. After that, it went back to a cattle ranch. Now it's an organic farm. There are some photographs of the place when it flooded out."

Starhawk turned to Etoile. "Isn't Widow Creek the place where those guys involved in the bank robbery were digging for Mendonca's cache?"

"Yes," Etoile replied. She had not mentioned her correspondence with Jordan Blake to anyone but Starhawk.

"Let's try to keep that part of story to ourselves. The thought of a bunch of idiots digging up Widow Creek Ranch again doesn't appeal to me," said Etoile.

It was nearly midnight and they were halfway through the story. Tom suggested they stop for the night and resume at a later date. They agreed to meet the following Tuesday and repeat their potluck.

Etoile helped Starhawk clean up after everyone left. "That was exhausting. So much drama in that story. My God, what that woman endured."

"Makes me ashamed of my soft life," said Starhawk with a chuckle. "Mariah can't seem to make up her mind about Pajaro, can she?" Starhawk turned to her friend. "He's a complicated guy, Etoile." "Aren't they all?" laughed Etoile.

⤳ 31 ⤶

PURDUE KNOCKED ON SHERIFF MILLER'S OFFICE door the next morning and waited for the signal to enter. Etoile looked up from her paperwork and motioned for him to come in. He went in with some hesitation. Purdue wasn't sure how to start this conversation. His relationship with Etoile was like *The Odd Couple.* He was organized where she was not, and he was prone to bursts of outrage while he kept her cool under extraordinary conditions. He admired her and yet he had no idea whether she liked him or not. She drove him nuts.

"You've got a voice mail from Folsom, Sheriff," he said, sidling up to her desk.

She looked up and then continued her paperwork.

"Sheriff Miller," he continued, "how many people have we sent to Folsom?" He didn't wait for answer. "One person. Jordan Blake."

Purdue watched her reaction. There was none. "Why were you asking about Jordan Blake down at Folsom?"

She finally looked up with her blue eyes—eyes that never revealed anything about what she was thinking. "What was the message?"

"He wants a meeting."

"Okay. Leave me the number. Thanks."

Purdue retreated to his desk. He felt dismissed and left out of the fun stuff. What was she after by meeting Jordan Blake? And what was she up to with flitting over hill and dale, first with Starhawk and then the Chinese guy? She had been distracted lately with all this nonsense about hidden rocks, manuscripts, and history. *It's like she's working an investigation*, Purdue thought.

And what did Jordan Blake have to do with all this?

Blake had written back to Etoile after she sent him the map indicating the location of the rocks. In his email, he said, "I found a better map of the area. It's from the 1840s. There's been quite a bit of logging up there in and around the spot indicated. It's amazing the place where the rocks are located has remained undisturbed. What exactly is written on the rocks? Is it just names? Or are their dates? I can't help you with the Chinese cowboy, though. Sheriff Miller, I am very happy to correspond with you about this."

Etoile called the number Purdue left her and spoke with an assistant warden about arranging a meeting. She gave the man a few details about the reason for the meeting and asked if she would be allowed to bring some documents with her. She was told that she would be allowed to do so after they were inspected by a guard. Blake would be allowed to sit at table with her in a secured area for a specific amount of time and their conversation would be monitored.

The following Monday, Etoile found herself seated in a room at Folsom Prison. It was painted a dull gray color. There was a row of windows near the ceiling, screened with thick wire mesh. The sun fought to get into the room. The metal table was anchored to the floor as were the bench seats beside it. A bright fluorescent fixture above the table scorched the table surface. She had brought copies of the photos of the rocks, which she placed on the table. She was now waiting for the buzzer to sound alerting her that a prisoner was in the area.

As she'd driven to the prison, Etoile had contemplated how much to tell Jordan about the manuscript. The last sentence of his email, in which he'd said he was happy to be in communication with her, was in the forefront of her thoughts. He might be interested to hear about the manuscript. On the other hand, he could just be desperately lonely and would talk to anyone about anything.

The buzzer alerted and Etoile looked up to see a small man in a prison-issue blue t-shirt and blue pants being escorted to the room. Blake was pale and puffy with a paunch around his midsection. The guard unlocked the door, which was half metal, half bulletproof glass, and led Blake inside. They sat opposite each other on the benches. Jordan had been allowed to bring a folder of papers. The guard stood in the corner staring off into space.

Blake ran his hands through his hair and looked at her with a sheepish grin. "Weird," he said. "Last time I saw you was not a great moment in my life."

"You get many visitors, Jordan?" asked Etoile.

"My mother came on my birthday six months ago. She acted like a deer in the headlights the entire time. My lawyer stops in occasionally. It's uncomfortable to see people here."

"I'm sorry if this is . . ." she started to say.

"No, no," he said. "This is good. There is a reason for you being here that has nothing to do with me. You know what I mean? I'm not the center of attention. That's the hard part. Being focused on and scrutinized. Difficult to explain."

"I think I understand. How are you holding up here?"

"Nice pun, Sheriff," said Blake. "Nah, don't worry about it," he added, noticing Etoile starting to say something. "Not like I haven't heard it before. I'm okay. There was an adjustment period in this place. At first, I just sat around feeling sorry for myself. Then I was kind of stuck in the middle of deciding what to do. Really stuck. They offer classes here but nothing I was interested in. And you can only read so many paperbacks, right? Then I thought about dragging out my research. Funny thing about that. I thought it would make things worse for me. Having no purpose for doing it. Not that anyone would ever read it or publish it. But then you gave me a reason to dig into my research again." Then, brightening up a bit, he said, "What did you bring?"

She looked at the guard before sliding the pictures around the table. He came over and picked up the photos, turned them over, and placed them down again with a grunt.

Jordan looked at each of the photos. Starhawk had enlarged them so the details were clearer. Another photo caught the bushes and some of the surrounding ground around the rocks.

Etoile told him that hikers had stumbled on the rocks by accident when they had diverted from the trail. The area had remained undisturbed except for the visits from Etoile, Starhawk, and Marcus. Jordan's eyes glistened as he examined each photograph, and Etoile found herself explaining who Starhawk and Marcus were and that they thought it might be a burial site. The road was rough getting to the area, she told him, and unless you knew what you were looking for, she couldn't imagine anyone finding it. Except by complete accident.

"Here's this map I was telling you about," Jordan said.

He opened the folder and pulled out a creased map that had some pencil markings on it. "It's an old mining map. These symbols indicate claims. You can see there are no roads, but these lines point out trails. I think the area where the rocks are located is just about here."

He pointed to a spot very near the corner of the map. Etoile brought her forest service map out and tried to get her bearings. She saw on her map where there was a rock spring from which a creek emerged. On her map it was called Robbers Creek. On Jordan's map, it was not named, but she could see the spring noted in the same approximate place. The rock spring was a few yards west of the rough road she had driven up. Tracing her finger from the spring on the old map, she followed a line to some words.

"What's that say?" she asked, squinting at the small lettering that was by a picture of something that looked like a shack.

Jordan sat back. "It says 'Purisima.' It was a very valuable mine."
Then he leaned forward. "Look carefully. I know the map is different.
But do you think this is near where you found the rocks?"

"It's pretty darn close, Jordan."

"What was the area like around it?"

"The spot was covered in manzanita at the base of a tall wall of
boulders. It looked like the wall extended back, but there must have
been a landslide. I couldn't get past it. Maybe somebody could climb
back there."

"If this is the Purisima, it is probably beyond that landslide. It would
make sense for Pajaro to be here. Or least a marker with his name."

This time it was Etoile who sat forward. "Why do think that?"

"Because one of the last known actions of Pajaro Mendonca's was
his work on the land dispute surrounding the Cañon of Purisima.
I only know this because Purisima was legendary and there is one
small reference to Mendonca about it in some old newspaper articles. Obscure, really. The articles allude to Mendonca as the dark
Californio with an interest in the Cañon. Something like that. There
are a lot of stories about the Cañon itself, though. The land holding
was deeded to the president of Mexico for some reason. Then the deed
was signed over to somebody else, probably as a bribe or payment
for favor. The new deed owner apparently didn't do anything with
the land. Or, if he did, there wasn't any record of it. The mine was
reportedly rich and pretty much untapped. Some say it was cursed
or just plain unlucky. Around the time Pajaro got involved, he was
mainly focused on the land part of Purisima. Down in the flatlands
near Susanville. Ten thousand acres, I believe. The mine disappeared
off the maps. This might be the last place you'd ever see it noted.
Whoever benefited from Pajaro's work on Purisima would have been
very fortunate."

"What does Californio mean?"

"It refers to a Spanish-speaking person of Latin American descent
born in the Alta California Province between 1769 and 1848."

Etoile nodded then asked, "So why didn't Pajaro take the land for himself?"

"Not his style, I think."

"Jordan, I remembered what you said. Back then during your arrest. Someone asked you if you really thought Mendonca's cache was buried up there. And you said no. You thought Pajaro had nothing to cache. You said he was a good guy and that the right stories were never told about him."

Jordan laughed quietly. "Did I say that? It's hard to imagine what life was like for him. His reputation, the one that history remembers, is that of a bandit, criminal, renegade, murderer. But he did a lot of work behind the scenes. The Californios were in desperate times with the new state of California. Their land was being slowly dragged away from them. And they had taken good care of the land, unlike the new breed coming from the East who just wanted to tear up the hills for gold and maybe try some ranching later on with their wealth. But they didn't understand the land or what it was good for. They'd just arrived and didn't bother asking the ones who had worked it quite successfully for decades. The Californios worked side by side with the indigenous tribes. It was the golden era of the state long before the gold era. Anyway, Pajaro was trying to restore that golden era, I guess. He might not have known it was a hopeless goal. He maintained this façade of the bandit because it suited him to live on the perimeter. Plenty of people were like that back then. They hid away or stayed in the shadows. The world was changing too rapidly."

"What ended up happening to Pajaro?"

"Like I said, he stayed in the shadows after Purisima. There was nothing more about him in any of the research I've done. Maybe this is the year he died," said Jordan, pointing at the year carved in the rock beneath Pajaro's name.

"Does the name Mariah Penngrove mean anything to you?"

"Yes. She was connected to Pajaro in some way. There was a newspaper article about a shootout involving the Mendonca brothers near

Widow Creek Station. It was reported that she was living there at the time of the shooting but disappeared soon after. Apparently, those rumors were true. There's her name on a rock right next to Pajaro's, right?" He showed her the copy of the article.

"It makes it sound like she was part of the gang or something."

"Who knows?" Jordan said.

"Do you know anything about a Chinese cowboy known as Sing from around that time?"

"You mentioned this Chinese cowboy before. Sing? No. Doesn't sound familiar."

"The Chinese writing on the rocks says 'eternally grateful.' Niou tsay. That means cowboy in Cantonese."

Jordan shook his head. "Nope. Haven't a clue." Then he placed his hands on the table and looked at Etoile. "What's this all about, Sheriff? It isn't just the rocks, is it?"

Etoile hesitated. Looking at the clock, she realized their time was nearly up. "Okay. There is something more."

She told him about the woman in St. Joseph and the trunk containing items belonging to Mariah Penngrove that had been sent to Missouri by Hetty Merrimack. There was a manuscript. There was also a little girl named Lucia Cravotti involved. As soon as she said Lucia's name, Etoile stopped talking. *Of course*, she thought. Lucia was the name of Pajaro's child. The one killed at Mendonca's mining claim.

"And?" asked Jordan, also noting the time. "You were saying something about Lucia Cravotti."

Etoile was quiet for a moment, deep in thought. "I just realized that Lucia is the name of Pajaro's child. The one who died long before all this happened. But it can't be the same girl who was sent to Missouri."

"Back up. What about this manuscript?" he asked.

"Mariah wrote the story of her early life."

"Time's up, folks," said the guard, a bit too loudly, for both Etoile and Jordan jumped. Etoile tried to read the expression on Jordan's face. He looked at her with pursed lips and was nodding, staring at the table. "I envy you. Finding something like that. Is it authenticated, by the way?"

"The curator seems to think it's the real deal."

"Wow. Finding something like that. Like a dream," he said. He glanced at the guard and rose from the bench.

Etoile stood as well. "Jordan?"

He was already turning to leave. "Yeah?"

"Would you like a copy of the manuscript? There's something in there you might find interesting."

"What's that?"

"I won't give it away."

"I'd be grateful to read it, Sheriff. Thank you," he said quietly and left with the guard closely behind him.

❧ 32 ❧

ETOILE HURRIED OUT TO HER CAR. She wanted to call Starhawk. She couldn't believe she was the only one who had picked up on the name Lucia.

Starhawk answered and listened to Etoile. "I feel like I need to sit down with that manuscript and read it a few more times. It's chock full of information. But now that you mention, I do recall Mariah and Pajaro talking about his wife and child and the fire in the cabin. Her name was Lucia. No, it couldn't be the same girl, of course."

"You know what I think? I think that Mariah and Pajaro had a child and named it after his dead daughter. Mariah died in 1859, or so we supposed by the date on the rock. The next time we see the name Lucia, she is now Lucy and is in a photograph of Sing's family dated 1865. We know Mariah and Pajaro were messing around at Widow Creek, right? That was around 1852. That would make that girl around twelve or thirteen in 1865. Then somebody named Lucia Cravotti is sent to live in Missouri by Hetty Merrimack when she was thirteen," said Etoile. "And we now know that Hetty Samuels became Hetty Merrimack."

"But Pajaro lived until 1871. That is, presuming all these dates are death dates. We can't know for sure. Why would he let his daughter go to Missouri?"

"I don't know. Maybe it was an opportunity for education and a better life than they had in Remington River. It's quite possible that Hetty Samuels kept in touch with Mariah. After all, they were in the same vicinity. Hetty might have cared for the child in some way and asked Pajaro if he would like to see her live in the East for a while. Who knows?"

"Perhaps all will be revealed in the second half of the manuscript. I can't wait for the next reading," said Starhawk.

"I'm surprising everyone by bringing chips and dip for the pot-luck," laughed Etoile.

§

They took the same seating arrangement as before. Once the food had been consumed and dishes cleared, the spiral notebooks were distributed and everyone settled in for the conclusion of the story.

"We ended at chapter six," said Tom.

Starhawk suggested he start reading and he opened the book. Whereas before when had Tom read in an almost lecture style, this time the chapter kept up such a rapid sequence of events and interludes between Mariah and Pajaro that Tom's voice now held a sense of urgency and drama. He read Pajaro's dialogue in a some-what deeper tone, and there was a slight hint of an accent, which delighted everyone.

When he finished, there was a long silence.

Etoile spoke. "I can't believe he died. It just can't be."

Starhawk looked at her friend and noted she was truly shaken.

She clapped. "Tom, that was magnificent. You're all too young to remember before television when radio programs had dramas like this. We'd sit in front of the radio and just listen to the performers.

You could picture all the action. Like being transported to the actual place and time of the story. Tom, you missed your calling. And I particularly like how you handled the juicy part. Very sensitive."

"Yeah, I got the hot stuff. How did that happen?" he laughed. "I wonder if Mariah ever intended for this to actually be read? Pretty racy for the time."

"Her daughter might have read it," said Etoile.

All eyes turned toward her. "Her daughter?" asked Penny.

Etoile told them about her theory. Marcus sat up and said, "You mean the girl in Sing's photo might be Pajaro and Mariah's child? I guess it's possible. There's no way of knowing for sure without a birth record or something. From what the woman in St. Louis says, Hetty Merrimack's name is linked to Lucia Cravotti. Maybe the girl was Hetty's daughter? Born out of wedlock? Sent away to hide her shame."

Starhawk snorted. "Not likely. If that woman had had an illegitimate child, you can bet she would have made sure she didn't stay around here until she was twelve or thirteen. Remember, she was a pillar of society, or what passed as society, in Remington River at the time."

Penny agreed. "She wasn't Hetty's child, I don't think. Look, we still have a lot of story left. Maybe it'll be in here. I believe it is my turn."

She began the next chapter. Penny read with an intensity that was evident by the way she turned the pages quickly to get to the next part. Breathless with anticipation, she started to read faster until she realized she was rushing it. Penny paused to take a sip of wine. "Sorry. I just can't believe Mariah is actually going to tell the Chinese woman about the gold. Why not keep it? She certainly could have used it."

Penny took a breath and continued reading. She returned to her excited recitation, and by the time she finished the chapter, her face was flushed and she was out of breath.

"Okay," said Penny. "Let's be practical here. How did Po Fong manage to smuggle a drugged body all the way to San Francisco? As I recall, going overland would have taken weeks and weeks."

Starhawk said, "I remember an old TV western called *Have Gun Will Travel*. The main character, Paladin, seemed to travel all over the place in record time."

Tom laughed. "For the convenience of a thirty-minute show, Hollywood shrunk the state to the size of a pea. I always liked that series, by the way. As to how Po Fong got her to San Francisco, once they got out of the mountains to, say, Sacramento—a three-day trip by stagecoach—she would have gone by steamer the rest of the way. In fact, if she's as wealthy as she sounds, she could have hired her own boat. Not out of the realm of possibility."

"He's alive," Etoile said. "I knew he would be."

Starhawk saw the glimmer of a smile on Etoile's face. "If she'd only been able to tell Po Fong about the gold right then and there," Etoile continued. "I wonder what would have happened."

Marcus picked up his copy and cleared his throat. "I suspect the story would have been cut much shorter, Sheriff. And so would Mariah's life. Po Fong doesn't sound very forgiving."

He started to read the next chapter, as it was his turn. It was a short chapter, and as it was revealed that Mariah had been brought to San Francisco, to Chinatown, Marcus smiled, shaking his head.

When he finished, he said, "From what I have heard about Chinatown during this era, it was possible to feel completely detached from the rest of the city. As if one were living in a province or in an entirely different world. I'm curious how she's going to get out of this jam."

"I have faith in our girl, Marcus," said Starhawk. "Your turn, Etoile. Let's rescue her."

Etoile opened her book and started reading a passage that was completely different from the rest of the story. It was another short chapter, and when it was completed, everyone around the table started talking at once.

"It doesn't quite fit," Marcus said. "Something is out of place here. She might have read a novel and got an idea to shake up the story."

"Shake it up? I don't know how much more shaking I can take," commented Tom.

Penny said, "It's as if she's trying to tell us something. A clue of some kind. I think she wrote this long after all these events happened. Like this is something she learned later on. Weird."

Starhawk shuddered. "A hand? God, what a scene that must have been. Who is the man bringing the hand all the way to Chinatown?"

"Your turn, Starhawk," said Etoile. "Hopefully we get to the bottom of this right now."

Starhawk began reading and with her familiar theatrics brought the scenes, action, and characters to life. The table was transfixed with the adventure unfolding. The long chapter kept a frantic pace, and Starhawk paused once or twice to drink water.

"That cup and saucer has seen a lot of activity," said Starhawk when she was finished. "I'm surprised they stayed in one piece."

"Just another fun fact," said Tom. "Mariah was correct about the cup and saucer. Part of a set belonging to Queen Victoria. I found it listed in an auction catalog."

Starhawk asked, "Is it worth a lot?"

"A tidy sum, if it were back with the original set."

"Mariah's still not sure about Pajaro, is she?" Etoile said. "After all this, she is still suspicious."

"Well, wouldn't you be? Even after their *thing* together," said Penny. "He's not telling her the whole story and she knows it. She's been carted all over the state in the hopes of flushing him out. Sure, she's glad to see him. But she still doesn't know why any of this is happening to her. And Pajaro isn't exactly the most trustworthy person."

"You're wrong about that," said Etoile. Starhawk shot her a look.

"What do you mean?" Penny asked.

"Well," Etoile began slowly, "you guys infected me with this history bug and I've been doing a little digging myself. I was going to tell you eventually, but now is as good a time as any. I contacted somebody who was researching land disputes in early California.

In fact, he was basing his master's thesis on the subject. He refutes much of what was written about Mendonca in the press at the time. To quote this person, 'He was a good guy.'

"We all know from what Mariah has written that Pajaro was involved in land disputes. That bit about switching the documents is just the tip of the iceberg. It is thought that Pajaro was working on the mother of disputes over a piece of land called Purisima. In fact, this land held a mine. My source thinks that the rocks placed way up there in the mountains might be very close to the Purisima mine."

Tom laughed. "You don't mean the Cañon of Purisima, do you? That place probably never existed. It was one of the richest mines in the state but reputedly was never properly worked. Which makes no sense. Who would leave a mine dormant when it could have produced a ton of gold? People back then didn't think about conservation or anything like that."

"So you've heard of this place, Tom?" asked Etoile.

"Oh sure. If you don't mind me asking, who is your source?"

Etoile paused. "A guy named Jordan Blake."

There was silence for a moment until Penny said, "You're not talking about the Jordan Blake who was a Chico student? God, I remember that whole story. He was in debt and figured he could bail himself out by finding the cache of gold or treasure buried by Pajaro Mendonca. Robbed a bank, too. How in the world did you get involved with him?"

"Actually, he knew there wasn't anything to find in terms of treasure. His theory was that Mendonca never had gold to spare. The digging idea was a ruse, according to him at the time. Those two others arrested were making all kinds of threats. He was in a bad corner," said Etoile. "And I arrested him. So that's how I know him. I remembered the whole Mendonca thing and asked him what he knew."

"And he thinks that the rocks are located near the Purisima? He's in prison, right? For a guy who's inside, he seems to know a lot about an area he probably has never seen," said Penny, barely hiding her sarcasm. "Look, I'm sorry. I'm sure it must have been a complete upheaval in his life. Maybe he was a bright student and he might have a few odds and ends in his research. But—"

"Etoile says he had all his research papers sent to him," Starhawk interjected. "She said he appeared to be quite interested in all this and is eager to help, if he can. Penny, remember when I first came to see you about the rocks? You showed me a document with both Pajaro's and Mariah's names on it. You couldn't quite make out the title of the deed. It was a poor copy. It's the only thing we had to go on at one point. I wonder if you could find it again and enhance the image."

"You don't think it's the Purisima deed?" Tom asked. He looked at Penny, who shrugged.

Penny said she would work on enhancing the image and, for the moment, dropped her ambivalence about Jordan Blake.

"Mariah never fails to enlighten us," Tom said. "I have a feeling we will learn more in the next chapter. Shall we proceed and find out what's in store next for this remarkable woman?"

The reading that followed was more complicated than previous chapters. Tom stopped several times to clarify certain details with the others. They could all feel the urgency of the story reaching its climax, and the plot was becoming a bit more convoluted. They all knew there was only one more chapter after this one.

Marcus spoke first after Tom finished. "Po Fong would certainly be a worthy adversary. She's a tough one. Boy, she just stands up and fights."

"No kidding," Etoile said. "They can't seem to shake that woman."

"So it is Purisima. I can't believe it. Tom, what do you think?" asked Penny.

"I think we've got a gold mine on our hands," he chuckled. "No, seriously. This is an incredible piece of history. Purisima is a fable. The El Dorado of the West. It is utterly astounding to read about its existence. If that deed with Pajaro and Mariah's signatures is in fact Purisima . . ."

"I think that Pajaro felt truly responsible for what happened in the valley with Sandro. He carried the weight of that incident on himself entirely," said Starhawk. "How that must have eaten away at him. And that he still is firmly set on keeping his tarnished reputation intact doesn't quite make sense. He could have easily walked away from it all, free and clear."

"He *was* a good guy," said Etoile. "He wanted to help as many people as he could. Jordan told me he kept up the façade so that, ironically, he would be trusted."

"Perhaps someday the right story will be told about him," said Starhawk, giving Etoile a nudge with her shoulder.

Before they started the next and final chapter, Etoile asked if she could send a copy of the manuscript to Jordan Blake. Tom and Penny were leery. "It's not copyrighted and the rights are not protected. We have to think what Mariah would have wanted."

Marcus spoke up. "The man's in prison. And I would imagine for a few more years. What's he going to do? Self-publish it on Amazon? If he was a serious student of history, which he sounds like he was, I feel he should have it. I put myself in his shoes. His whole life was ruined by his own inadequacies. This may help him back on his feet. Give him a purpose. He apparently knows a good deal about these times and events. I think it would be a gesture of goodwill for this man."

"And," Marcus added, "I believe Mariah would have seen it the same way. She is certainly coming to conclusions about Pajaro. Perhaps she is finally going to see the man for who is he. I think she is a careful judge of character, just as I believe Sheriff Miller is, too. Mariah would give him the book."

"Here we go," said Starhawk after a suitable pause following Marcus' heartfelt words. "The last chapter."

It was fitting for Starhawk to tackle this last bit of story, and she took to the task with her usual flair and keen interpretation. She paused at moments, allowing for the story to sink in. When she finally finished, she dropped her hands in her lap. "It's not what I expected. She was a master storyteller. She drove us to the end. And yet it is not the end, is it?"

Marcus Choy stood up and walked to the coffee urn. It was cold, but he still filled his cup. He would not sleep tonight.

"It seems that I will have another ancestor to research now. Manuelito Gonzalvo. It makes sense that I could not find a trace of Sing in China. He wasn't born there, and he was only part Chinese," said Marcus.

"Sing," he continued. "It was Sing all along. No wonder he placed those stones up there. He owed a great deal to Pajaro and Mariah. With the land, he became what he wanted. A cowboy. Niou tsay. Of course, it is Bird who is commemorated on the third stone. I told Sheriff Miller he always wanted to befriend another wild bird. Perhaps you only get one chance in life to tame something wild."

"My God," said Tom. "They blew it up. The mine. Gone."

"And what happened to Po Fong? She just walked away and went on to raise roses?" asked Starhawk.

"Pajaro had her from several angles," Etoile said. "Not just destroying the mine that she wanted. Don't forget Ah Wong's hand. Pajaro was making sure that if she crossed him again, he'd have ample ammunition to fight her."

Starhawk produced a cake that she had baked for the special occasion. She had managed to make a rendition of a bird in black icing, along with "PM+MP 4 EVER." This brought a round of laughter. The cake was cut and enjoyed. When all was said and done, Etoile summed it up with more questions than answers.

"We still don't know everything, do we? What happened to Pajaro and Mariah? It's so sad that she might have died before him. Leaving a little girl behind. They probably had a few years together. But where? And what did they do?"

Starhawk forked a piece of cake in her mouth and swallowed. "We know one thing that she did, Etoile. She wrote this manuscript."

℘ 33 ℘

ETOILE SENT THE MANUSCRIPT TO JORDAN Blake.

He replied upon receiving it with one word: "Thanks."

Etoile's work caught up with her finally, and for several weeks she was involved with investigating a suspicious death at a lakeside house.

Meanwhile, Starhawk pestered Penny enough so that she, at last, enlarged and enhanced the document. It was certainly a deed, and by carefully examining it, Penny discovered it was the Cañon de Purisima. Sing had taken over the land in the valley when he turned twenty-one and had evidently prospered. Eventually, he sold off bits and pieces of it, and now it was a subdivision of upscale houses just outside of Susanville. It had taken considerable work to track down the long line of owners of the original property. In the end, it had been one of the sons who sold it off and moved to Los Angeles.

The placing of the stones at the collapsed entry to the Cañon was, thought Marcus, Sing's tribute to those who had brought him his fortune and a reminder of his loss.

As for Lucia Cravotti, Starhawk called Sharon Hollister and said that they had turned up nothing about her in California. But they suspected she might have been the daughter of Pajaro and Mariah, an idea that Sharon had tossed around herself.

It occurred to Tom that since Mendonca was closely connected to the mission in San Francisco, perhaps more information about him could be found at the mission. All mission records were archived at Mission Santa Barbara, and he started his search there. He was rewarded on several points.

A birth was recorded in 1852: Lucia Mendonca. Her parents were listed as Pajaro Mendonca and Mariah Hardwick Penngrove. A log kept track of any individuals searching records at the missions. This was almost as revealing as anything else Tom had found. He could look back and see anyone who had queried for birth, death, or marriage records. He discovered a signature dated 1880 for a Lucia Mendonca-Cravotti searching for a death record for Pajaro Mendonca. Tom found an entry from an old mission bulletin announcing his death. Apparently, the priests had allowed him to live quietly and reclusively in his final years.

Tom used a genealogy site to track down Lucia Mendonca-Cravotti and was successful. The entry in the Bible did not include her hyphenated name or her use of the more familiar Lucy as her first name. According to the genealogy site, she remained in Missouri, married, and lived well into her eighties. Her obituary read, "She was the beloved daughter of the late, great Pajaro Mendonca and Mariah Penngrove. Cherished parents from Remington River, California."

Starhawk called Sharon Hollister. "It's like we had two parts of the puzzle and just needed to find each other to fit them together."

"Lucia Mendonca-Cravotti. I wonder if she left a trace anywhere about her parents. A story? Letters? I have a feeling this is only the beginning of her story." Starhawk wished her luck on her new area of research.

Sheriff Miller finally found time to send an email to Jordan Blake and ask whether he had read the manuscript. His response came quickly. "Please come down for a visit."

She went through the usual process before finding herself in the same room waiting for Jordan to be escorted to the visit. He showed up looking considerably more fit and happy than he had the previous time. He had a jump to his step, and he smiled broadly when he saw her.

"The manuscript is extraordinary," said Jordan. "What a story."

Etoile nodded. "I'd like to know what happened to Mariah. Did she die in Remington River? We never found out what happened to her. One of the curators at the Susanville Historical Society discovered that Pajaro died at Mission Santa Barbara and apparently lived there until his death."

"That doesn't surprise me. I'm sure he was welcome there after all the work he had done for the Californios," Jordan said.

"What do you think happened to Mariah and Pajaro after the explosion?" asked Etoile.

"They needed to wait until Sing came of age," he said. "Mariah and Pajaro probably helped him get ready to take over the Cañon. Educated him. Taught him the skills he would need. I guess Mariah never returned to Missouri. She'd found her 'Beyond.' Then, once Sing was old enough, I think Pajaro faded into the background. As he'd always wanted to do. With Mariah and Lucia, I imagine he was a happy man. They stayed in the area while Sing started his family. But all that changed with Mariah's death. We only get Mariah's version of Pajaro. Who knows what the man was really like? Raising Lucia by himself, even with Sing's family around him, might have been difficult for him. Hetty Samuels offered an opportunity for Lucia. Although, that can't have been easy for Lucia. Leaving her home and heading east."

"Still a lot of unanswered questions," said Etoile after a long silence.

Jordan cocked his head and looked at Etoile thoughtfully. "Even the most dedicated diarists leave out stuff. It's as if to say, 'This is who I am and the rest is for you to decide.' And a lot of people don't have nice, neat endings, Sheriff. Do you really need to know everything? You have to make up your own mind about how much you want to understand."

❧ 34 ❧

THE CALL HAD COME IN AROUND three in the afternoon from a rancher out in Sunrise Valley. He was moving a half dozen horses and had them loaded in their carrier for transport out to Nevada. Before coupling the trailer to his truck, he'd gone back into the barn for no more than twenty minutes to bring out some tack and feed. When he returned, the carrier and the horses were not there. He'd heard a truck engine while he was in the barn but thought it was one of his sons pulling out.

But he was wrong.

Somebody else had arrived with a truck, hitched up the horse carrier, and taken off. He surmised that whoever took his rig was heading to the main highway. He called the sheriff's department immediately and then set off on his own after the horses.

Etoile and Purdue responded rapidly and caught up to the rancher's truck in his own pursuit to catch up with whoever took his horses. The rancher, seeing them in his rearview mirror, waved to them and continued on.

The highway rose up over Engle's Summit and descended into a narrow river gorge. The road twisted and turned to a degree that vehicles had to slow down significantly. Etoile would catch a glimpse of the rancher's truck, then it would disappear around a bend. The truck hauling the horses surely must have been slowed down, but the rancher had not caught up to it. After twenty minutes, the rancher pulled over, and Etoile followed him into the turnout.

The rancher, Calvin West, shook hands with Etoile and Purdue. His expression was unreadable but Etoile knew he was angry. West said, "We would have caught up with them by now. No way they could have taken these turns."

Purdue nodded. "They turned off somewhere."

Cal kicked his front tire. "Shit. Who in God's name would do this?"

"We're going to find out, Cal. But right now, we have to backtrack and see where they went. Your sons would be a big help if they could start taking a few of these side roads. Purdue, radio back for some help," Etoile directed. "I say we start with A-14. It's the easiest turn off the highway."

"A-14?" Cal said incredulously. "That's way too narrow for my carrier. They gotta be up ahead, Sheriff."

"It's possible, but there's that big road project five miles down. If whoever took your horses knows the area, they won't go this way because they know they'll get stopped."

Cal grunted. "Should have thought of that myself. Wasting time going this way. Damn it."

She called the highway division and instructed them to be on the lookout for any horse carriers at the construction stops. Then she turned to Cal, "In the meantime, let's go back and start following these roads."

An hour later, with ten volunteers and Cal West's two sons, the search continued. Cell service was spotty, and by nightfall, Etoile had only heard back from a few members of the search party. They'd come up empty.

Etoile, Purdue, and Cal had taken A-14 for fifteen miles and then turned onto a logging road before returning to the main highway.

It was nearly midnight and they'd seen no trace of the horses. She stopped at the turnout for the highway and joined Cal as he stood outside his truck. It was pitch black except for the glows from their cellphones as they checked for reports.

Her phone found a couple of bars of signal and a series of texts popped up. She could hear Cal's anguished groan as he read his texts. The news was not good.

One of Cal's sons had found the carrier. It had left a logging road and fallen into a ditch with the truck still coupled to the carrier. However, there was nobody in the truck. Somehow, the driver had escaped. The six horses were all severely injured, and Etoile could only imagine what was happening at this point.

They left immediately for the accident site. Etoile called in for the heavy equipment rescue team and a veterinarian. Etoile and Purdue drove in silence following Cal on the logging road until they drew near to where the carrier had gone off the road. Only then did they turn and look at each other as the sounds of rifle shots pierced the darkness.

A group of search and rescue team members combed the ditch and surrounding area. There were boot prints suggesting there had been another person along with the driver. Etoile and Purdue followed the logging road for miles. Whoever had stolen the horses had vanished into the forest.

"Either they're lost or they know this area better than I do," said Etoile.

"I got a hunch we'll get them, Sheriff. When the word gets out about the crash, somebody's going to talk." Purdue tried to sound convincing.

The sun was coming up when Etoile and Purdue returned to the main highway and headed back to Remington River. As they drove west, the white cap of Hasten Peak suddenly poked up above the trees. Having grown up beneath it, Etoile had spent little time studying Hasten. It was just there, changing through the seasons, never wavering in its vigil over Remington River. And yet she hadn't paid much attention. She had never noticed how the peak stayed hidden and then just seemed to pop up. *With no other tall ranges nearby, its starkness is remarkable*, thought Etoile.

She tried to picture the mountain through Mariah's eyes. Despite having traveled over the Rocky Mountains, surely taller and grander than anything in California, it had been Hasten Peak that had captured Mariah's heart. Was it the isolation of the peak along with its strength and beauty that had drawn her in? Like the West. Like Mariah and the other hearty souls who had ventured here back in Mariah's time. Etoile could understand this. She knew the feeling well.

Hours later, Etoile slumped in her chair with a cup of lukewarm coffee while a late summer storm gathered outside the office window. There would be lightning strikes. She'd have to stay glued to the weather report today.

Deputy Purdue had been by her side for the last thirteen hours. She watched as he rested his head on his desk, knowing that he shared her discouragement about the outcome of the long night.

All the horses had been put down. There was still no sign of the thieves.

Etoile got up from her chair and went to the outer office. She put her hand on Purdue's shoulder. "Go on home and get some sleep."

He didn't argue and grabbed his coat and hat. "See you later," he mumbled.

"Oh," he said, before reaching the door. "Starhawk left you a package. It's there on my desk."

It was a large padded envelope with, "For Etoile. Happy Birthday. See page 208," written with black marker on the front.

Etoile had completely forgotten that today was her birthday.

She picked up the envelope and went back to her desk to open it. Inside was a book: a copy of *The Journals of Lewis and Clark*.

Etoile smiled and thought about Mariah and her mother reading the entries together. Later, Mariah had derived inspiration from them during troubling times.

It was a new edition with annotated notes and historical backgrounds, much different from Mariah's copy. It included some illustrations and a full-page map indicating the route of the expedition as it went westward then returned to the East. Etoile found a plate of Meriwether Lewis, a portrait of him, his face turned to the right. He was dressed in a dark jacket with a white, high-necked, ruffled collar. The painting showed a sharp nose, narrowly set eyes, and black hair combed forward in the style of the time. The date indicated that it had been painted prior to the expedition. There were no further illustrations of the man, and Etoile wondered how the journey had changed him; whether the eyes shown in this portrait, casually directed beyond the canvas, would be different in the years that followed his return. Would all that he had experienced and seen over those two years be revealed in his eyes?

She opened the book to the page Starhawk mentioned. The chapter heading was "Crossing the Great Divide." Halfway down the page, Meriwether Lewis logged an entry for August 18, 1805. It began with Lewis bargaining with the Shoshone. He offered them clothing and other articles in exchange for help with transporting the expedition's equipment. They were taking to the river for the next part of the journey and needed all their men at the water's edge to work on the canoes.

As the entry concluded, Etoile realized why Starhawk wanted her to read that entry in particular: it was Lewis's birthday entry, in which he laments about how little he has accomplished in his thirty-one years. It was the entry that Mariah and her mother read every August 18 to commemorate their hero. It was also Etoile Miller's birthday.

After she finished reading, Etoile reflected on the man. In the midst of detailing a laundry list of items and purchase prices for what he would use to bargain with the Shoshone, worrying about a decision to abandon travel by land in favor of an unknown river, he paused to take stock of his own life. It was as if, momentarily, Lewis wanted to step out of the journals and uncover this part of himself.

Etoile recalled Jordan Blake's comments about diarists. "This is who I am and the rest of it is for you to decide." Meriwether Lewis could not have known how history would portray him. Just as Mariah Hardwick Penngrove had not known how her manuscript would be interpreted. Etoile could not be sure if Mariah had wanted her story to be a just a brief glimpse into her life or a speculation on who she was as a person. In retrospect, it made sense to Etoile that Mariah had turned to someone like Lewis for guidance. Like Lewis, Mariah wasn't sure where she would find The Beyond; she only knew she wanted to get there.

Etoile set the book aside, fatigue enveloping her. She couldn't shake the vision of Cal and his sons, down in that ditch, hovering over their horses, flashlights in hand. Hoping. She felt cold and empty.

She should go home, get some sleep. But before she did, she picked up *The Journals*, Placing the book on its spine, she let it fall open to a random page.

Wednesday May 29ᵗʰ 1805 [Lewis]:

Last night we were all alarmed by a large buffalo bull which swam over from the opposite shore and coming alongside of the white pirogue, climbed over it to land. He ran full speed directly towards our fires and was within 18 inches of the heads of some of the men. When he came near the tent, my dog saved us by causing him to change his course. We were happy to find no one hurt in the aftermath. In the morning, it was discovered that the bull had trampled in the pirogue and trodden on a rifle and shattered the stock of one of the blunderbushes on board. It appears that the white pirogue which contains most of our most valuable stores is attended by some evil geniie.

Etoile laughed. Leaving weapons in the pirogue? Mariah would have heartily disapproved.

Acknowledgements

I am grateful to Michael A. McLellan for his support and advice. There are no words to express my love and appreciation to my family for giving me the space and time for writing. A big thanks to Jessica Santina at Lucky Bat Books for her input and suggestions. Lastly, none of this is possible without Tim.

About the author

Sarah Margolis Pearce lives and writes in Northern California. She divides her time between San Francisco and Lassen County.